SPIDER-MAN
SPIDER-VERSE
FEARSOME FOES

AMAZING SPIDER-MAN (1963) #20
WRITER/EDITOR: **STAN LEE**
ARTIST: **STEVE DITKO**
LETTERER: **SAM ROSEN**

AMAZING SPIDER-MAN (1963) #197
WRITER/EDITOR: **MARV WOLFMAN**
LAYOUTS: **KEITH POLLARD**
FINISHER: **JIM MOONEY**
COLORIST: **BEN SEAN**
LETTERER: **JOE ROSEN**
CONSULTING EDITOR: **JIM SHOOTER**

SPECTACULAR SPIDER-MAN (1976) #139
WRITER: **GERRY CONWAY**
ARTIST: **SAL BUSCEMA**
COLORIST: **BOB SHAREN**
LETTERER: **RICK PARKER**
EDITOR: **JIM SALICRUP**

ULTIMATE SPIDER-MAN (2000) #7
STORY: **BILL JEMAS
& BRIAN MICHAEL BENDIS**
WRITER: **BRIAN MICHAEL BENDIS**
PENCILER: **MARK BAGLEY**
INKER: **ART THIBERT**
COLORIST: **JUNG CHOI**
LETTERER: **RS & COMICRAFT's
ALBERT DESCHESNE**
COVER ART: **MARK BAGLEY
& TRANSPARENCY DIGITAL**
ASSISTANT EDITOR: **BRIAN SMITH**
EDITOR: **RALPH MACCHIO**

ULTIMATE COMICS SPIDER-MAN (2011) #11
WRITER: **BRIAN MICHAEL BENDIS**
ARTIST: **DAVID MARQUEZ**
COLORIST: **JUSTIN PONSOR**
LETTERER: **VC's CORY PETIT**
COVER ART: **KAARE ANDREWS**
ASSISTANT EDITOR: **JON MOISAN**
ASSOCIATE EDITOR: **SANA AMANAT**
EDITOR: **MARK PANICCIA**

SPIDER-MAN CREATED BY STAN LEE & STEVE DITKO

COLLECTION EDITOR: **JENNIFER GRÜNWALD**
ASSOCIATE MANAGING EDITOR: **KATERI WOO**
VP PRODUCTION & SPECIAL PROJECTS: **JEFF YOUNG**
BOOK DESIGN

EDITOR IN CHIEF: **C.B. CEBULSKI**
PRESIDENT: **DAN BUCKLEY**

EL

SPIDER-MAN: SPIDER-VERSE — FEARSOME FOES. Contains material originally published in magazine form as AMAZING SPIDER-MAN #20 and #197, SPECTACULAR SPIDER-MAN #139, ULTIMATE SPIDER-MAN #7, and ULTIMATE COMICS SPIDER-MAN #11. First printing 2018. ISBN 978-1-302-91412-7. Published by MARVEL WORLDWIDE, INC., a subsidiary of MARVEL ENTERTAINMENT, LLC. OFFICE OF PUBLICATION: 135 West 50th Street, New York, NY 10020. Copyright © 2018 MARVEL No similarity between any of the names, characters, persons, and/or institutions in this magazine with those of any living or dead person or institution is intended, and any such similarity which may exist is purely coincidental. **Printed in Canada.** DAN BUCKLEY, President, Marvel Entertainment; JOHN NEE, Publisher; JOE QUESADA, Chief Creative Officer; TOM BREVOORT, SVP of Publishing; DAVID BOGART, SVP of Business Affairs & Operations, Publishing & Partnership; DAVID GABRIEL, SVP of Sales & Marketing, Publishing; JEFF YOUNGQUIST, VP of Production & Special Projects; DAN CARR, Executive Director of Publishing Technology; ALEX MORALES, Director of Publishing Operations; DAN EDINGTON, Managing Editor; SUSAN CRESPI, Production Manager; STAN LEE, Chairman Emeritus. For information regarding advertising in Marvel Comics or on Marvel.com, please contact Vit DeBellis, Custom Solutions & Integrated Advertising Manager, at vdebellis@marvel.com. For Marvel subscription inquiries, please call 888-511-5480. **Manufactured between 9/7/2018 and 10/9/2018 by SOLISCO PRINTERS, SCOTT, QC, CANADA.**

10 9 8 7 6 5 4 3 2 1

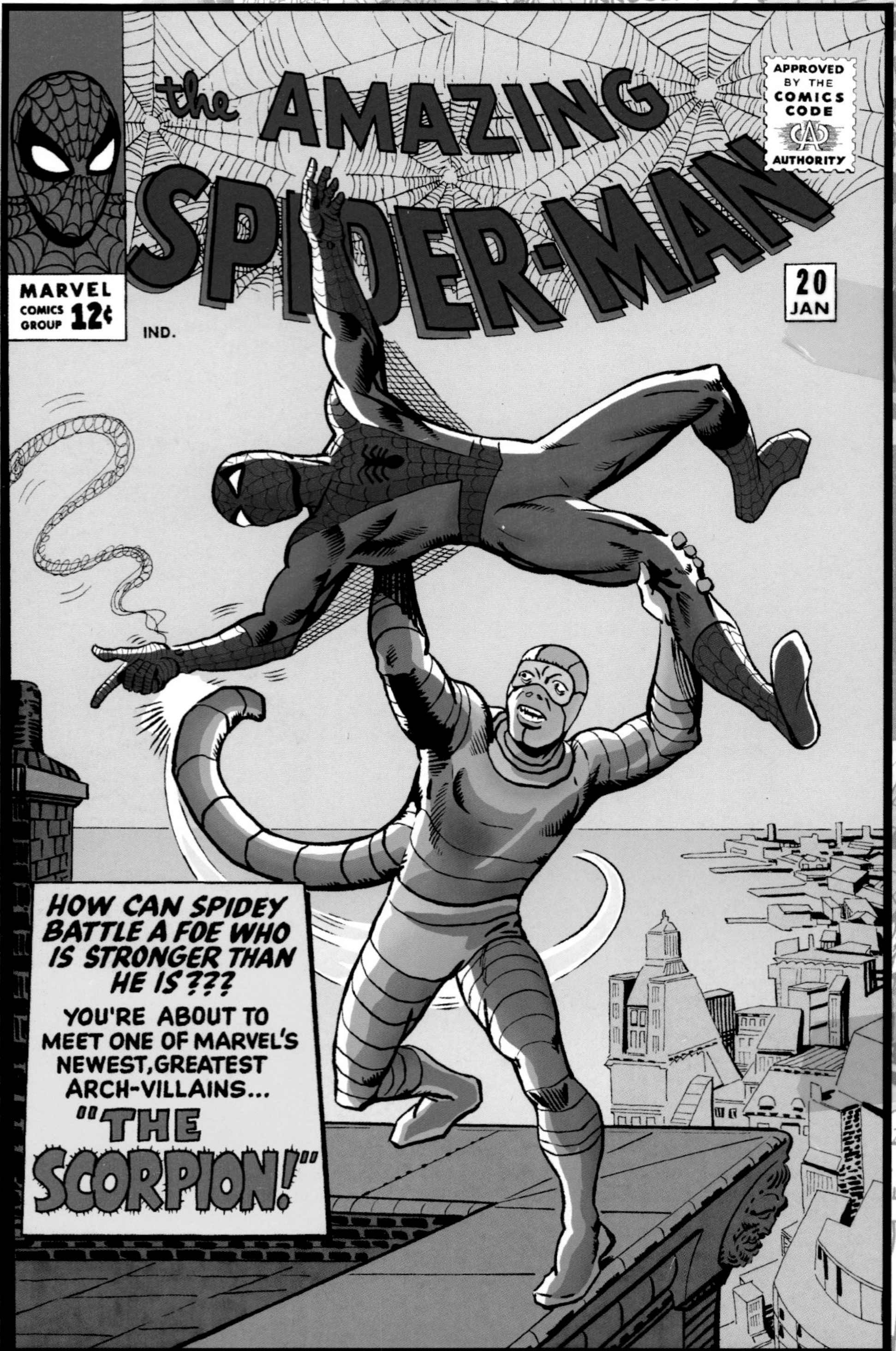
the AMAZING SPIDER-MAN
APPROVED BY THE COMICS CODE AUTHORITY
MARVEL COMICS GROUP 12¢
IND.
20 JAN
HOW CAN SPIDEY BATTLE A FOE WHO IS STRONGER THAN HE IS???
YOU'RE ABOUT TO MEET ONE OF MARVEL'S NEWEST, GREATEST ARCH-VILLAINS...
"THE SCORPION!"

AMAZING SPIDER-MAN (1963) #20

J. JONAH JAMESON WILL DO ANYTHING TO FIND OUT WHO SPIDER-MAN IS — EVEN HAVING PRIVATE INVESTIGATOR MAC GARGAN TURNED INTO THE

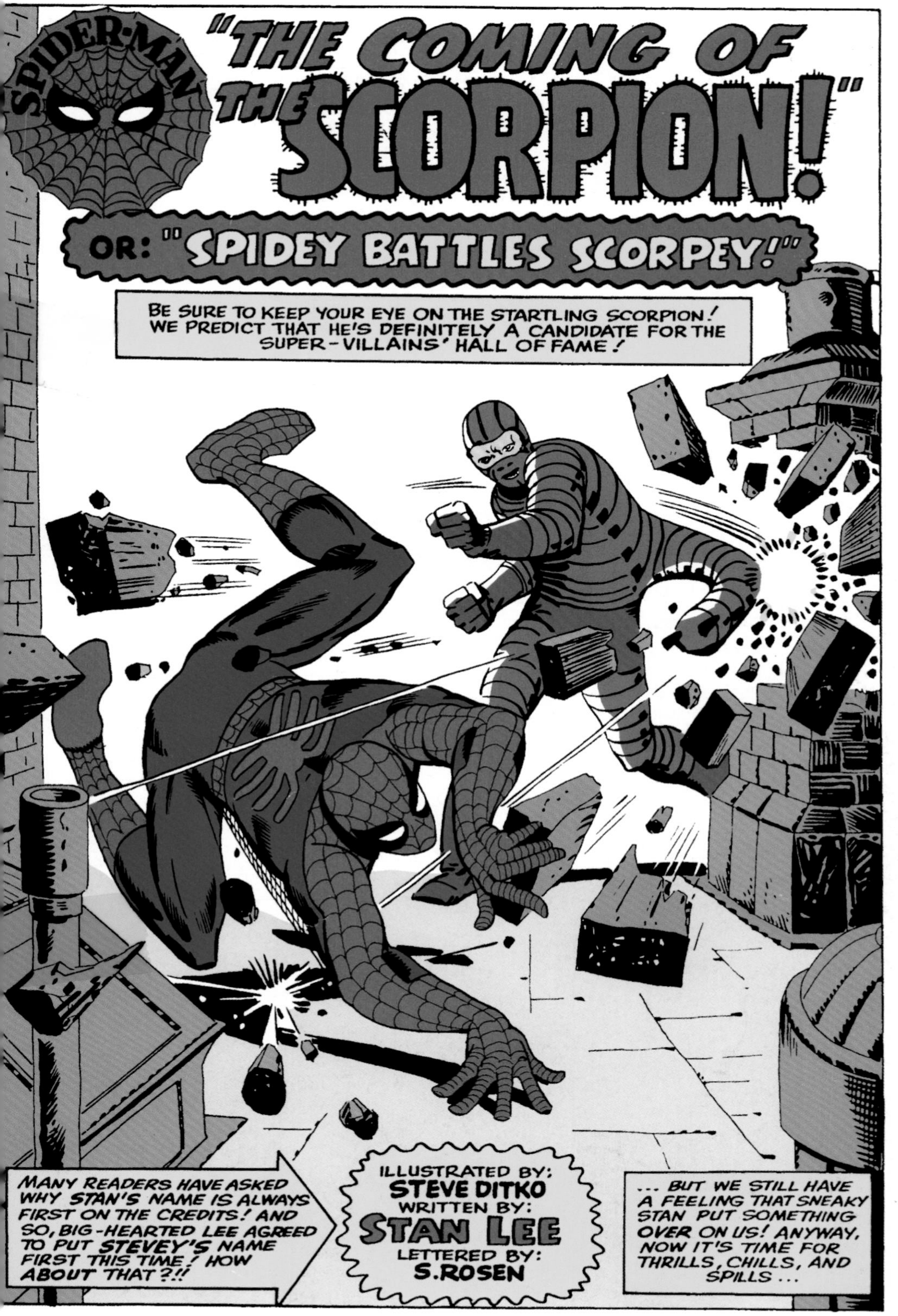
SPIDER-MAN
"THE COMING OF THE SCORPION!"
OR: "SPIDEY BATTLES SCORPEY!"
BE SURE TO KEEP YOUR EYE ON THE STARTLING SCORPION! WE PREDICT THAT HE'S DEFINITELY A CANDIDATE FOR THE SUPER-VILLAINS' HALL OF FAME!
MANY READERS HAVE ASKED WHY STAN'S NAME IS ALWAYS FIRST ON THE CREDITS! AND SO, BIG-HEARTED LEE AGREED TO PUT STEVEY'S NAME FIRST THIS TIME! HOW ABOUT THAT?!!
ILLUSTRATED BY: STEVE DITKO WRITTEN BY: STAN LEE LETTERED BY: S.ROSEN
... BUT WE STILL HAVE A FEELING THAT SNEAKY STAN PUT SOMETHING OVER ON US! ANYWAY, NOW IT'S TIME FOR THRILLS, CHILLS, AND SPILLS ...

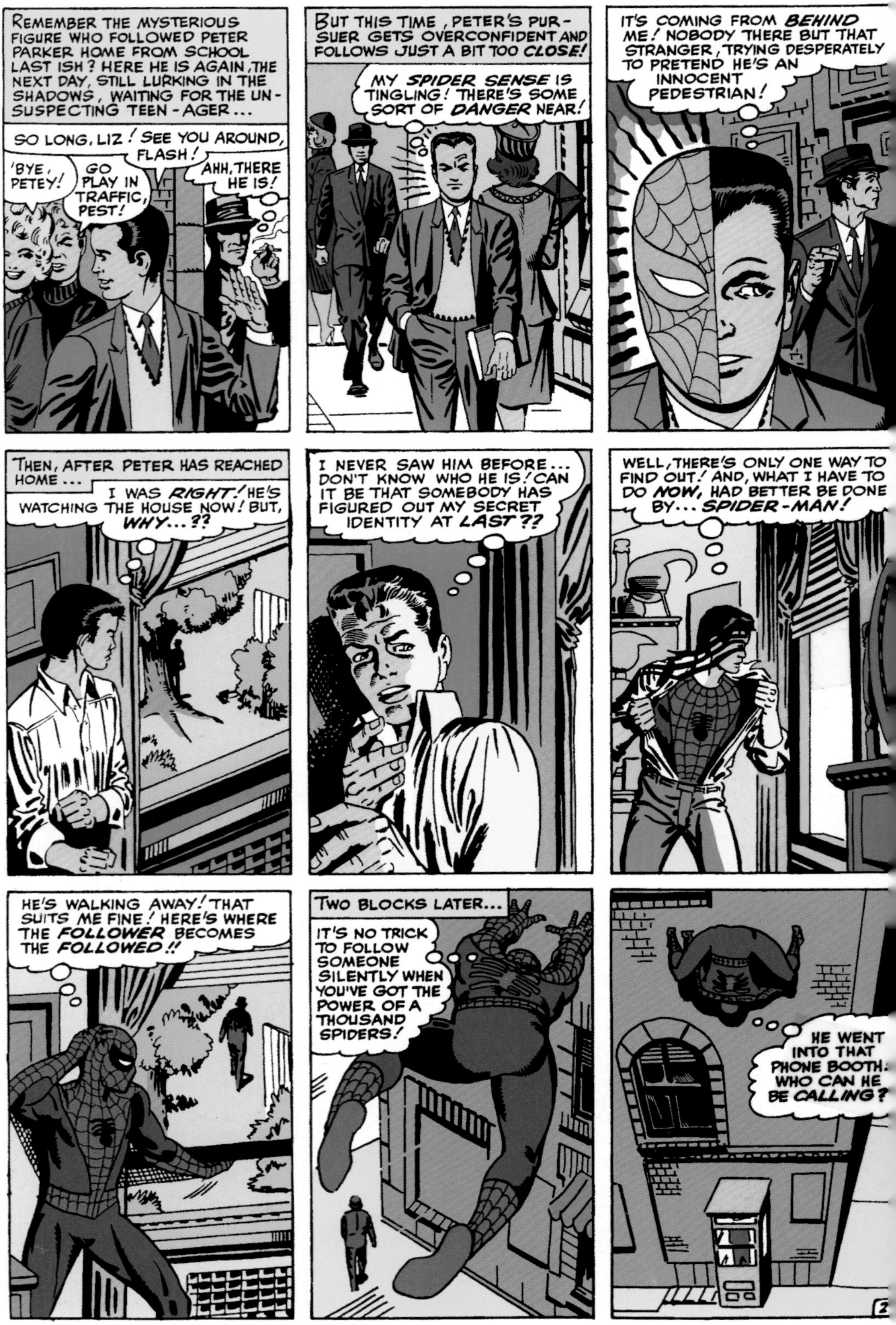
REMEMBER THE MYSTERIOUS FIGURE WHO FOLLOWED PETER PARKER HOME FROM SCHOOL LAST ISH? HERE HE IS AGAIN, THE NEXT DAY, STILL LURKING IN THE SHADOWS, WAITING FOR THE UN-SUSPECTING TEEN-AGER...
SO LONG, LIZ! SEE YOU AROUND, FLASH!
'BYE, PETEY!
GO PLAY IN TRAFFIC, PEST!
AHH, THERE HE IS!
BUT THIS TIME, PETER'S PUR-SUER GETS OVERCONFIDENT AND FOLLOWS JUST A BIT TOO CLOSE!
MY SPIDER SENSE IS TINGLING! THERE'S SOME SORT OF DANGER NEAR!
IT'S COMING FROM BEHIND ME! NOBODY THERE BUT THAT STRANGER, TRYING DESPERATELY TO PRETEND HE'S AN INNOCENT PEDESTRIAN!
THEN, AFTER PETER HAS REACHED HOME...
I WAS RIGHT! HE'S WATCHING THE HOUSE NOW! BUT, WHY...??
I NEVER SAW HIM BEFORE... DON'T KNOW WHO HE IS! CAN IT BE THAT SOMEBODY HAS FIGURED OUT MY SECRET IDENTITY AT LAST??
WELL, THERE'S ONLY ONE WAY TO FIND OUT! AND, WHAT I HAVE TO DO NOW, HAD BETTER BE DONE BY... SPIDER-MAN!
HE'S WALKING AWAY! THAT SUITS ME FINE! HERE'S WHERE THE FOLLOWER BECOMES THE FOLLOWED!!
TWO BLOCKS LATER...
IT'S NO TRICK TO FOLLOW SOMEONE SILENTLY WHEN YOU'VE GOT THE POWER OF A THOUSAND SPIDERS!
HE WENT INTO THAT PHONE BOOTH! WHO CAN HE BE CALLING?
2

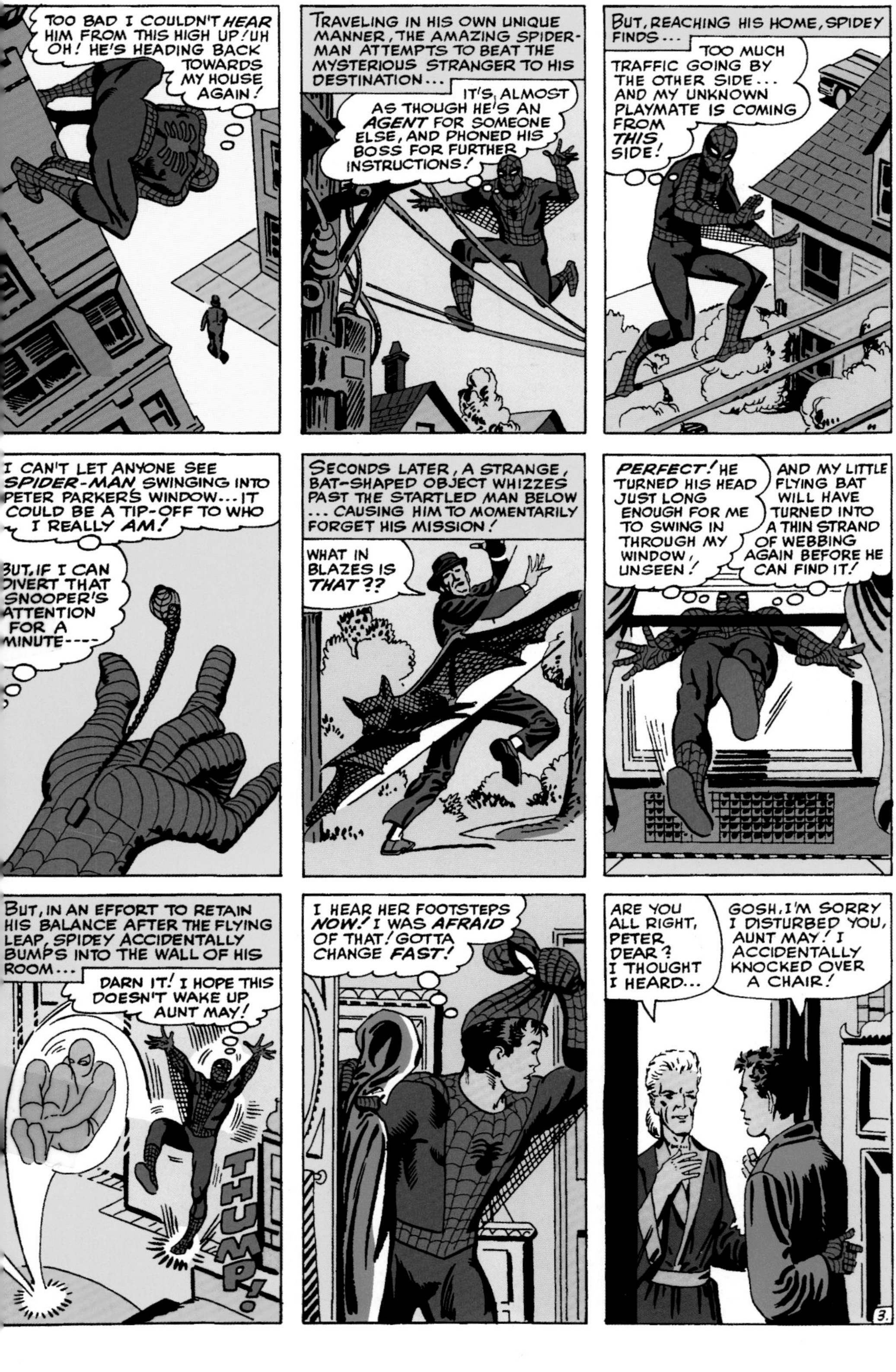
TOO BAD I COULDN'T HEAR HIM FROM THIS HIGH UP! UH OH! HE'S HEADING BACK TOWARDS MY HOUSE AGAIN!
TRAVELING IN HIS OWN UNIQUE MANNER, THE AMAZING SPIDER-MAN ATTEMPTS TO BEAT THE MYSTERIOUS STRANGER TO HIS DESTINATION...
IT'S ALMOST AS THOUGH HE'S AN AGENT FOR SOMEONE ELSE, AND PHONED HIS BOSS FOR FURTHER INSTRUCTIONS!
BUT, REACHING HIS HOME, SPIDEY FINDS...
TOO MUCH TRAFFIC GOING BY THE OTHER SIDE... AND MY UNKNOWN PLAYMATE IS COMING FROM THIS SIDE!
I CAN'T LET ANYONE SEE SPIDER-MAN SWINGING INTO PETER PARKER'S WINDOW... IT COULD BE A TIP-OFF TO WHO I REALLY AM!
BUT, IF I CAN DIVERT THAT SNOOPER'S ATTENTION FOR A MINUTE----
SECONDS LATER, A STRANGE, BAT-SHAPED OBJECT WHIZZES PAST THE STARTLED MAN BELOW ... CAUSING HIM TO MOMENTARILY FORGET HIS MISSION!
WHAT IN BLAZES IS THAT??
PERFECT! HE TURNED HIS HEAD JUST LONG ENOUGH FOR ME TO SWING IN THROUGH MY WINDOW, UNSEEN!
AND MY LITTLE FLYING BAT WILL HAVE TURNED INTO A THIN STRAND OF WEBBING AGAIN BEFORE HE CAN FIND IT!
BUT, IN AN EFFORT TO RETAIN HIS BALANCE AFTER THE FLYING LEAP, SPIDEY ACCIDENTALLY BUMPS INTO THE WALL OF HIS ROOM...
DARN IT! I HOPE THIS DOESN'T WAKE UP AUNT MAY!
THUMP!
I HEAR HER FOOTSTEPS NOW! I WAS AFRAID OF THAT! GOTTA CHANGE FAST!
ARE YOU ALL RIGHT, PETER DEAR? I THOUGHT I HEARD...
GOSH, I'M SORRY I DISTURBED YOU, AUNT MAY! I ACCIDENTALLY KNOCKED OVER A CHAIR!
3.

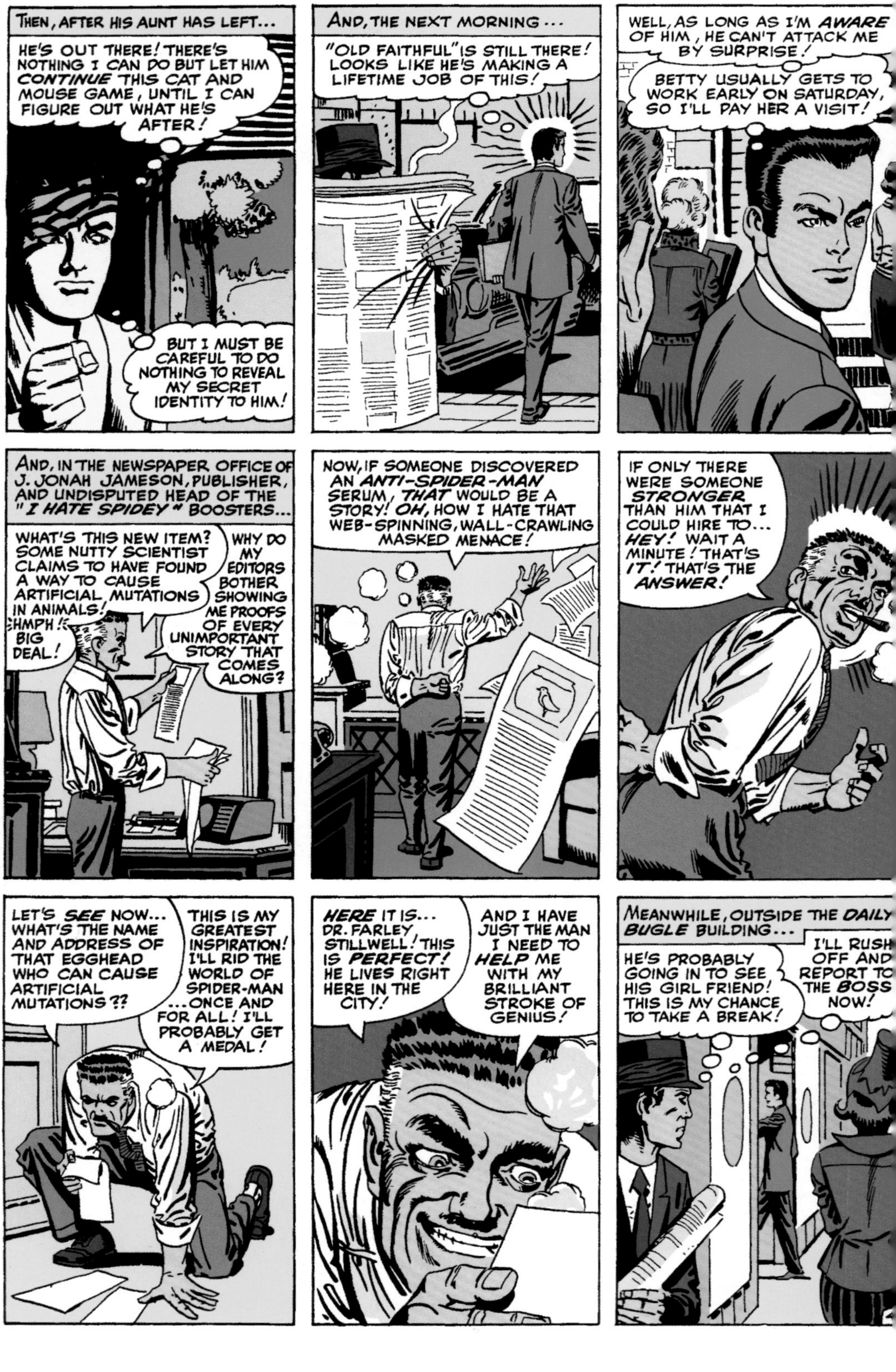

THEN, AFTER HIS AUNT HAS LEFT...
HE'S OUT THERE! THERE'S NOTHING I CAN DO BUT LET HIM CONTINUE THIS CAT AND MOUSE GAME, UNTIL I CAN FIGURE OUT WHAT HE'S AFTER!
BUT I MUST BE CAREFUL TO DO NOTHING TO REVEAL MY SECRET IDENTITY TO HIM!
AND, THE NEXT MORNING...
"OLD FAITHFUL" IS STILL THERE! LOOKS LIKE HE'S MAKING A LIFETIME JOB OF THIS!
WELL, AS LONG AS I'M AWARE OF HIM, HE CAN'T ATTACK ME BY SURPRISE!
BETTY USUALLY GETS TO WORK EARLY ON SATURDAY, SO I'LL PAY HER A VISIT!
AND, IN THE NEWSPAPER OFFICE OF J. JONAH JAMESON, PUBLISHER, AND UNDISPUTED HEAD OF THE "I HATE SPIDEY" BOOSTERS...
WHAT'S THIS NEW ITEM? SOME NUTTY SCIENTIST CLAIMS TO HAVE FOUND A WAY TO CAUSE ARTIFICIAL MUTATIONS IN ANIMALS!
HMPH!! BIG DEAL!
WHY DO MY EDITORS BOTHER SHOWING ME PROOFS OF EVERY UNIMPORTANT STORY THAT COMES ALONG?
NOW, IF SOMEONE DISCOVERED AN ANTI-SPIDER-MAN SERUM, THAT WOULD BE A STORY! OH, HOW I HATE THAT WEB-SPINNING, WALL-CRAWLING MASKED MENACE!
IF ONLY THERE WERE SOMEONE STRONGER THAN HIM THAT I COULD HIRE TO... HEY! WAIT A MINUTE! THAT'S IT! THAT'S THE ANSWER!
LET'S SEE NOW... WHAT'S THE NAME AND ADDRESS OF THAT EGGHEAD WHO CAN CAUSE ARTIFICIAL MUTATIONS ??
THIS IS MY GREATEST INSPIRATION! I'LL RID THE WORLD OF SPIDER-MAN ...ONCE AND FOR ALL! I'LL PROBABLY GET A MEDAL!
HERE IT IS... DR. FARLEY STILLWELL! THIS IS PERFECT! HE LIVES RIGHT HERE IN THE CITY!
AND I HAVE JUST THE MAN I NEED TO HELP ME WITH MY BRILLIANT STROKE OF GENIUS!
MEANWHILE, OUTSIDE THE DAILY BUGLE BUILDING...
HE'S PROBABLY GOING IN TO SEE HIS GIRL FRIEND! THIS IS MY CHANCE TO TAKE A BREAK!
I'LL RUSH OFF AND REPORT TO THE BOSS NOW!

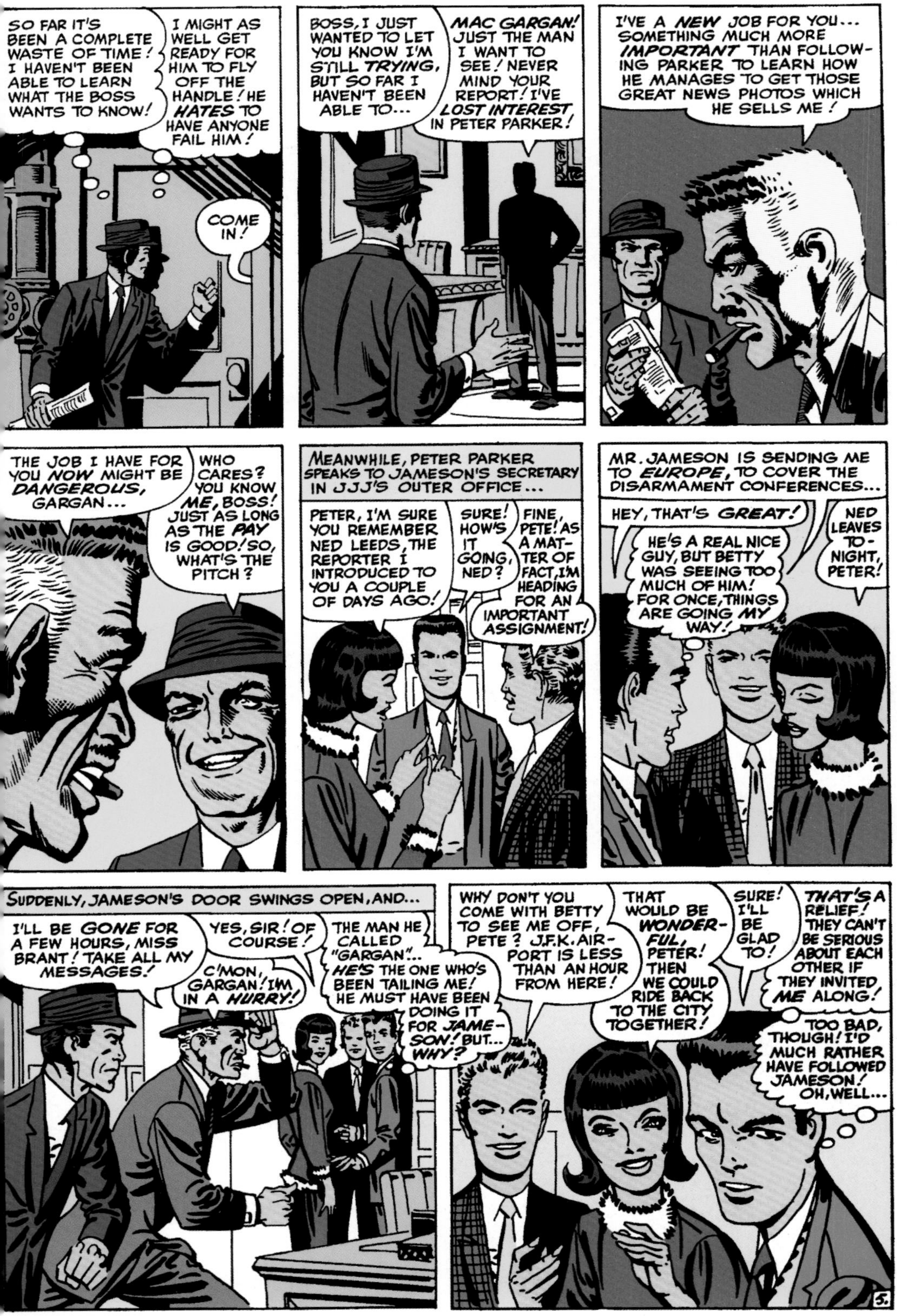
SO FAR IT'S BEEN A COMPLETE WASTE OF TIME! I HAVEN'T BEEN ABLE TO LEARN WHAT THE BOSS WANTS TO KNOW!
I MIGHT AS WELL GET READY FOR HIM TO FLY OFF THE HANDLE! HE HATES TO HAVE ANYONE FAIL HIM!
COME IN!
BOSS, I JUST WANTED TO LET YOU KNOW I'M STILL TRYING, BUT SO FAR I HAVEN'T BEEN ABLE TO...
MAC GARGAN! JUST THE MAN I WANT TO SEE! NEVER MIND YOUR REPORT! I'VE LOST INTEREST IN PETER PARKER!
I'VE A NEW JOB FOR YOU... SOMETHING MUCH MORE IMPORTANT THAN FOLLOWING PARKER TO LEARN HOW HE MANAGES TO GET THOSE GREAT NEWS PHOTOS WHICH HE SELLS ME!
THE JOB I HAVE FOR YOU NOW MIGHT BE DANGEROUS, GARGAN...
WHO CARES? YOU KNOW ME, BOSS! JUST AS LONG AS THE PAY IS GOOD! SO, WHAT'S THE PITCH?
MEANWHILE, PETER PARKER SPEAKS TO JAMESON'S SECRETARY IN JJJ'S OUTER OFFICE...
PETER, I'M SURE YOU REMEMBER NED LEEDS, THE REPORTER I INTRODUCED TO YOU A COUPLE OF DAYS AGO!
SURE! HOW'S IT GOING, NED?
FINE, PETE! AS A MATTER OF FACT, I'M HEADING FOR AN IMPORTANT ASSIGNMENT!
MR. JAMESON IS SENDING ME TO EUROPE, TO COVER THE DISARMAMENT CONFERENCES...
HEY, THAT'S GREAT!
HE'S A REAL NICE GUY, BUT BETTY WAS SEEING TOO MUCH OF HIM! FOR ONCE, THINGS ARE GOING MY WAY!
NED LEAVES TONIGHT, PETER!
SUDDENLY, JAMESON'S DOOR SWINGS OPEN, AND...
I'LL BE GONE FOR A FEW HOURS, MISS BRANT! TAKE ALL MY MESSAGES!
YES, SIR! OF COURSE!
C'MON, GARGAN! I'M IN A HURRY!
THE MAN HE CALLED "GARGAN"... HE'S THE ONE WHO'S BEEN TAILING ME! HE MUST HAVE BEEN DOING IT FOR JAMESON! BUT... WHY?
WHY DON'T YOU COME WITH BETTY TO SEE ME OFF, PETE? J.F.K. AIRPORT IS LESS THAN AN HOUR FROM HERE!
THAT WOULD BE WONDERFUL, PETER! THEN WE COULD RIDE BACK TO THE CITY TOGETHER!
SURE! I'LL BE GLAD TO!
THAT'S A RELIEF! THEY CAN'T BE SERIOUS ABOUT EACH OTHER IF THEY INVITED ME ALONG!
TOO BAD, THOUGH! I'D MUCH RATHER HAVE FOLLOWED JAMESON! OH, WELL...
5.

A SHORT TIME LATER, AT THE LABORATORY OF DR. FARLEY STILLWELL...

YOU MEAN YOU ACTUALLY MUTATED A RAT SO IT CAN SWIM LIKE A FISH... AND ENABLED A FISH TO BREATHE AIR LIKE A RAT?

WELL, "MUTATED" IS NOT THE EXACT SCIENTIFIC WORD, MR. JAMESON!...BUT I BELIEVE YOU SUMMED IT UP ACCURATELY ENOUGH!

MY WORK, IF PROPERLY DEVELOPED, MIGHT BE OF GREAT VALUE TO FARMERS, BOTANISTS AND THE LIKE! I'M DELIGHTED THAT YOU'VE SHOWN SUCH INTEREST! AN INFLUENTIAL MAN LIKE YOU, PUBLICIZING MY FINDINGS COULD FURTHER THE CAUSE OF SCIENCE IMMEASURABLY!

SURE, SURE! NATURALLY! BUT IT'S NOT *SCIENCE* I'M INTERESTED IN RIGHT NOW! I WANT YOU TO WORK ON A *SPECIAL PROJECT* FOR ME! IF IT WORKS, I'LL PAY YOU $10,000!

I'M A RESEARCH SCIENTIST! I DON'T ACCEPT PRIVATE JOBS FOR PAY! AND YET... WITH $10,000 I COULD BUY NEW EQUIPMENT... NEW MATERIALS! I...I'M JUST NOT IN A POSITION TO *REFUSE* YOU, MR. JAMESON! WHAT IS YOUR PROJECT?

I WANT YOU TO TRY YOUR EXPERIMENT ON A *HUMAN BEING*! I WANT YOU TO GIVE A MAN POWERS WHICH ARE GREATER THAN *SPIDER-MAN'S*!

I HAVE ENOUGH SERUM... I HAVE THE KNOW-HOW... AND, YET, IT MIGHT BE *DANGEROUS*! I CAN'T GUARANTEE THE RESULTS!

THAT'S OKAY, DOC! I'M WILLING TO CHANCE IT!

MOMENTS LATER...AFTER DR. STILLWELL HAS SHAVED GARGAN'S HEAD...

I CAN GIVE YOU THE POWERS OF A *SCORPION*, FOR INSTANCE! YOUR BODY WOULD BECOME MORE POWERFUL THAN SPIDER-MAN'S...BUT I DON'T KNOW HOW IT WOULD AFFECT YOUR *BRAIN*!

WHO CARES? I'M GETTING $10,000 *ALSO* FOR *MY* PART IN THIS...AND I'D DO *ANYTHING* FOR THAT KIND OF DOUGH!

VERY WELL, THEN, DRINK THIS! I *KNOW* I SHOULDN'T AGREE TO THIS MAD SCHEME, BUT HEAVEN FORGIVE ME, I *MUST* HAVE THE MONEY TO CARRY ON MY WORK!

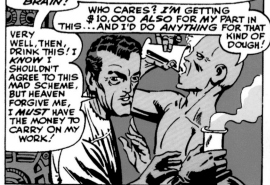

THEN, THE LONG ARDUOUS PERIOD OF *TESTING* BEGINS, UNTIL...

HE'S REACTING *PERFECTLY*! SEE HOW HIS *STRENGTH* HAS INCREASED! AND HIS COORDINATION IS ALREADY SUPER-HUMAN!

GOOD! GOOD! JUST SO LONG AS I'M SURE HE CAN BEAT THAT BLASTED *SPIDER MAN*! THAT'S ALL I *WANT*!!

6.

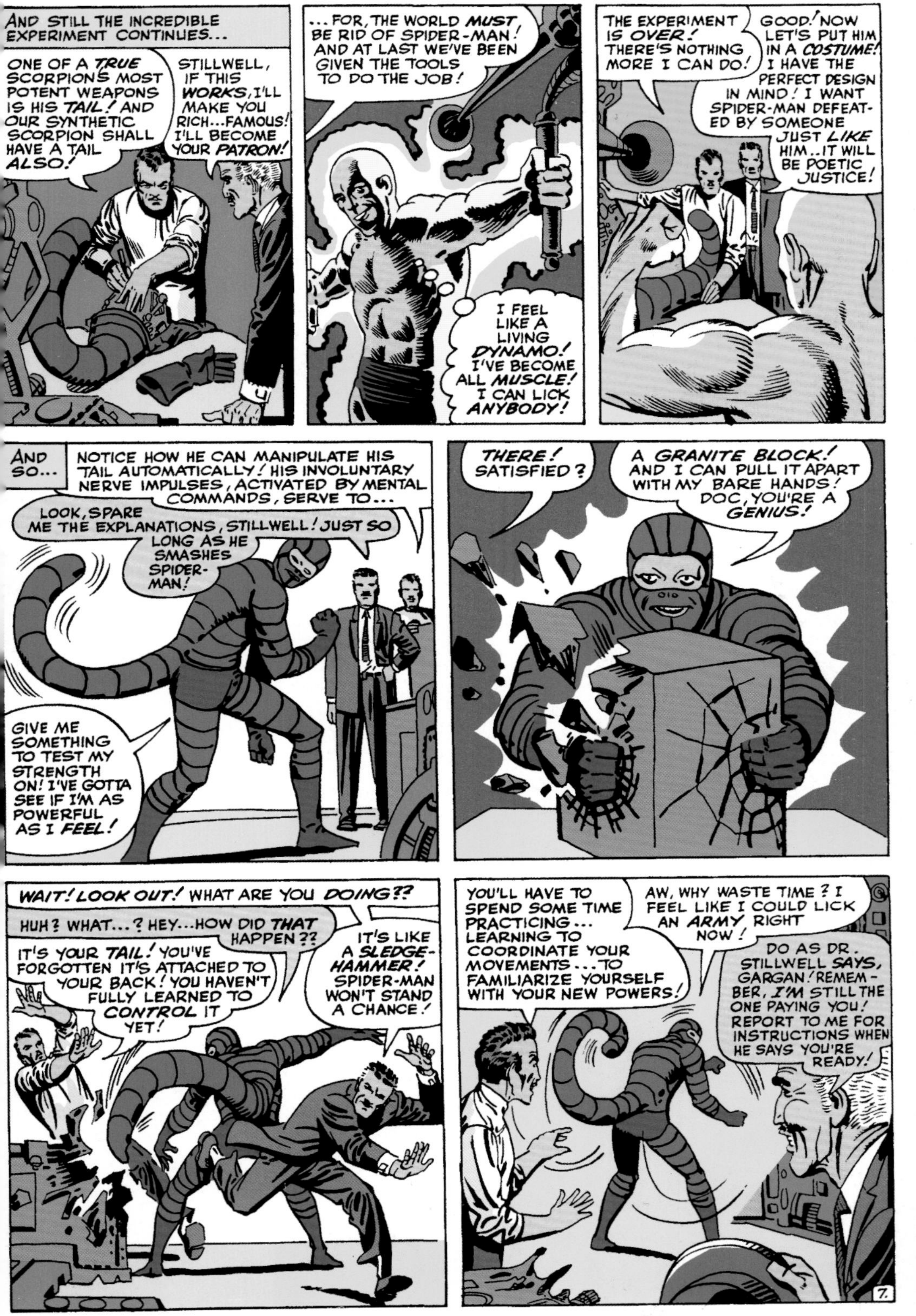
AND STILL THE INCREDIBLE EXPERIMENT CONTINUES...
ONE OF A TRUE SCORPION'S MOST POTENT WEAPONS IS HIS TAIL! AND OUR SYNTHETIC SCORPION SHALL HAVE A TAIL ALSO!
STILLWELL, IF THIS WORKS, I'LL MAKE YOU RICH...FAMOUS! I'LL BECOME YOUR PATRON!
...FOR, THE WORLD MUST BE RID OF SPIDER-MAN! AND AT LAST WE'VE BEEN GIVEN THE TOOLS TO DO THE JOB!
I FEEL LIKE A LIVING DYNAMO! I'VE BECOME ALL MUSCLE! I CAN LICK ANYBODY!
THE EXPERIMENT IS OVER! THERE'S NOTHING MORE I CAN DO!
GOOD! NOW LET'S PUT HIM IN A COSTUME! I HAVE THE PERFECT DESIGN IN MIND! I WANT SPIDER-MAN DEFEATED BY SOMEONE JUST LIKE HIM...IT WILL BE POETIC JUSTICE!
AND SO...
NOTICE HOW HE CAN MANIPULATE HIS TAIL AUTOMATICALLY! HIS INVOLUNTARY NERVE IMPULSES, ACTIVATED BY MENTAL COMMANDS, SERVE TO...
LOOK, SPARE ME THE EXPLANATIONS, STILLWELL! JUST SO LONG AS HE SMASHES SPIDER-MAN!
GIVE ME SOMETHING TO TEST MY STRENGTH ON! I'VE GOTTA SEE IF I'M AS POWERFUL AS I FEEL!
THERE! SATISFIED?
A GRANITE BLOCK! AND I CAN PULL IT APART WITH MY BARE HANDS! DOC, YOU'RE A GENIUS!
WAIT! LOOK OUT! WHAT ARE YOU DOING??
HUH? WHAT...? HEY...HOW DID THAT HAPPEN??
IT'S YOUR TAIL! YOU'VE FORGOTTEN IT'S ATTACHED TO YOUR BACK! YOU HAVEN'T FULLY LEARNED TO CONTROL IT YET!
IT'S LIKE A SLEDGE-HAMMER! SPIDER-MAN WON'T STAND A CHANCE!
YOU'LL HAVE TO SPEND SOME TIME PRACTICING... LEARNING TO COORDINATE YOUR MOVEMENTS...TO FAMILIARIZE YOURSELF WITH YOUR NEW POWERS!
AW, WHY WASTE TIME? I FEEL LIKE I COULD LICK AN ARMY RIGHT NOW!
DO AS DR. STILLWELL SAYS, GARGAN! REMEMBER, I'M STILL THE ONE PAYING YOU! REPORT TO ME FOR INSTRUCTIONS WHEN HE SAYS YOU'RE READY!
7.

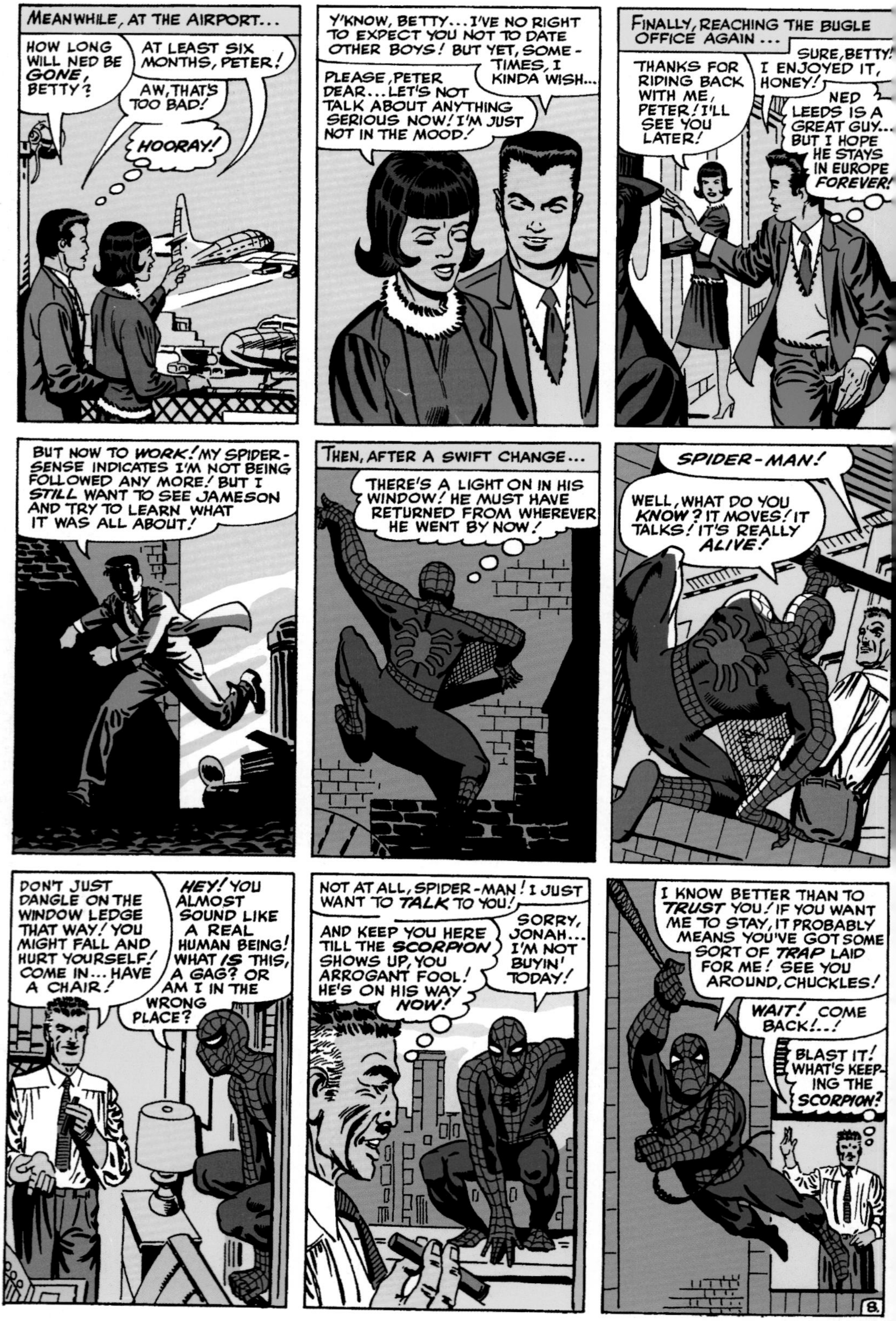

MEANWHILE, AT THE AIRPORT...
HOW LONG WILL NED BE GONE, BETTY?
AT LEAST SIX MONTHS, PETER!
AW, THAT'S TOO BAD!
HOORAY!
Y'KNOW, BETTY... I'VE NO RIGHT TO EXPECT YOU NOT TO DATE OTHER BOYS! BUT YET, SOME-TIMES, I KINDA WISH...
PLEASE, PETER DEAR... LET'S NOT TALK ABOUT ANYTHING SERIOUS NOW! I'M JUST NOT IN THE MOOD!
FINALLY, REACHING THE BUGLE OFFICE AGAIN...
THANKS FOR RIDING BACK WITH ME, PETER! I'LL SEE YOU LATER!
SURE, BETTY! I ENJOYED IT, HONEY!
NED LEEDS IS A GREAT GUY... BUT I HOPE HE STAYS IN EUROPE FOREVER!
BUT NOW TO WORK! MY SPIDER-SENSE INDICATES I'M NOT BEING FOLLOWED ANY MORE! BUT I STILL WANT TO SEE JAMESON AND TRY TO LEARN WHAT IT WAS ALL ABOUT!
THEN, AFTER A SWIFT CHANGE...
THERE'S A LIGHT ON IN HIS WINDOW! HE MUST HAVE RETURNED FROM WHEREVER HE WENT BY NOW!
SPIDER-MAN!
WELL, WHAT DO YOU KNOW? IT MOVES! IT TALKS! IT'S REALLY ALIVE!
DON'T JUST DANGLE ON THE WINDOW LEDGE THAT WAY! YOU MIGHT FALL AND HURT YOURSELF! COME IN... HAVE A CHAIR!
HEY! YOU ALMOST SOUND LIKE A REAL HUMAN BEING! WHAT IS THIS, A GAG? OR AM I IN THE WRONG PLACE?
NOT AT ALL, SPIDER-MAN! I JUST WANT TO TALK TO YOU!
AND KEEP YOU HERE TILL THE SCORPION SHOWS UP, YOU ARROGANT FOOL! HE'S ON HIS WAY NOW!
SORRY, JONAH... I'M NOT BUYIN' TODAY!
I KNOW BETTER THAN TO TRUST YOU! IF YOU WANT ME TO STAY, IT PROBABLY MEANS YOU'VE GOT SOME SORT OF TRAP LAID FOR ME! SEE YOU AROUND, CHUCKLES!
WAIT! COME BACK!..!
BLAST IT! WHAT'S KEEP-ING THE SCORPION?
8.

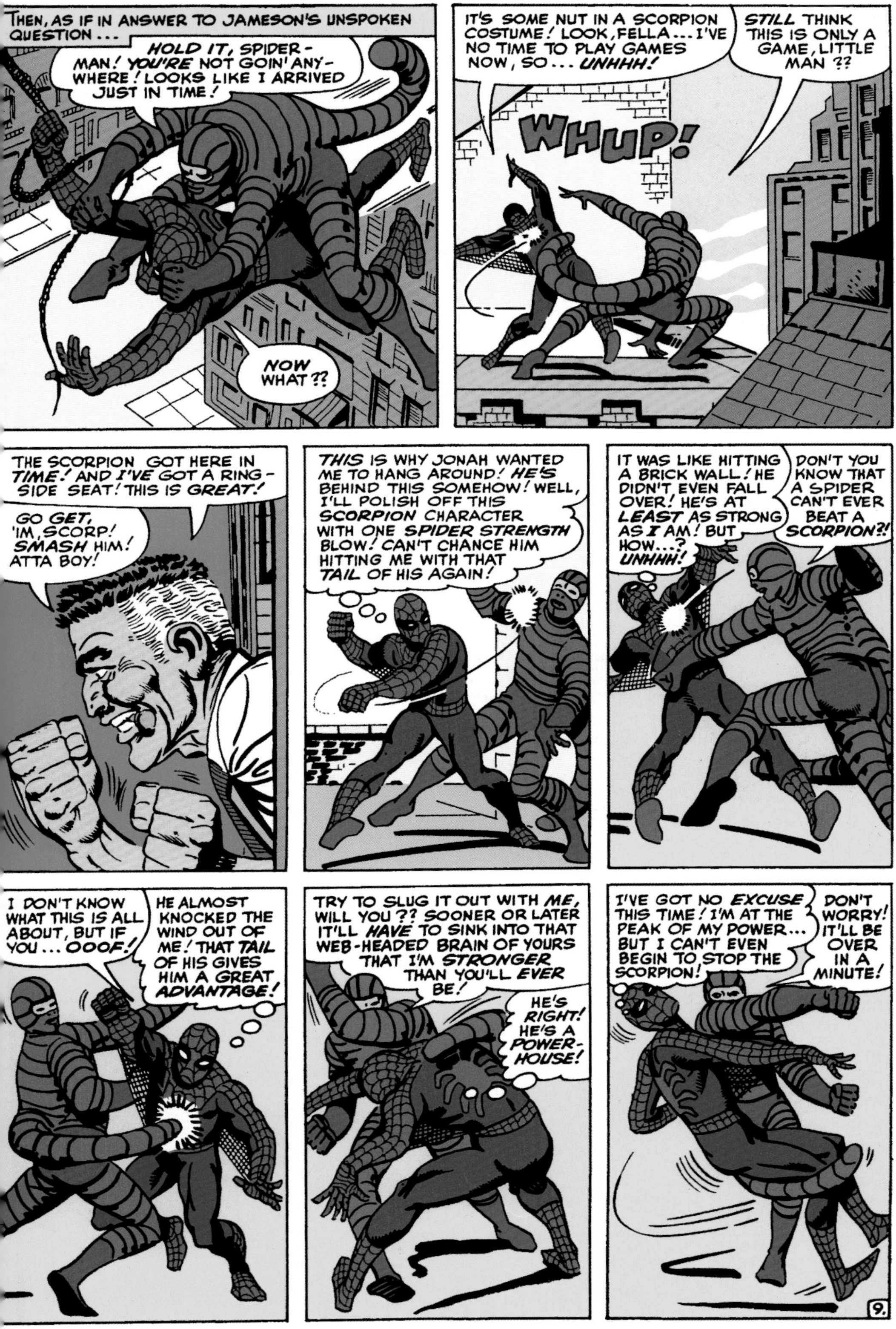

THEN, AS IF IN ANSWER TO JAMESON'S UNSPOKEN QUESTION...
HOLD IT, SPIDER-MAN! YOU'RE NOT GOIN' ANYWHERE! LOOKS LIKE I ARRIVED JUST IN TIME!
NOW WHAT??
IT'S SOME NUT IN A SCORPION COSTUME! LOOK, FELLA... I'VE NO TIME TO PLAY GAMES NOW, SO... UNHHH!
STILL THINK THIS IS ONLY A GAME, LITTLE MAN??
WHUP!
THE SCORPION GOT HERE IN TIME! AND I'VE GOT A RING-SIDE SEAT! THIS IS GREAT!
GO GET 'IM, SCORP! SMASH HIM! ATTA BOY!
THIS IS WHY JONAH WANTED ME TO HANG AROUND! HE'S BEHIND THIS SOMEHOW! WELL, I'LL POLISH OFF THIS SCORPION CHARACTER WITH ONE SPIDER STRENGTH BLOW! CAN'T CHANCE HIM HITTING ME WITH THAT TAIL OF HIS AGAIN!
IT WAS LIKE HITTING A BRICK WALL! HE DIDN'T EVEN FALL OVER! HE'S AT LEAST AS STRONG AS I AM! BUT HOW...? UNHHH!
DON'T YOU KNOW THAT A SPIDER CAN'T EVER BEAT A SCORPION?!
I DON'T KNOW WHAT THIS IS ALL ABOUT, BUT IF YOU... OOOF!
HE ALMOST KNOCKED THE WIND OUT OF ME! THAT TAIL OF HIS GIVES HIM A GREAT ADVANTAGE!
TRY TO SLUG IT OUT WITH ME, WILL YOU?? SOONER OR LATER IT'LL HAVE TO SINK INTO THAT WEB-HEADED BRAIN OF YOURS THAT I'M STRONGER THAN YOU'LL EVER BE!
HE'S RIGHT! HE'S A POWER-HOUSE!
I'VE GOT NO EXCUSE THIS TIME! I'M AT THE PEAK OF MY POWER... BUT I CAN'T EVEN BEGIN TO STOP THE SCORPION!
DON'T WORRY! IT'LL BE OVER IN A MINUTE!
9.

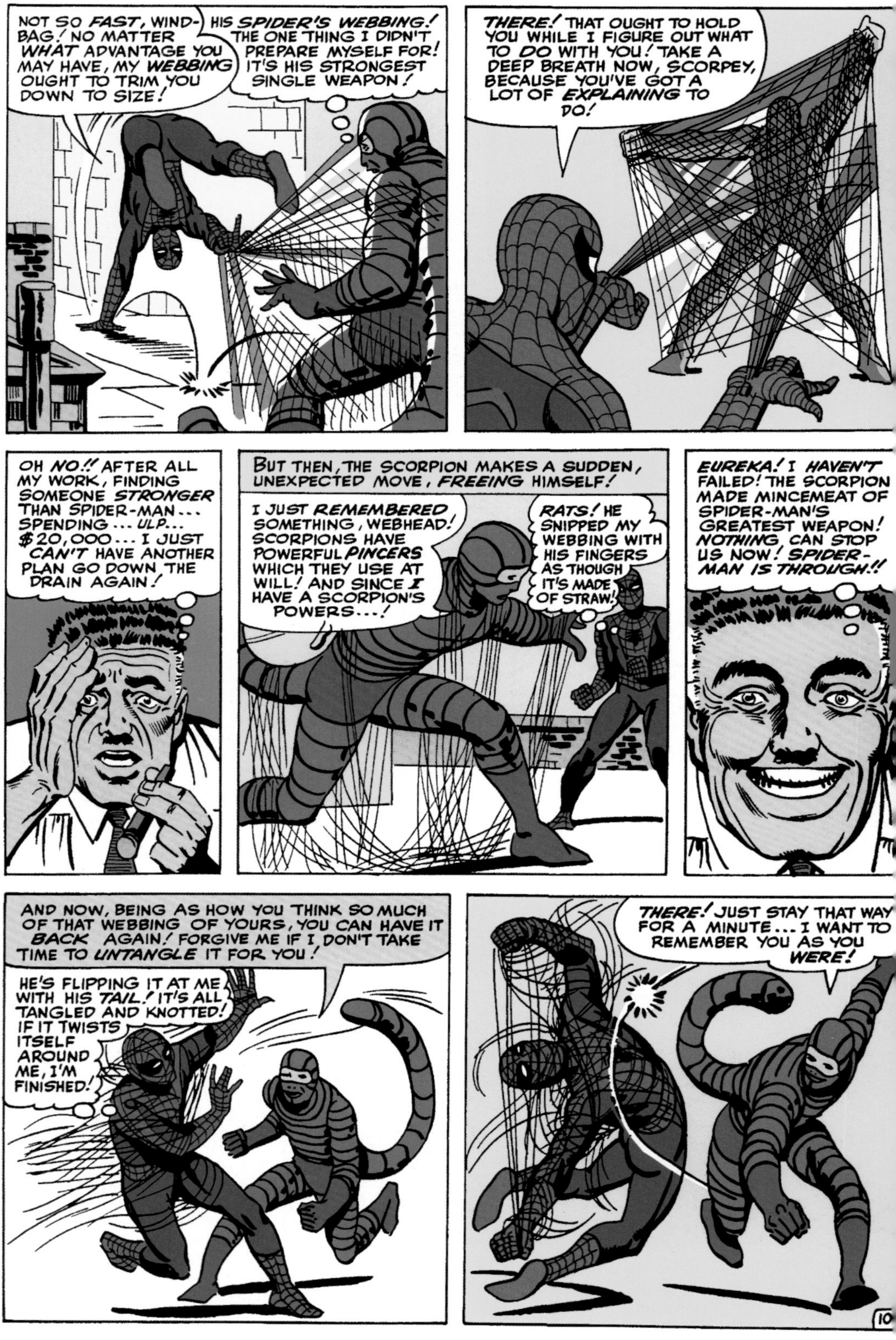

NOT SO *FAST*, WIND-BAG! NO MATTER *WHAT* ADVANTAGE YOU MAY HAVE, MY *WEBBING* OUGHT TO TRIM YOU DOWN TO SIZE!
HIS *SPIDER'S WEBBING!* THE ONE THING I DIDN'T PREPARE MYSELF FOR! IT'S HIS STRONGEST SINGLE WEAPON!
THERE! THAT OUGHT TO HOLD YOU WHILE I FIGURE OUT WHAT TO *DO* WITH YOU! TAKE A DEEP BREATH NOW, SCORPEY, BECAUSE YOU'VE GOT A LOT OF *EXPLAINING* TO DO!
OH *NO!!* AFTER ALL MY WORK, FINDING SOMEONE *STRONGER* THAN SPIDER-MAN... SPENDING... *ULP...* $20,000... I JUST *CAN'T* HAVE ANOTHER PLAN GO DOWN THE DRAIN AGAIN!
BUT THEN, THE SCORPION MAKES A SUDDEN, UNEXPECTED MOVE, *FREEING* HIMSELF!
I JUST *REMEMBERED* SOMETHING, WEBHEAD! SCORPIONS HAVE POWERFUL *PINCERS* WHICH THEY USE AT WILL! AND SINCE *I* HAVE A SCORPION'S POWERS...!
RATS! HE SNIPPED MY WEBBING WITH HIS FINGERS AS THOUGH IT'S MADE OF STRAW!
EUREKA! I *HAVEN'T* FAILED! THE SCORPION MADE MINCEMEAT OF SPIDER-MAN'S GREATEST WEAPON! *NOTHING* CAN STOP US NOW! *SPIDER-MAN IS THROUGH!!*
AND NOW, BEING AS HOW YOU THINK SO MUCH OF THAT WEBBING OF YOURS, YOU CAN HAVE IT *BACK* AGAIN! FORGIVE ME IF I DON'T TAKE TIME TO *UNTANGLE* IT FOR YOU!
HE'S FLIPPING IT AT ME WITH HIS *TAIL!* IT'S ALL TANGLED AND KNOTTED! IF IT TWISTS ITSELF AROUND ME, I'M FINISHED!
THERE! JUST STAY THAT WAY FOR A MINUTE... I WANT TO REMEMBER YOU AS YOU *WERE!*
10

MEANWHILE, STILL WORKING IN HIS LAB, DR. FARLEY STILLWELL HAS SOME VERY SERIOUS MISGIVINGS...

ACCORDING TO THESE NEW TESTS, THE *SCORPION* WILL BE EVEN MORE POWERFUL THAN I THOUGHT!

AND THE MORE HIS *STRENGTH* INCREASES, THE MORE HIS *EVIL NATURE* WILL TAKE OVER!

I MUST HAVE BEEN *MAD* TO DO WHAT I DID! MONEY ISN'T *THAT* IMPORTANT! I MAY HAVE UNLEASHED ONE OF THE WORST DANGERS OF ALL TIME UPON MANKIND!

BUT THERE'S STILL A CHANCE TO MAKE AMENDS... IF I MOVE FAST ENOUGH!

IF I CAN GET THIS *SERUM* TO HIM IN TIME, IT WILL SERVE AS AN *ANTIDOTE!* HE'LL LOSE HIS DEADLY POWERS BEFORE IT IS TOO LATE!

AND, AS THE DESPERATE SCIENTIST RUSHES INTO THE *STREET*, THE SCORPION PROVES TO BE AS POWERFUL AS STILLWELL FEARED...

HOW DOES IT *FEEL* TO BE ON *RECEIVING END* FOR ONCE, LITTLE MAN ?? WHAT'S A MATTER? CAT GOT YOUR TONGUE ?

HOW *ABOUT* THAT? I KNOCKED HIM OUT !! THIS IS THE EASIEST TEN GRAND ANYONE'S EVER MADE !

OKAY, USELESS... YOU CAN SLEEP IT OFF IN THAT EMPTY WATER TOWER! I'VE GOT *OTHER* THINGS TO DO NOW !

THUS SPIDER-MAN SUFFERS ONE OF HIS GREATEST DEFEATS, AS HE LIES MOTIONLESS ATOP THE ROOF, HIS MIGHTY MUSCLES STILLED... HIS POTENT SPIDER POWER TEMPORARILY DORMANT... ONLY THE BEATING OF HIS VALIANT HEART TESTIFYING TO THE LIFE WHICH REMAINS... TO THE AWESOME ENERGY WHICH IS SLOWLY RETURNING...

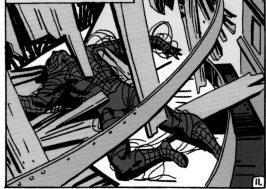

13.

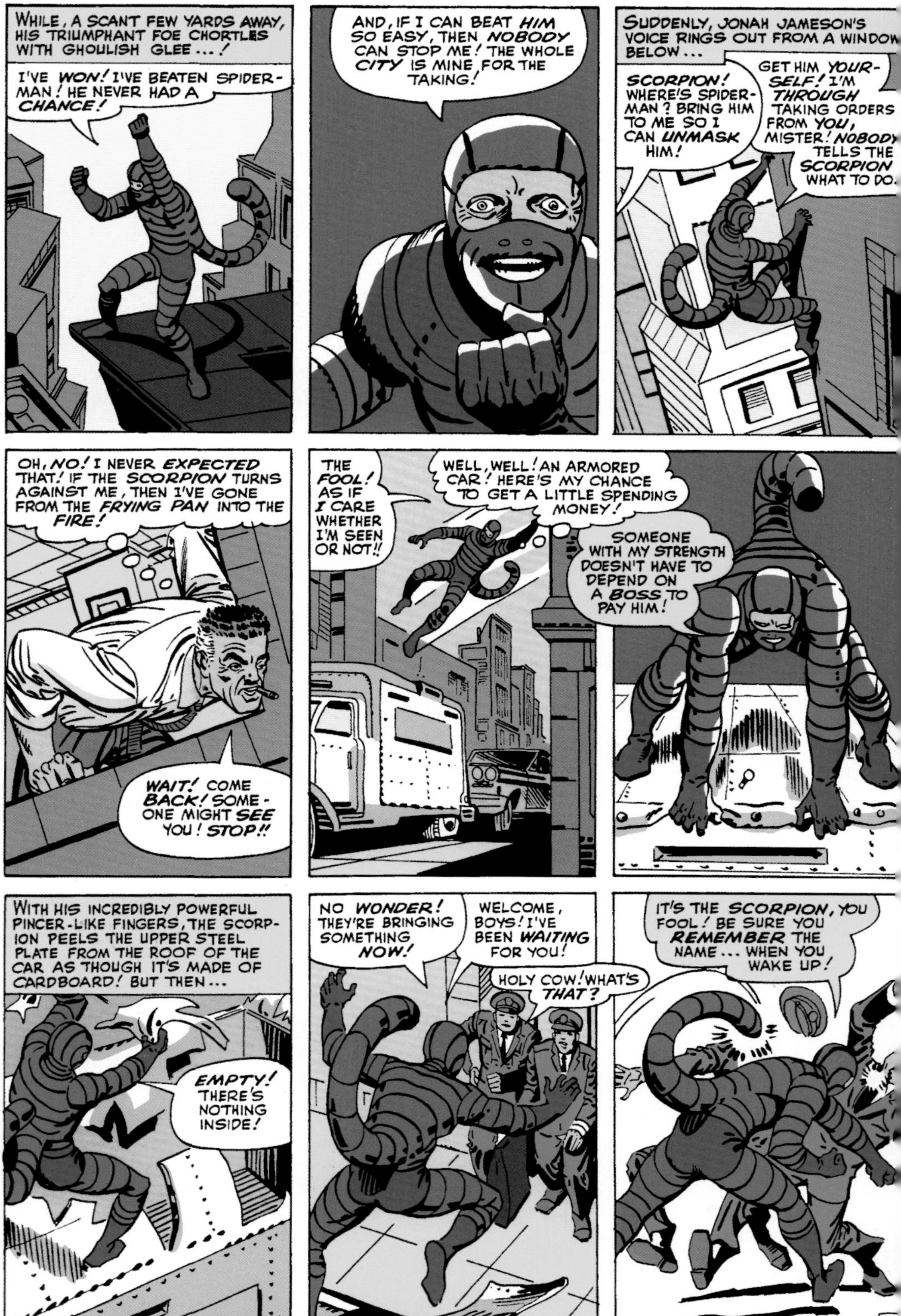
WHILE, A SCANT FEW YARDS AWAY, HIS TRIUMPHANT FOE CHORTLES WITH GHOULISH GLEE...!
I'VE WON! I'VE BEATEN SPIDER-MAN! HE NEVER HAD A CHANCE!
AND, IF I CAN BEAT HIM SO EASY, THEN NOBODY CAN STOP ME! THE WHOLE CITY IS MINE, FOR THE TAKING!
SUDDENLY, JONAH JAMESON'S VOICE RINGS OUT FROM A WINDOW BELOW...
SCORPION! WHERE'S SPIDER-MAN? BRING HIM TO ME SO I CAN UNMASK HIM!
GET HIM YOURSELF! I'M THROUGH TAKING ORDERS FROM YOU, MISTER! NOBODY TELLS THE SCORPION WHAT TO DO.
OH, NO! I NEVER EXPECTED THAT! IF THE SCORPION TURNS AGAINST ME, THEN I'VE GONE FROM THE FRYING PAN INTO THE FIRE!
WAIT! COME BACK! SOME-ONE MIGHT SEE YOU! STOP!!
THE FOOL! AS IF I CARE WHETHER I'M SEEN OR NOT!!
WELL, WELL! AN ARMORED CAR! HERE'S MY CHANCE TO GET A LITTLE SPENDING MONEY!
SOMEONE WITH MY STRENGTH DOESN'T HAVE TO DEPEND ON A BOSS TO PAY HIM!
WITH HIS INCREDIBLY POWERFUL PINCER-LIKE FINGERS, THE SCORPION PEELS THE UPPER STEEL PLATE FROM THE ROOF OF THE CAR AS THOUGH IT'S MADE OF CARDBOARD! BUT THEN...
EMPTY! THERE'S NOTHING INSIDE!
NO WONDER! THEY'RE BRINGING SOMETHING NOW!
WELCOME, BOYS! I'VE BEEN WAITING FOR YOU!
HOLY COW! WHAT'S THAT?
IT'S THE SCORPION, YOU FOOL! BE SURE YOU REMEMBER THE NAME... WHEN YOU WAKE UP!
12

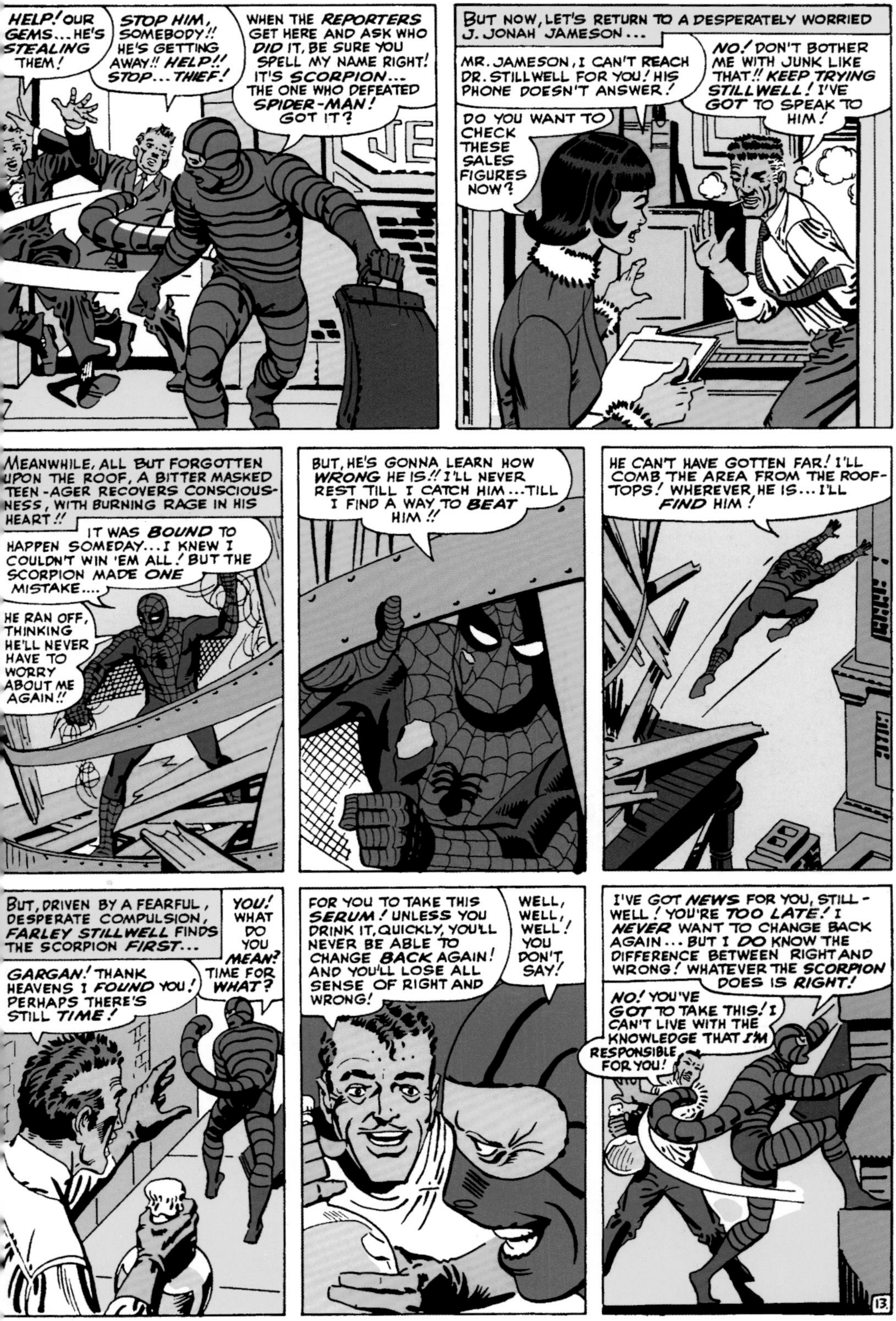
HELP! OUR GEMS... HE'S STEALING THEM!
STOP HIM, SOMEBODY!! HE'S GETTING AWAY!! HELP!! STOP... THIEF!
WHEN THE REPORTERS GET HERE AND ASK WHO DID IT, BE SURE YOU SPELL MY NAME RIGHT! IT'S SCORPION... THE ONE WHO DEFEATED SPIDER-MAN! GOT IT?
BUT NOW, LET'S RETURN TO A DESPERATELY WORRIED J. JONAH JAMESON...
MR. JAMESON, I CAN'T REACH DR. STILLWELL FOR YOU! HIS PHONE DOESN'T ANSWER!
DO YOU WANT TO CHECK THESE SALES FIGURES NOW?
NO! DON'T BOTHER ME WITH JUNK LIKE THAT!! KEEP TRYING STILLWELL! I'VE GOT TO SPEAK TO HIM!
MEANWHILE, ALL BUT FORGOTTEN UPON THE ROOF, A BITTER MASKED TEEN-AGER RECOVERS CONSCIOUSNESS, WITH BURNING RAGE IN HIS HEART!!
IT WAS BOUND TO HAPPEN SOMEDAY... I KNEW I COULDN'T WIN 'EM ALL! BUT THE SCORPION MADE ONE MISTAKE....
HE RAN OFF, THINKING HE'LL NEVER HAVE TO WORRY ABOUT ME AGAIN!!
BUT, HE'S GONNA LEARN HOW WRONG HE IS!! I'LL NEVER REST TILL I CATCH HIM... TILL I FIND A WAY TO BEAT HIM!!
HE CAN'T HAVE GOTTEN FAR! I'LL COMB THE AREA FROM THE ROOF-TOPS! WHEREVER HE IS... I'LL FIND HIM!
BUT, DRIVEN BY A FEARFUL, DESPERATE COMPULSION, FARLEY STILLWELL FINDS THE SCORPION FIRST...
GARGAN! THANK HEAVENS I FOUND YOU! PERHAPS THERE'S STILL TIME!
YOU! WHAT DO YOU MEAN? TIME FOR WHAT?
FOR YOU TO TAKE THIS SERUM! UNLESS YOU DRINK IT, QUICKLY, YOU'LL NEVER BE ABLE TO CHANGE BACK AGAIN! AND YOU'LL LOSE ALL SENSE OF RIGHT AND WRONG!
WELL, WELL, WELL! YOU DON'T SAY!
I'VE GOT NEWS FOR YOU, STILL-WELL! YOU'RE TOO LATE! I NEVER WANT TO CHANGE BACK AGAIN... BUT I DO KNOW THE DIFFERENCE BETWEEN RIGHT AND WRONG! WHATEVER THE SCORPION DOES IS RIGHT!
NO! YOU'VE GOT TO TAKE THIS! I CAN'T LIVE WITH THE KNOWLEDGE THAT I'M RESPONSIBLE FOR YOU!
13

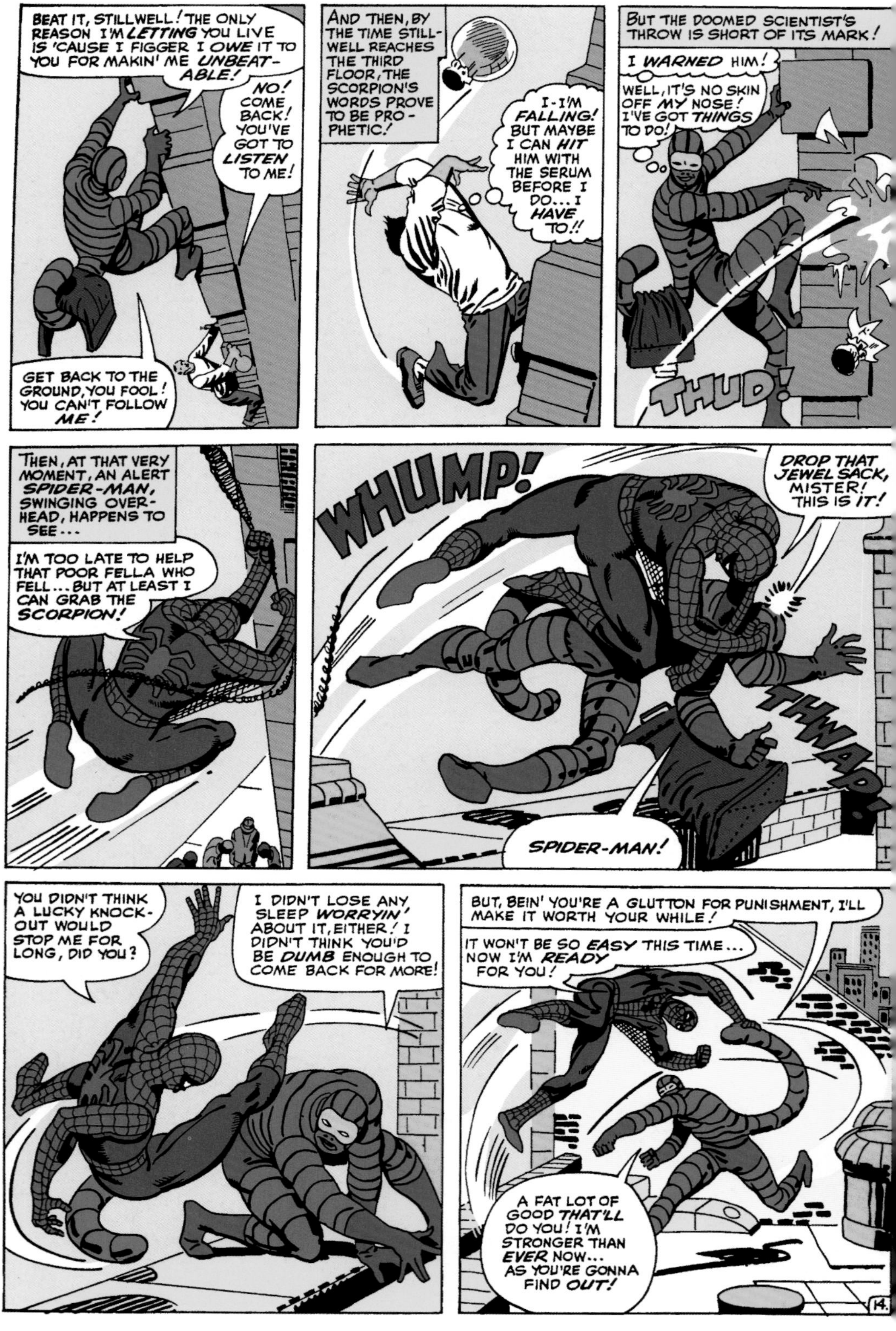
BEAT IT, STILLWELL! THE ONLY REASON I'M LETTING YOU LIVE IS 'CAUSE I FIGGER I OWE IT TO YOU FOR MAKIN' ME UNBEATABLE!
NO! COME BACK! YOU'VE GOT TO LISTEN TO ME!
GET BACK TO THE GROUND, YOU FOOL! YOU CAN'T FOLLOW ME!
AND THEN, BY THE TIME STILLWELL REACHES THE THIRD FLOOR, THE SCORPION'S WORDS PROVE TO BE PROPHETIC!
I-I'M FALLING! BUT MAYBE I CAN HIT HIM WITH THE SERUM BEFORE I DO... I HAVE TO!!
BUT THE DOOMED SCIENTIST'S THROW IS SHORT OF ITS MARK!
I WARNED HIM!
WELL, IT'S NO SKIN OFF MY NOSE! I'VE GOT THINGS TO DO!
THUD!
THEN, AT THAT VERY MOMENT, AN ALERT SPIDER-MAN, SWINGING OVERHEAD, HAPPENS TO SEE...
I'M TOO LATE TO HELP THAT POOR FELLA WHO FELL... BUT AT LEAST I CAN GRAB THE SCORPION!
WHUMP!
DROP THAT JEWEL SACK, MISTER! THIS IS IT!
THWAP!
SPIDER-MAN!
YOU DIDN'T THINK A LUCKY KNOCK-OUT WOULD STOP ME FOR LONG, DID YOU?
I DIDN'T LOSE ANY SLEEP WORRYIN' ABOUT IT, EITHER! I DIDN'T THINK YOU'D BE DUMB ENOUGH TO COME BACK FOR MORE!
BUT, BEIN' YOU'RE A GLUTTON FOR PUNISHMENT, I'LL MAKE IT WORTH YOUR WHILE!
IT WON'T BE SO EASY THIS TIME... NOW I'M READY FOR YOU!
A FAT LOT OF GOOD THAT'LL DO YOU! I'M STRONGER THAN EVER NOW... AS YOU'RE GONNA FIND OUT!
14.

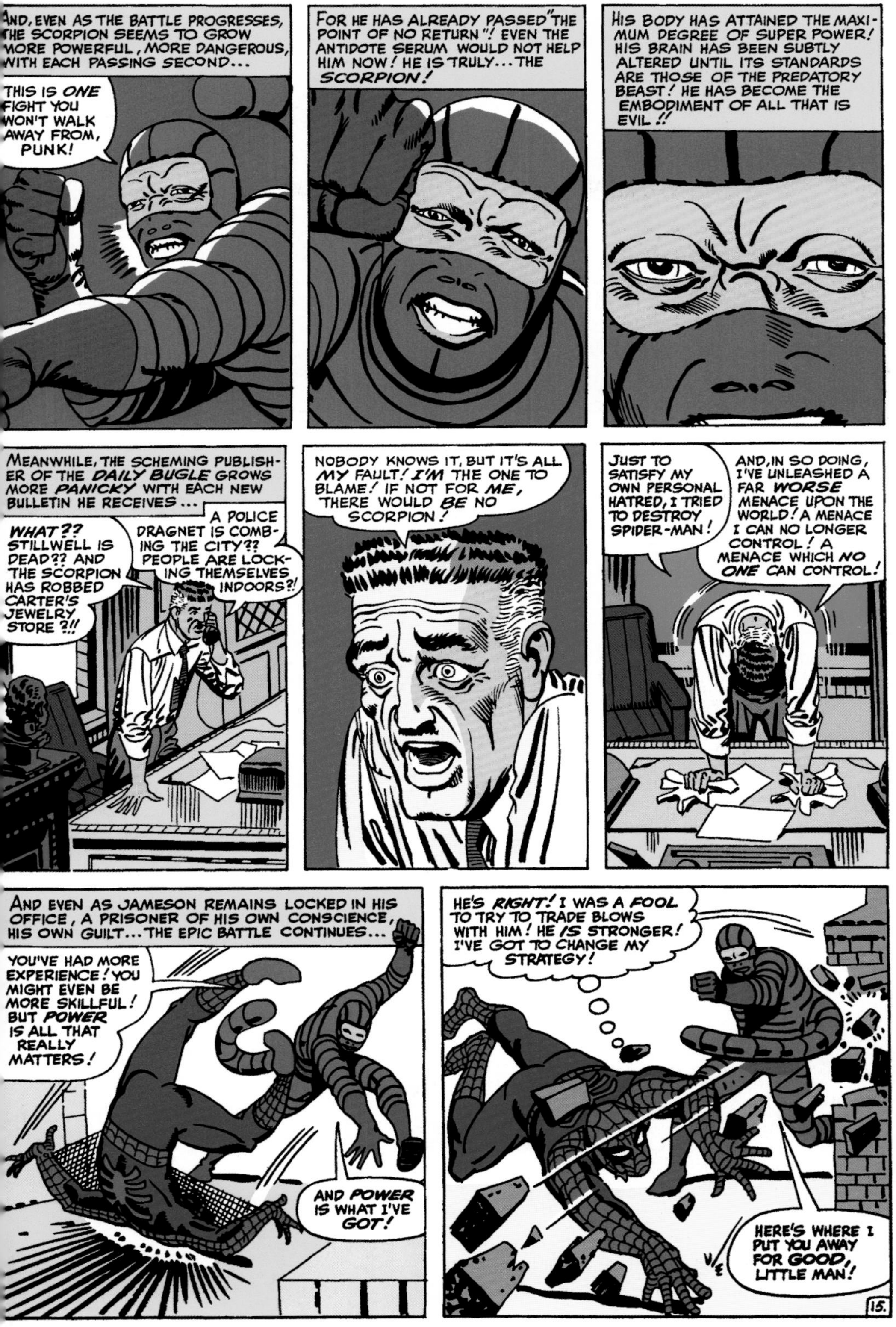
AND, EVEN AS THE BATTLE PROGRESSES, THE SCORPION SEEMS TO GROW MORE POWERFUL, MORE DANGEROUS, WITH EACH PASSING SECOND...
THIS IS ONE FIGHT YOU WON'T WALK AWAY FROM, PUNK!
FOR HE HAS ALREADY PASSED "THE POINT OF NO RETURN"! EVEN THE ANTIDOTE SERUM WOULD NOT HELP HIM NOW! HE IS TRULY... THE SCORPION!
HIS BODY HAS ATTAINED THE MAXIMUM DEGREE OF SUPER POWER! HIS BRAIN HAS BEEN SUBTLY ALTERED UNTIL ITS STANDARDS ARE THOSE OF THE PREDATORY BEAST! HE HAS BECOME THE EMBODIMENT OF ALL THAT IS EVIL!!
MEANWHILE, THE SCHEMING PUBLISHER OF THE DAILY BUGLE GROWS MORE PANICKY WITH EACH NEW BULLETIN HE RECEIVES...
WHAT?? STILLWELL IS DEAD?? AND THE SCORPION HAS ROBBED CARTER'S JEWELRY STORE?!!
A POLICE DRAGNET IS COMBING THE CITY?? PEOPLE ARE LOCKING THEMSELVES INDOORS?!
NOBODY KNOWS IT, BUT IT'S ALL MY FAULT! I'M THE ONE TO BLAME! IF NOT FOR ME, THERE WOULD BE NO SCORPION!
JUST TO SATISFY MY OWN PERSONAL HATRED, I TRIED TO DESTROY SPIDER-MAN!
AND, IN SO DOING, I'VE UNLEASHED A FAR WORSE MENACE UPON THE WORLD! A MENACE I CAN NO LONGER CONTROL! A MENACE WHICH NO ONE CAN CONTROL!
AND EVEN AS JAMESON REMAINS LOCKED IN HIS OFFICE, A PRISONER OF HIS OWN CONSCIENCE, HIS OWN GUILT... THE EPIC BATTLE CONTINUES...
YOU'VE HAD MORE EXPERIENCE! YOU MIGHT EVEN BE MORE SKILLFUL! BUT POWER IS ALL THAT REALLY MATTERS!
AND POWER IS WHAT I'VE GOT!
HE'S RIGHT! I WAS A FOOL TO TRY TO TRADE BLOWS WITH HIM! HE IS STRONGER! I'VE GOT TO CHANGE MY STRATEGY!
HERE'S WHERE I PUT YOU AWAY FOR GOOD, LITTLE MAN!

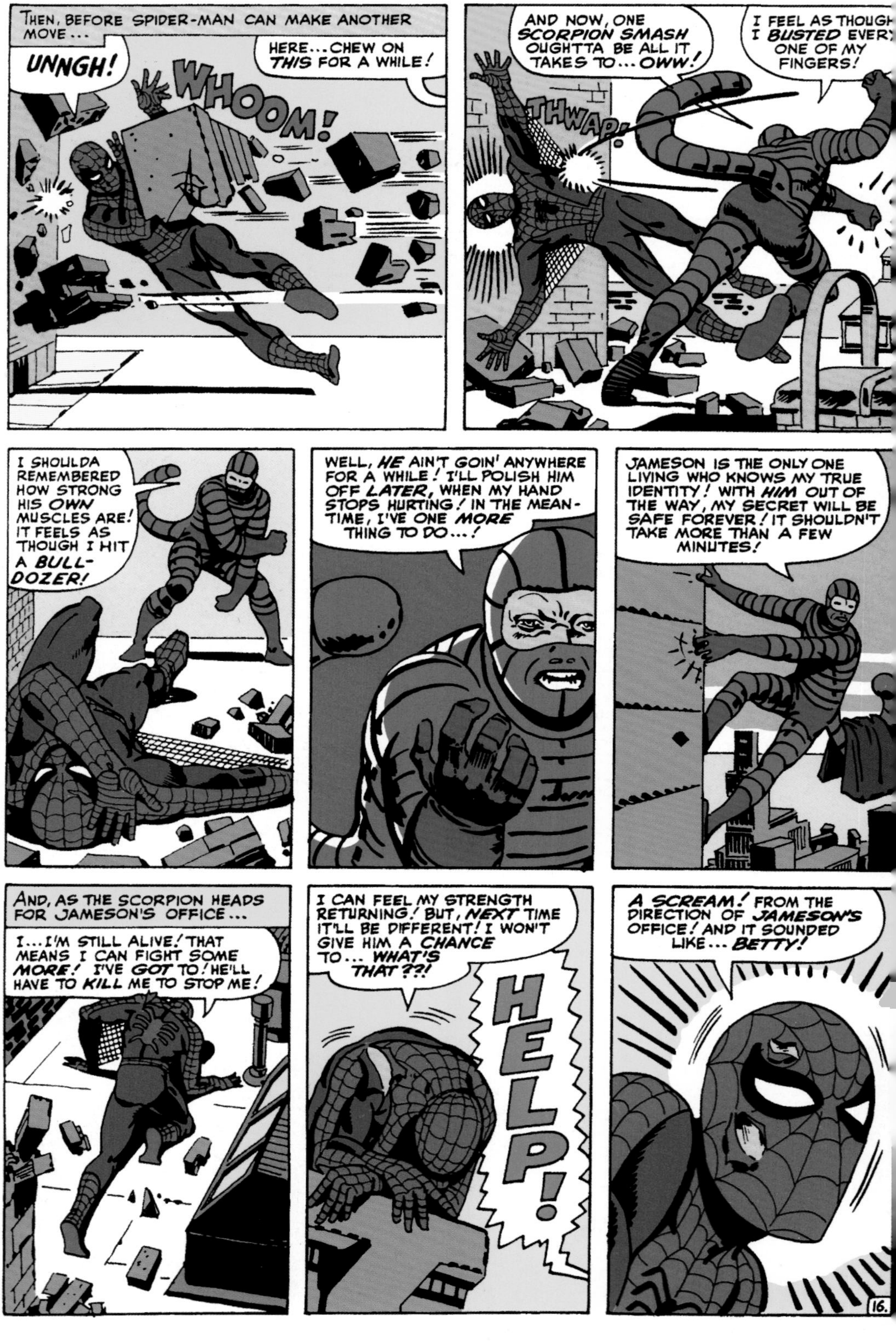
THEN, BEFORE SPIDER-MAN CAN MAKE ANOTHER MOVE...
UNNGH!
HERE...CHEW ON THIS FOR A WHILE!
WHOOM!
AND NOW, ONE SCORPION SMASH OUGHTTA BE ALL IT TAKES TO... OWW!
THWAP!
I FEEL AS THOUGH I BUSTED EVERY ONE OF MY FINGERS!
I SHOULDA REMEMBERED HOW STRONG HIS OWN MUSCLES ARE! IT FEELS AS THOUGH I HIT A BULL-DOZER!
WELL, HE AIN'T GOIN' ANYWHERE FOR A WHILE! I'LL POLISH HIM OFF LATER, WHEN MY HAND STOPS HURTING! IN THE MEAN-TIME, I'VE ONE MORE THING TO DO...!
JAMESON IS THE ONLY ONE LIVING WHO KNOWS MY TRUE IDENTITY! WITH HIM OUT OF THE WAY, MY SECRET WILL BE SAFE FOREVER! IT SHOULDN'T TAKE MORE THAN A FEW MINUTES!
AND, AS THE SCORPION HEADS FOR JAMESON'S OFFICE...
I...I'M STILL ALIVE! THAT MEANS I CAN FIGHT SOME MORE! I'VE GOT TO! HE'LL HAVE TO KILL ME TO STOP ME!
I CAN FEEL MY STRENGTH RETURNING! BUT, NEXT TIME IT'LL BE DIFFERENT! I WON'T GIVE HIM A CHANCE TO... WHAT'S THAT??!
HELP!
A SCREAM! FROM THE DIRECTION OF JAMESON'S OFFICE! AND IT SOUNDED LIKE... BETTY!
16.

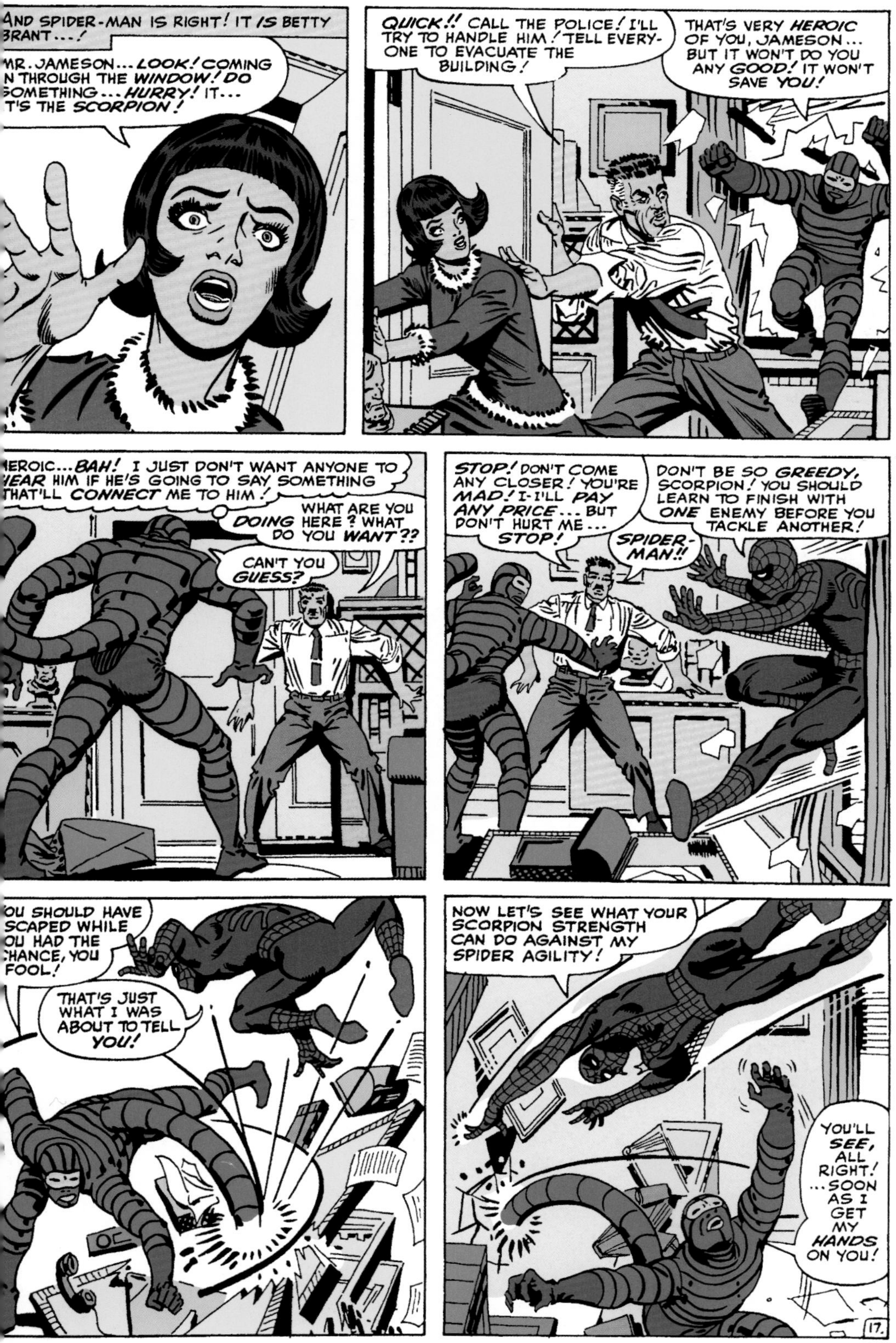
AND SPIDER-MAN IS RIGHT! IT IS BETTY BRANT...!
MR. JAMESON... LOOK! COMING IN THROUGH THE WINDOW! DO SOMETHING... HURRY! IT... IT'S THE SCORPION!
QUICK!! CALL THE POLICE! I'LL TRY TO HANDLE HIM! TELL EVERYONE TO EVACUATE THE BUILDING!
THAT'S VERY HEROIC OF YOU, JAMESON... BUT IT WON'T DO YOU ANY GOOD! IT WON'T SAVE YOU!
HEROIC... BAH! I JUST DON'T WANT ANYONE TO HEAR HIM IF HE'S GOING TO SAY SOMETHING THAT'LL CONNECT ME TO HIM!
WHAT ARE YOU DOING HERE? WHAT DO YOU WANT??
CAN'T YOU GUESS?
STOP! DON'T COME ANY CLOSER! YOU'RE MAD! I-I'LL PAY ANY PRICE... BUT DON'T HURT ME... STOP!
DON'T BE SO GREEDY, SCORPION! YOU SHOULD LEARN TO FINISH WITH ONE ENEMY BEFORE YOU TACKLE ANOTHER!
SPIDER-MAN!!
YOU SHOULD HAVE ESCAPED WHILE YOU HAD THE CHANCE, YOU FOOL!
THAT'S JUST WHAT I WAS ABOUT TO TELL YOU!
NOW LET'S SEE WHAT YOUR SCORPION STRENGTH CAN DO AGAINST MY SPIDER AGILITY!
YOU'LL SEE, ALL RIGHT! ...SOON AS I GET MY HANDS ON YOU!
17.

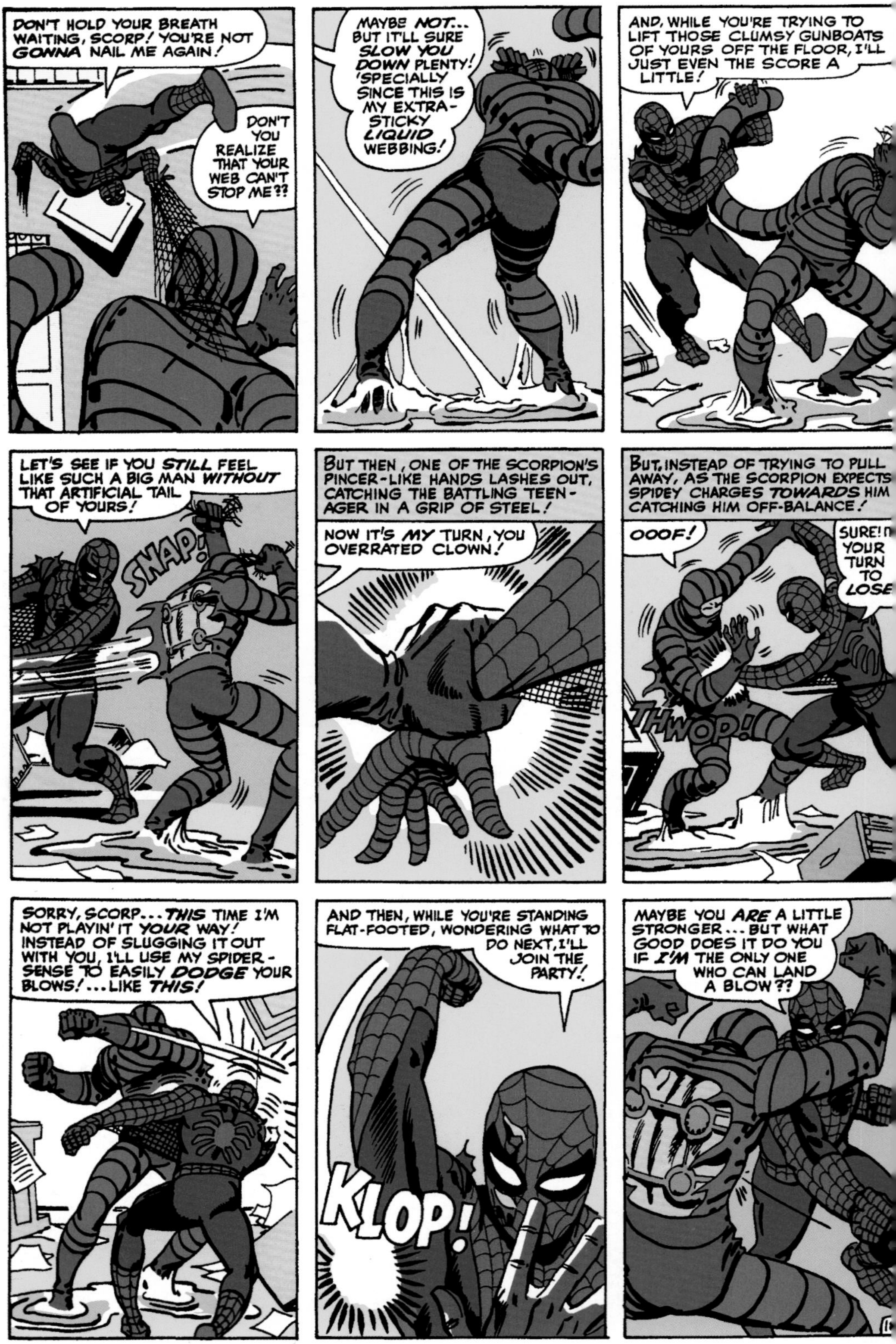
DON'T HOLD YOUR BREATH WAITING, SCORP! YOU'RE NOT GONNA NAIL ME AGAIN!
DON'T YOU REALIZE THAT YOUR WEB CAN'T STOP ME??
MAYBE NOT... BUT IT'LL SURE SLOW YOU DOWN PLENTY! 'SPECIALLY SINCE THIS IS MY EXTRA-STICKY LIQUID WEBBING!
AND, WHILE YOU'RE TRYING TO LIFT THOSE CLUMSY GUNBOATS OF YOURS OFF THE FLOOR, I'LL JUST EVEN THE SCORE A LITTLE!
LET'S SEE IF YOU STILL FEEL LIKE SUCH A BIG MAN WITHOUT THAT ARTIFICIAL TAIL OF YOURS!
SNAP!
BUT THEN, ONE OF THE SCORPION'S PINCER-LIKE HANDS LASHES OUT, CATCHING THE BATTLING TEEN-AGER IN A GRIP OF STEEL!
NOW IT'S MY TURN, YOU OVERRATED CLOWN!
BUT, INSTEAD OF TRYING TO PULL AWAY, AS THE SCORPION EXPECTS SPIDEY CHARGES TOWARDS HIM CATCHING HIM OFF-BALANCE!
OOOF!
THWOP!
SORRY, SCORP... THIS TIME I'M NOT PLAYIN' IT YOUR WAY! INSTEAD OF SLUGGING IT OUT WITH YOU, I'LL USE MY SPIDER-SENSE TO EASILY DODGE YOUR BLOWS!... LIKE THIS!
AND THEN, WHILE YOU'RE STANDING FLAT-FOOTED, WONDERING WHAT TO DO NEXT, I'LL JOIN THE PARTY!
KLOP!
MAYBE YOU ARE A LITTLE STRONGER... BUT WHAT GOOD DOES IT DO YOU IF I'M THE ONLY ONE WHO CAN LAND A BLOW??

THAT'S *IT*, SPIDEY! HIT HIM *AGAIN!* AND AGAIN! BE SURE HE'S *BEATEN!* DON'T TAKE ANY CHANCES! GOOD... GOOD!

WHAT'S *HAPPENING??* HAVE I GONE *MAD?* HERE I AM, CHEERING FOR SPIDER-MAN... THE ONE I HATE *WORST* IN ALL THE WORLD!

PTOW!

ALL RIGHT, JAMESON...HE'S ALL *YOURS!* BE SURE THE POLICE GET HERE BEFORE HE COMES TO AGAIN!

YOU *BEAT* HIM! YOU DEFEATED SOMEONE WHO'S *STRONGER* THAN YOU!

IT HAPPENS ALL THE TIME! EVER HEAR OF DAVID AND GOLIATH?

MY SECRET IS SAFE...FOR *NOW!* BUT WHAT SUPREME IRONY! I WAS SAVED FROM A MENACE WHOM I MYSELF HELPED TO CREATE... SAVED BY THE ONE HE WAS CREATED TO DESTROY!

A SHORT TIME LATER...

GOSH, I'M ALL CUT AND BRUISED! WHAT'LL I SAY TO AUNT MAY? ...AND THE KIDS AT SCHOOL?

I'D BETTER THINK OF SOMETHING *FAST!*

AND THEN...

I GUESS THE BEST THING IS TO CRUMPLE UP MY CLOTHES AS THOUGH I'VE BEEN IN SOME SORT OF ACCIDENT! I'LL SAY I GOT BOWLED OVER PLAYING TOUCH FOOTBALL! AT LEAST NO ONE WILL BE ABLE TO DIS-PROVE IT!

AND SO...

UH-OH! WOULDN'T YOU KNOW I'D BUMP INTO THE WHOLE BLAMED CROWD ALL AT ONCE!!

WELL, WELL! IF IT ISN'T PUNY PARKER WITH HIS ITTY BITTY FACE ALL SCRATCHED UP!

DON'T TELL ME A JELLYFISH LIKE *YOU* ACTUALLY GOT INTO A *FIGHT!*

WHAT *HAPPENED*, USELESS? DID SOME *INFANT* IN A CARRIAGE BEAT YOU UP FOR TRYING TO TAKE ITS LOLLIPOP AWAY?!

OKAY, THOMP-SON! I'VE TAKEN ALL I *CAN* FROM YOU! NOW I'M GONNA MAKE YOU *EAT* THOSE WORDS!

OH, *NO* YOU DON'T! YOU'RE NOT GONNA TRICK ME INTO FIGHTING YOU WHILE YOU'RE ALL BRUISED, SO THAT YOU'LL HAVE AN *EXCUSE* FOR LOSING! WHEN I WALLOP YOU, I DON'T WANT YOU TO HAVE ANY ALIBI!

HE'LL NEVER KNOW HOW *LUCKY* HE IS! I ALMOST LOST CONTROL OF MY TEMPER! I'D HAVE *PUL-VERIZED* HIM!

19.

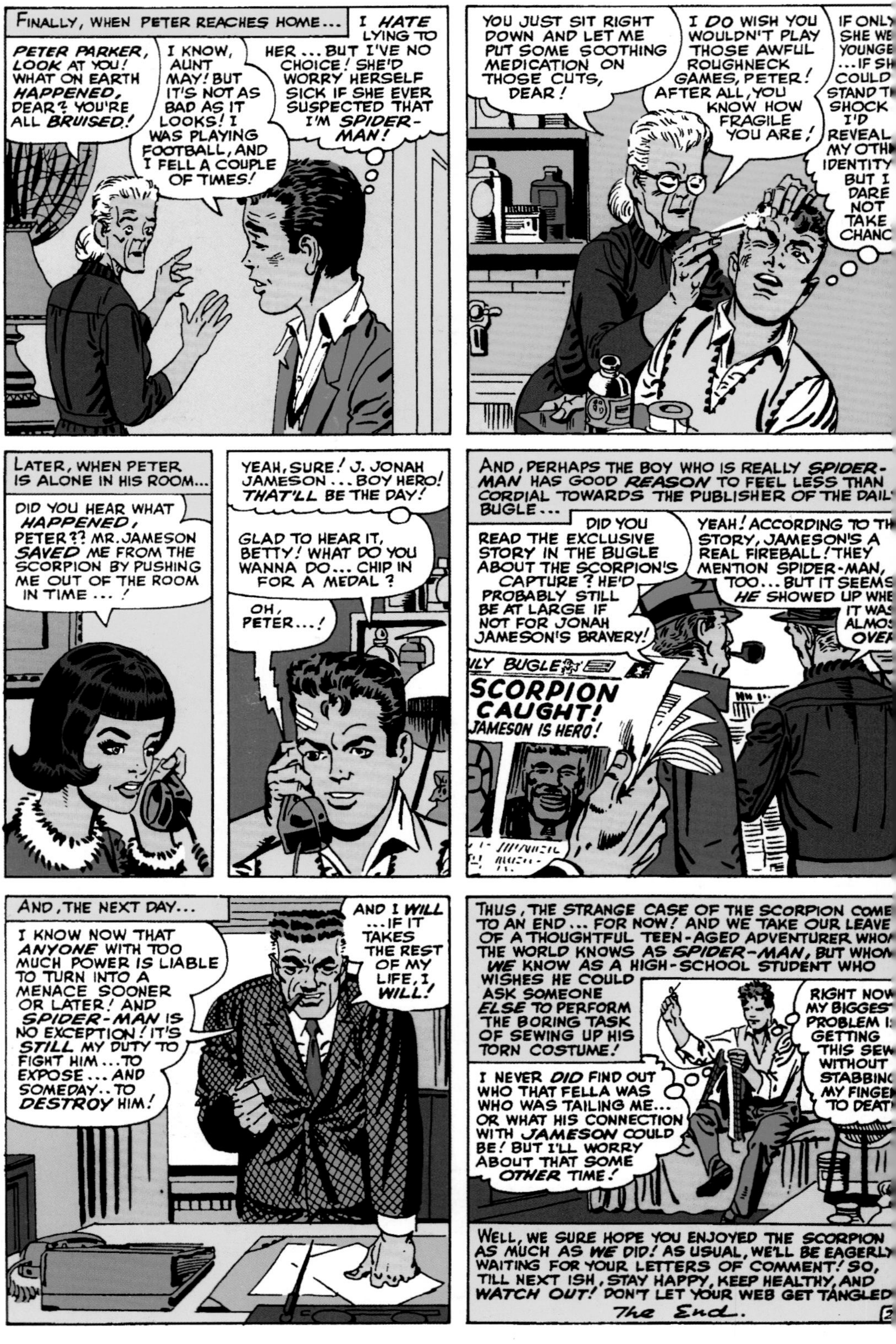
FINALLY, WHEN PETER REACHES HOME...
PETER PARKER, LOOK AT YOU! WHAT ON EARTH HAPPENED, DEAR?? YOU'RE ALL BRUISED!
I KNOW, AUNT MAY! BUT IT'S NOT AS BAD AS IT LOOKS! I WAS PLAYING FOOTBALL, AND I FELL A COUPLE OF TIMES!
I HATE LYING TO HER ... BUT I'VE NO CHOICE! SHE'D WORRY HERSELF SICK IF SHE EVER SUSPECTED THAT I'M SPIDER-MAN!
YOU JUST SIT RIGHT DOWN AND LET ME PUT SOME SOOTHING MEDICATION ON THOSE CUTS, DEAR!
I DO WISH YOU WOULDN'T PLAY THOSE AWFUL ROUGHNECK GAMES, PETER! AFTER ALL, YOU KNOW HOW FRAGILE YOU ARE!
IF ONLY SHE WE YOUNGE ...IF SH COULD STAND T SHOCK I'D REVEAL MY OTH IDENTITY BUT I DARE NOT TAKE CHANC
LATER, WHEN PETER IS ALONE IN HIS ROOM...
DID YOU HEAR WHAT HAPPENED, PETER?? MR. JAMESON SAVED ME FROM THE SCORPION BY PUSHING ME OUT OF THE ROOM IN TIME ... !
YEAH, SURE! J. JONAH JAMESON ... BOY HERO! THAT'LL BE THE DAY!
GLAD TO HEAR IT, BETTY! WHAT DO YOU WANNA DO... CHIP IN FOR A MEDAL?
OH, PETER...!
AND, PERHAPS THE BOY WHO IS REALLY SPIDER-MAN HAS GOOD REASON TO FEEL LESS THAN CORDIAL TOWARDS THE PUBLISHER OF THE DAIL BUGLE...
DID YOU READ THE EXCLUSIVE STORY IN THE BUGLE ABOUT THE SCORPION'S CAPTURE? HE'D PROBABLY STILL BE AT LARGE IF NOT FOR JONAH JAMESON'S BRAVERY!
YEAH! ACCORDING TO TH STORY, JAMESON'S A REAL FIREBALL! THEY MENTION SPIDER-MAN, TOO... BUT IT SEEMS HE SHOWED UP WHE IT WAS ALMOS OVER
ILY BUGLE
SCORPION CAUGHT!
JAMESON IS HERO!
AND, THE NEXT DAY...
I KNOW NOW THAT ANYONE WITH TOO MUCH POWER IS LIABLE TO TURN INTO A MENACE SOONER OR LATER! AND SPIDER-MAN IS NO EXCEPTION! IT'S STILL MY DUTY TO FIGHT HIM...TO EXPOSE... AND SOMEDAY..TO DESTROY HIM!
AND I WILL ...IF IT TAKES THE REST OF MY LIFE, I WILL!
THUS, THE STRANGE CASE OF THE SCORPION COME TO AN END ... FOR NOW! AND WE TAKE OUR LEAVE OF A THOUGHTFUL TEEN-AGED ADVENTURER WHOM THE WORLD KNOWS AS SPIDER-MAN, BUT WHOM WE KNOW AS A HIGH-SCHOOL STUDENT WHO WISHES HE COULD ASK SOMEONE ELSE TO PERFORM THE BORING TASK OF SEWING UP HIS TORN COSTUME!
RIGHT NOW MY BIGGEST PROBLEM IS GETTING THIS SEW WITHOUT STABBING MY FINGER TO DEAT
I NEVER DID FIND OUT WHO THAT FELLA WAS WHO WAS TAILING ME... OR WHAT HIS CONNECTION WITH JAMESON COULD BE! BUT I'LL WORRY ABOUT THAT SOME OTHER TIME!
WELL, WE SURE HOPE YOU ENJOYED THE SCORPION AS MUCH AS WE DID! AS USUAL, WE'LL BE EAGERLY WAITING FOR YOUR LETTERS OF COMMENT! SO, TILL NEXT ISH, STAY HAPPY, KEEP HEALTHY, AND WATCH OUT! DON'T LET YOUR WEB GET TANGLED
The End.

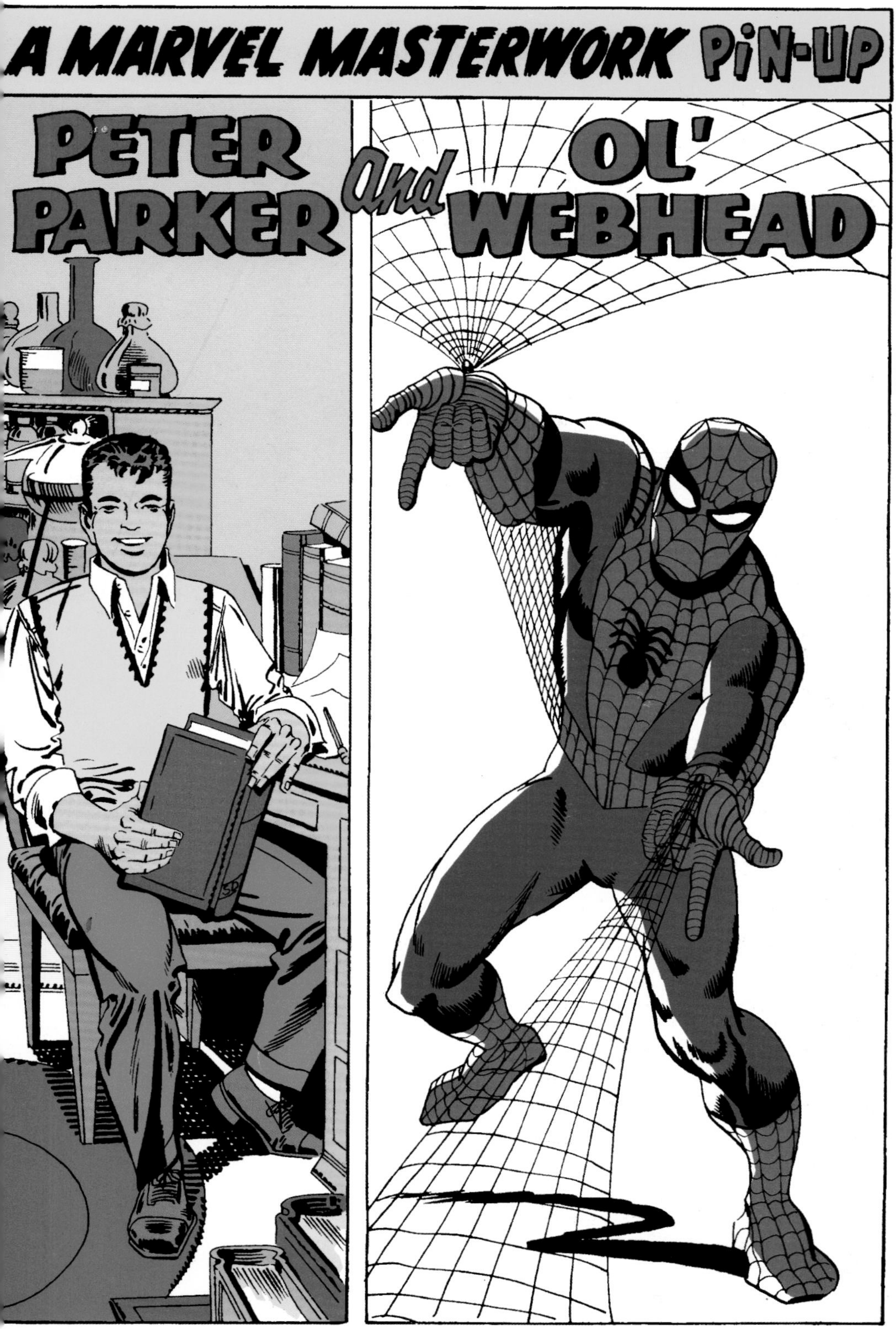
A MARVEL MASTERWORK PiN-UP
PETER PARKER
And
OL' WEBHEAD

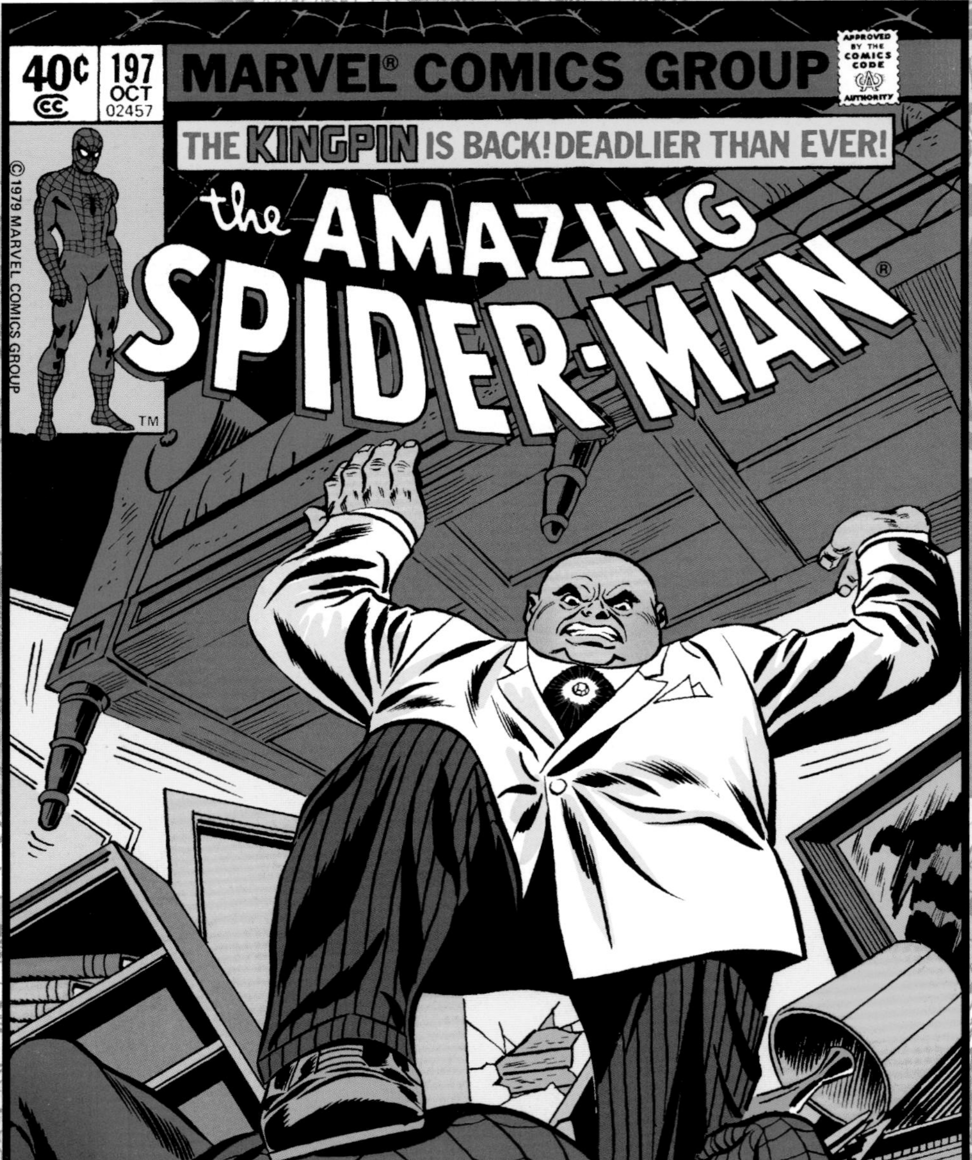
40¢
197
OCT
02457
MARVEL® COMICS GROUP
APPROVED BY THE COMICS CODE AUTHORITY
THE KINGPIN IS BACK! DEADLIER THAN EVER!
the AMAZING SPIDER-MAN®
© 1979 MARVEL COMICS GROUP
TM

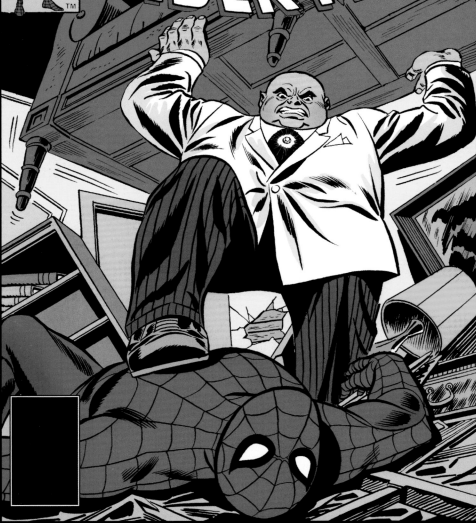

AMAZING SPIDER-MAN (1963) #197

THE KINGPIN IS BACK FROM THE DEAD, AND HE HAS HIS SIGHTS SET ON

While attending a demonstration in radiology, student PETER PARKER was bitten by a spider which had accidentally been exposed to RADIOACTIVE RAYS. Through a miracle of science, Peter soon found that he had GAINED the insect's powers...and had, in effect, become a human spider...

Stan Lee PRESENTS: THE AMAZING SPIDER-MAN®

MARV WOLFMAN WRITER / EDITOR · KEITH POLLARD & JIM MOONEY LAYOUTS · FINISHER · JOE ROSEN LETTERER · BEN SEAN COLORIST · JIM SHOOTER CONSULTING ED.

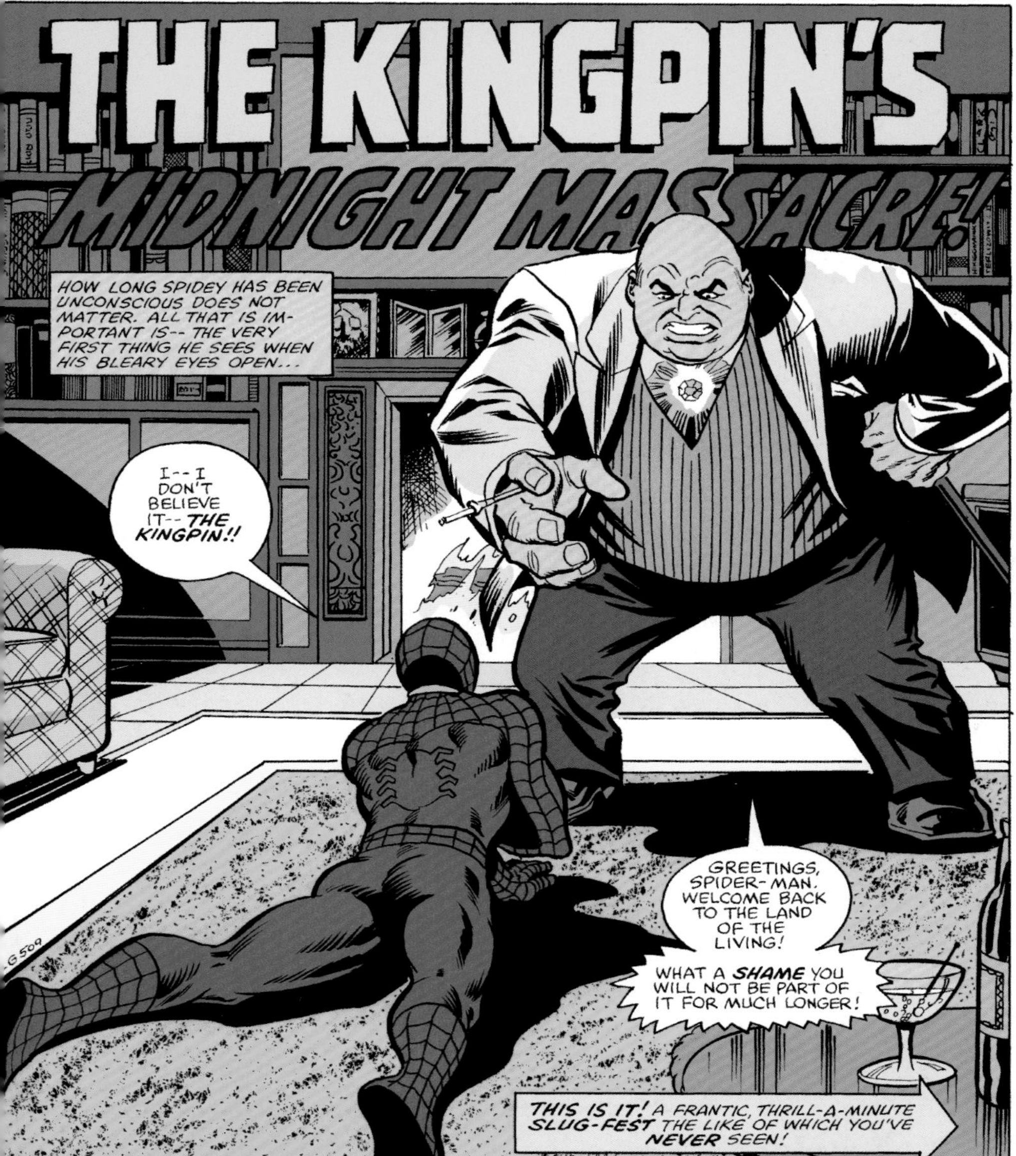
THE KINGPIN'S
MIDNIGHT MASSACRE!
HOW LONG SPIDEY HAS BEEN UNCONSCIOUS DOES NOT MATTER. ALL THAT IS IMPORTANT IS-- THE VERY FIRST THING HE SEES WHEN HIS BLEARY EYES OPEN...
I-- I DON'T BELIEVE IT-- THE KINGPIN!!
GREETINGS, SPIDER-MAN. WELCOME BACK TO THE LAND OF THE LIVING!
WHAT A SHAME YOU WILL NOT BE PART OF IT FOR MUCH LONGER!
THIS IS IT! A FRANTIC, THRILL-A-MINUTE SLUG-FEST THE LIKE OF WHICH YOU'VE NEVER SEEN!

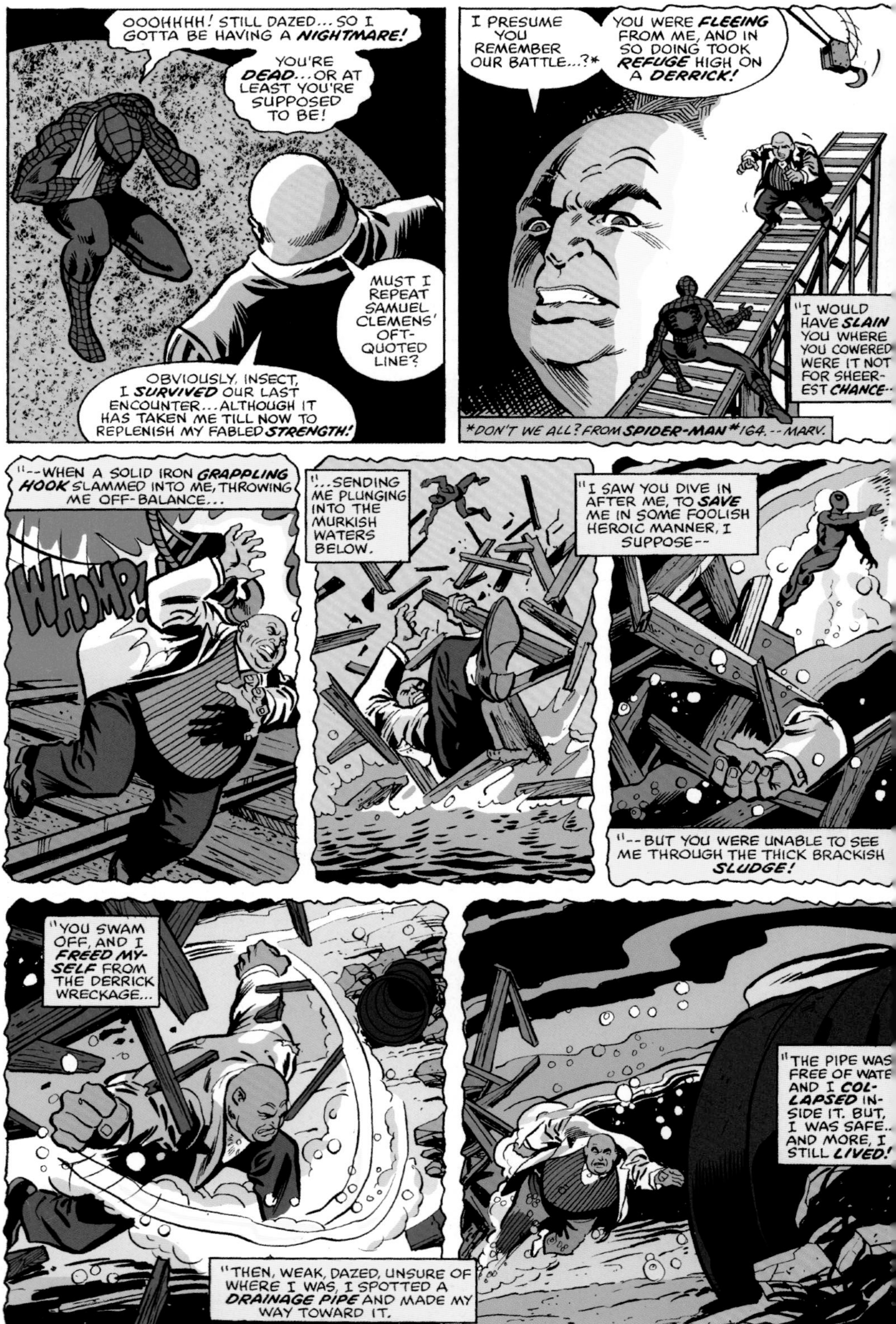
OOOHHHH! STILL DAZED... SO I GOTTA BE HAVING A NIGHTMARE!
YOU'RE DEAD...OR AT LEAST YOU'RE SUPPOSED TO BE!
MUST I REPEAT SAMUEL CLEMENS' OFT-QUOTED LINE?
OBVIOUSLY, INSECT, I SURVIVED OUR LAST ENCOUNTER...ALTHOUGH IT HAS TAKEN ME TILL NOW TO REPLENISH MY FABLED STRENGTH!
I PRESUME YOU REMEMBER OUR BATTLE...?*
YOU WERE FLEEING FROM ME, AND IN SO DOING TOOK REFUGE HIGH ON A DERRICK!
"I WOULD HAVE SLAIN YOU WHERE YOU COWERED WERE IT NOT FOR SHEER-EST CHANCE--
*DON'T WE ALL? FROM SPIDER-MAN #164. --MARV.
"--WHEN A SOLID IRON GRAPPLING HOOK SLAMMED INTO ME, THROWING ME OFF-BALANCE...
WHOMP!
"...SENDING ME PLUNGING INTO THE MURKISH WATERS BELOW.
"I SAW YOU DIVE IN AFTER ME, TO SAVE ME IN SOME FOOLISH HEROIC MANNER, I SUPPOSE--
"--BUT YOU WERE UNABLE TO SEE ME THROUGH THE THICK BRACKISH SLUDGE!
"YOU SWAM OFF, AND I FREED MY-SELF FROM THE DERRICK WRECKAGE...
"THEN, WEAK, DAZED, UNSURE OF WHERE I WAS, I SPOTTED A DRAINAGE PIPE AND MADE MY WAY TOWARD IT.
"THE PIPE WAS FREE OF WATE AND I COL-LAPSED IN-SIDE IT. BUT, I WAS SAFE... AND MORE, I STILL LIVED!

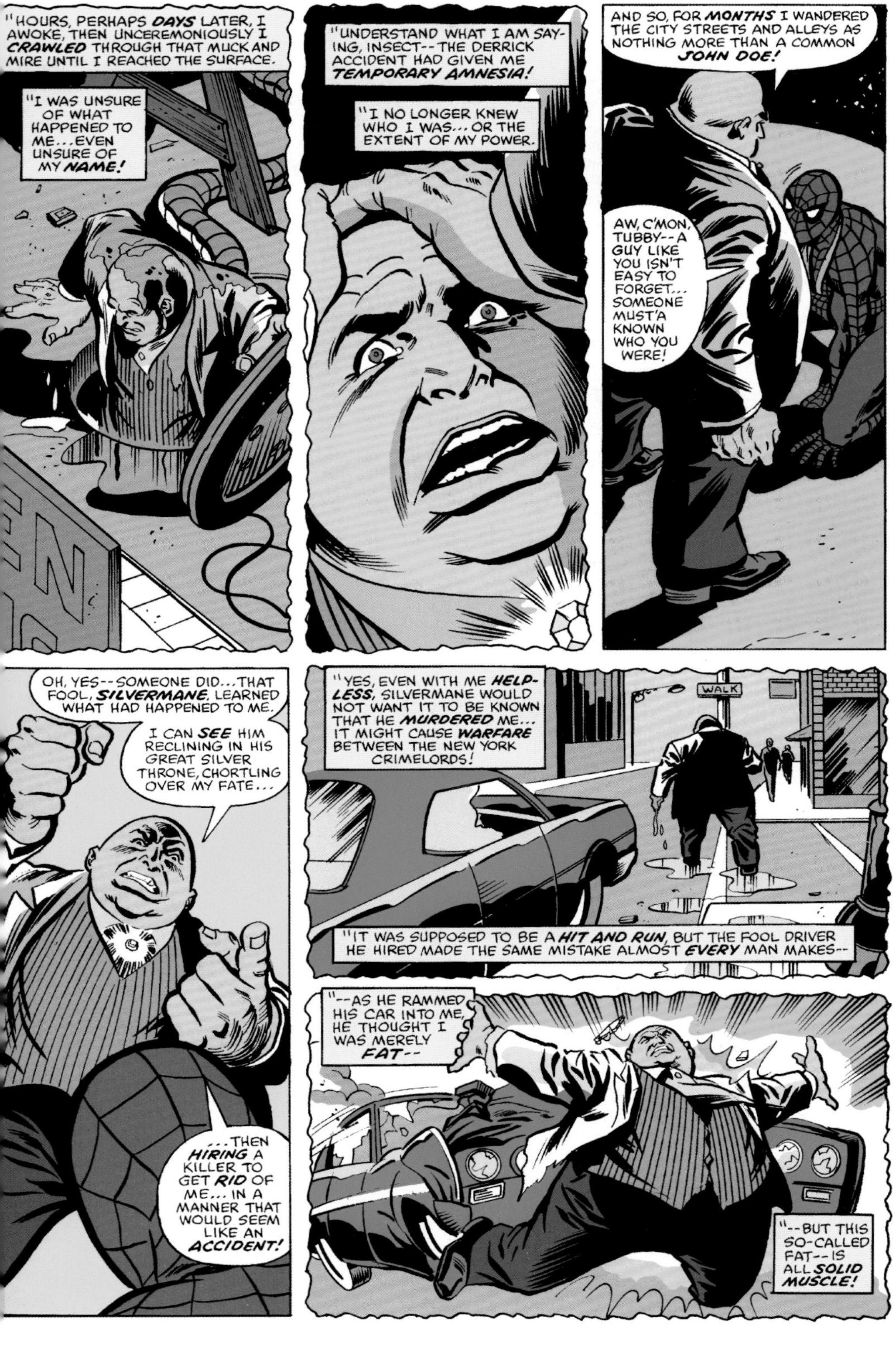
"HOURS, PERHAPS DAYS LATER, I AWOKE, THEN UNCEREMONIOUSLY I CRAWLED THROUGH THAT MUCK AND MIRE UNTIL I REACHED THE SURFACE.
"I WAS UNSURE OF WHAT HAPPENED TO ME... EVEN UNSURE OF MY NAME!
"UNDERSTAND WHAT I AM SAYING, INSECT-- THE DERRICK ACCIDENT HAD GIVEN ME TEMPORARY AMNESIA!
"I NO LONGER KNEW WHO I WAS... OR THE EXTENT OF MY POWER.
AND SO, FOR MONTHS I WANDERED THE CITY STREETS AND ALLEYS AS NOTHING MORE THAN A COMMON JOHN DOE!
AW, C'MON, TUBBY-- A GUY LIKE YOU ISN'T EASY TO FORGET... SOMEONE MUST'A KNOWN WHO YOU WERE!
OH, YES-- SOMEONE DID... THAT FOOL, SILVERMANE, LEARNED WHAT HAD HAPPENED TO ME.
I CAN SEE HIM RECLINING IN HIS GREAT SILVER THRONE, CHORTLING OVER MY FATE...
...THEN HIRING A KILLER TO GET RID OF ME... IN A MANNER THAT WOULD SEEM LIKE AN ACCIDENT!
"YES, EVEN WITH ME HELPLESS, SILVERMANE WOULD NOT WANT IT TO BE KNOWN THAT HE MURDERED ME... IT MIGHT CAUSE WARFARE BETWEEN THE NEW YORK CRIMELORDS!
WALK
"IT WAS SUPPOSED TO BE A HIT AND RUN, BUT THE FOOL DRIVER HE HIRED MADE THE SAME MISTAKE ALMOST EVERY MAN MAKES--
"--AS HE RAMMED HIS CAR INTO ME, HE THOUGHT I WAS MERELY FAT--
"--BUT THIS SO-CALLED FAT-- IS ALL SOLID MUSCLE!

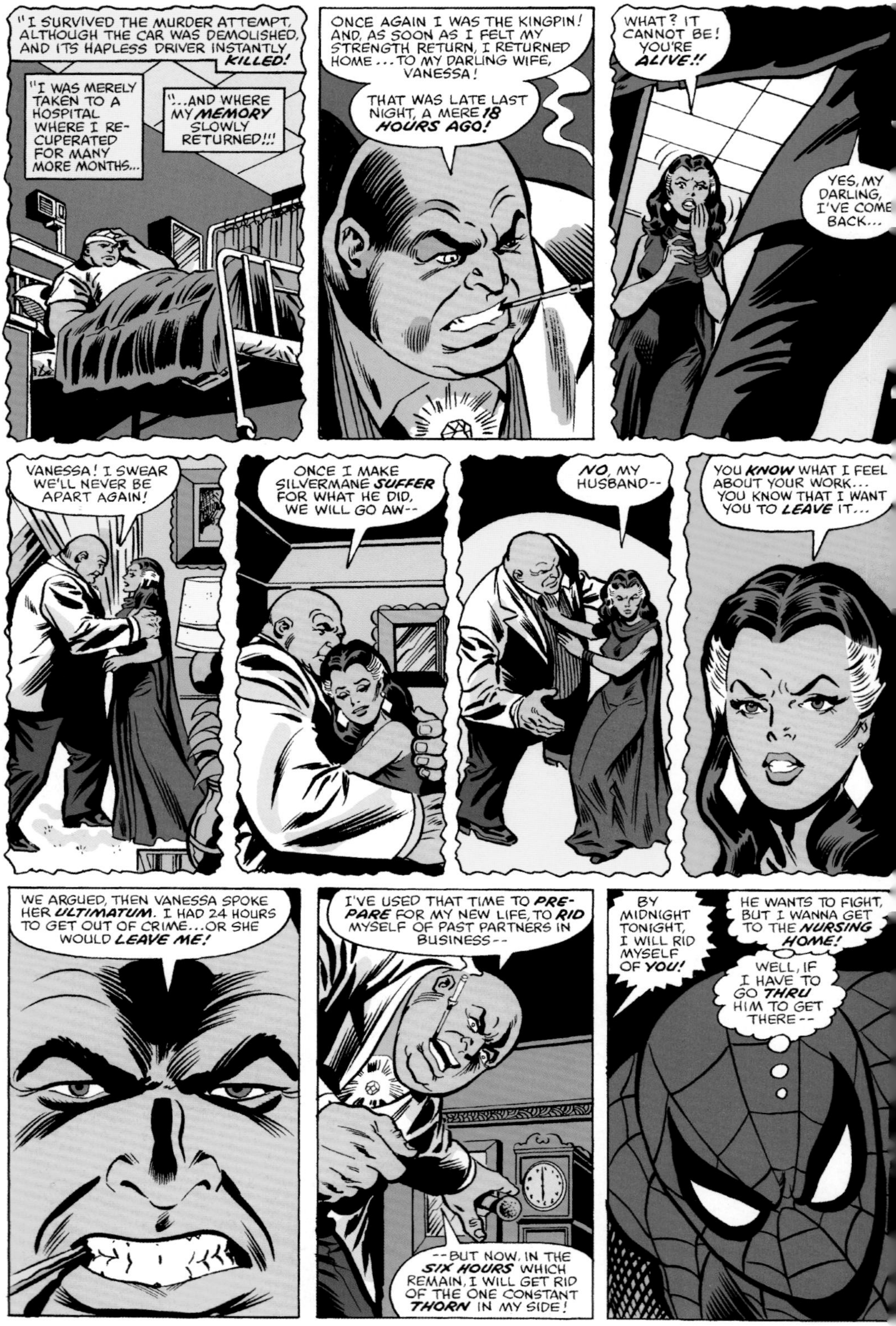
"I SURVIVED THE MURDER ATTEMPT, ALTHOUGH THE CAR WAS DEMOLISHED, AND ITS HAPLESS DRIVER INSTANTLY KILLED!
"I WAS MERELY TAKEN TO A HOSPITAL WHERE I RE-CUPERATED FOR MANY MORE MONTHS...
"...AND WHERE MY MEMORY SLOWLY RETURNED!!!
ONCE AGAIN I WAS THE KINGPIN! AND, AS SOON AS I FELT MY STRENGTH RETURN, I RETURNED HOME... TO MY DARLING WIFE, VANESSA!
THAT WAS LATE LAST NIGHT, A MERE 18 HOURS AGO!
WHAT? IT CANNOT BE! YOU'RE ALIVE!!
YES, MY DARLING, I'VE COME BACK...
VANESSA! I SWEAR WE'LL NEVER BE APART AGAIN!
ONCE I MAKE SILVERMANE SUFFER FOR WHAT HE DID, WE WILL GO AW--
NO, MY HUSBAND--
YOU KNOW WHAT I FEEL ABOUT YOUR WORK... YOU KNOW THAT I WANT YOU TO LEAVE IT...
WE ARGUED, THEN VANESSA SPOKE HER ULTIMATUM. I HAD 24 HOURS TO GET OUT OF CRIME...OR SHE WOULD LEAVE ME!
I'VE USED THAT TIME TO PRE-PARE FOR MY NEW LIFE, TO RID MYSELF OF PAST PARTNERS IN BUSINESS--
--BUT NOW, IN THE SIX HOURS WHICH REMAIN, I WILL GET RID OF THE ONE CONSTANT THORN IN MY SIDE!
BY MIDNIGHT TONIGHT, I WILL RID MYSELF OF YOU!
HE WANTS TO FIGHT, BUT I WANNA GET TO THE NURSING HOME!
WELL, IF I HAVE TO GO THRU HIM TO GET THERE--

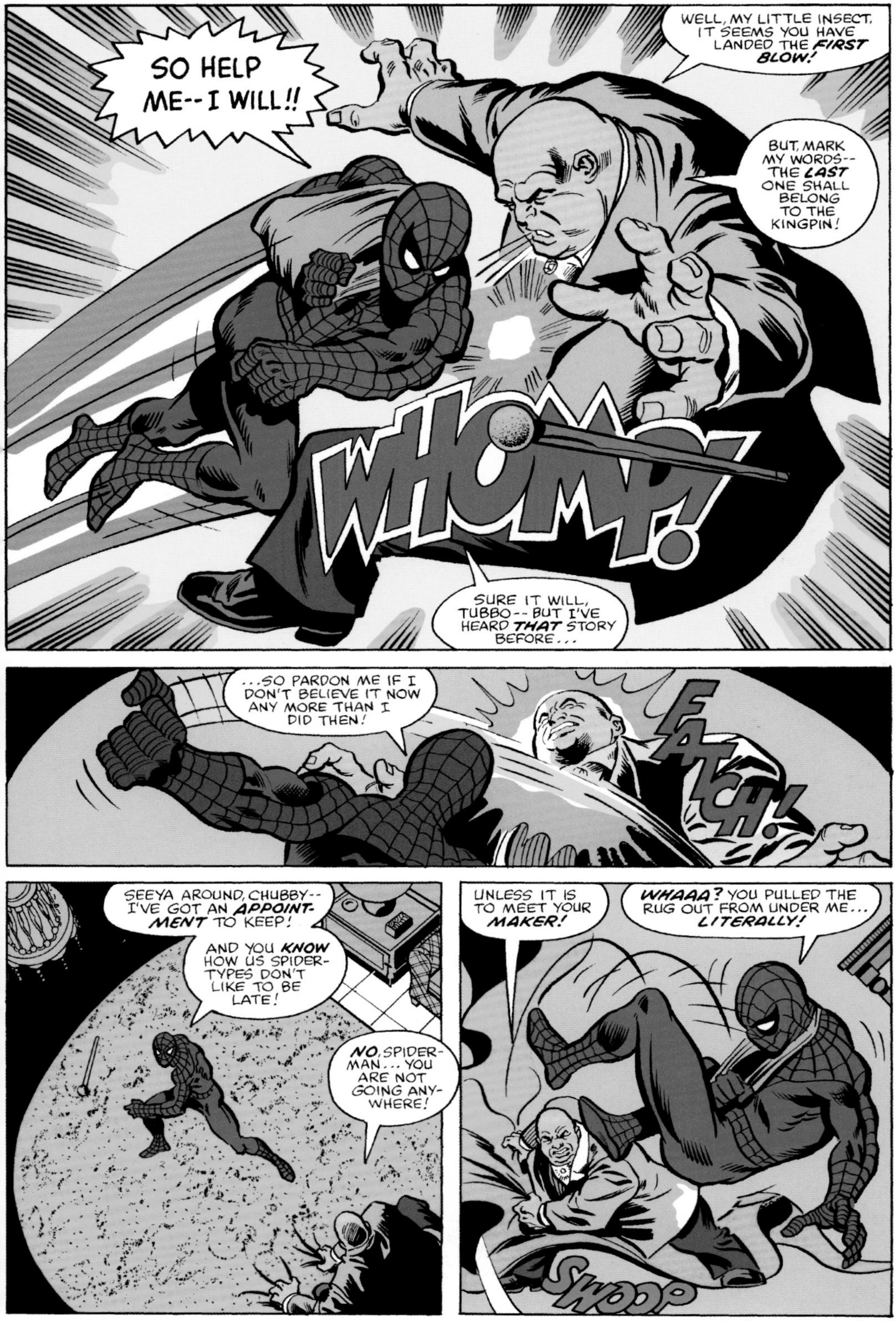
SO HELP ME--I WILL!!
WELL, MY LITTLE INSECT, IT SEEMS YOU HAVE LANDED THE FIRST BLOW!
BUT, MARK MY WORDS--THE LAST ONE SHALL BELONG TO THE KINGPIN!
WHOMP!
SURE IT WILL, TUBBO--BUT I'VE HEARD THAT STORY BEFORE...
...SO PARDON ME IF I DON'T BELIEVE IT NOW ANY MORE THAN I DID THEN!
FATCH!
SEEYA AROUND, CHUBBY--I'VE GOT AN APPOINTMENT TO KEEP!
AND YOU KNOW HOW US SPIDER-TYPES DON'T LIKE TO BE LATE!
NO, SPIDER-MAN... YOU ARE NOT GOING ANYWHERE!
UNLESS IT IS TO MEET YOUR MAKER!
WHAAA? YOU PULLED THE RUG OUT FROM UNDER ME... LITERALLY!
SWOOP

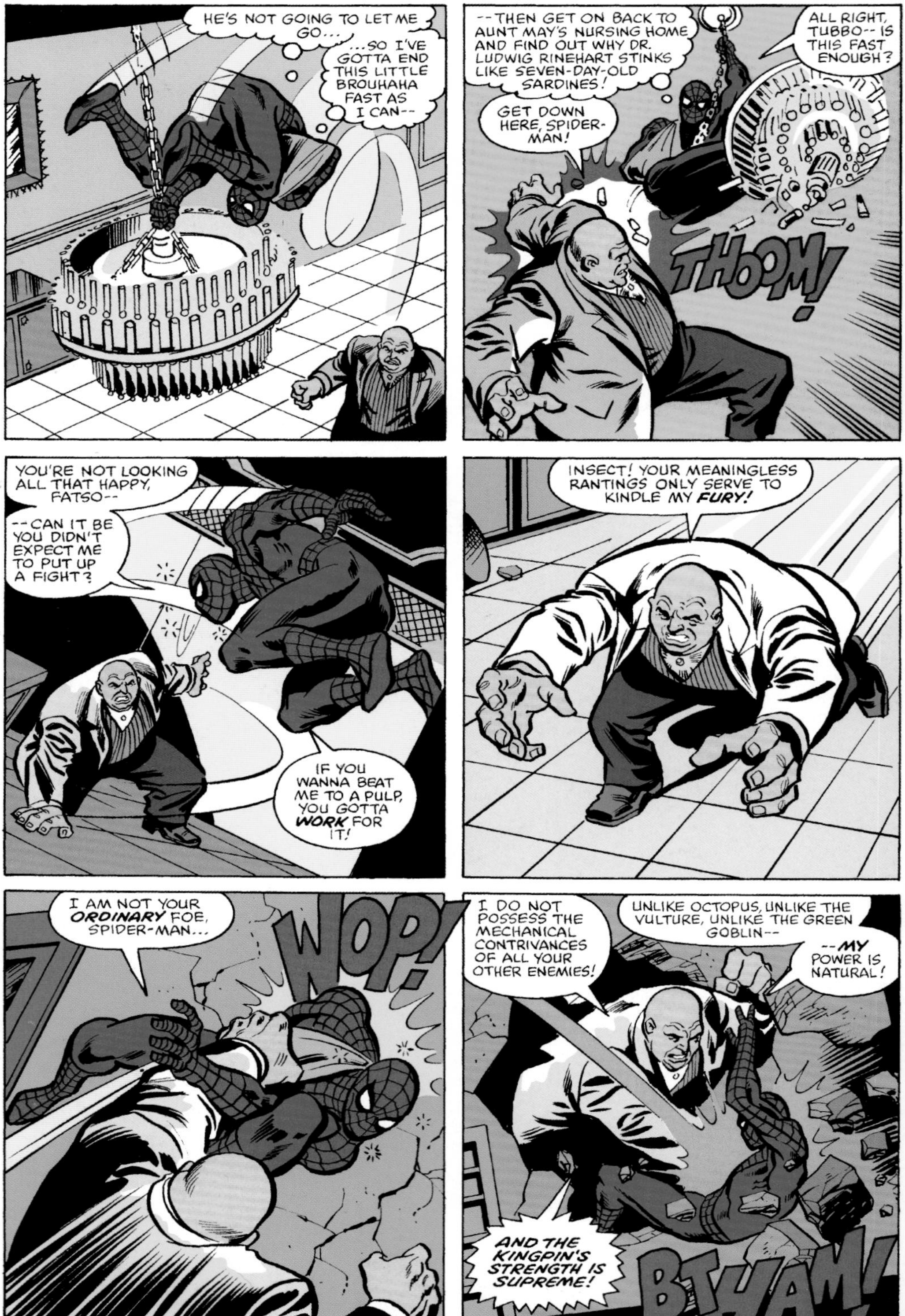
HE'S NOT GOING TO LET ME GO...
...SO I'VE GOTTA END THIS LITTLE BROUHAHA FAST AS I CAN--
--THEN GET ON BACK TO AUNT MAY'S NURSING HOME AND FIND OUT WHY DR. LUDWIG RINEHART STINKS LIKE SEVEN-DAY-OLD SARDINES!
GET DOWN HERE, SPIDER-MAN!
ALL RIGHT, TUBBO-- IS THIS FAST ENOUGH?
THOOM!
YOU'RE NOT LOOKING ALL THAT HAPPY, FATSO--
--CAN IT BE YOU DIDN'T EXPECT ME TO PUT UP A FIGHT?
IF YOU WANNA BEAT ME TO A PULP, YOU GOTTA **WORK** FOR IT!
INSECT! YOUR MEANINGLESS RANTINGS ONLY SERVE TO KINDLE MY **FURY!**
I AM NOT YOUR **ORDINARY** FOE, SPIDER-MAN...
WOP!
I DO NOT POSSESS THE MECHANICAL CONTRIVANCES OF ALL YOUR OTHER ENEMIES!
UNLIKE OCTOPUS, UNLIKE THE VULTURE, UNLIKE THE GREEN GOBLIN--
--**MY** POWER IS NATURAL!
AND THE KINGPIN'S STRENGTH IS SUPREME!
BTHAM!

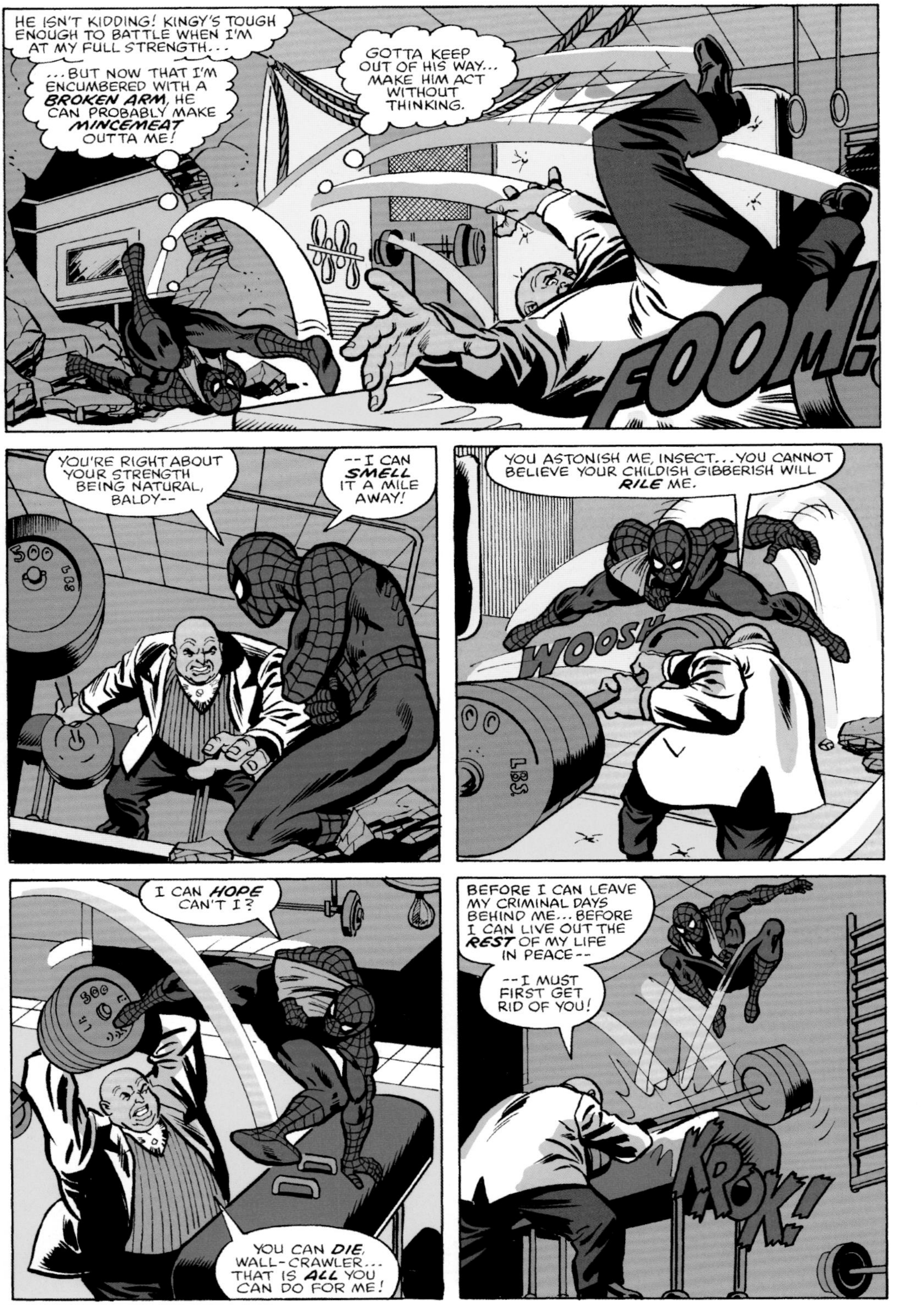
HE ISN'T KIDDING! KINGY'S TOUGH ENOUGH TO BATTLE WHEN I'M AT MY FULL STRENGTH...
...BUT NOW THAT I'M ENCUMBERED WITH A BROKEN ARM, HE CAN PROBABLY MAKE MINCEMEAT OUTTA ME!
GOTTA KEEP OUT OF HIS WAY... MAKE HIM ACT WITHOUT THINKING.
FOOM!
YOU'RE RIGHT ABOUT YOUR STRENGTH BEING NATURAL, BALDY--
--I CAN SMELL IT A MILE AWAY!
500
YOU ASTONISH ME, INSECT...YOU CANNOT BELIEVE YOUR CHILDISH GIBBERISH WILL RILE ME.
WOOSH
LBS.
I CAN HOPE CAN'T I?
YOU CAN DIE, WALL-CRAWLER... THAT IS ALL YOU CAN DO FOR ME!
BEFORE I CAN LEAVE MY CRIMINAL DAYS BEHIND ME... BEFORE I CAN LIVE OUT THE REST OF MY LIFE IN PEACE--
--I MUST FIRST GET RID OF YOU!
KROK!

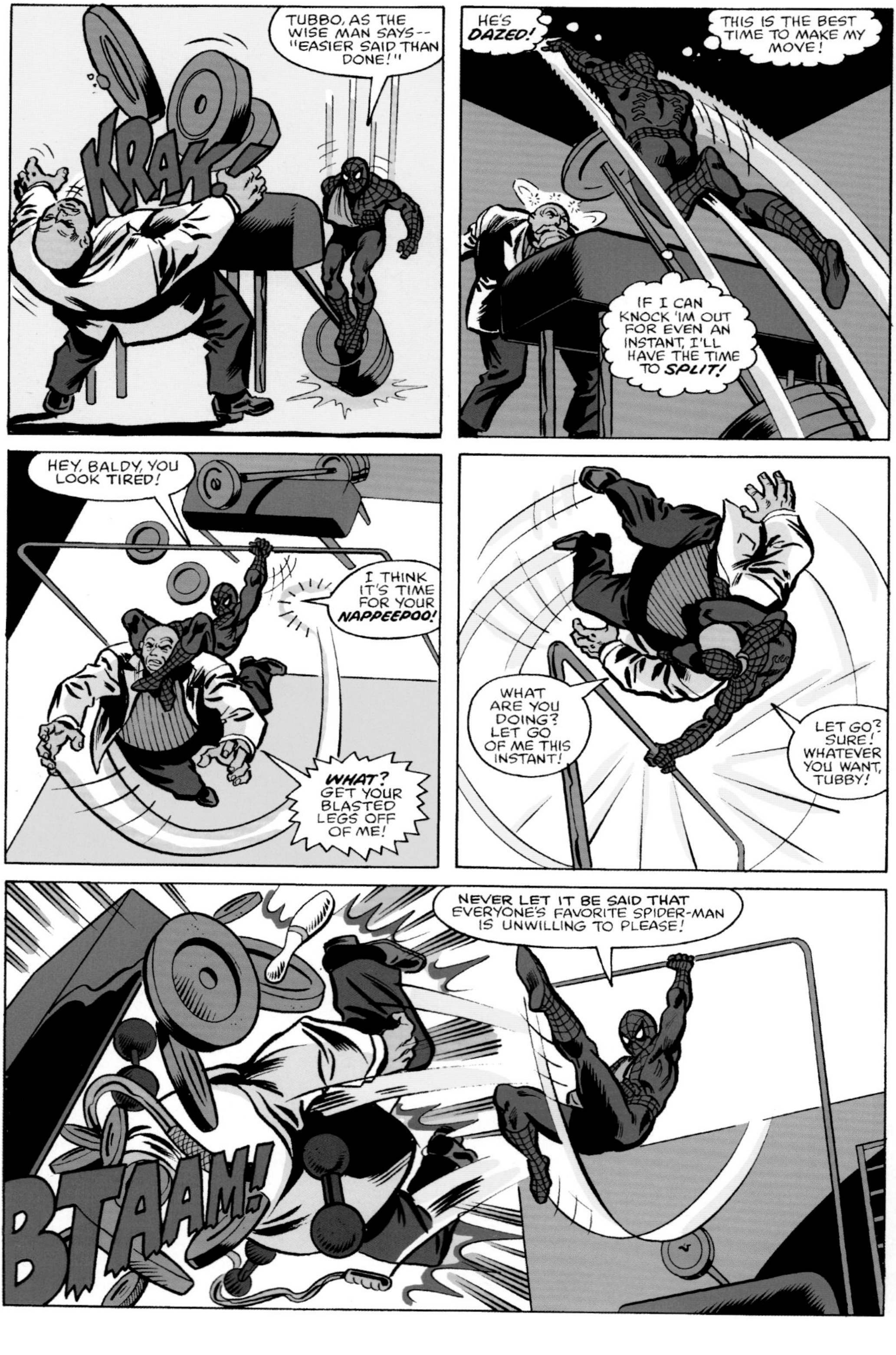
TUBBO, AS THE WISE MAN SAYS-- "EASIER SAID THAN DONE!"
KRAK!
HE'S DAZED!
THIS IS THE BEST TIME TO MAKE MY MOVE!
IF I CAN KNOCK 'IM OUT FOR EVEN AN INSTANT, I'LL HAVE THE TIME TO SPLIT!
HEY, BALDY, YOU LOOK TIRED!
I THINK IT'S TIME FOR YOUR NAPPEEPOO!
WHAT? GET YOUR BLASTED LEGS OFF OF ME!
WHAT ARE YOU DOING? LET GO OF ME THIS INSTANT!
LET GO? SURE! WHATEVER YOU WANT, TUBBY!
NEVER LET IT BE SAID THAT EVERYONE'S FAVORITE SPIDER-MAN IS UNWILLING TO PLEASE!
BTAAM!

HE'S DOWN... ...AND IN A MINUTE, I'LL BE OUT!

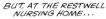

BUT, AT THE RESTWELL NURSING HOME...

I DID AS YOU *TOLD* ME ME... PETER PARKER WON'T BE SNOOPING ABOUT HERE ANY LONGER.

NOW, WHY DON'T YOU TELL ME WHY YOU WANTED MAY PARKER?

YA REALLY WANNA KNOW, EH? SEEIN' AS I'M GONNA *KILL* YA WHEN THIS IS ALL OVER, SURE, I'LL TALK...

ARROGANT CRETIN! WE SHALL SEE WHO WILL GET RID OF WHOM!

MEANWHILE...

UH OH... I HEAR TUBBO CLOMPING THIS WAY!

HE RECOVERED FASTER THAN I EXPECTED-- *CRIPES!*

SPIDER-SENSES ARE BUZZING! WHAT'S HE UP TO?

WHAT INDEED? SILENTLY, A PUDGY FINGER PRESSES A SMALL BUTTON ON A SEEMINGLY INNOCENT WALKING CANE...

AND...

YEOW! THE CEILING'S *ELECTRIFIED!*

ZTAK!

IF I STAY UP HERE ANY LONGER, I'LL GET FRENCH FRIED *FEET!*

WELL, WELL, IT SEEMS THE TIDE HAS TURNED... AS I KNEW IT WOULD!

NOW YOU ARE DOWN, AND THE KINGPIN IS READY TO *DESTROY* YOU!

HEAD'S STILL REELING... CAN'T FOCUS...

THE KINGPIN'S GOT ME, AND I CAN'T DO ANYTHING ABOUT IT!

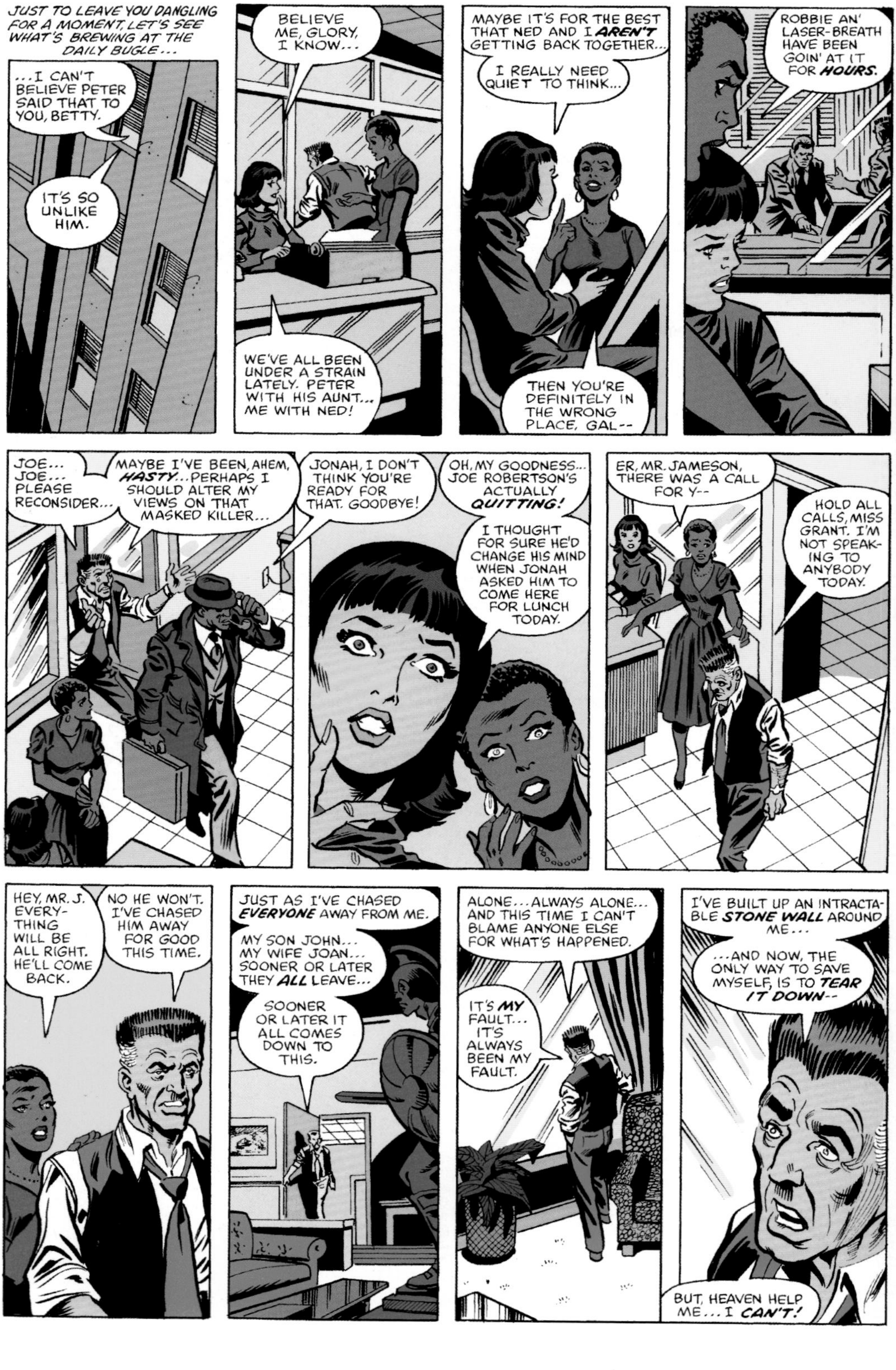
JUST TO LEAVE YOU DANGLING FOR A MOMENT, LET'S SEE WHAT'S BREWING AT THE DAILY BUGLE...
...I CAN'T BELIEVE PETER SAID THAT TO YOU, BETTY.
IT'S SO UNLIKE HIM.
BELIEVE ME, GLORY, I KNOW...
WE'VE ALL BEEN UNDER A STRAIN LATELY. PETER WITH HIS AUNT... ME WITH NED!
MAYBE IT'S FOR THE BEST THAT NED AND I AREN'T GETTING BACK TOGETHER...
I REALLY NEED QUIET TO THINK...
THEN YOU'RE DEFINITELY IN THE WRONG PLACE, GAL--
ROBBIE AN' LASER-BREATH HAVE BEEN GOIN' AT IT FOR HOURS.
JOE... JOE... PLEASE RECONSIDER...
MAYBE I'VE BEEN, AHEM, HASTY... PERHAPS I SHOULD ALTER MY VIEWS ON THAT MASKED KILLER...
JONAH, I DON'T THINK YOU'RE READY FOR THAT. GOODBYE!
OH, MY GOODNESS... JOE ROBERTSON'S ACTUALLY QUITTING!
I THOUGHT FOR SURE HE'D CHANGE HIS MIND WHEN JONAH ASKED HIM TO COME HERE FOR LUNCH TODAY.
ER, MR. JAMESON, THERE WAS A CALL FOR Y--
HOLD ALL CALLS, MISS GRANT. I'M NOT SPEAKING TO ANYBODY TODAY.
HEY, MR. J. EVERYTHING WILL BE ALL RIGHT. HE'LL COME BACK.
NO HE WON'T. I'VE CHASED HIM AWAY FOR GOOD THIS TIME.
JUST AS I'VE CHASED EVERYONE AWAY FROM ME.
MY SON JOHN... MY WIFE JOAN... SOONER OR LATER THEY ALL LEAVE...
SOONER OR LATER IT ALL COMES DOWN TO THIS.
ALONE... ALWAYS ALONE... AND THIS TIME I CAN'T BLAME ANYONE ELSE FOR WHAT'S HAPPENED.
IT'S MY FAULT... IT'S ALWAYS BEEN MY FAULT.
I'VE BUILT UP AN INTRACTABLE STONE WALL AROUND ME...
...AND NOW, THE ONLY WAY TO SAVE MYSELF, IS TO TEAR IT DOWN--
BUT, HEAVEN HELP ME... I CAN'T!

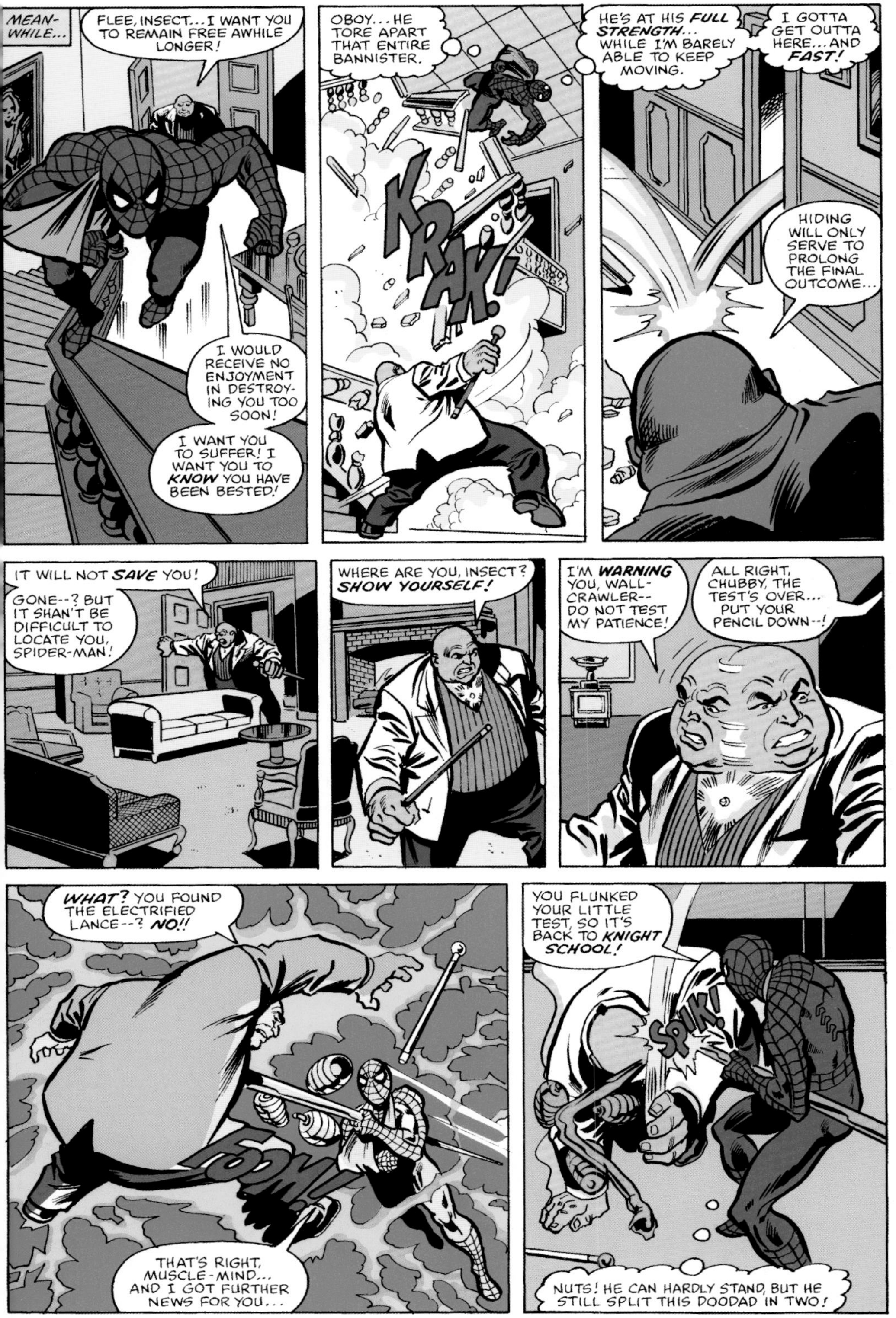
MEAN-WHILE...
FLEE, INSECT... I WANT YOU TO REMAIN FREE AWHILE LONGER!
I WOULD RECEIVE NO ENJOYMENT IN DESTROYING YOU TOO SOON!
I WANT YOU TO SUFFER! I WANT YOU TO KNOW YOU HAVE BEEN BESTED!
OBOY... HE TORE APART THAT ENTIRE BANNISTER.
KRAK!
HE'S AT HIS FULL STRENGTH... WHILE I'M BARELY ABLE TO KEEP MOVING.
I GOTTA GET OUTTA HERE... AND FAST!
HIDING WILL ONLY SERVE TO PROLONG THE FINAL OUTCOME...
IT WILL NOT SAVE YOU!
GONE--? BUT IT SHAN'T BE DIFFICULT TO LOCATE YOU, SPIDER-MAN!
WHERE ARE YOU, INSECT? SHOW YOURSELF!
I'M WARNING YOU, WALL-CRAWLER-- DO NOT TEST MY PATIENCE!
ALL RIGHT, CHUBBY, THE TEST'S OVER... PUT YOUR PENCIL DOWN--!
WHAT? YOU FOUND THE ELECTRIFIED LANCE--? NO!!
FOOM!
THAT'S RIGHT, MUSCLE-MIND... AND I GOT FURTHER NEWS FOR YOU...
YOU FLUNKED YOUR LITTLE TEST, SO IT'S BACK TO KNIGHT SCHOOL!
SPIK!
NUTS! HE CAN HARDLY STAND, BUT HE STILL SPLIT THIS DOODAD IN TWO!

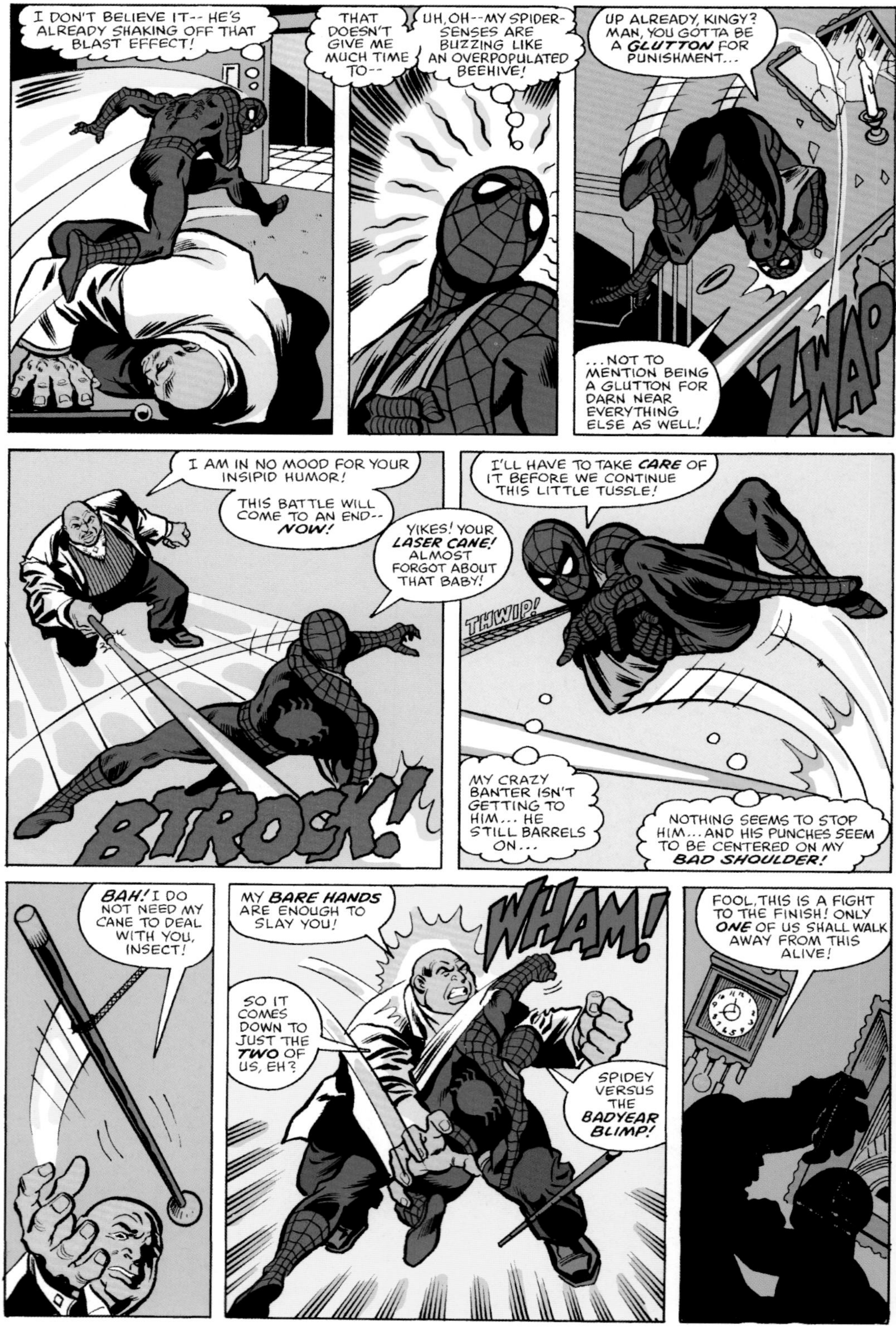
I DON'T BELIEVE IT-- HE'S ALREADY SHAKING OFF THAT BLAST EFFECT!
THAT DOESN'T GIVE ME MUCH TIME TO--
UH, OH--MY SPIDER-SENSES ARE BUZZING LIKE AN OVERPOPULATED BEEHIVE!
UP ALREADY, KINGY? MAN, YOU GOTTA BE A **GLUTTON** FOR PUNISHMENT...
...NOT TO MENTION BEING A GLUTTON FOR DARN NEAR EVERYTHING ELSE AS WELL!
ZWAP
I AM IN NO MOOD FOR YOUR INSIPID HUMOR!
THIS BATTLE WILL COME TO AN END-- **NOW!**
YIKES! YOUR **LASER CANE!** ALMOST FORGOT ABOUT THAT BABY!
BTROCK!
I'LL HAVE TO TAKE **CARE** OF IT BEFORE WE CONTINUE THIS LITTLE TUSSLE!
THWIP!
MY CRAZY BANTER ISN'T GETTING TO HIM... HE STILL BARRELS ON...
NOTHING SEEMS TO STOP HIM... AND HIS PUNCHES SEEM TO BE CENTERED ON MY **BAD SHOULDER!**
BAH! I DO NOT NEED MY CANE TO DEAL WITH YOU, INSECT!
MY **BARE HANDS** ARE ENOUGH TO SLAY YOU!
WHAM!
SO IT COMES DOWN TO JUST THE **TWO** OF US, EH?
SPIDEY VERSUS THE **BADYEAR BLIMP!**
FOOL, THIS IS A FIGHT TO THE FINISH! ONLY **ONE** OF US SHALL WALK AWAY FROM THIS ALIVE!

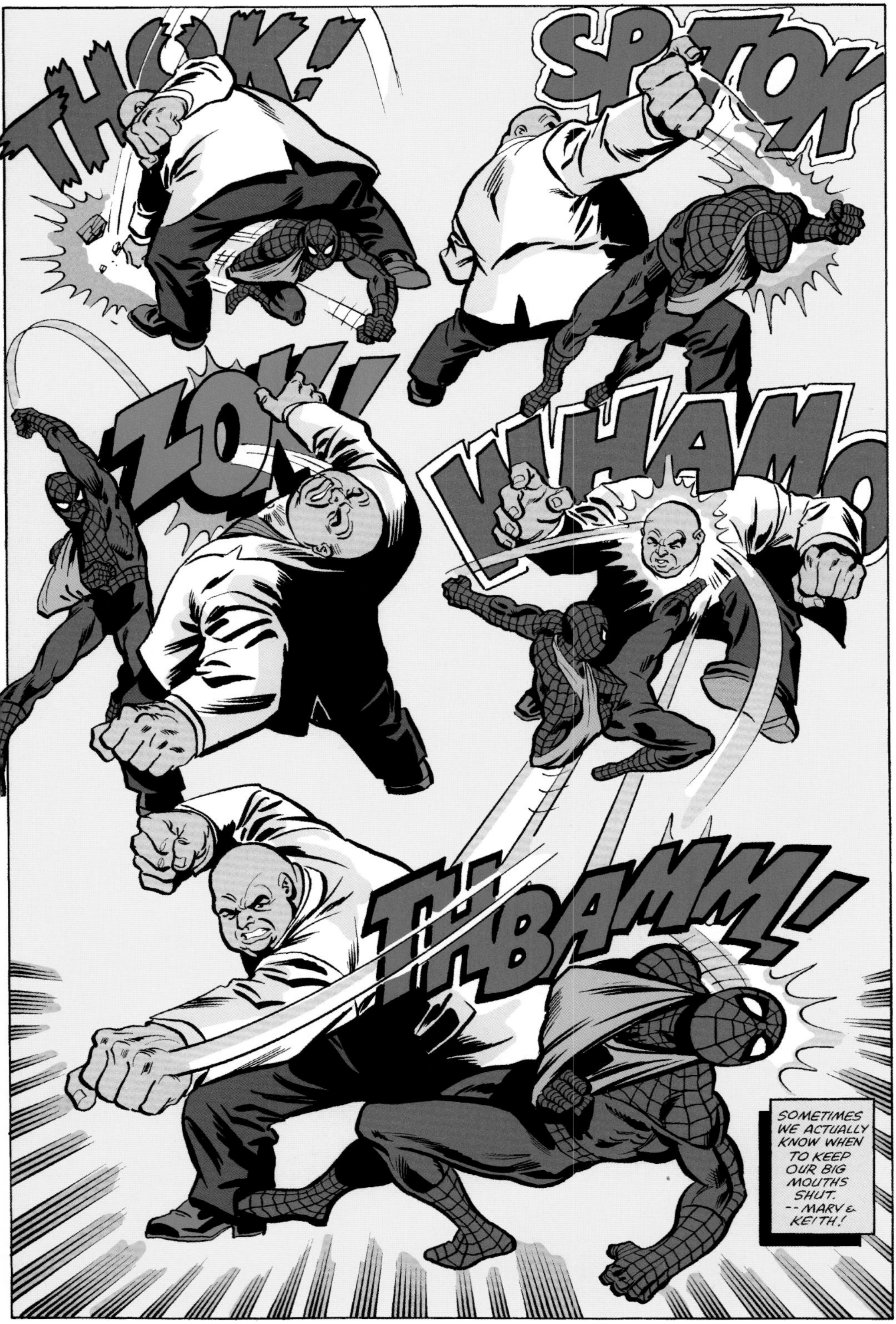
THOOK!
SPTOK
ZOK!
WHAM
THBAMM!
SOMETIMES WE ACTUALLY KNOW WHEN TO KEEP OUR BIG MOUTHS SHUT. --MARV & KEITH!

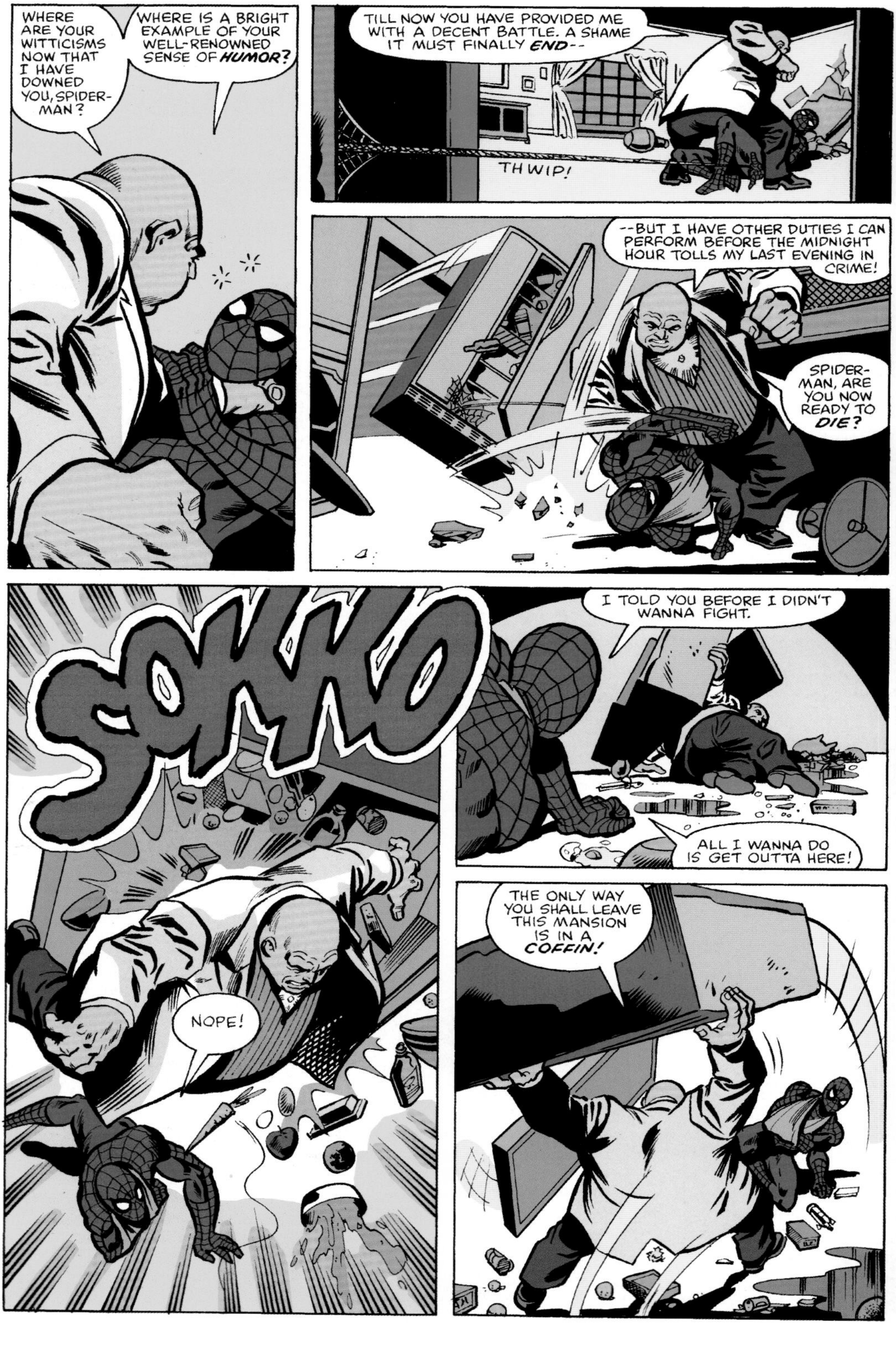
WHERE ARE YOUR WITTICISMS NOW THAT I HAVE DOWNED YOU, SPIDER-MAN?
WHERE IS A BRIGHT EXAMPLE OF YOUR WELL-RENOWNED SENSE OF HUMOR?
TILL NOW YOU HAVE PROVIDED ME WITH A DECENT BATTLE. A SHAME IT MUST FINALLY END--
THWIP!
--BUT I HAVE OTHER DUTIES I CAN PERFORM BEFORE THE MIDNIGHT HOUR TOLLS MY LAST EVENING IN CRIME!
SPIDER-MAN, ARE YOU NOW READY TO DIE?
SOKKO
NOPE!
I TOLD YOU BEFORE I DIDN'T WANNA FIGHT.
ALL I WANNA DO IS GET OUTTA HERE!
THE ONLY WAY YOU SHALL LEAVE THIS MANSION IS IN A COFFIN!

DO YOU UNDERSTAND THAT, INSECT?

ACTUALLY, I DON'T!

BUT I CAN SEE YOU WON'T LISTEN TO REASON, SO I'M GETTING OUT OF HERE ON MY OWN--

KRASH

--THROUGH THIS *HOLE* IN THE FLOOR WHICH YOU SO KINDLY PROVIDED!

SEEYA, CUDDLES, AND PLEASE TRY'N REMEMBER THAT *WEIGHT WATCHERS* MEETS EVERY WEDNESDAY!

NO! THAT INFERNAL PEST IS GONE...

BUT I MUSTN'T ALLOW HIM TO LEAVE --

MY FUTURE SERENITY DEPENDS ON HIS IMMEDIATE REMOVAL!

FOR THE KINGPIN TO LIVE, SPIDER-MAN MUST *DIE!!*

HOWEVER, THAT'S ABOUT THE *LAST* THING ON THE WEB-WEAVER'S MIND...

DON'T WANNA TURN ON THE SPIDER-SIGNAL... THAT COULD PINPOINT MY POSITION TO TUBBO.

GUESS I'VE GOTTA *FEEL* MY WAY THRU THIS BASEMENT JUNK AND--

BLAST! IT'S MY SPIDER-SENSES AGAIN... KINGY'S DIRECTLY BEHIND ME!

THE GUY'S BUILT LIKE A MOUNTAIN, BUT HE MOVES LIKE *MERCURY!*

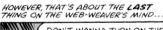

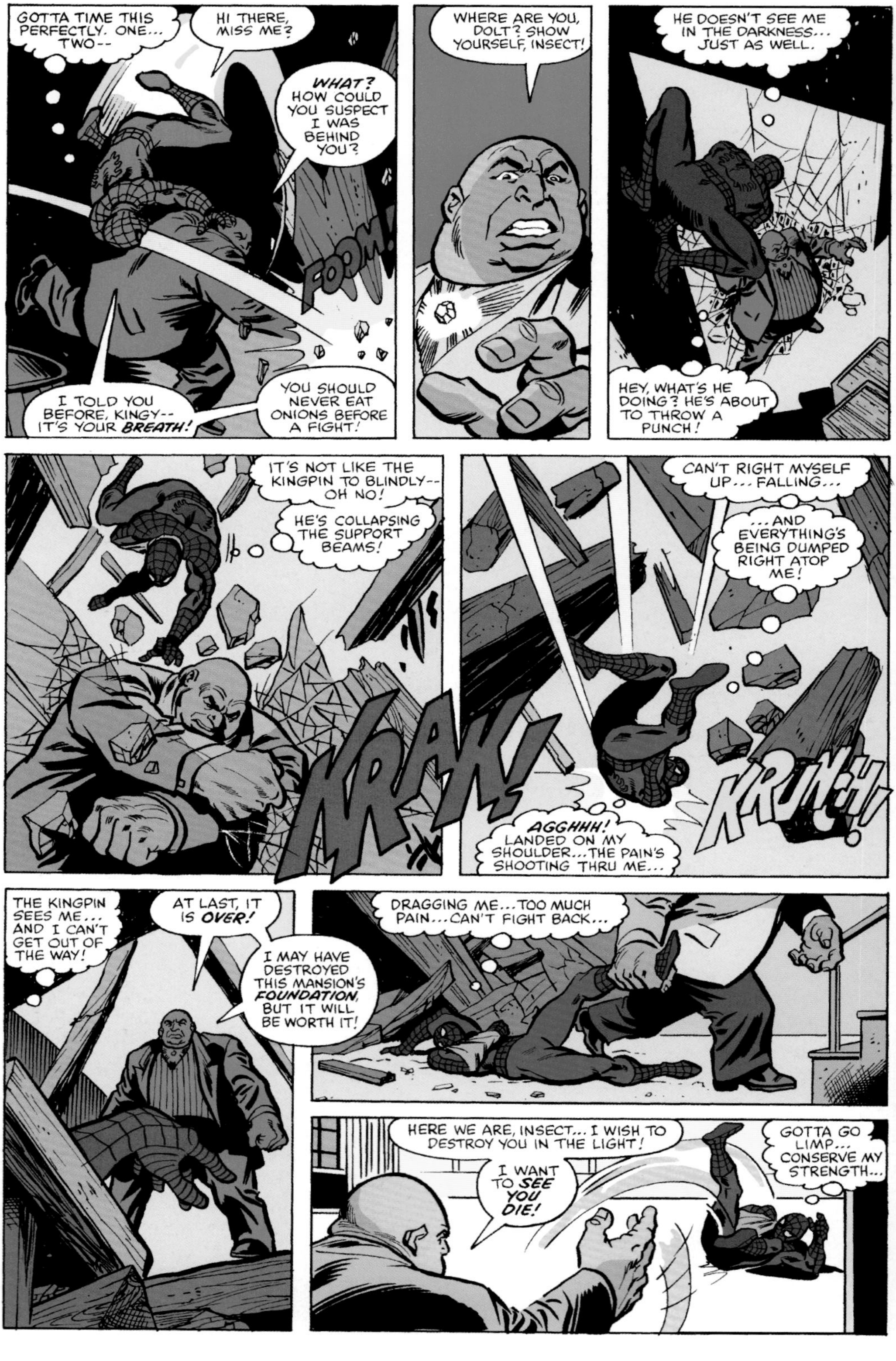
GOTTA TIME THIS PERFECTLY. ONE... TWO--
HI THERE, MISS ME?
WHAT? HOW COULD YOU SUSPECT I WAS BEHIND YOU?
FOOM!
I TOLD YOU BEFORE, KINGY-- IT'S YOUR BREATH!
YOU SHOULD NEVER EAT ONIONS BEFORE A FIGHT!
WHERE ARE YOU, DOLT? SHOW YOURSELF, INSECT!
HE DOESN'T SEE ME IN THE DARKNESS... JUST AS WELL.
HEY, WHAT'S HE DOING? HE'S ABOUT TO THROW A PUNCH!
IT'S NOT LIKE THE KINGPIN TO BLINDLY-- OH NO!
HE'S COLLAPSING THE SUPPORT BEAMS!
KRAK!
CAN'T RIGHT MYSELF UP... FALLING...
...AND EVERYTHING'S BEING DUMPED RIGHT ATOP ME!
KRUNCH!
AGGHHH! LANDED ON MY SHOULDER... THE PAIN'S SHOOTING THRU ME...
THE KINGPIN SEES ME... AND I CAN'T GET OUT OF THE WAY!
AT LAST, IT IS OVER!
I MAY HAVE DESTROYED THIS MANSION'S FOUNDATION, BUT IT WILL BE WORTH IT!
DRAGGING ME... TOO MUCH PAIN... CAN'T FIGHT BACK...
HERE WE ARE, INSECT... I WISH TO DESTROY YOU IN THE LIGHT!
I WANT TO SEE YOU DIE!
GOTTA GO LIMP... CONSERVE MY STRENGTH...

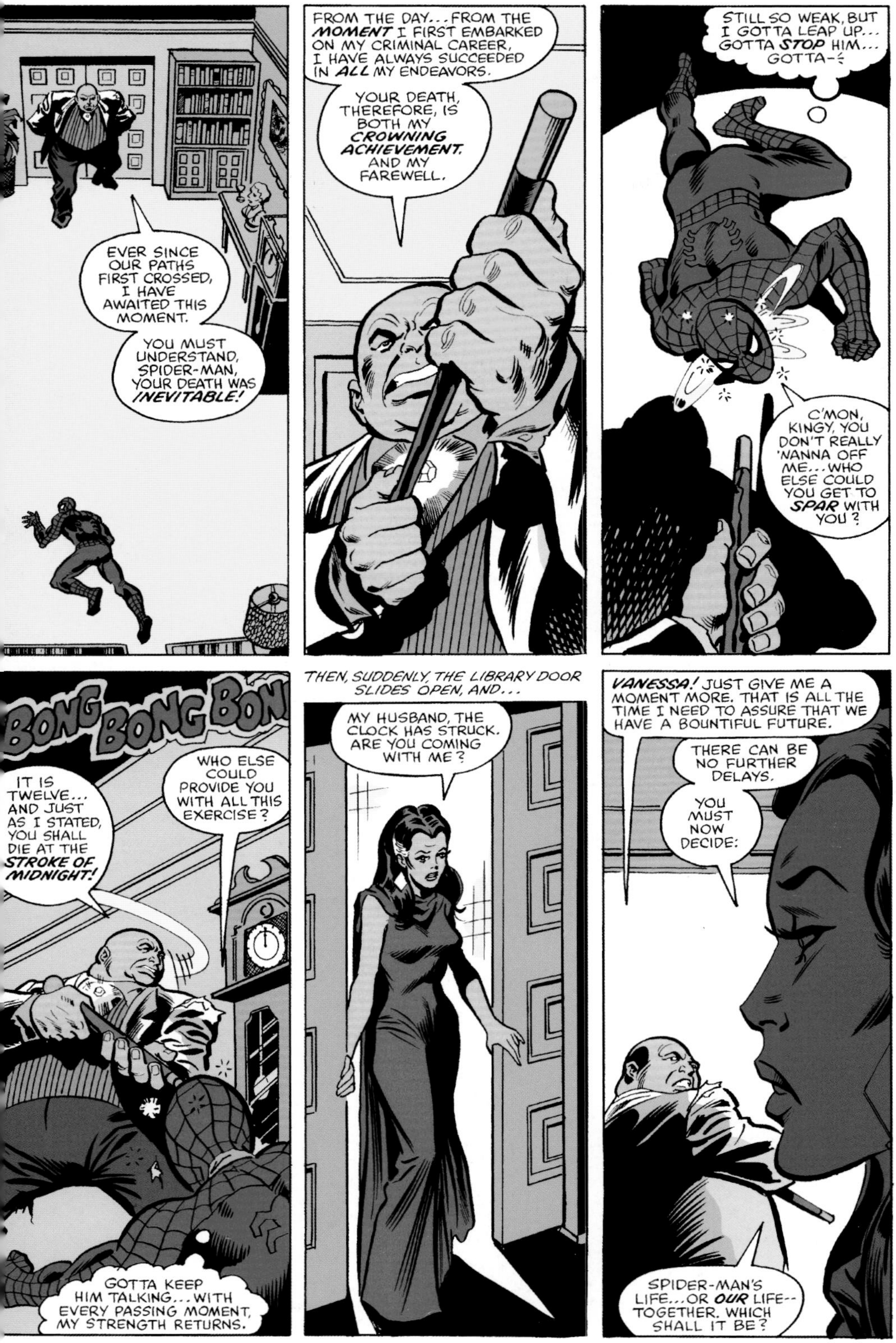
EVER SINCE OUR PATHS FIRST CROSSED, I HAVE AWAITED THIS MOMENT.
YOU MUST UNDERSTAND, SPIDER-MAN, YOUR DEATH WAS INEVITABLE!
FROM THE DAY... FROM THE MOMENT I FIRST EMBARKED ON MY CRIMINAL CAREER, I HAVE ALWAYS SUCCEEDED IN ALL MY ENDEAVORS.
YOUR DEATH, THEREFORE, IS BOTH MY CROWNING ACHIEVEMENT AND MY FAREWELL.
STILL SO WEAK, BUT I GOTTA LEAP UP... GOTTA STOP HIM... GOTTA--!
C'MON, KINGY, YOU DON'T REALLY 'NANNA OFF ME... WHO ELSE COULD YOU GET TO SPAR WITH YOU?
BONG BONG BON
IT IS TWELVE... AND JUST AS I STATED, YOU SHALL DIE AT THE STROKE OF MIDNIGHT!
WHO ELSE COULD PROVIDE YOU WITH ALL THIS EXERCISE?
GOTTA KEEP HIM TALKING... WITH EVERY PASSING MOMENT, MY STRENGTH RETURNS.
THEN, SUDDENLY, THE LIBRARY DOOR SLIDES OPEN, AND...
MY HUSBAND, THE CLOCK HAS STRUCK. ARE YOU COMING WITH ME?
VANESSA! JUST GIVE ME A MOMENT MORE. THAT IS ALL THE TIME I NEED TO ASSURE THAT WE HAVE A BOUNTIFUL FUTURE.
THERE CAN BE NO FURTHER DELAYS.
YOU MUST NOW DECIDE:
SPIDER-MAN'S LIFE... OR OUR LIFE-- TOGETHER. WHICH SHALL IT BE?

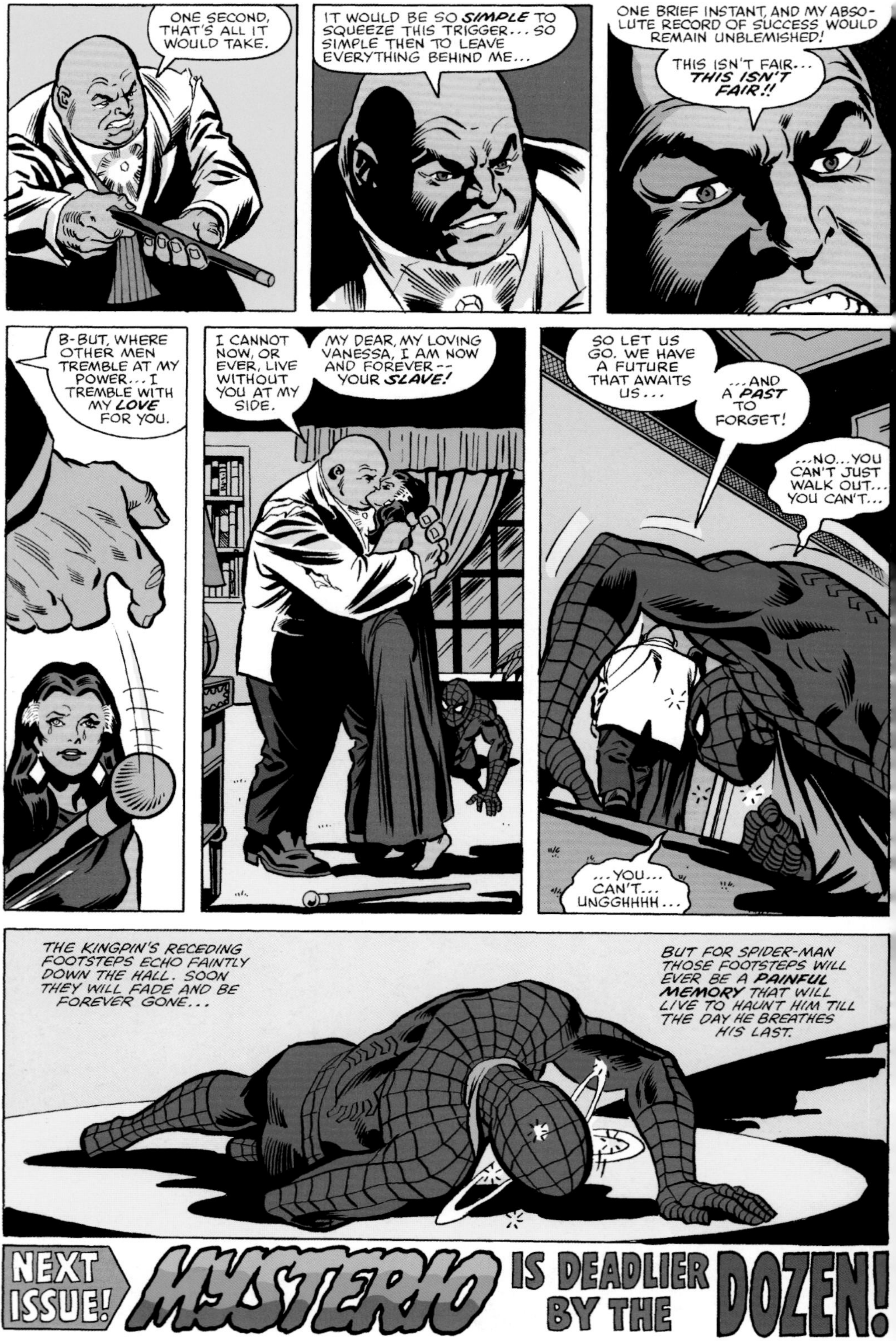
ONE SECOND, THAT'S ALL IT WOULD TAKE.
IT WOULD BE SO SIMPLE TO SQUEEZE THIS TRIGGER... SO SIMPLE THEN TO LEAVE EVERYTHING BEHIND ME...
ONE BRIEF INSTANT, AND MY ABSOLUTE RECORD OF SUCCESS WOULD REMAIN UNBLEMISHED!
THIS ISN'T FAIR... THIS ISN'T FAIR!!
B-BUT, WHERE OTHER MEN TREMBLE AT MY POWER... I TREMBLE WITH MY LOVE FOR YOU.
I CANNOT NOW, OR EVER, LIVE WITHOUT YOU AT MY SIDE.
MY DEAR, MY LOVING VANESSA, I AM NOW AND FOREVER -- YOUR SLAVE!
SO LET US GO. WE HAVE A FUTURE THAT AWAITS US...
...AND A PAST TO FORGET!
...NO... YOU CAN'T JUST WALK OUT... YOU CAN'T...
...YOU... CAN'T... UNGGHHHH...
THE KINGPIN'S RECEDING FOOTSTEPS ECHO FAINTLY DOWN THE HALL. SOON THEY WILL FADE AND BE FOREVER GONE...
BUT FOR SPIDER-MAN THOSE FOOTSTEPS WILL EVER BE A PAINFUL MEMORY THAT WILL LIVE TO HAUNT HIM TILL THE DAY HE BREATHES HIS LAST.
NEXT ISSUE!
MYSTERIO IS DEADLIER BY THE DOZEN!

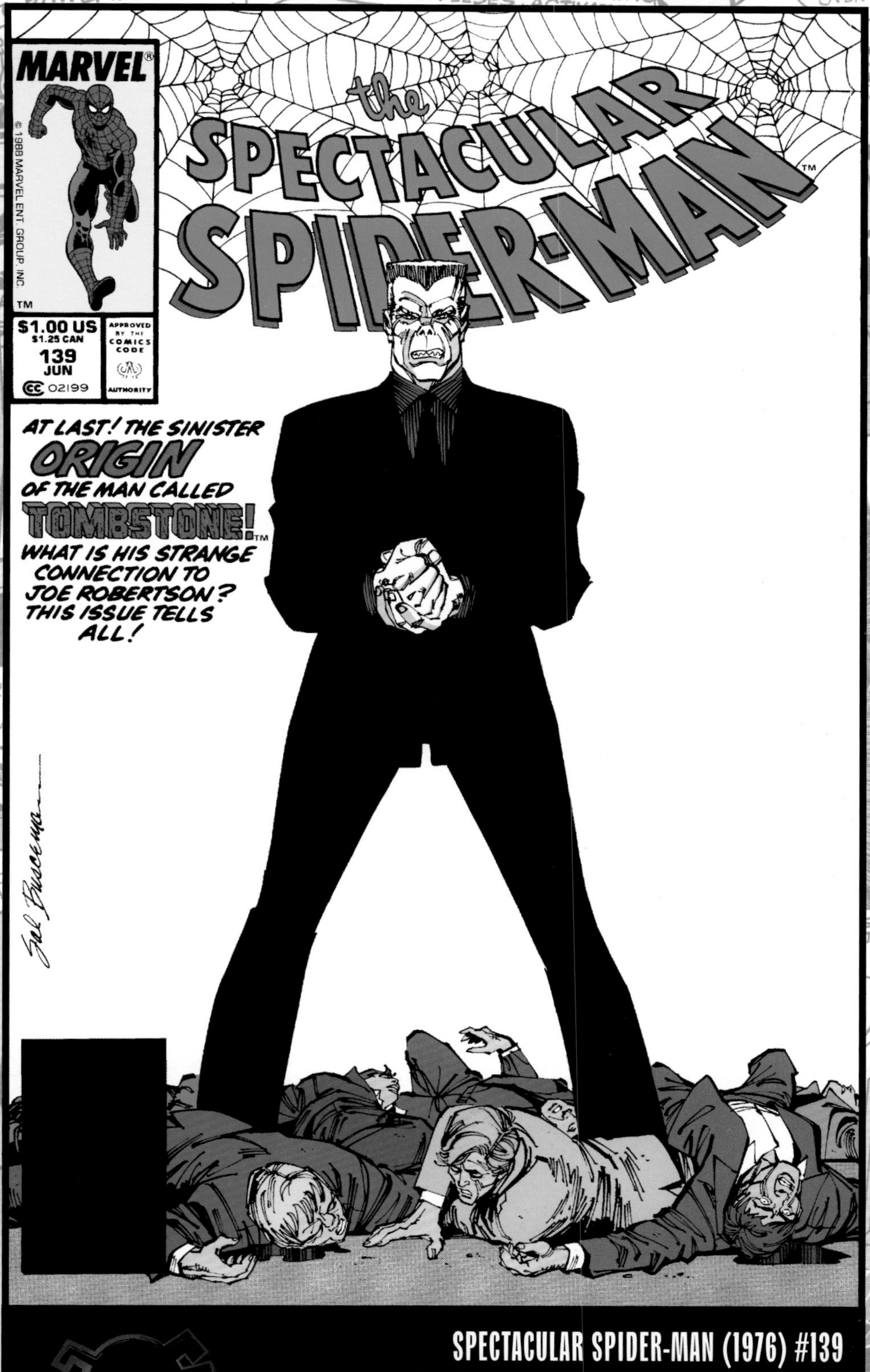
MARVEL
© 1988 MARVEL ENT. GROUP, INC.
$1.00 US
$1.25 CAN
139
JUN
02199
APPROVED BY THE COMICS CODE AUTHORITY
the SPECTACULAR SPIDER-MAN
AT LAST! THE SINISTER ORIGIN OF THE MAN CALLED TOMBSTONE! WHAT IS HIS STRANGE CONNECTION TO JOE ROBERTSON? THIS ISSUE TELLS ALL!

SPECTACULAR SPIDER-MAN (1976) #139

THE PAST COMES BACK TO HAUNT JOE "ROBBIE" ROBERTSON AS THE SINISTER HISTORY OF HITMAN TOMBSTONE IS REVEALED.

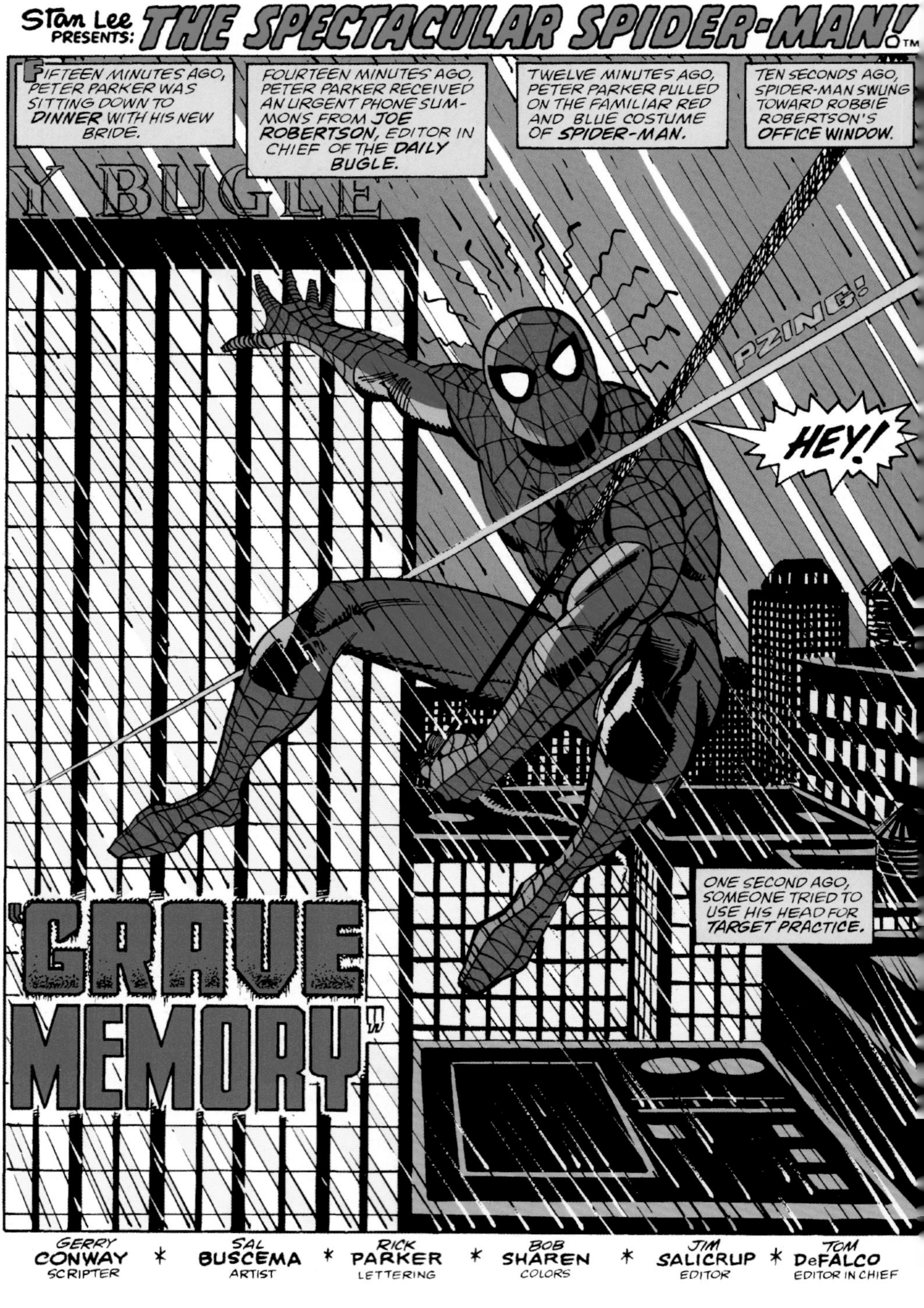
Stan Lee PRESENTS: THE SPECTACULAR SPIDER-MAN!
FIFTEEN MINUTES AGO, PETER PARKER WAS SITTING DOWN TO DINNER WITH HIS NEW BRIDE.
FOURTEEN MINUTES AGO, PETER PARKER RECEIVED AN URGENT PHONE SUMMONS FROM JOE ROBERTSON, EDITOR IN CHIEF OF THE DAILY BUGLE.
TWELVE MINUTES AGO, PETER PARKER PULLED ON THE FAMILIAR RED AND BLUE COSTUME OF SPIDER-MAN.
TEN SECONDS AGO, SPIDER-MAN SWUNG TOWARD ROBBIE ROBERTSON'S OFFICE WINDOW.
Y BUGLE
PZING!
HEY!
ONE SECOND AGO, SOMEONE TRIED TO USE HIS HEAD FOR TARGET PRACTICE.
"GRAVE MEMORY"
GERRY CONWAY SCRIPTER * SAL BUSCEMA ARTIST * RICK PARKER LETTERING * BOB SHAREN COLORS * JIM SALICRUP EDITOR * TOM DeFALCO EDITOR IN CHIEF

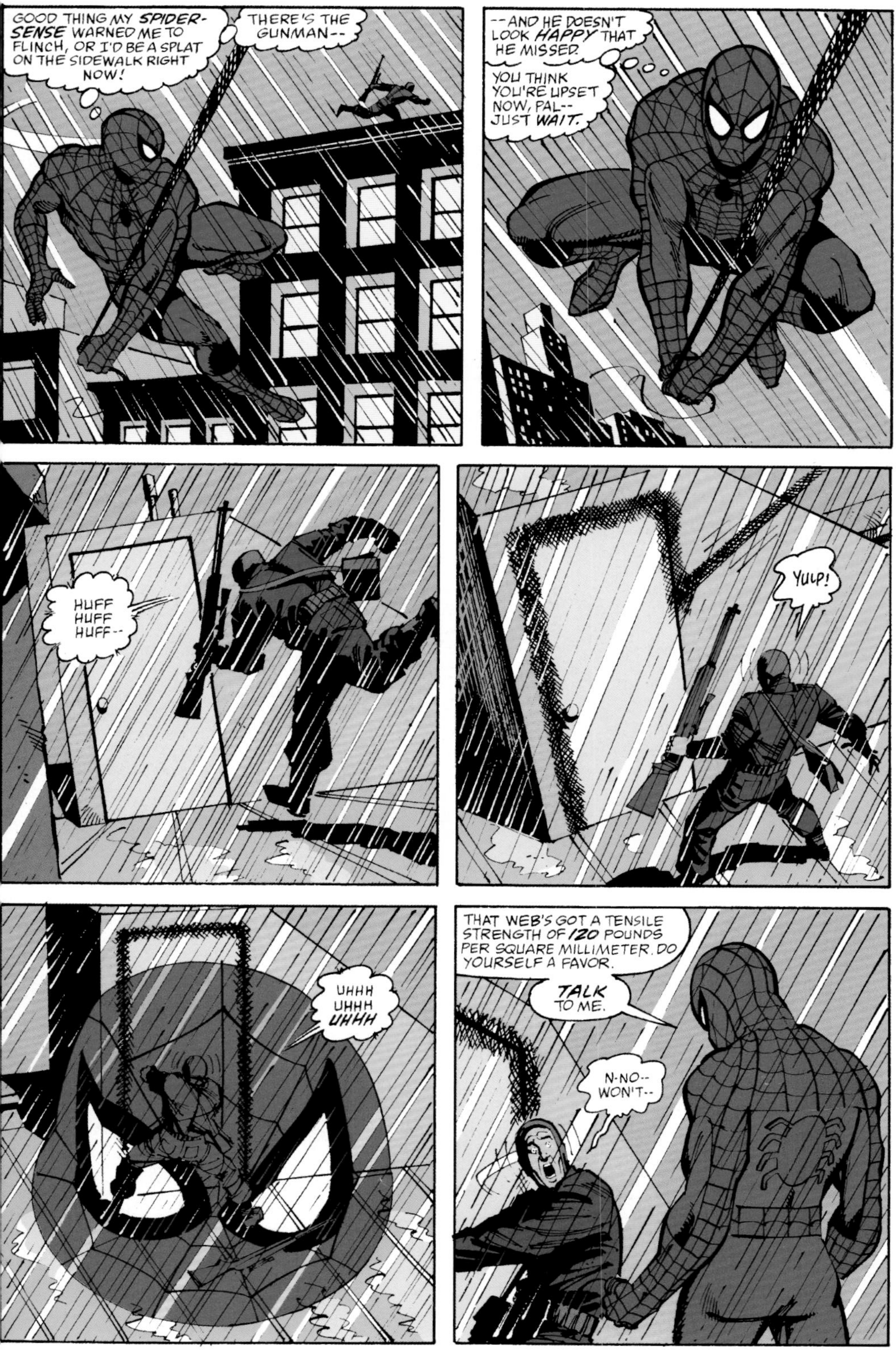
GOOD THING MY SPIDER-SENSE WARNED ME TO FLINCH, OR I'D BE A SPLAT ON THE SIDEWALK RIGHT NOW!
THERE'S THE GUNMAN--
--AND HE DOESN'T LOOK HAPPY THAT HE MISSED.
YOU THINK YOU'RE UPSET NOW, PAL--JUST WAIT.
HUFF HUFF HUFF--
YULP!
UHHH UHHH UHHH
THAT WEB'S GOT A TENSILE STRENGTH OF 120 POUNDS PER SQUARE MILLIMETER. DO YOURSELF A FAVOR.
TALK TO ME.
N-NO-- WON'T--

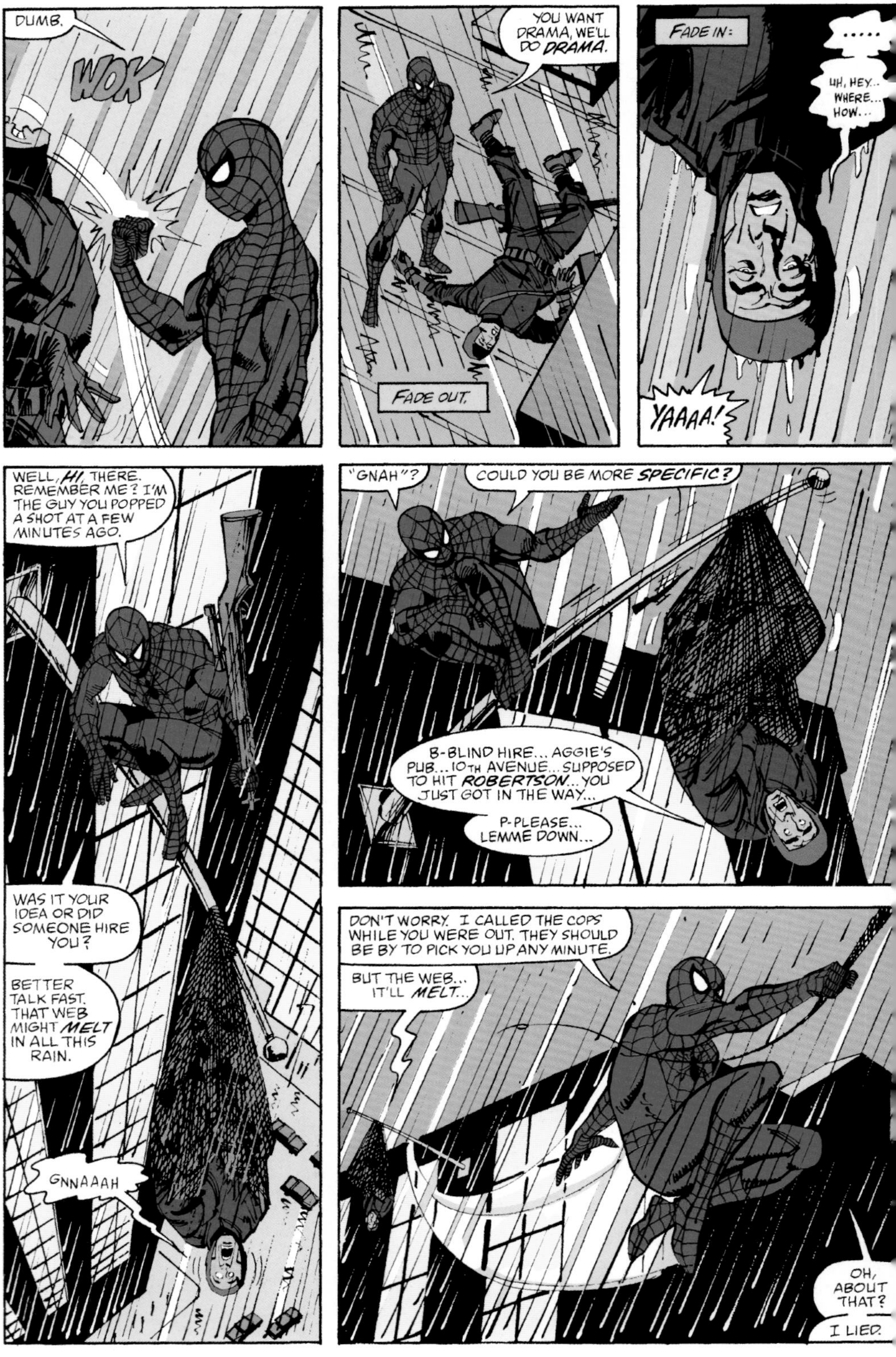

DUMB.
WOK
YOU WANT DRAMA, WE'LL DO DRAMA.
FADE OUT.
FADE IN:
......
UH, HEY... WHERE... HOW...
YAAAA!
WELL, HI, THERE. REMEMBER ME? I'M THE GUY YOU POPPED A SHOT AT A FEW MINUTES AGO.
WAS IT YOUR IDEA OR DID SOMEONE HIRE YOU?
BETTER TALK FAST. THAT WEB MIGHT MELT IN ALL THIS RAIN.
GNNAAAH
"GNAH"?
COULD YOU BE MORE SPECIFIC?
B-BLIND HIRE... AGGIE'S PUB... 10TH AVENUE... SUPPOSED TO HIT ROBERTSON... YOU JUST GOT IN THE WAY...
P-PLEASE... LEMME DOWN...
DON'T WORRY. I CALLED THE COPS WHILE YOU WERE OUT. THEY SHOULD BE BY TO PICK YOU UP ANY MINUTE.
BUT THE WEB... IT'LL MELT...
OH, ABOUT THAT?
I LIED.

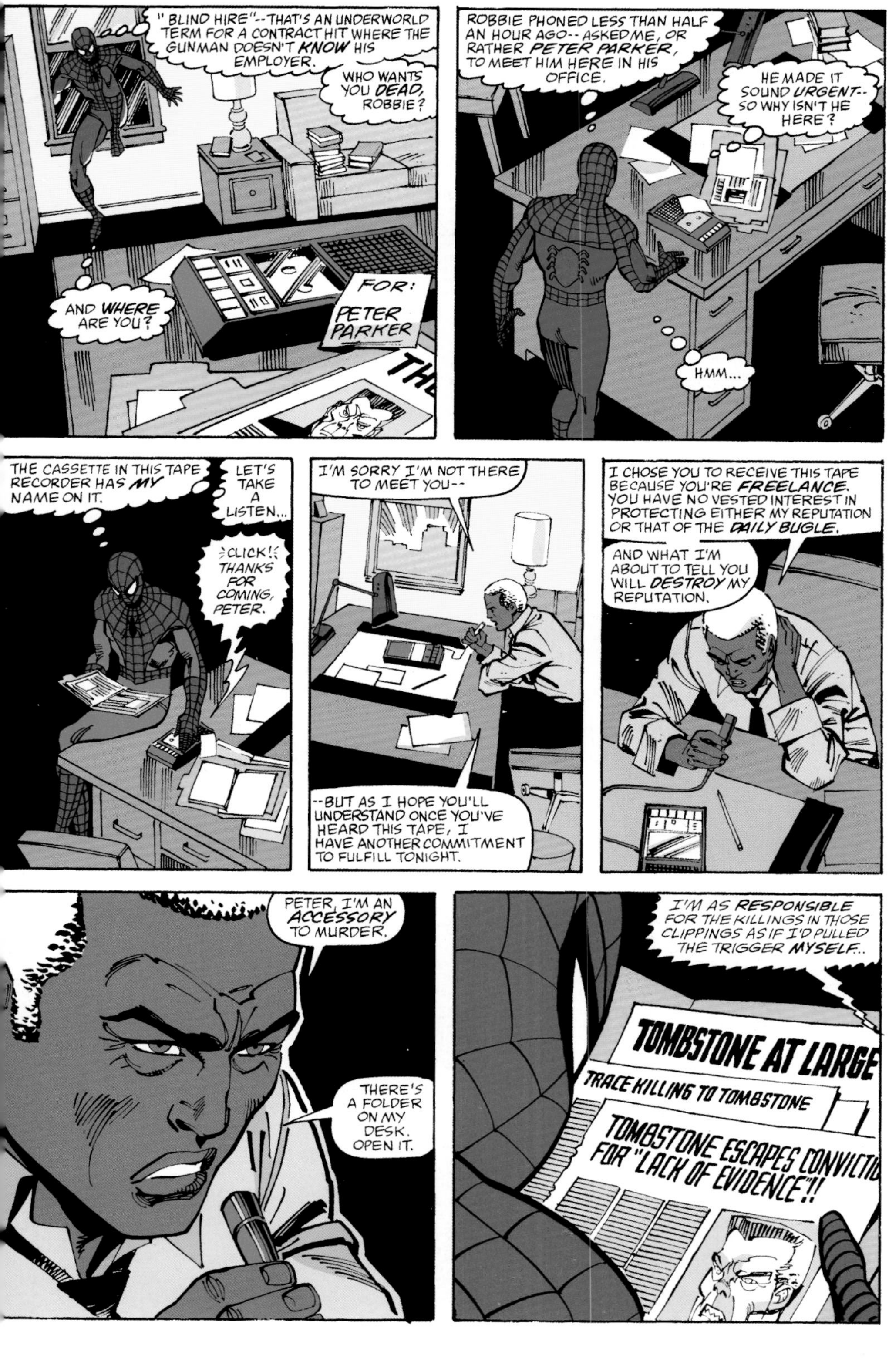
"BLIND HIRE"--THAT'S AN UNDERWORLD TERM FOR A CONTRACT HIT WHERE THE GUNMAN DOESN'T KNOW HIS EMPLOYER.
WHO WANTS YOU DEAD, ROBBIE?
AND WHERE ARE YOU?
FOR: PETER PARKER
ROBBIE PHONED LESS THAN HALF AN HOUR AGO-- ASKED ME, OR RATHER PETER PARKER, TO MEET HIM HERE IN HIS OFFICE.
HE MADE IT SOUND URGENT-- SO WHY ISN'T HE HERE?
HMM...
THE CASSETTE IN THIS TAPE RECORDER HAS MY NAME ON IT.
LET'S TAKE A LISTEN...
CLICK!
THANKS FOR COMING, PETER.
I'M SORRY I'M NOT THERE TO MEET YOU--
--BUT AS I HOPE YOU'LL UNDERSTAND ONCE YOU'VE HEARD THIS TAPE, I HAVE ANOTHER COMMITMENT TO FULFILL TONIGHT.
I CHOSE YOU TO RECEIVE THIS TAPE BECAUSE YOU'RE FREELANCE. YOU HAVE NO VESTED INTEREST IN PROTECTING EITHER MY REPUTATION OR THAT OF THE DAILY BUGLE.
AND WHAT I'M ABOUT TO TELL YOU WILL DESTROY MY REPUTATION.
PETER, I'M AN ACCESSORY TO MURDER.
THERE'S A FOLDER ON MY DESK. OPEN IT.
I'M AS RESPONSIBLE FOR THE KILLINGS IN THOSE CLIPPINGS AS IF I'D PULLED THE TRIGGER MYSELF...
TOMBSTONE AT LARGE
TRACE KILLING TO TOMBSTONE
TOMBSTONE ESCAPES CONVICTIO
FOR "LACK OF EVIDENCE"!!

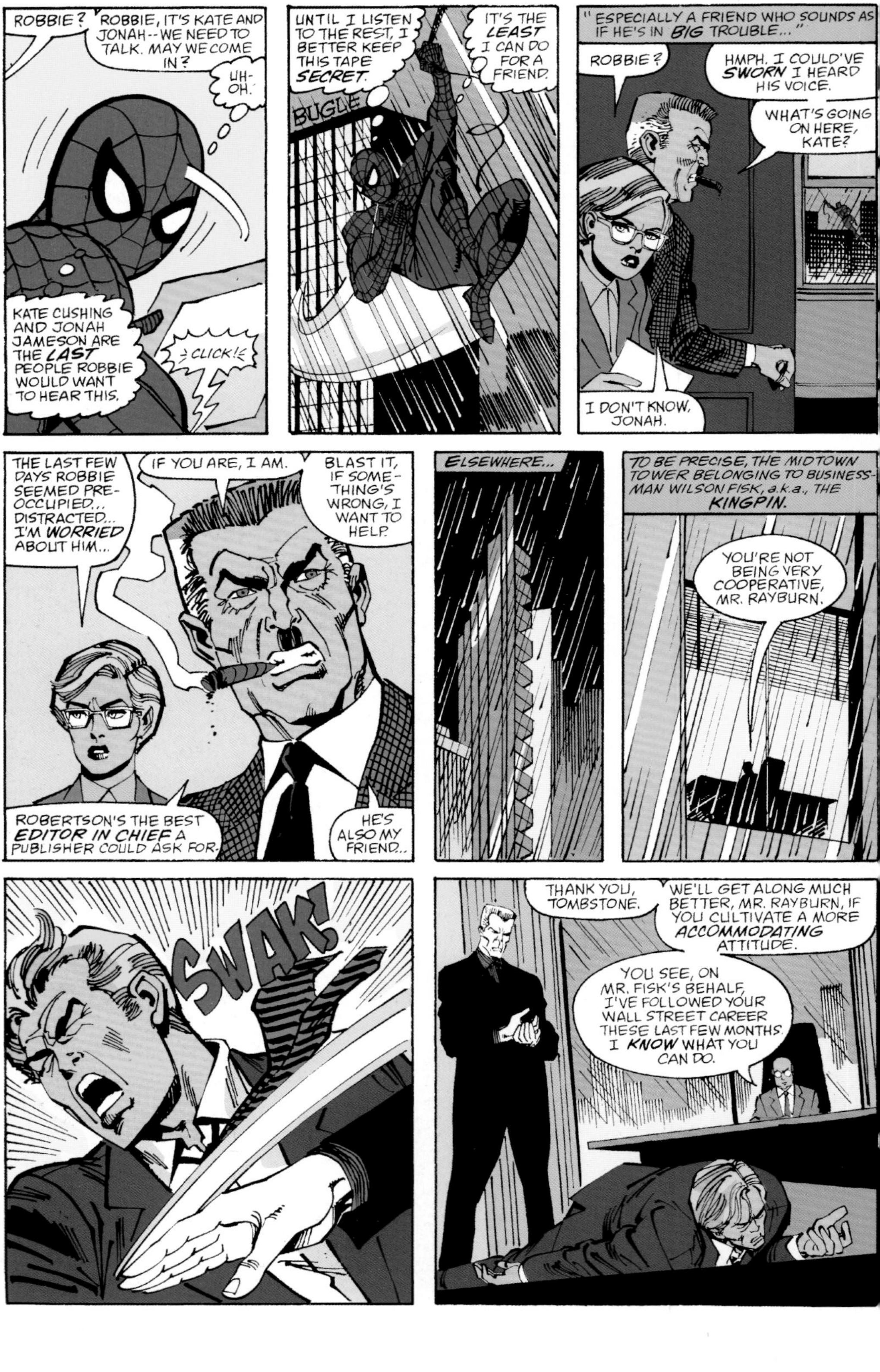
ROBBIE?
ROBBIE, IT'S KATE AND JONAH--WE NEED TO TALK. MAY WE COME IN?
UH-OH.
KATE CUSHING AND JONAH JAMESON ARE THE LAST PEOPLE ROBBIE WOULD WANT TO HEAR THIS.
CLICK!
UNTIL I LISTEN TO THE REST, I BETTER KEEP THIS TAPE SECRET.
IT'S THE LEAST I CAN DO FOR A FRIEND.
BUGLE
"ESPECIALLY A FRIEND WHO SOUNDS AS IF HE'S IN BIG TROUBLE..."
ROBBIE?
HMPH. I COULD'VE SWORN I HEARD HIS VOICE.
WHAT'S GOING ON HERE, KATE?
I DON'T KNOW, JONAH.
THE LAST FEW DAYS ROBBIE SEEMED PRE-OCCUPIED... DISTRACTED... I'M WORRIED ABOUT HIM...
IF YOU ARE, I AM.
BLAST IT, IF SOME-THING'S WRONG, I WANT TO HELP.
ROBERTSON'S THE BEST EDITOR IN CHIEF A PUBLISHER COULD ASK FOR.
HE'S ALSO MY FRIEND...
ELSEWHERE...
TO BE PRECISE, THE MIDTOWN TOWER BELONGING TO BUSINESS-MAN WILSON FISK, a.k.a., THE KINGPIN.
YOU'RE NOT BEING VERY COOPERATIVE, MR. RAYBURN.
SWAK!
THANK YOU, TOMBSTONE.
WE'LL GET ALONG MUCH BETTER, MR. RAYBURN, IF YOU CULTIVATE A MORE ACCOMMODATING ATTITUDE.
YOU SEE, ON MR. FISK'S BEHALF, I'VE FOLLOWED YOUR WALL STREET CAREER THESE LAST FEW MONTHS. I KNOW WHAT YOU CAN DO.

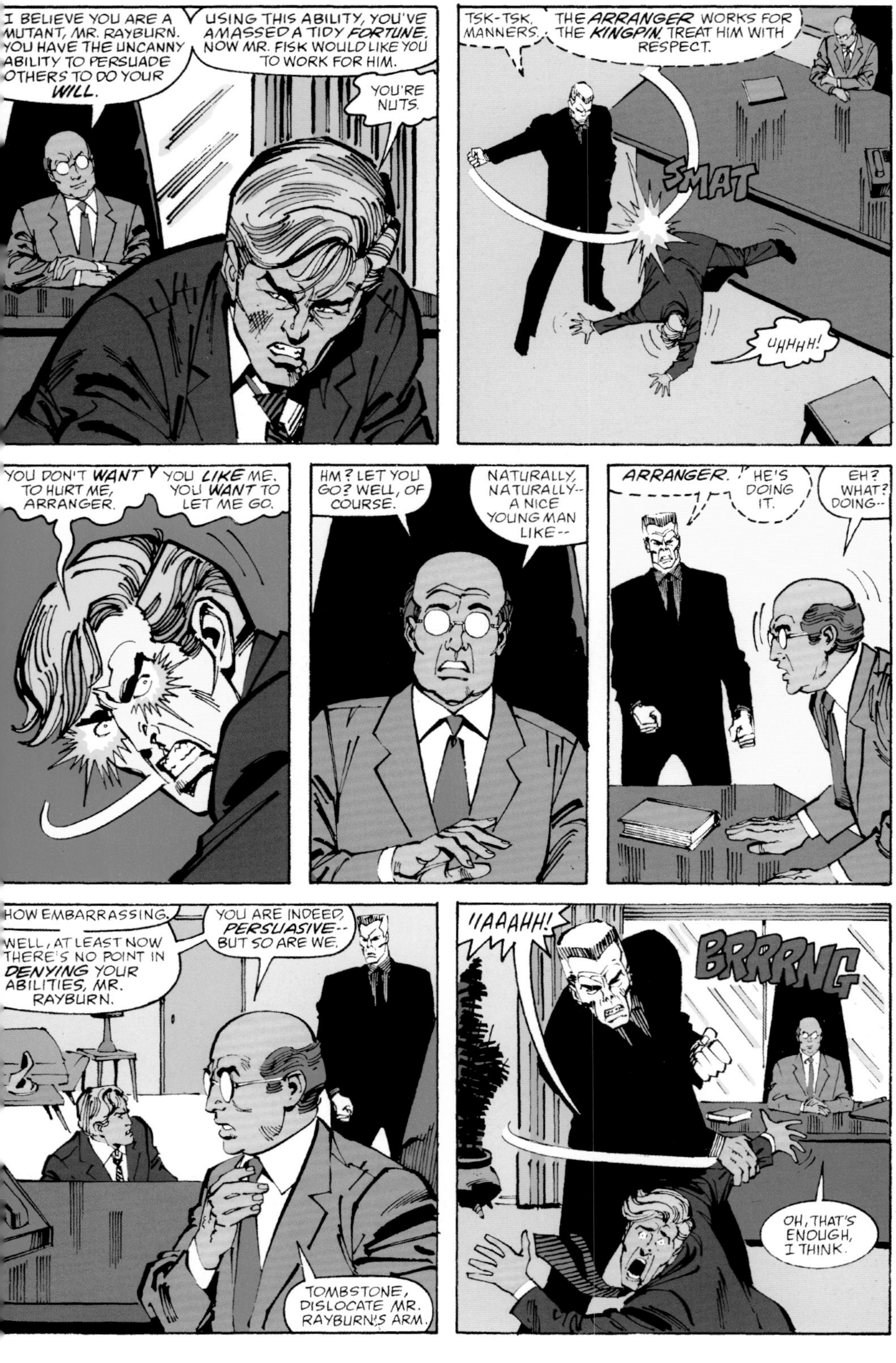

I BELIEVE YOU ARE A MUTANT, MR. RAYBURN. YOU HAVE THE UNCANNY ABILITY TO PERSUADE OTHERS TO DO YOUR WILL.
USING THIS ABILITY, YOU'VE AMASSED A TIDY FORTUNE. NOW MR. FISK WOULD LIKE YOU TO WORK FOR HIM.
YOU'RE NUTS.
TSK-TSK, MANNERS.
THE ARRANGER WORKS FOR THE KINGPIN. TREAT HIM WITH RESPECT.
SMAT
UHHHH!
YOU DON'T WANT TO HURT ME, ARRANGER.
YOU LIKE ME. YOU WANT TO LET ME GO.
HM? LET YOU GO? WELL, OF COURSE.
NATURALLY, NATURALLY-- A NICE YOUNG MAN LIKE--
ARRANGER.
HE'S DOING IT.
EH? WHAT? DOING--
HOW EMBARRASSING.
WELL, AT LEAST NOW THERE'S NO POINT IN DENYING YOUR ABILITIES, MR. RAYBURN.
YOU ARE INDEED PERSUASIVE-- BUT SO ARE WE.
TOMBSTONE, DISLOCATE MR. RAYBURN'S ARM.
!!AAAHH!
BRRRNG
OH, THAT'S ENOUGH, I THINK.

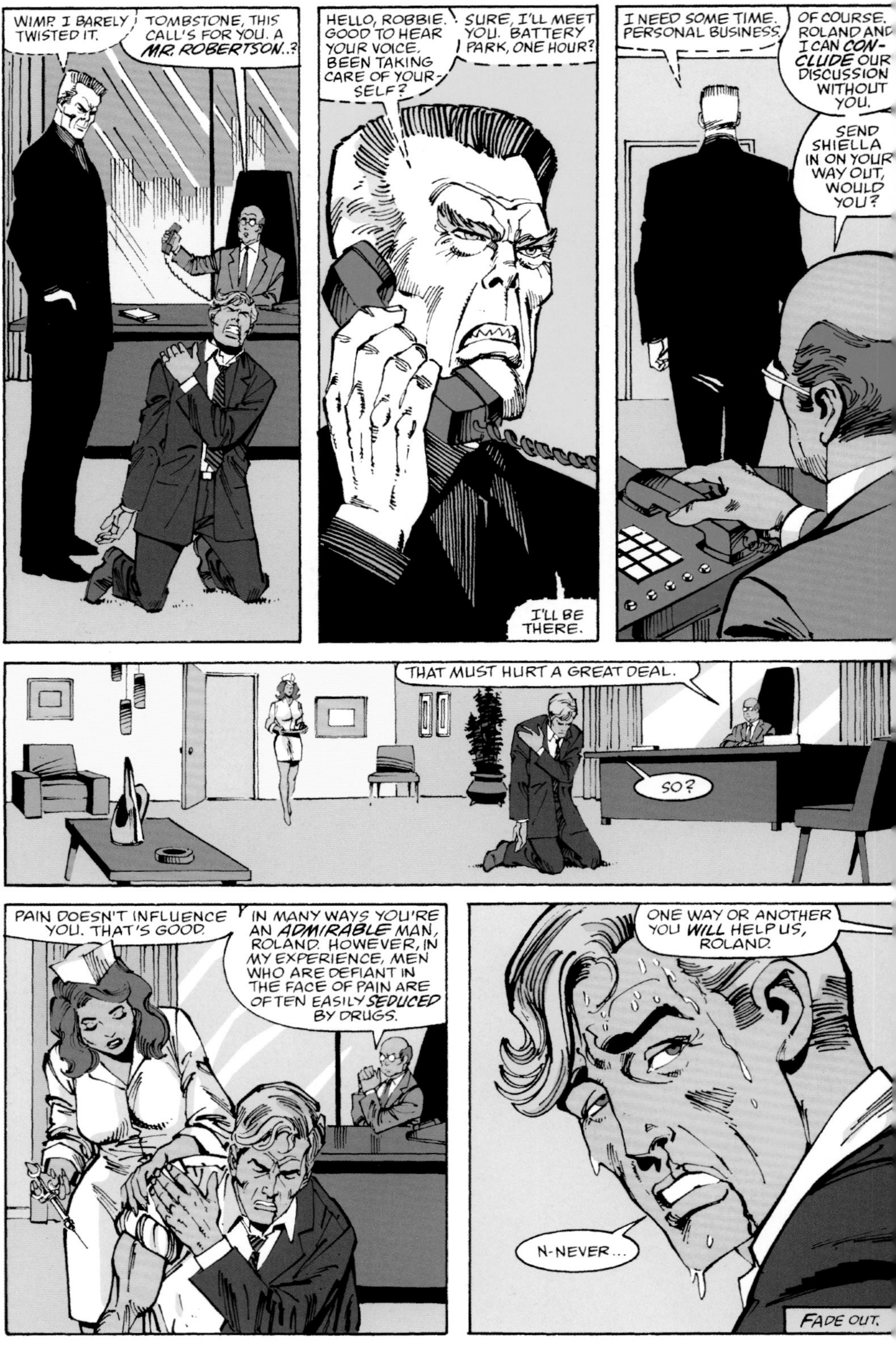
WIMP. I BARELY TWISTED IT.
TOMBSTONE, THIS CALL'S FOR YOU. A MR. ROBERTSON..?
HELLO, ROBBIE. GOOD TO HEAR YOUR VOICE. BEEN TAKING CARE OF YOURSELF?
SURE, I'LL MEET YOU. BATTERY PARK, ONE HOUR?
I'LL BE THERE.
I NEED SOME TIME. PERSONAL BUSINESS.
OF COURSE. ROLAND AND I CAN CONCLUDE OUR DISCUSSION WITHOUT YOU.
SEND SHIELLA IN ON YOUR WAY OUT, WOULD YOU?
THAT MUST HURT A GREAT DEAL.
SO?
PAIN DOESN'T INFLUENCE YOU. THAT'S GOOD.
IN MANY WAYS YOU'RE AN ADMIRABLE MAN, ROLAND. HOWEVER, IN MY EXPERIENCE, MEN WHO ARE DEFIANT IN THE FACE OF PAIN ARE OFTEN EASILY SEDUCED BY DRUGS.
ONE WAY OR ANOTHER YOU WILL HELP US, ROLAND.
N-NEVER...
FADE OUT.

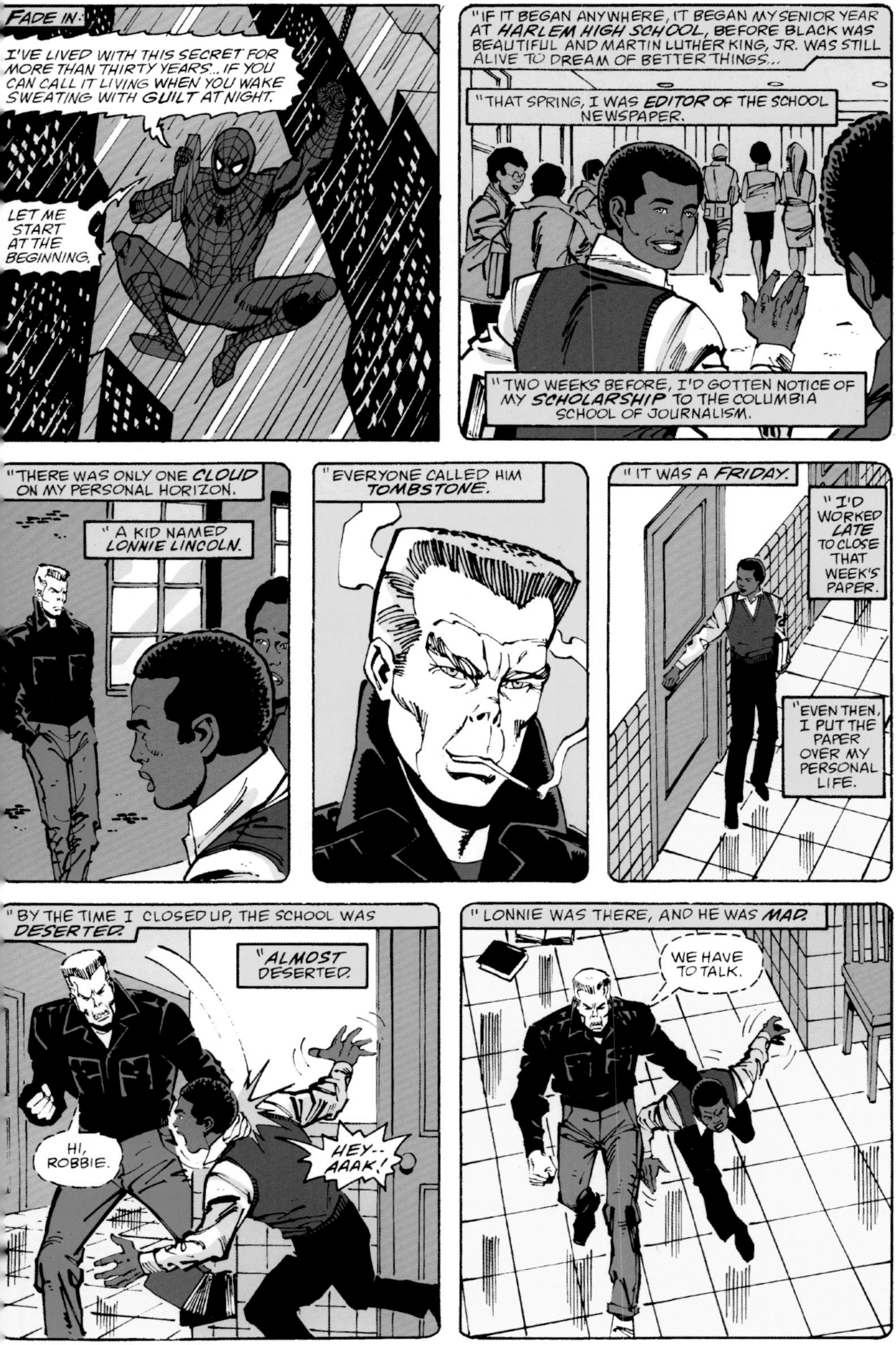
FADE IN:
I'VE LIVED WITH THIS SECRET FOR MORE THAN THIRTY YEARS... IF YOU CAN CALL IT LIVING WHEN YOU WAKE SWEATING WITH GUILT AT NIGHT.
LET ME START AT THE BEGINNING.
"IF IT BEGAN ANYWHERE, IT BEGAN MY SENIOR YEAR AT HARLEM HIGH SCHOOL, BEFORE BLACK WAS BEAUTIFUL AND MARTIN LUTHER KING, JR. WAS STILL ALIVE TO DREAM OF BETTER THINGS...
"THAT SPRING, I WAS EDITOR OF THE SCHOOL NEWSPAPER.
"TWO WEEKS BEFORE, I'D GOTTEN NOTICE OF MY SCHOLARSHIP TO THE COLUMBIA SCHOOL OF JOURNALISM.
"THERE WAS ONLY ONE CLOUD ON MY PERSONAL HORIZON.
"A KID NAMED LONNIE LINCOLN.
"EVERYONE CALLED HIM TOMBSTONE.
"IT WAS A FRIDAY.
"I'D WORKED LATE TO CLOSE THAT WEEK'S PAPER.
"EVEN THEN, I PUT THE PAPER OVER MY PERSONAL LIFE.
"BY THE TIME I CLOSED UP, THE SCHOOL WAS DESERTED.
"ALMOST DESERTED.
HI, ROBBIE.
HEY-- AAAK!
"LONNIE WAS THERE, AND HE WAS MAD.
WE HAVE TO TALK.

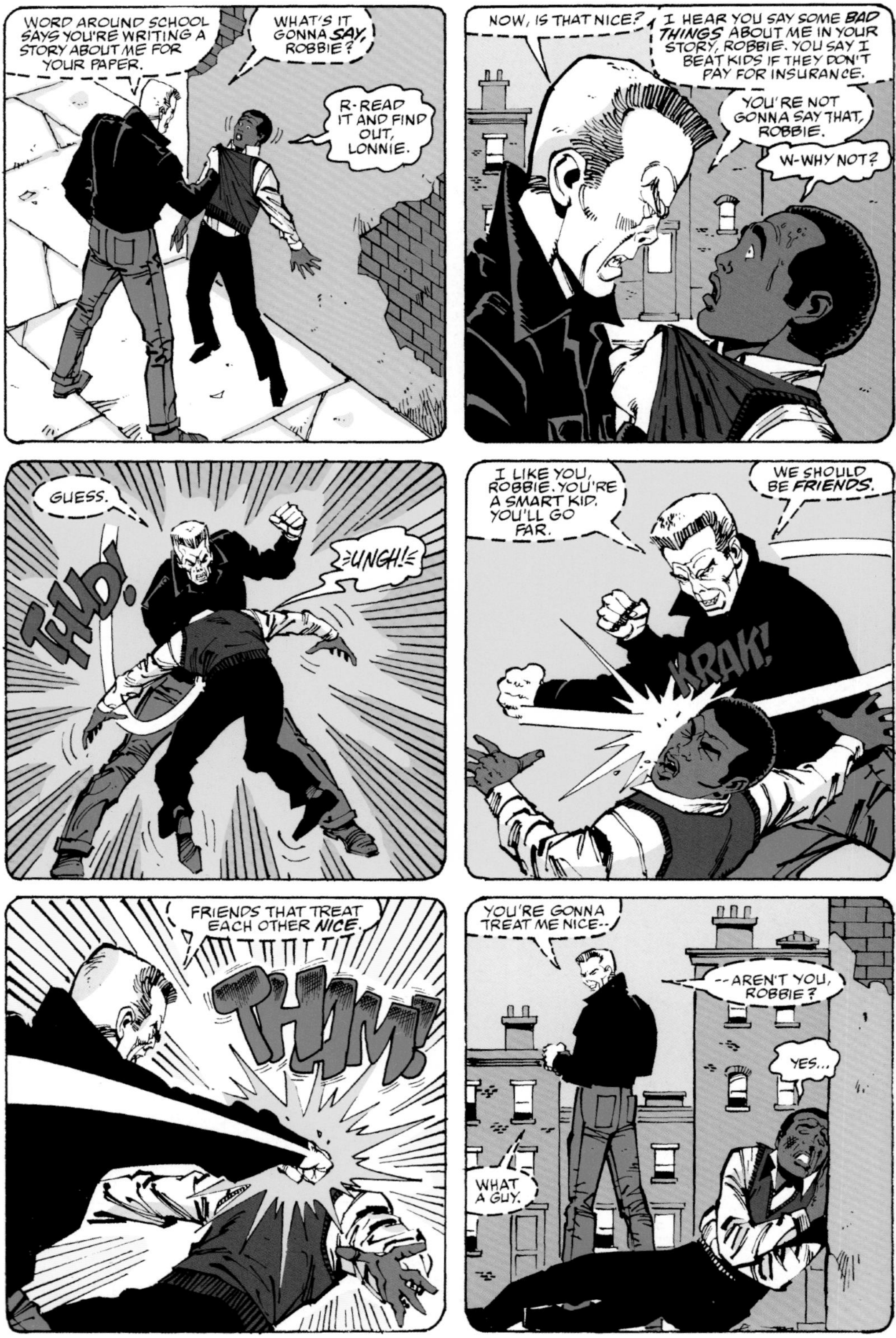
WORD AROUND SCHOOL SAYS YOU'RE WRITING A STORY ABOUT ME FOR YOUR PAPER.
WHAT'S IT GONNA SAY, ROBBIE?
R-READ IT AND FIND OUT, LONNIE.
NOW, IS THAT NICE?
I HEAR YOU SAY SOME BAD THINGS ABOUT ME IN YOUR STORY, ROBBIE. YOU SAY I BEAT KIDS IF THEY DON'T PAY FOR INSURANCE.
YOU'RE NOT GONNA SAY THAT, ROBBIE.
W-WHY NOT?
GUESS.
THUD!
UNGH!
I LIKE YOU, ROBBIE. YOU'RE A SMART KID. YOU'LL GO FAR.
WE SHOULD BE FRIENDS.
KRAK!
FRIENDS THAT TREAT EACH OTHER NICE.
THOM!
YOU'RE GONNA TREAT ME NICE--
--AREN'T YOU, ROBBIE?
YES...
WHAT A GUY.

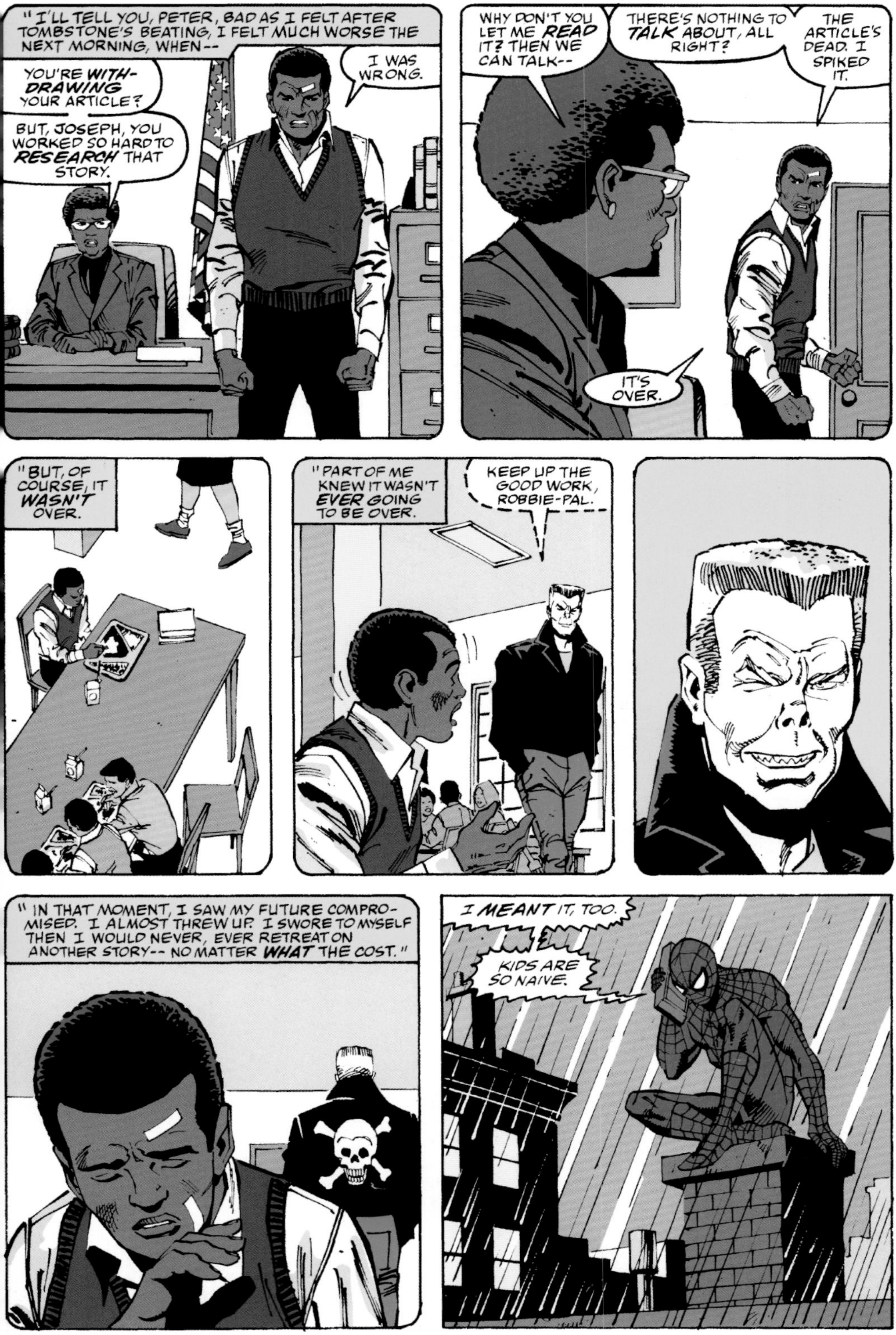
"I'LL TELL YOU, PETER, BAD AS I FELT AFTER TOMBSTONE'S BEATING, I FELT MUCH WORSE THE NEXT MORNING, WHEN--
YOU'RE WITH-DRAWING YOUR ARTICLE?
BUT, JOSEPH, YOU WORKED SO HARD TO RESEARCH THAT STORY.
I WAS WRONG.
WHY DON'T YOU LET ME READ IT? THEN WE CAN TALK--
THERE'S NOTHING TO TALK ABOUT, ALL RIGHT?
THE ARTICLE'S DEAD. I SPIKED IT.
IT'S OVER.
"BUT, OF COURSE, IT WASN'T OVER.
"PART OF ME KNEW IT WASN'T EVER GOING TO BE OVER.
KEEP UP THE GOOD WORK, ROBBIE-PAL.
"IN THAT MOMENT, I SAW MY FUTURE COMPROMISED. I ALMOST THREW UP. I SWORE TO MYSELF THEN I WOULD NEVER, EVER RETREAT ON ANOTHER STORY-- NO MATTER WHAT THE COST."
I MEANT IT, TOO.
KIDS ARE SO NAIVE.

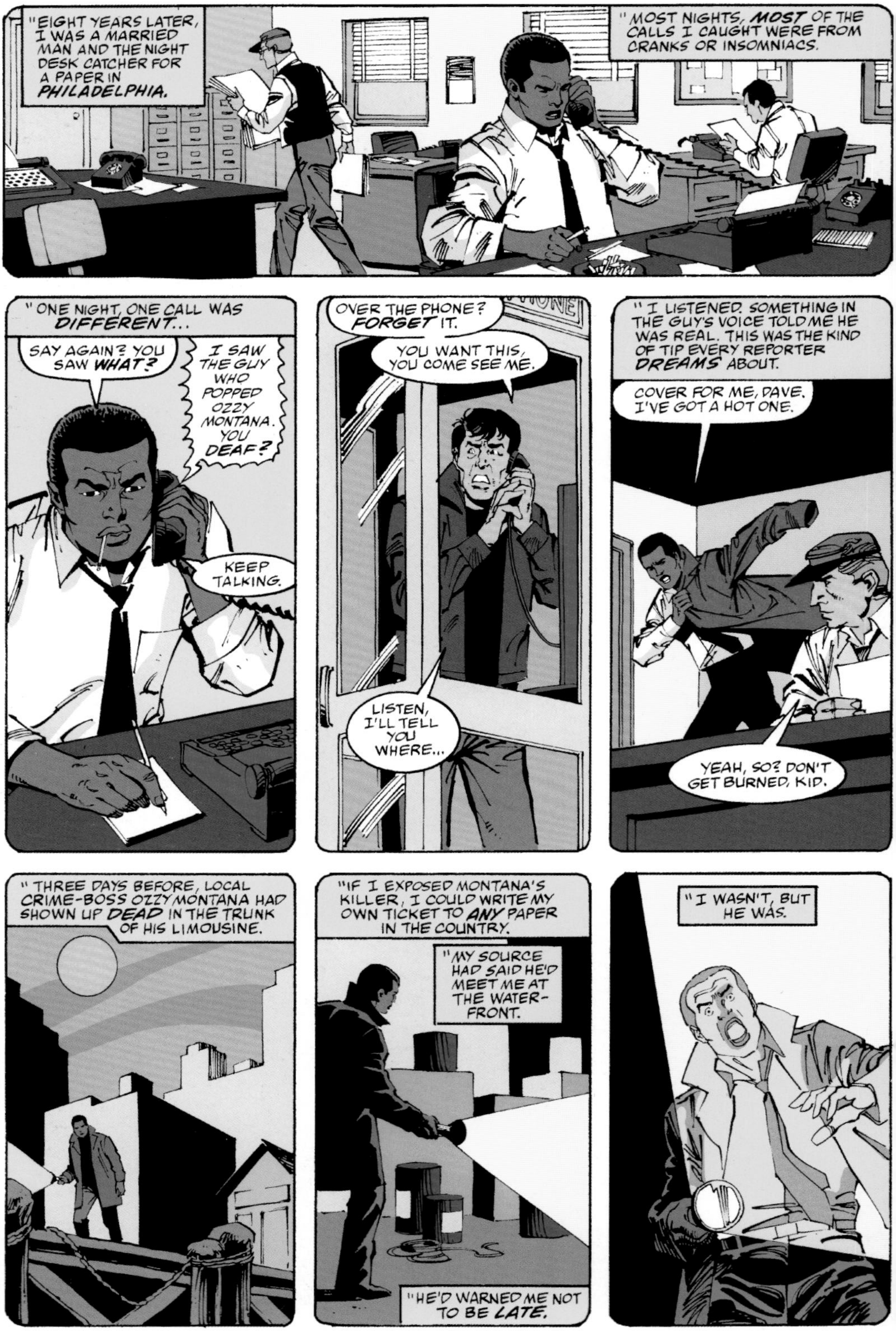
"EIGHT YEARS LATER, I WAS A MARRIED MAN AND THE NIGHT DESK CATCHER FOR A PAPER IN PHILADELPHIA.
"MOST NIGHTS, MOST OF THE CALLS I CAUGHT WERE FROM CRANKS OR INSOMNIACS.
"ONE NIGHT, ONE CALL WAS DIFFERENT...
SAY AGAIN? YOU SAW WHAT?
I SAW THE GUY WHO POPPED OZZY MONTANA. YOU DEAF?
KEEP TALKING.
OVER THE PHONE? FORGET IT.
YOU WANT THIS, YOU COME SEE ME.
LISTEN, I'LL TELL YOU WHERE...
"I LISTENED. SOMETHING IN THE GUY'S VOICE TOLD ME HE WAS REAL. THIS WAS THE KIND OF TIP EVERY REPORTER DREAMS ABOUT.
COVER FOR ME, DAVE. I'VE GOT A HOT ONE.
YEAH, SO? DON'T GET BURNED, KID.
"THREE DAYS BEFORE, LOCAL CRIME-BOSS OZZY MONTANA HAD SHOWN UP DEAD IN THE TRUNK OF HIS LIMOUSINE.
"IF I EXPOSED MONTANA'S KILLER, I COULD WRITE MY OWN TICKET TO ANY PAPER IN THE COUNTRY.
"MY SOURCE HAD SAID HE'D MEET ME AT THE WATER-FRONT.
"HE'D WARNED ME NOT TO BE LATE.
"I WASN'T, BUT HE WAS.

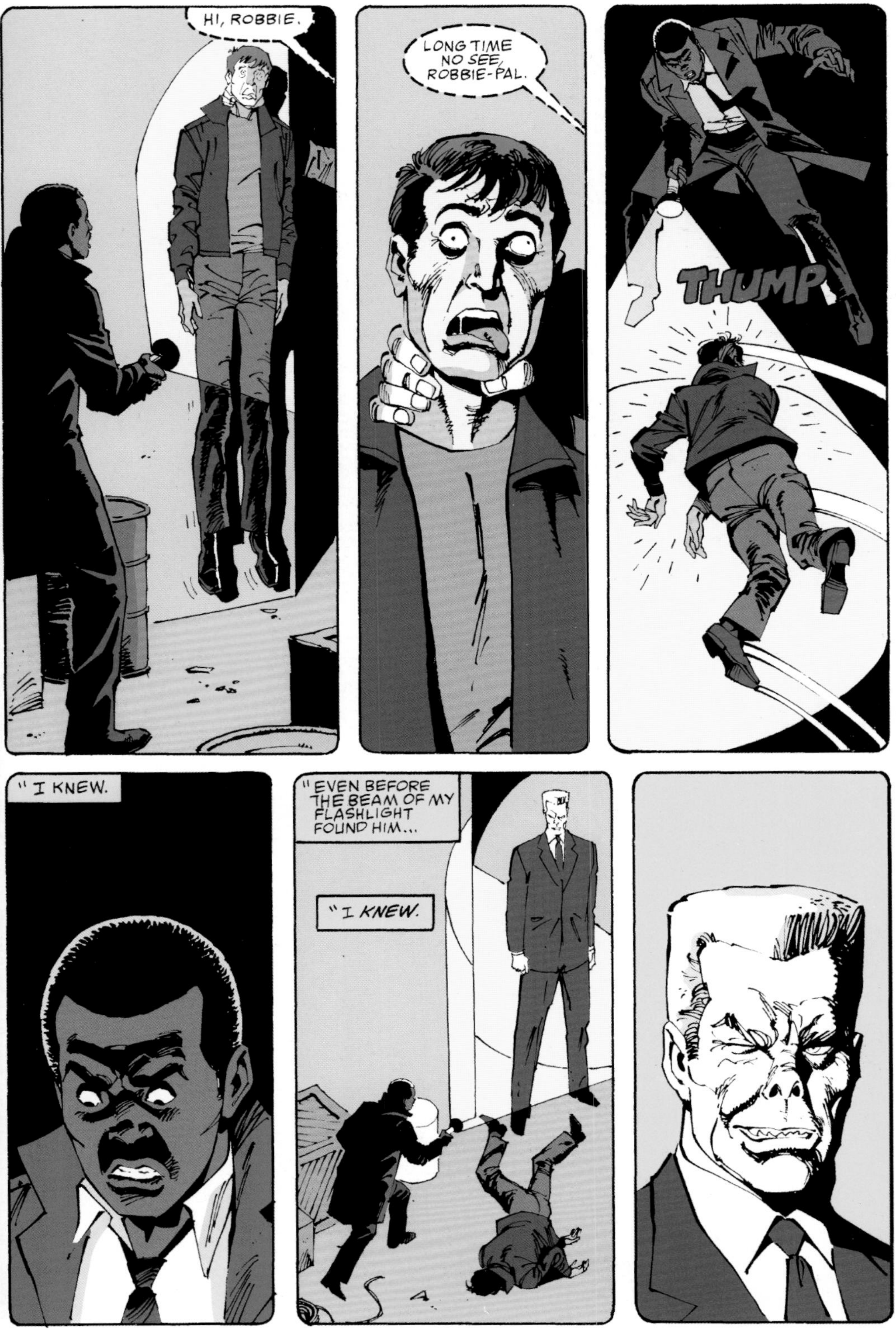
HI, ROBBIE.
LONG TIME NO SEE, ROBBIE-PAL.
THUMP
"I KNEW.
"EVEN BEFORE THE BEAM OF MY FLASHLIGHT FOUND HIM...
"I KNEW.

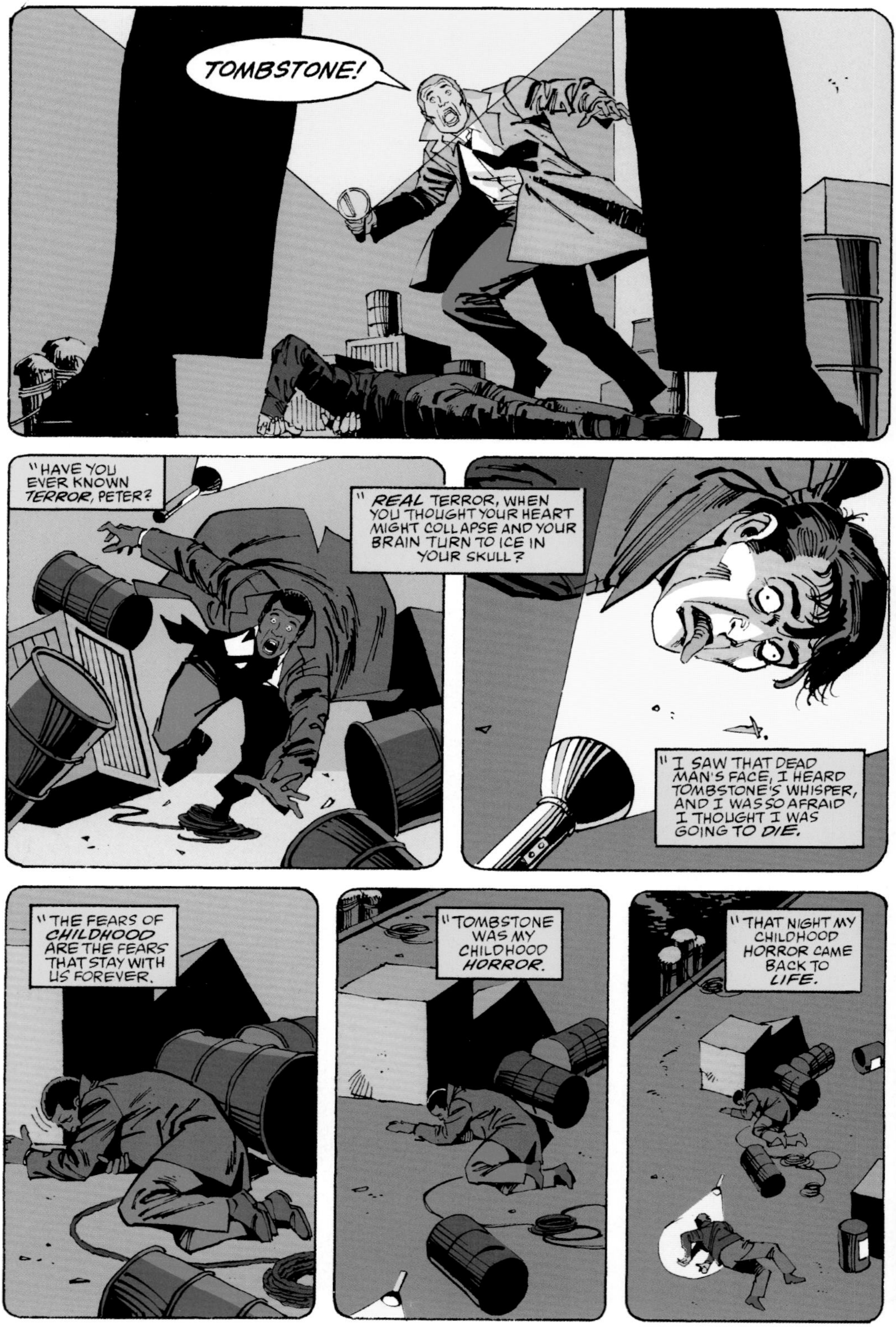
TOMBSTONE!
"HAVE YOU EVER KNOWN TERROR, PETER?
"REAL TERROR, WHEN YOU THOUGHT YOUR HEART MIGHT COLLAPSE AND YOUR BRAIN TURN TO ICE IN YOUR SKULL?
"I SAW THAT DEAD MAN'S FACE, I HEARD TOMBSTONE'S WHISPER, AND I WAS SO AFRAID I THOUGHT I WAS GOING TO DIE.
"THE FEARS OF CHILDHOOD ARE THE FEARS THAT STAY WITH US FOREVER.
"TOMBSTONE WAS MY CHILDHOOD HORROR.
"THAT NIGHT MY CHILDHOOD HORROR CAME BACK TO LIFE.

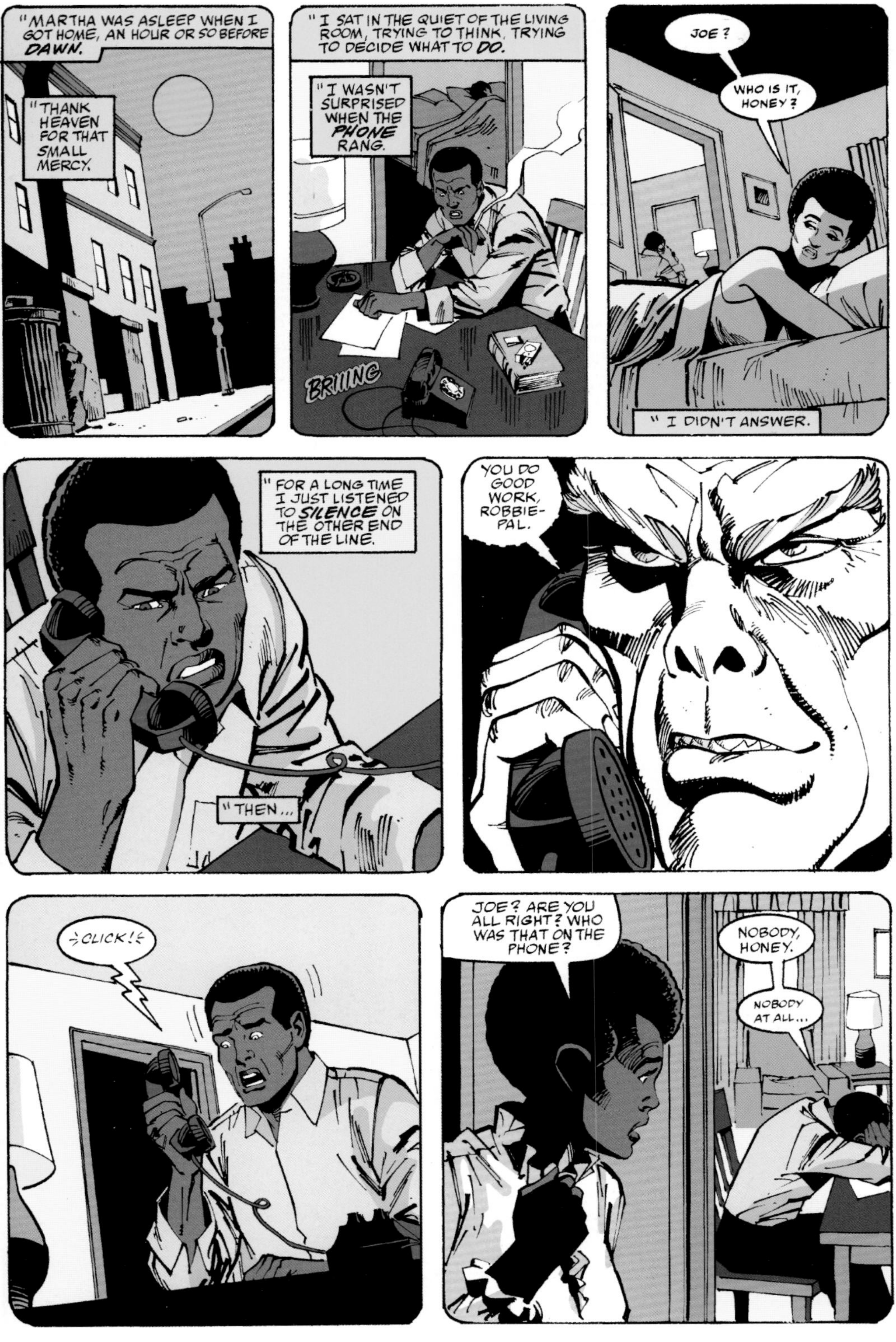
"MARTHA WAS ASLEEP WHEN I GOT HOME, AN HOUR OR SO BEFORE DAWN.
"THANK HEAVEN FOR THAT SMALL MERCY.
"I SAT IN THE QUIET OF THE LIVING ROOM, TRYING TO THINK, TRYING TO DECIDE WHAT TO DO.
"I WASN'T SURPRISED WHEN THE PHONE RANG.
BRIIING
JOE?
WHO IS IT, HONEY?
"I DIDN'T ANSWER.
"FOR A LONG TIME I JUST LISTENED TO SILENCE ON THE OTHER END OF THE LINE.
"THEN...
YOU DO GOOD WORK, ROBBIE-PAL.
CLICK!
JOE? ARE YOU ALL RIGHT? WHO WAS THAT ON THE PHONE?
NOBODY, HONEY.
NOBODY AT ALL...

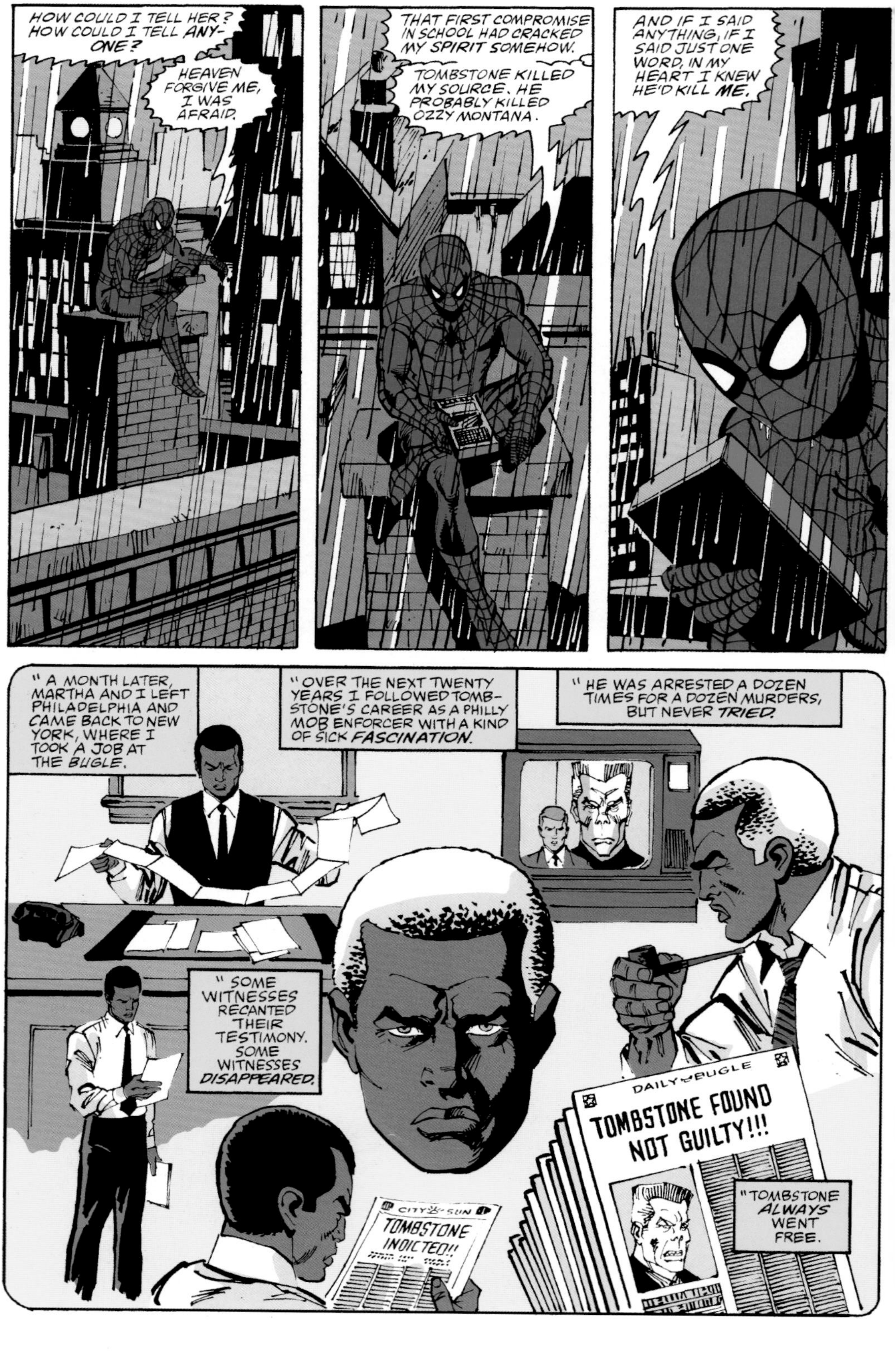
HOW COULD I TELL HER? HOW COULD I TELL ANY-ONE?
HEAVEN FORGIVE ME, I WAS AFRAID.
THAT FIRST COMPROMISE IN SCHOOL HAD CRACKED MY SPIRIT SOMEHOW.
TOMBSTONE KILLED MY SOURCE. HE PROBABLY KILLED OZZY MONTANA.
AND IF I SAID ANYTHING, IF I SAID JUST ONE WORD, IN MY HEART I KNEW HE'D KILL ME.
"A MONTH LATER, MARTHA AND I LEFT PHILADELPHIA AND CAME BACK TO NEW YORK, WHERE I TOOK A JOB AT THE BUGLE.
"OVER THE NEXT TWENTY YEARS I FOLLOWED TOMB-STONE'S CAREER AS A PHILLY MOB ENFORCER WITH A KIND OF SICK FASCINATION.
"HE WAS ARRESTED A DOZEN TIMES FOR A DOZEN MURDERS, BUT NEVER TRIED.
"SOME WITNESSES RECANTED THEIR TESTIMONY. SOME WITNESSES DISAPPEARED.
CITY SUN
TOMBSTONE INDICTED!!
DAILY BUGLE
TOMBSTONE FOUND NOT GUILTY!!!
"TOMBSTONE ALWAYS WENT FREE.

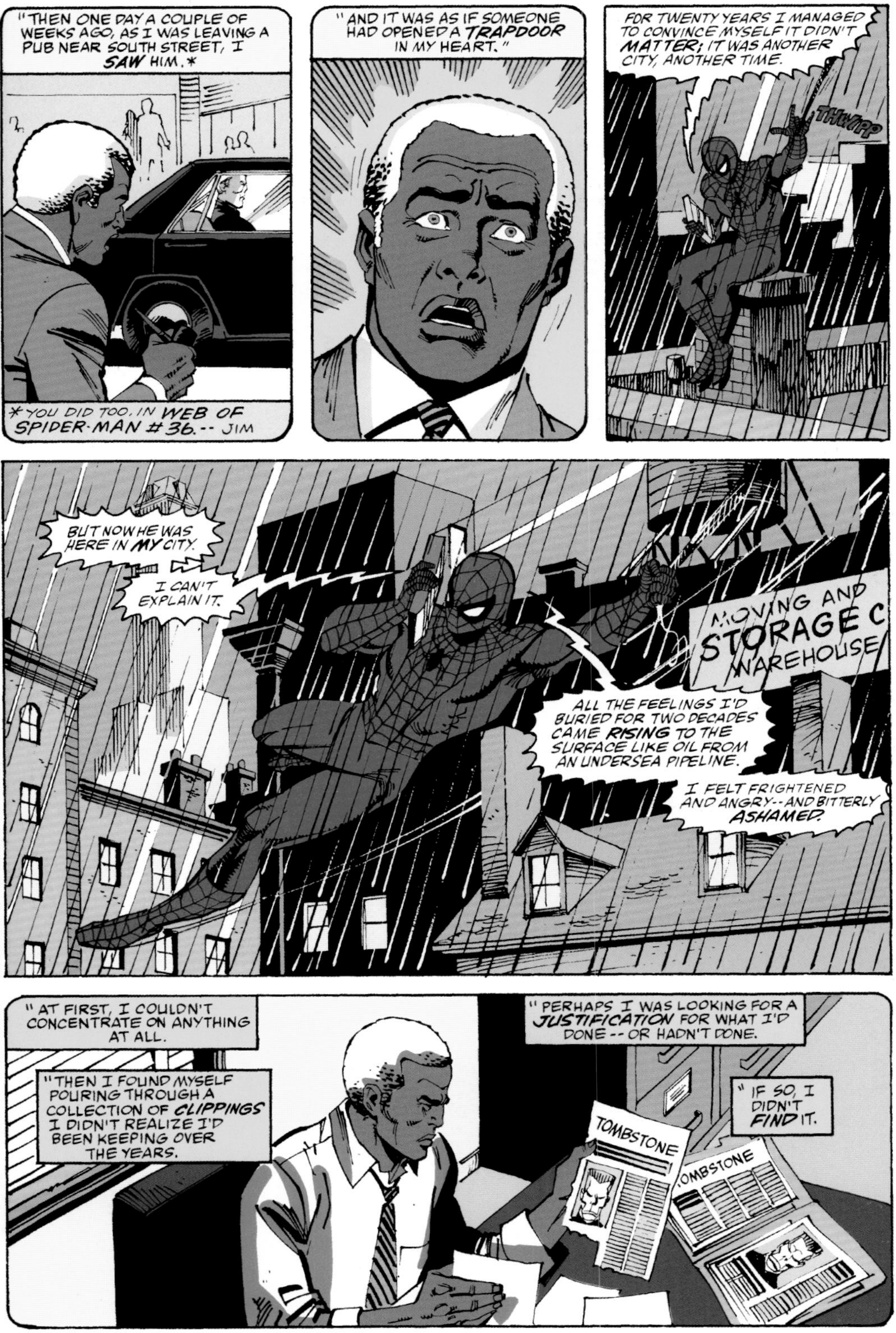
"THEN ONE DAY A COUPLE OF WEEKS AGO, AS I WAS LEAVING A PUB NEAR SOUTH STREET, I SAW HIM.*
*YOU DID TOO, IN WEB OF SPIDER-MAN #36.-- JIM
"AND IT WAS AS IF SOMEONE HAD OPENED A TRAPDOOR IN MY HEART."
FOR TWENTY YEARS I MANAGED TO CONVINCE MYSELF IT DIDN'T MATTER; IT WAS ANOTHER CITY, ANOTHER TIME.
THWIPP
BUT NOW HE WAS HERE IN MY CITY.
I CAN'T EXPLAIN IT.
MOVING AND STORAGE C WAREHOUSE
ALL THE FEELINGS I'D BURIED FOR TWO DECADES CAME RISING TO THE SURFACE LIKE OIL FROM AN UNDERSEA PIPELINE.
I FELT FRIGHTENED AND ANGRY--AND BITTERLY ASHAMED.
"AT FIRST, I COULDN'T CONCENTRATE ON ANYTHING AT ALL.
"THEN I FOUND MYSELF POURING THROUGH A COLLECTION OF CLIPPINGS I DIDN'T REALIZE I'D BEEN KEEPING OVER THE YEARS.
"PERHAPS I WAS LOOKING FOR A JUSTIFICATION FOR WHAT I'D DONE -- OR HADN'T DONE.
"IF SO, I DIDN'T FIND IT.
TOMBSTONE
TOMBSTONE

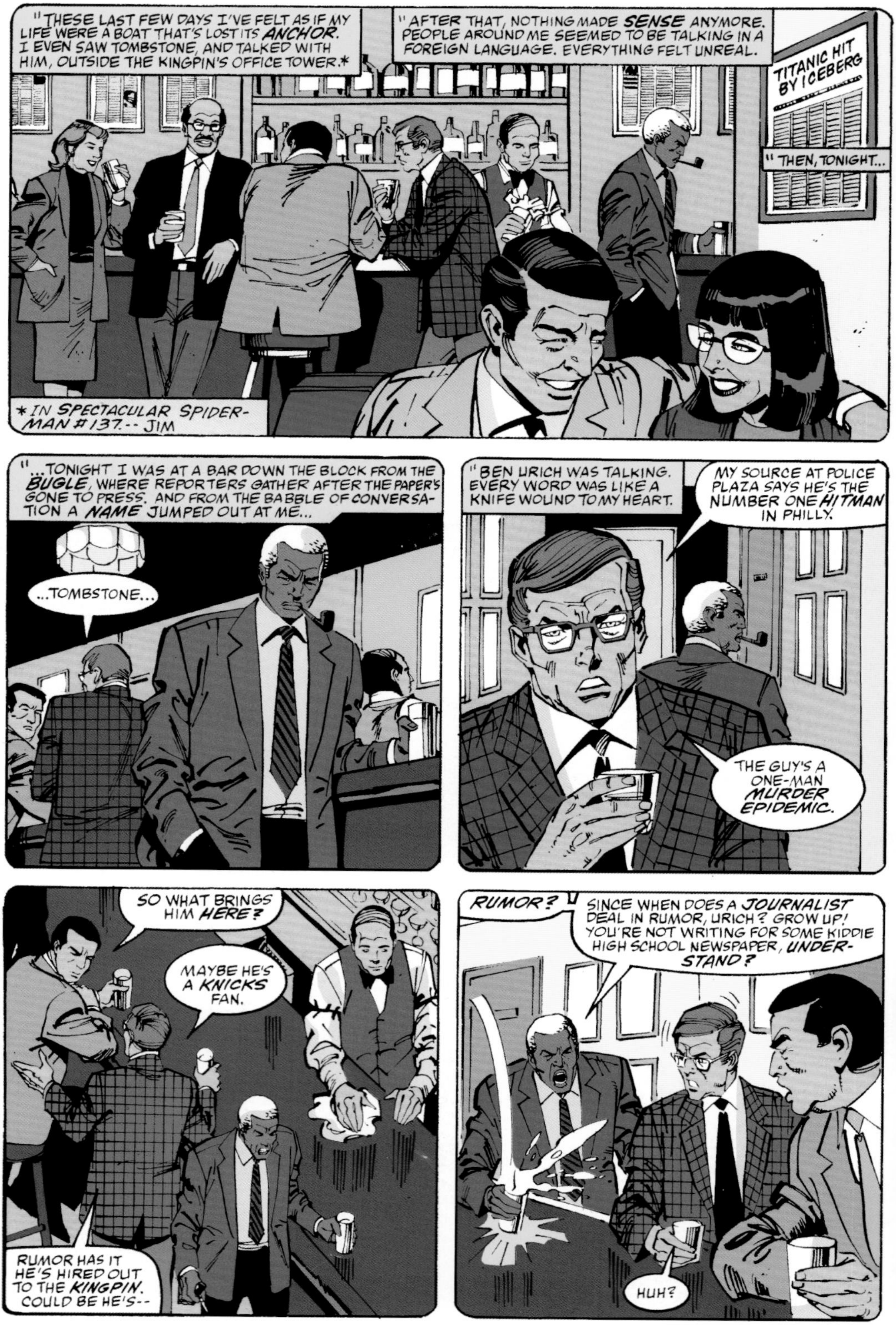
"THESE LAST FEW DAYS I'VE FELT AS IF MY LIFE WERE A BOAT THAT'S LOST ITS ANCHOR. I EVEN SAW TOMBSTONE, AND TALKED WITH HIM, OUTSIDE THE KINGPIN'S OFFICE TOWER.*
"AFTER THAT, NOTHING MADE SENSE ANYMORE. PEOPLE AROUND ME SEEMED TO BE TALKING IN A FOREIGN LANGUAGE. EVERYTHING FELT UNREAL.
TITANIC HIT BY ICEBERG
"THEN, TONIGHT...
*IN SPECTACULAR SPIDER-MAN #137.-- JIM
"...TONIGHT I WAS AT A BAR DOWN THE BLOCK FROM THE BUGLE, WHERE REPORTERS GATHER AFTER THE PAPER'S GONE TO PRESS. AND FROM THE BABBLE OF CONVERSATION A NAME JUMPED OUT AT ME...
...TOMBSTONE...
"BEN URICH WAS TALKING. EVERY WORD WAS LIKE A KNIFE WOUND TO MY HEART.
MY SOURCE AT POLICE PLAZA SAYS HE'S THE NUMBER ONE HITMAN IN PHILLY.
THE GUY'S A ONE-MAN MURDER EPIDEMIC.
SO WHAT BRINGS HIM HERE?
MAYBE HE'S A KNICKS FAN.
RUMOR HAS IT HE'S HIRED OUT TO THE KINGPIN. COULD BE HE'S--
RUMOR?
SINCE WHEN DOES A JOURNALIST DEAL IN RUMOR, URICH? GROW UP! YOU'RE NOT WRITING FOR SOME KIDDIE HIGH SCHOOL NEWSPAPER, UNDERSTAND?
HUH?

SURE, ROBBIE.

WE WERE JUST SCHMOOZING.

ROBBIE?

ARE YOU OKAY?

Ol's PUB
OPEN

DAILY BUGLE

"WAS I OKAY?

"OH, I WAS FINE.

DAILY BUGLE

MOB HITS MULTIPLY!!

25¢

SMASH

"HOW MANY PEOPLE HAD TOMBSTONE KILLED? THIRTY? FIFTY?

"A HUNDRED?

"THOSE DEATHS WERE ON MY HEAD, TOO.

"IF I'D HAD THE COURAGE TO FACE TOMBSTONE DOWN TWENTY YEARS AGO, HIS VICTIMS WOULD BE ALIVE TODAY.

"I CAN'T CHANGE THE PAST, PETER, BUT I CAN CHANGE THE FUTURE. I'M GOING TO MEET HIM TONIGHT.

"TONIGHT IT ENDS.

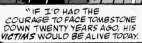

FADE OUT.

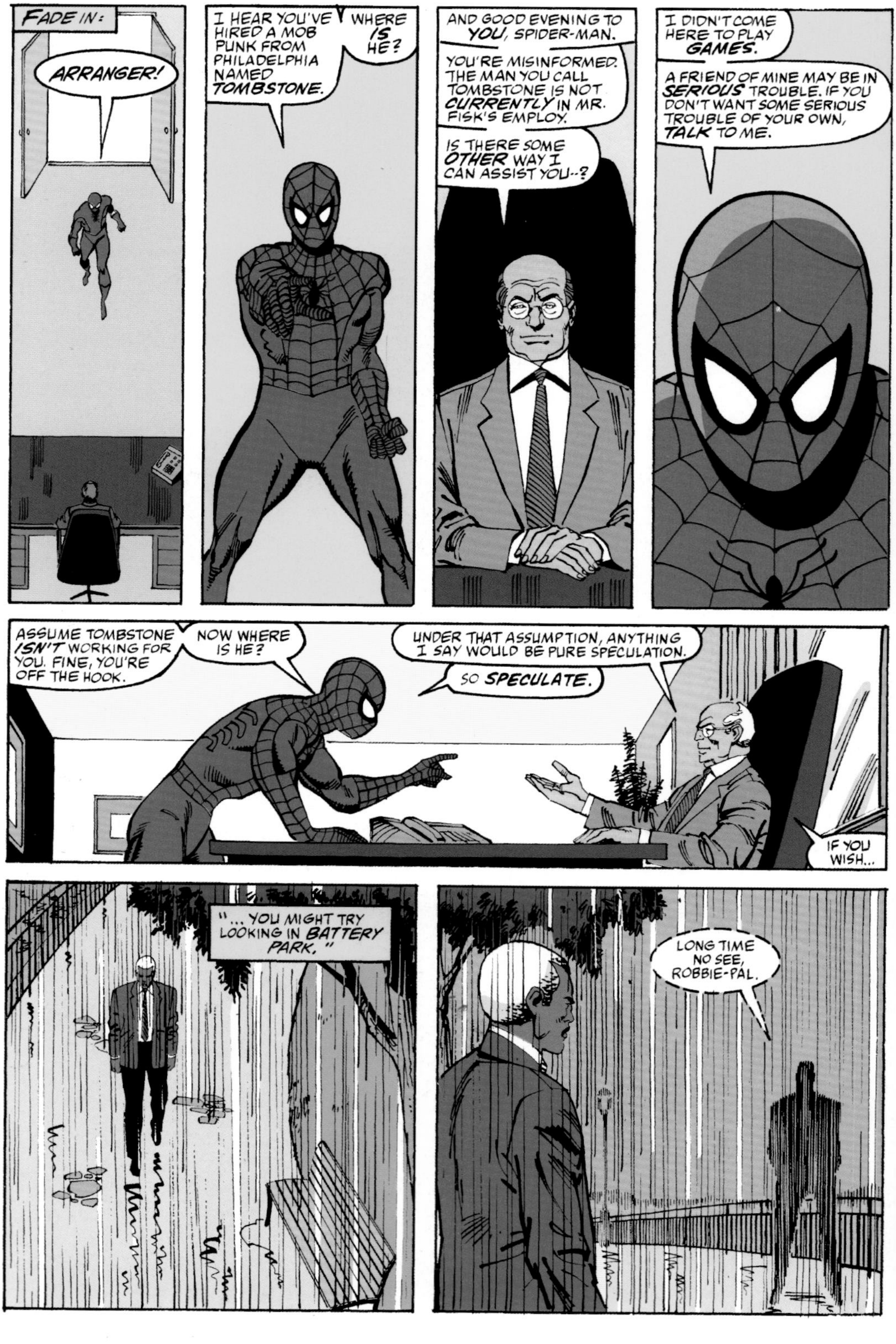
FADE IN:
ARRANGER!
I HEAR YOU'VE HIRED A MOB PUNK FROM PHILADELPHIA NAMED TOMBSTONE.
WHERE IS HE?
AND GOOD EVENING TO YOU, SPIDER-MAN.
YOU'RE MISINFORMED. THE MAN YOU CALL TOMBSTONE IS NOT CURRENTLY IN MR. FISK'S EMPLOY.
IS THERE SOME OTHER WAY I CAN ASSIST YOU--?
I DIDN'T COME HERE TO PLAY GAMES.
A FRIEND OF MINE MAY BE IN SERIOUS TROUBLE. IF YOU DON'T WANT SOME SERIOUS TROUBLE OF YOUR OWN, TALK TO ME.
ASSUME TOMBSTONE ISN'T WORKING FOR YOU. FINE, YOU'RE OFF THE HOOK.
NOW WHERE IS HE?
UNDER THAT ASSUMPTION, ANYTHING I SAY WOULD BE PURE SPECULATION.
SO SPECULATE.
IF YOU WISH...
"... YOU MIGHT TRY LOOKING IN BATTERY PARK."
LONG TIME NO SEE, ROBBIE-PAL.

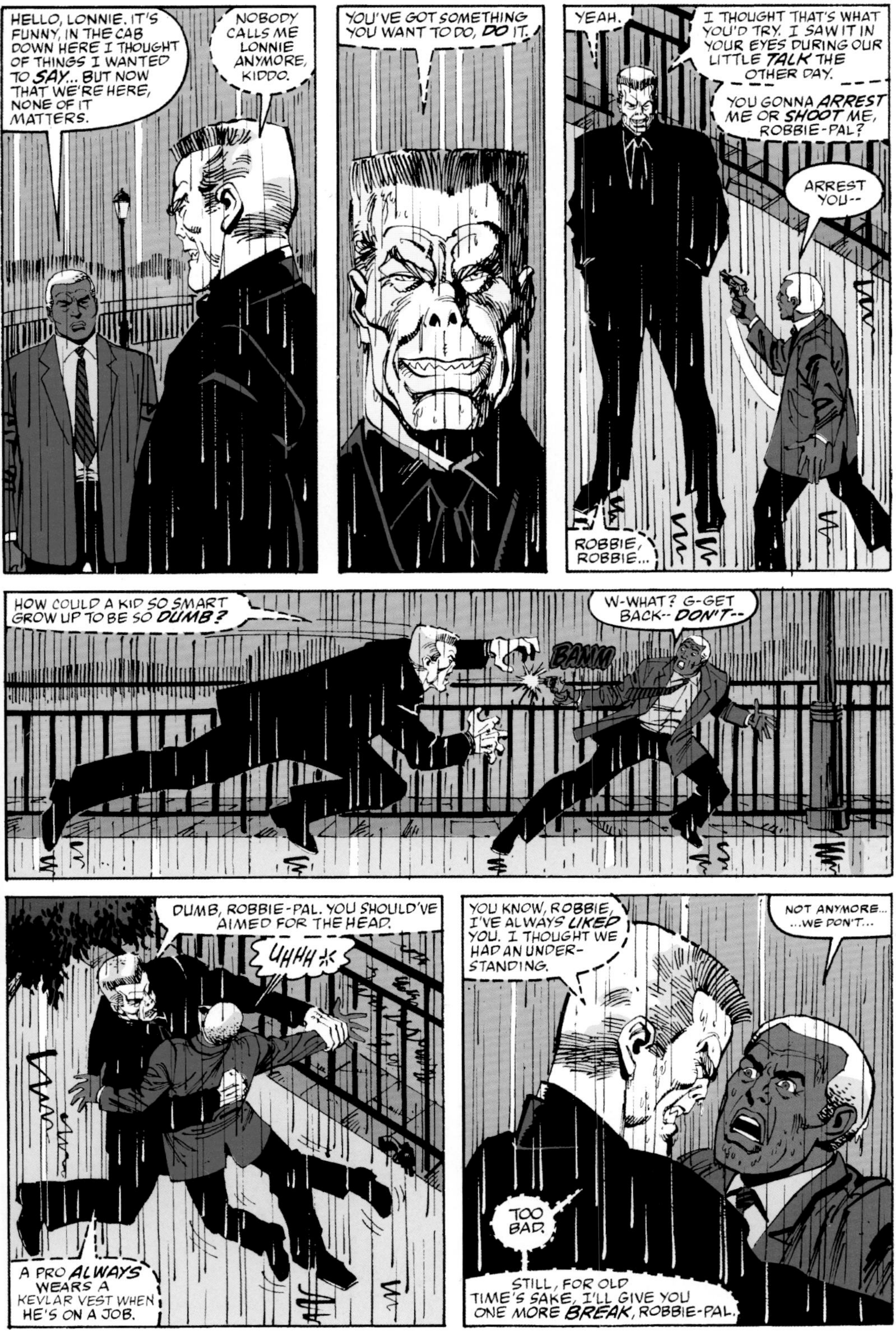

HELLO, LONNIE. IT'S FUNNY, IN THE CAB DOWN HERE I THOUGHT OF THINGS I WANTED TO SAY... BUT NOW THAT WE'RE HERE, NONE OF IT MATTERS.
NOBODY CALLS ME LONNIE ANYMORE, KIDDO.
YOU'VE GOT SOMETHING YOU WANT TO DO, DO IT.
YEAH.
I THOUGHT THAT'S WHAT YOU'D TRY. I SAW IT IN YOUR EYES DURING OUR LITTLE TALK THE OTHER DAY.
YOU GONNA ARREST ME OR SHOOT ME, ROBBIE-PAL?
ARREST YOU--
ROBBIE, ROBBIE...
HOW COULD A KID SO SMART GROW UP TO BE SO DUMB?
W-WHAT? G-GET BACK-- DON'T--
BAMM
DUMB, ROBBIE-PAL. YOU SHOULD'VE AIMED FOR THE HEAD.
UHHH
A PRO ALWAYS WEARS A KEVLAR VEST WHEN HE'S ON A JOB.
YOU KNOW, ROBBIE, I'VE ALWAYS LIKED YOU. I THOUGHT WE HAD AN UNDER-STANDING.
NOT ANYMORE... ...WE DON'T...
TOO BAD.
STILL, FOR OLD TIME'S SAKE, I'LL GIVE YOU ONE MORE BREAK, ROBBIE-PAL.

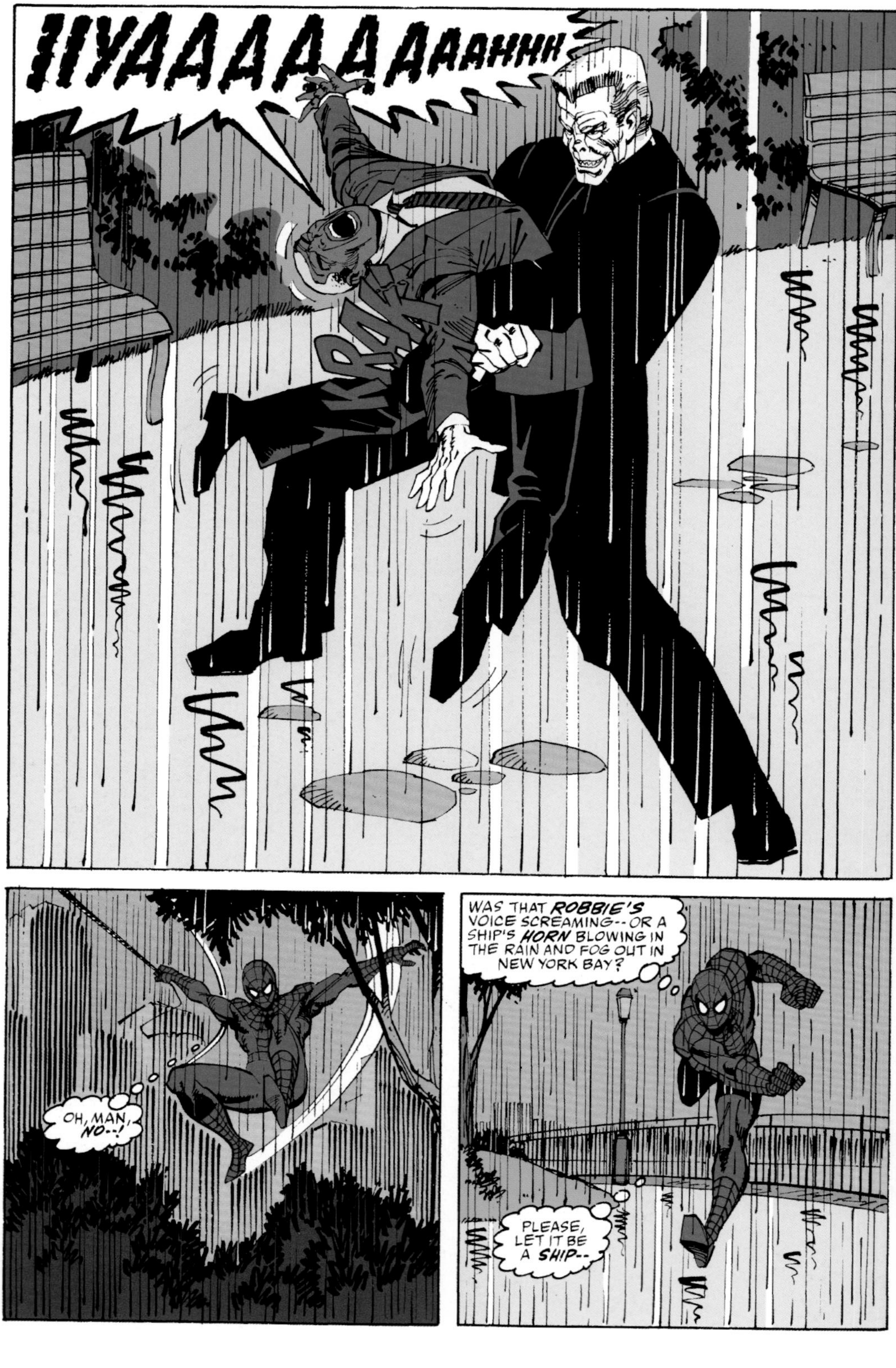
IIYAAAAAAAAHHH
WAS THAT ROBBIE'S VOICE SCREAMING-- OR A SHIP'S HORN BLOWING IN THE RAIN AND FOG OUT IN NEW YORK BAY?
OH, MAN, NO--!
PLEASE, LET IT BE A SHIP--

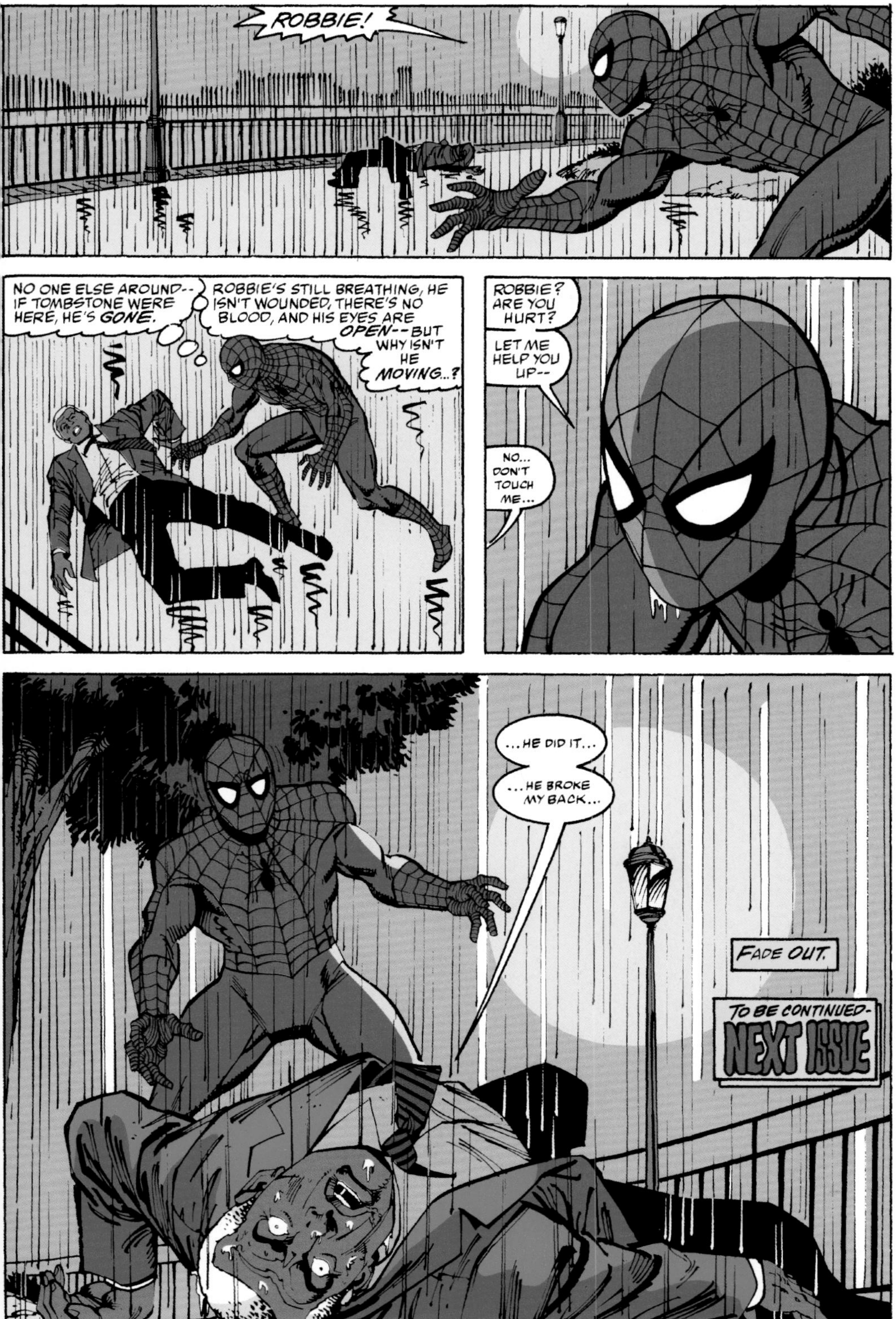
ROBBIE!
NO ONE ELSE AROUND-- IF TOMBSTONE WERE HERE, HE'S GONE.
ROBBIE'S STILL BREATHING, HE ISN'T WOUNDED, THERE'S NO BLOOD, AND HIS EYES ARE OPEN--BUT WHY ISN'T HE MOVING...?
ROBBIE? ARE YOU HURT?
LET ME HELP YOU UP--
NO... DON'T TOUCH ME...
...HE DID IT...
...HE BROKE MY BACK...
FADE OUT.
TO BE CONTINUED- NEXT ISSUE

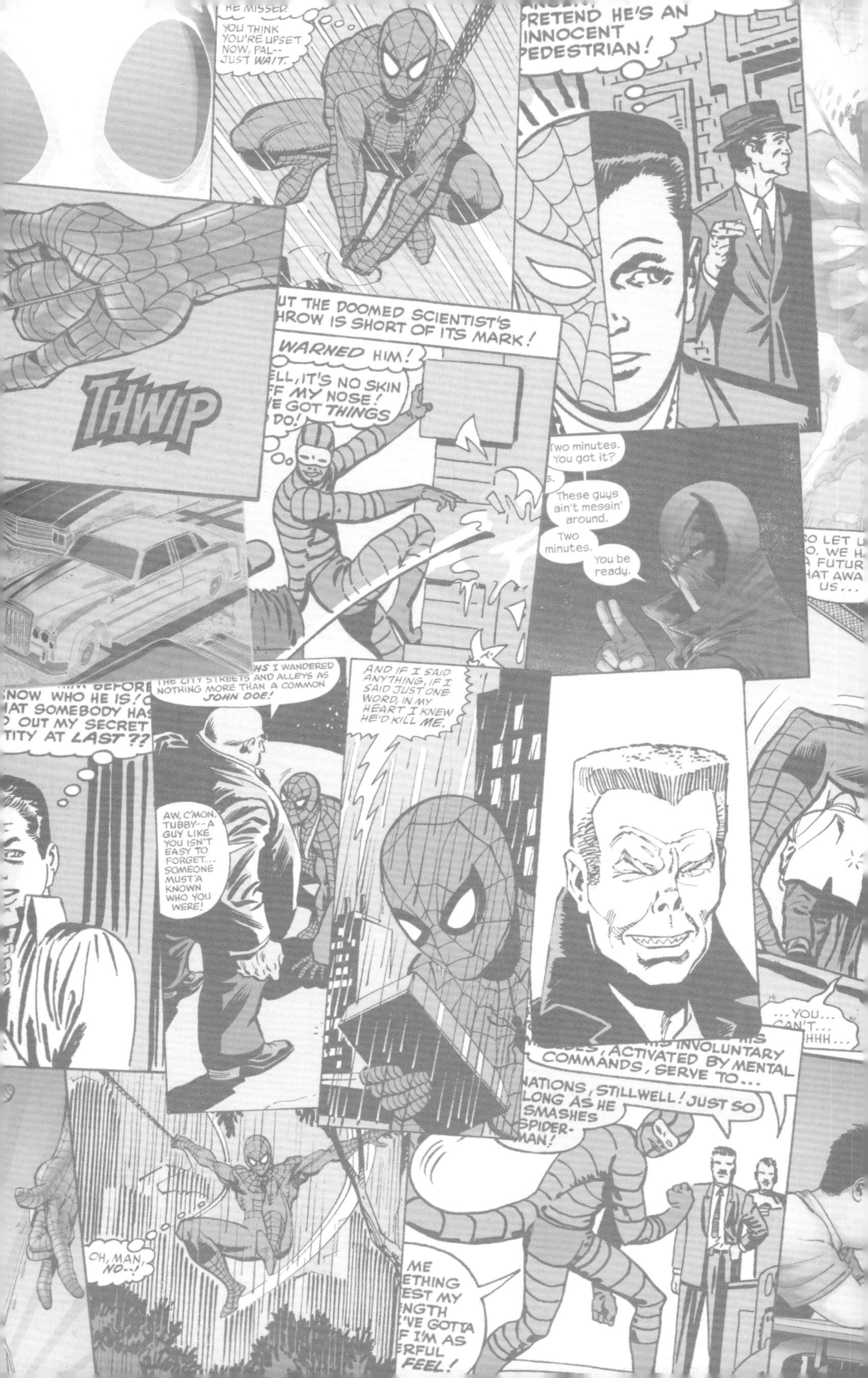
HE MISSED.
YOU THINK YOU'RE UPSET NOW, PAL-- JUST WAIT.
PRETEND HE'S AN INNOCENT PEDESTRIAN!
THWIP
UT THE DOOMED SCIENTIST'S HROW IS SHORT OF ITS MARK!
WARNED HIM!
ELL, IT'S NO SKIN FF MY NOSE! 'VE GOT THINGS DO!
Two minutes. You got it?
These guys ain't messin' around.
Two minutes.
You be ready.
O LET U O, WE HA A FUTUR HAT AWA US...
NOW WHO HE IS!
HAT SOMEBODY HAS D OUT MY SECRET TITY AT LAST??
THE CITY STREETS AND ALLEYS AS NOTHING MORE THAN A COMMON JOHN DOE!
AND IF I SAID ANYTHING, IF I SAID JUST ONE WORD, IN MY HEART I KNEW HE'D KILL ME.
AW, C'MON, TUBBY-- A GUY LIKE YOU ISN'T EASY TO FORGET... SOMEONE MUST'A KNOWN WHO YOU WERE!
...YOU... CAN'T...
COMMANDS, ACTIVATED BY MENTAL
NATIONS, STILLWELL! JUST SO LONG AS HE SMASHES SPIDER-MAN!
OH, MAN, NO--!
ME ETHING EST MY NGTH 'VE GOTTA F I'M AS ERFUL FEEL!

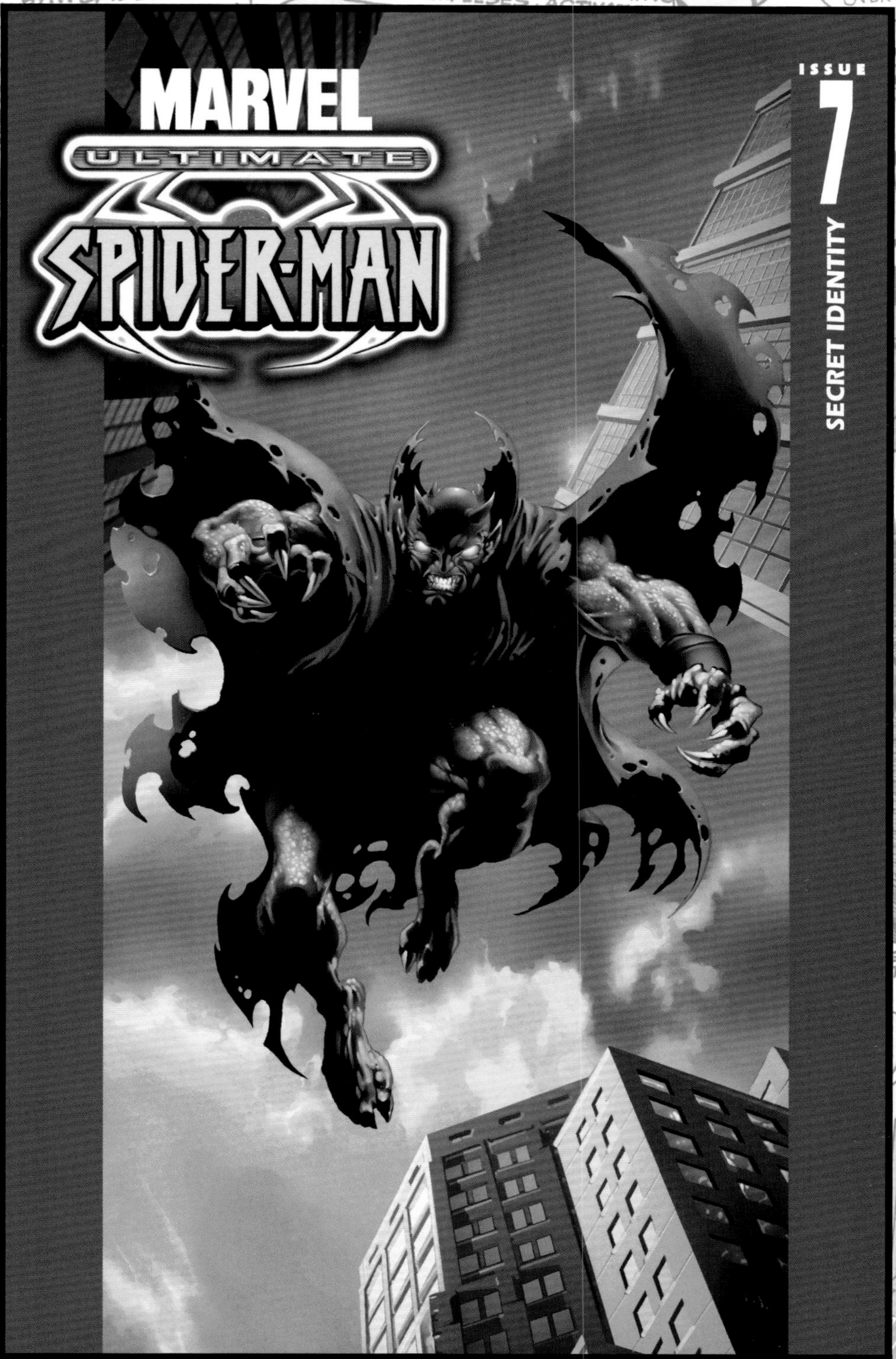
MARVEL
ULTIMATE
SPIDER-MAN
ISSUE
7
SECRET IDENTITY

ULTIMATE SPIDER-MAN (2000) #7

JOURNEY TO THE ULTIMATE UNIVERSE WHERE TEENAGE PETER PARKER FINDS HIMSELF FIGHTING AGAINST A MONSTROUS

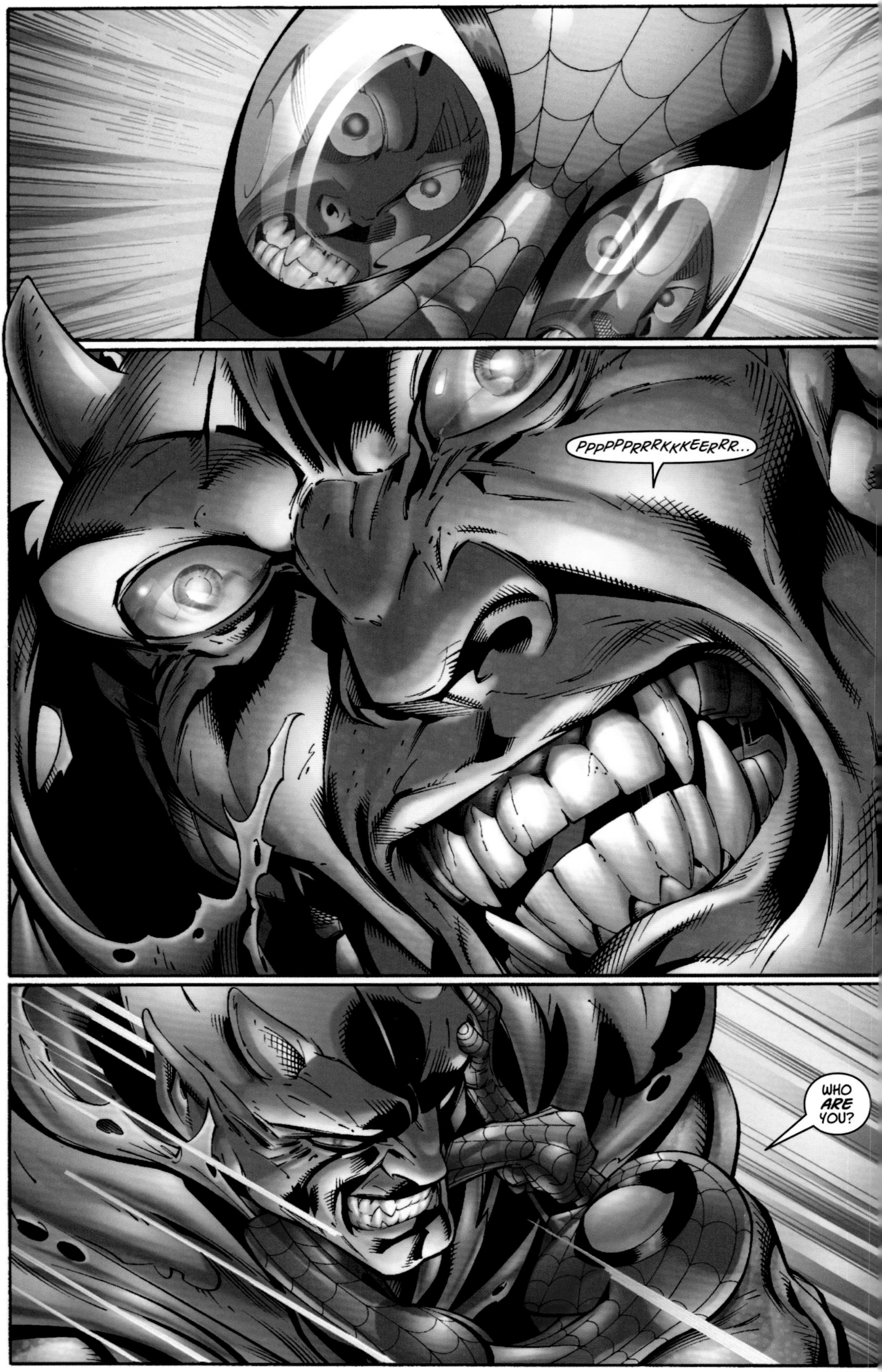
PPPPPPRRRKKKEERRR...
WHO ARE YOU?

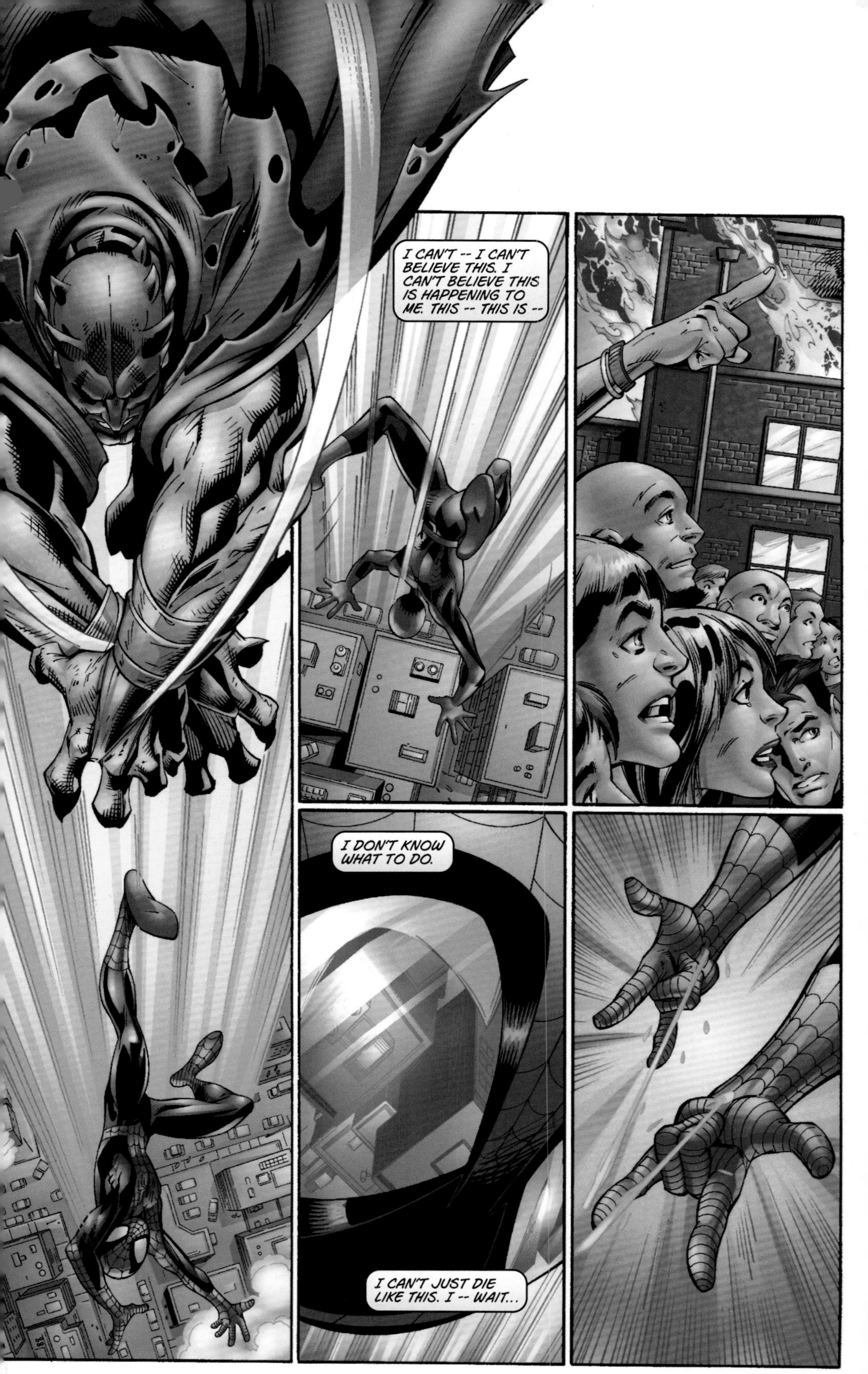

I CAN'T -- I CAN'T BELIEVE THIS. I CAN'T BELIEVE THIS IS HAPPENING TO ME. THIS -- THIS IS --
I DON'T KNOW WHAT TO DO.
I CAN'T JUST DIE LIKE THIS. I -- WAIT...

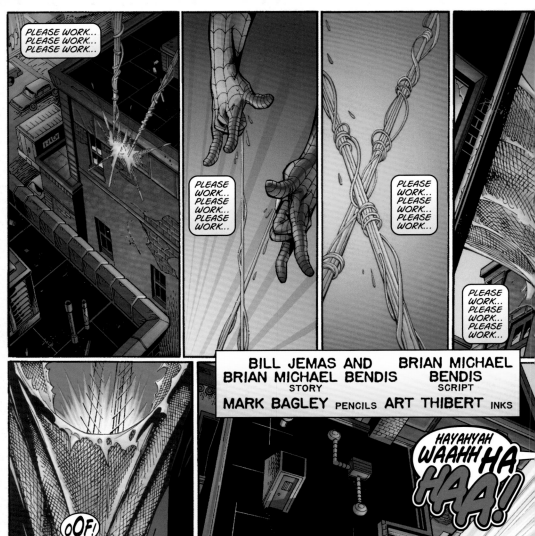

PLEASE WORK...
PLEASE WORK...
PLEASE WORK...
PLEASE WORK...
PLEASE WORK...
PLEASE WORK...
PLEASE WORK...
PLEASE WORK...
PLEASE WORK...
PLEASE WORK...
PLEASE WORK...
PLEASE WORK...
BILL JEMAS AND BRIAN MICHAEL BENDIS STORY
BRIAN MICHAEL BENDIS SCRIPT
MARK BAGLEY PENCILS ART THIBERT INKS
OOF!
HAYAHYAH WAAHH HA HAA!
RS & COMICRAFT'S ALBERT DESCHESNE LETTERS
JC COLORS BRIAN SMITH ASSISTANT EDITOR
RALPH MACCHIO EDITOR JOE QUESADA EDITOR IN CHIEF

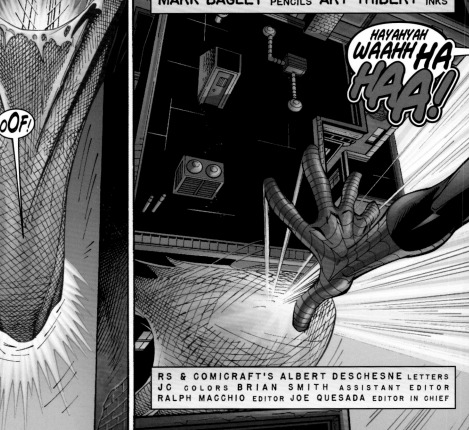

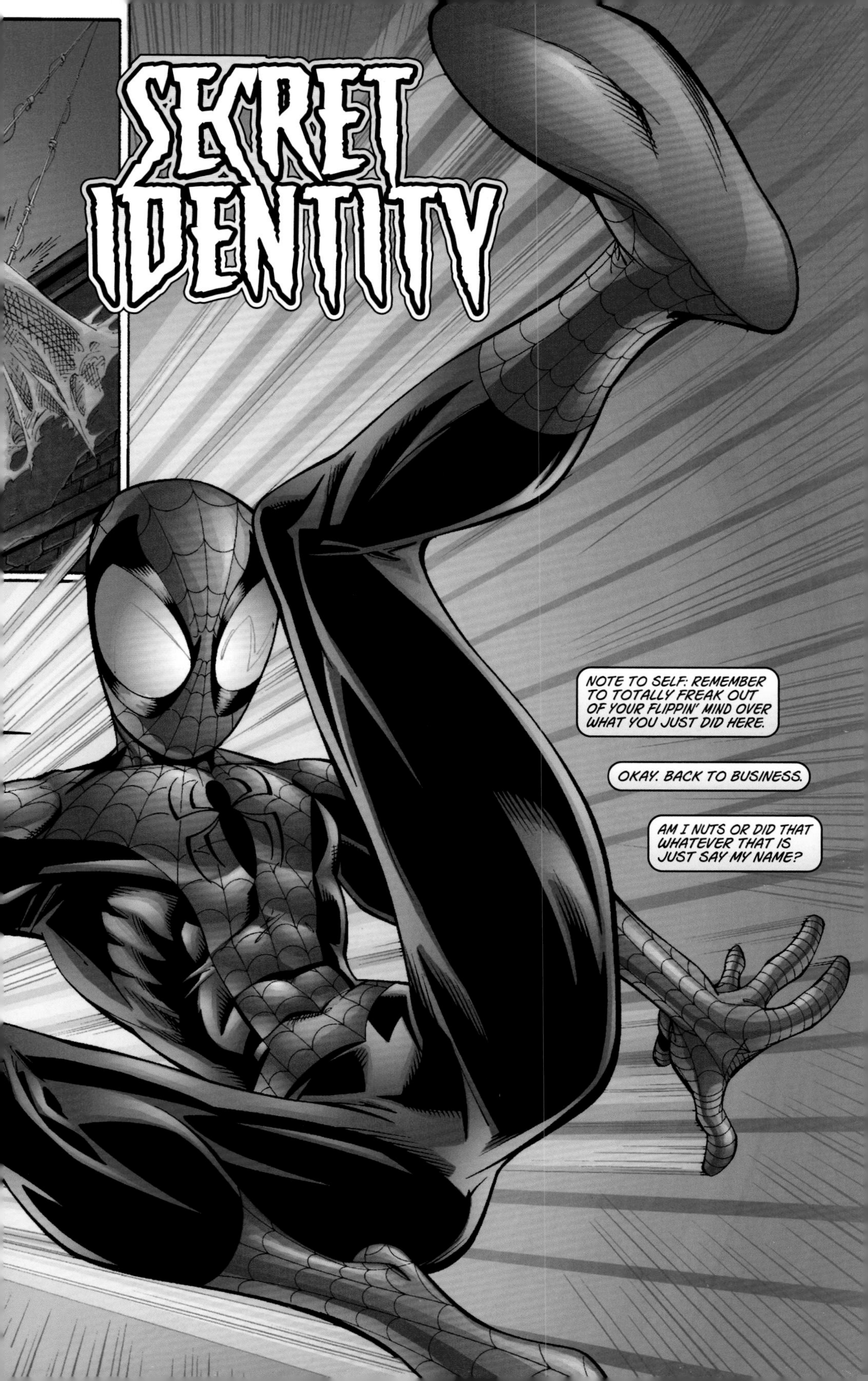
SECRET IDENTITY
NOTE TO SELF: REMEMBER TO TOTALLY FREAK OUT OF YOUR FLIPPIN' MIND OVER WHAT YOU JUST DID HERE.
OKAY. BACK TO BUSINESS.
AM I NUTS OR DID THAT WHATEVER THAT IS JUST SAY MY NAME?

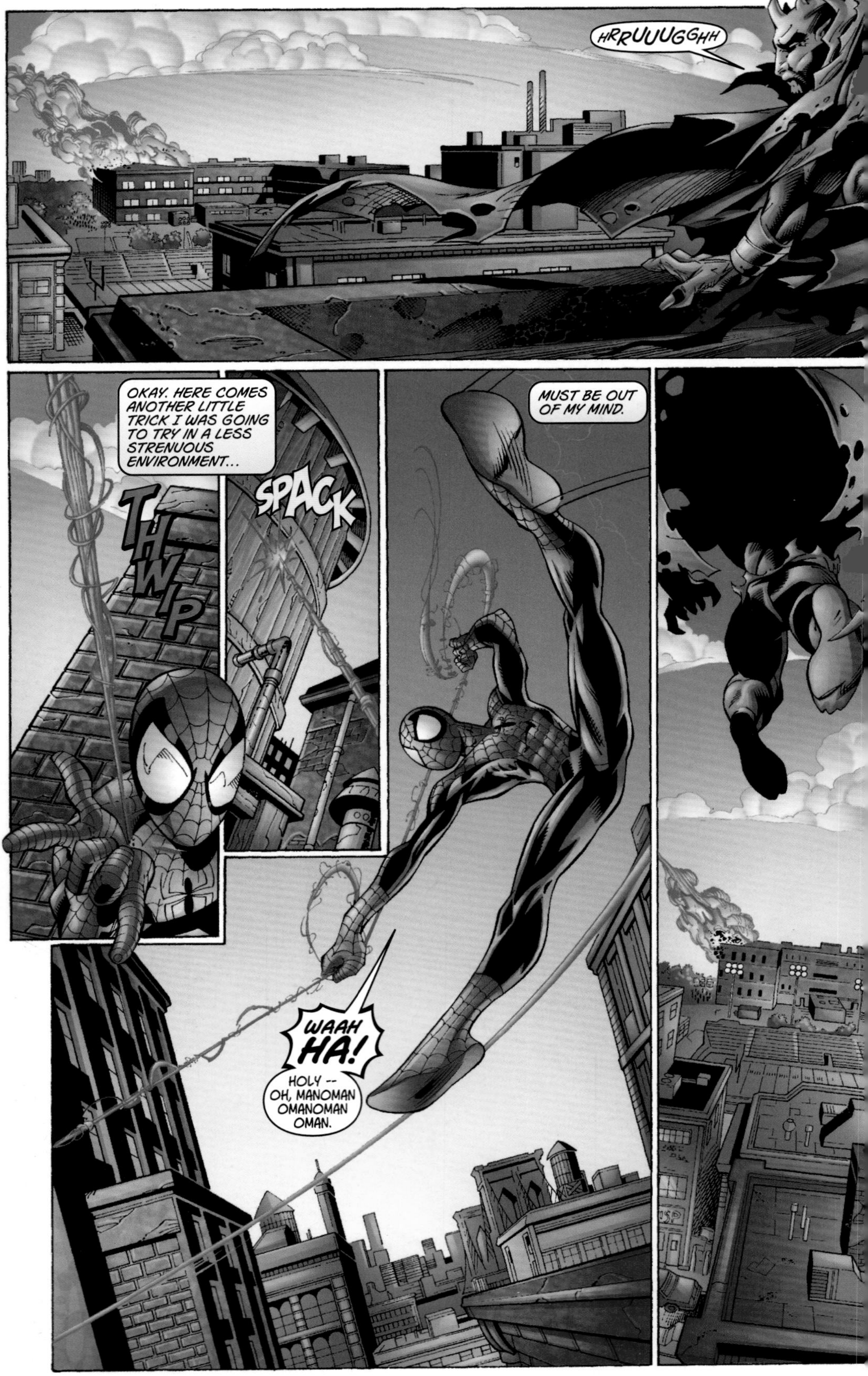
HRRUUUGGHH
OKAY. HERE COMES ANOTHER LITTLE TRICK I WAS GOING TO TRY IN A LESS STRENUOUS ENVIRONMENT...
THWIP
SPACK
MUST BE OUT OF MY MIND.
WAAH HA!
HOLY -- OH, MANOMAN OMANOMAN OMAN.

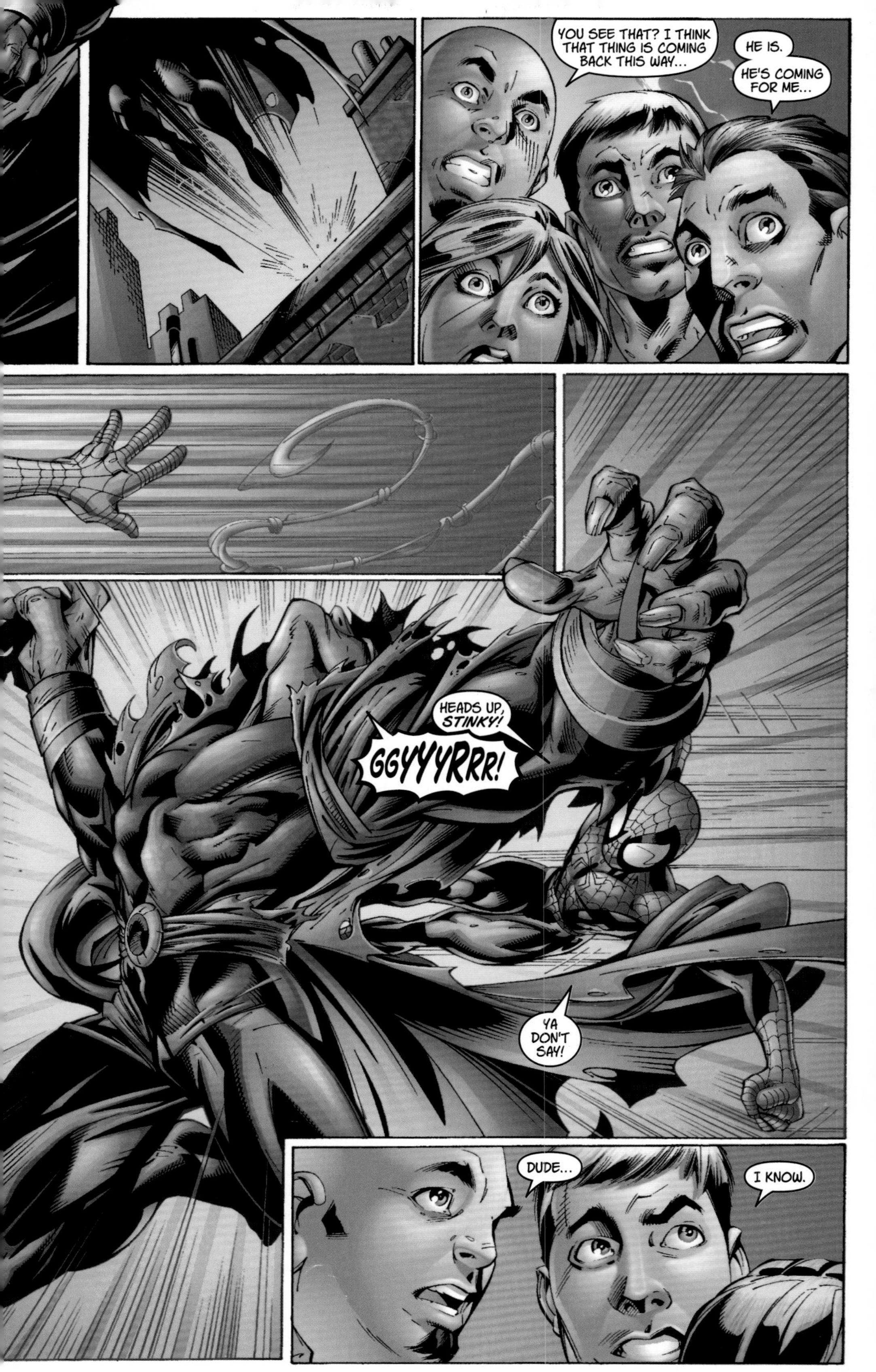
YOU SEE THAT? I THINK THAT THING IS COMING BACK THIS WAY...
HE IS.
HE'S COMING FOR ME...
HEADS UP, STINKY!
GGYYYRRR!
YA DON'T SAY!
DUDE...
I KNOW.

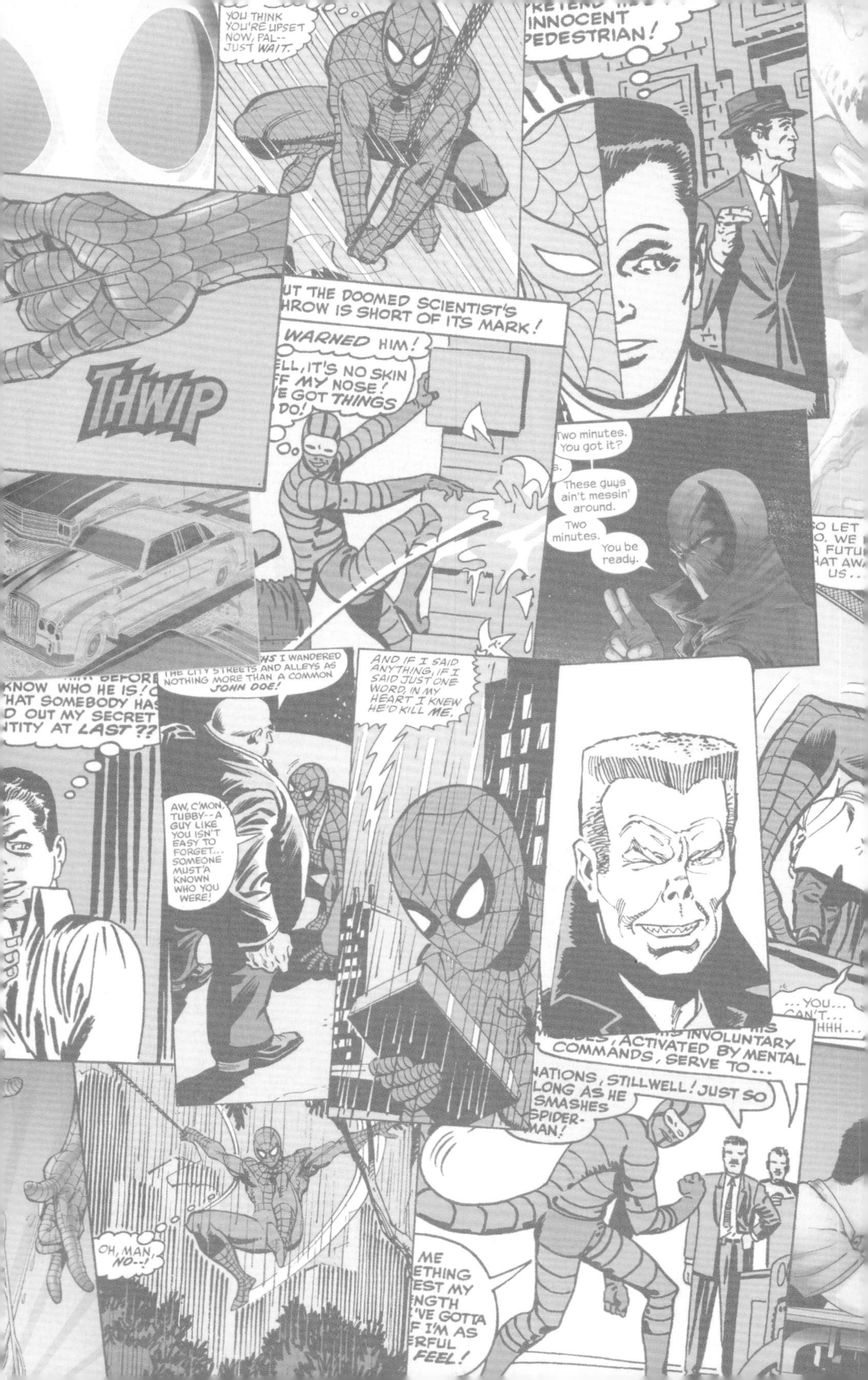
YOU THINK YOU'RE UPSET NOW, PAL-- JUST WAIT.
INNOCENT PEDESTRIAN!
UT THE DOOMED SCIENTIST'S HROW IS SHORT OF ITS MARK!
WARNED HIM!
ELL, IT'S NO SKIN FF MY NOSE! E GOT THINGS DO!
THWIP
Two minutes. You got it?
These guys ain't messin' around.
Two minutes.
You be ready.
SO LET O, WE A FUTU HAT AWA US...
KNOW WHO HE IS!
HAT SOMEBODY HAS D OUT MY SECRET NTITY AT LAST??
THE CITY STREETS AND ALLEYS AS NOTHING MORE THAN A COMMON JOHN DOE!
AW, C'MON, TUBBY-- A GUY LIKE YOU ISN'T EASY TO FORGET... SOMEONE MUST'A KNOWN WHO YOU WERE!
AND IF I SAID ANYTHING, IF I SAID JUST ONE WORD, IN MY HEART I KNEW HE'D KILL ME.
...YOU... CAN'T... HHHH...
INVOLUNTARY COMMANDS, ACTIVATED BY MENTAL SERVE TO...
NATIONS, STILLWELL! JUST SO LONG AS HE SMASHES SPIDER-MAN!
OH, MAN, NO--!
ME ETHING EST MY NGTH 'VE GOTTA F I'M AS ERFUL FEEL!

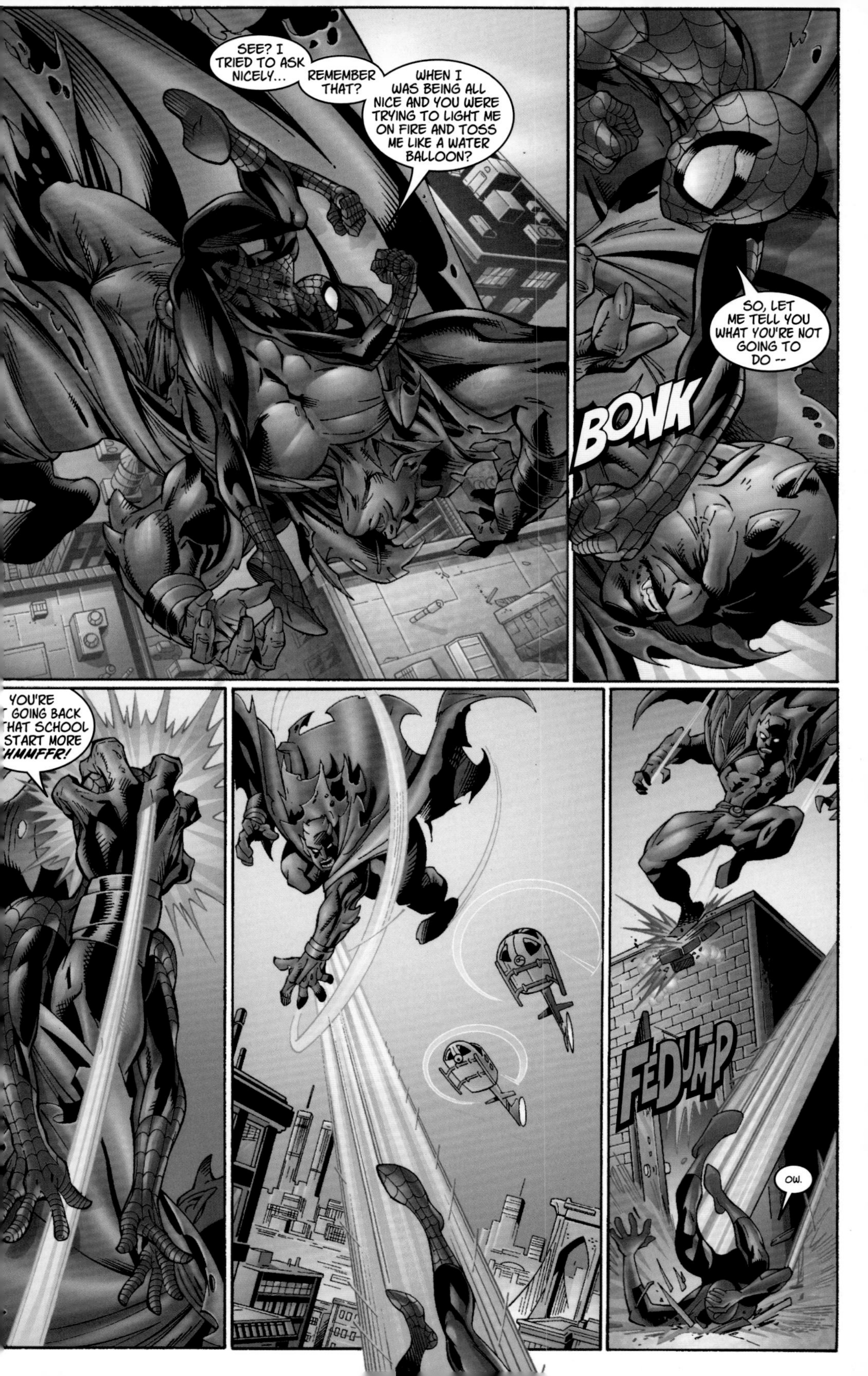
SEE? I TRIED TO ASK NICELY...
REMEMBER THAT?
WHEN I WAS BEING ALL NICE AND YOU WERE TRYING TO LIGHT ME ON FIRE AND TOSS ME LIKE A WATER BALLOON?
SO, LET ME TELL YOU WHAT YOU'RE NOT GOING TO DO --
BONK
YOU'RE
GOING BACK
THAT SCHOOL
START MORE
HMMFFR!
FEDUMP
OW.

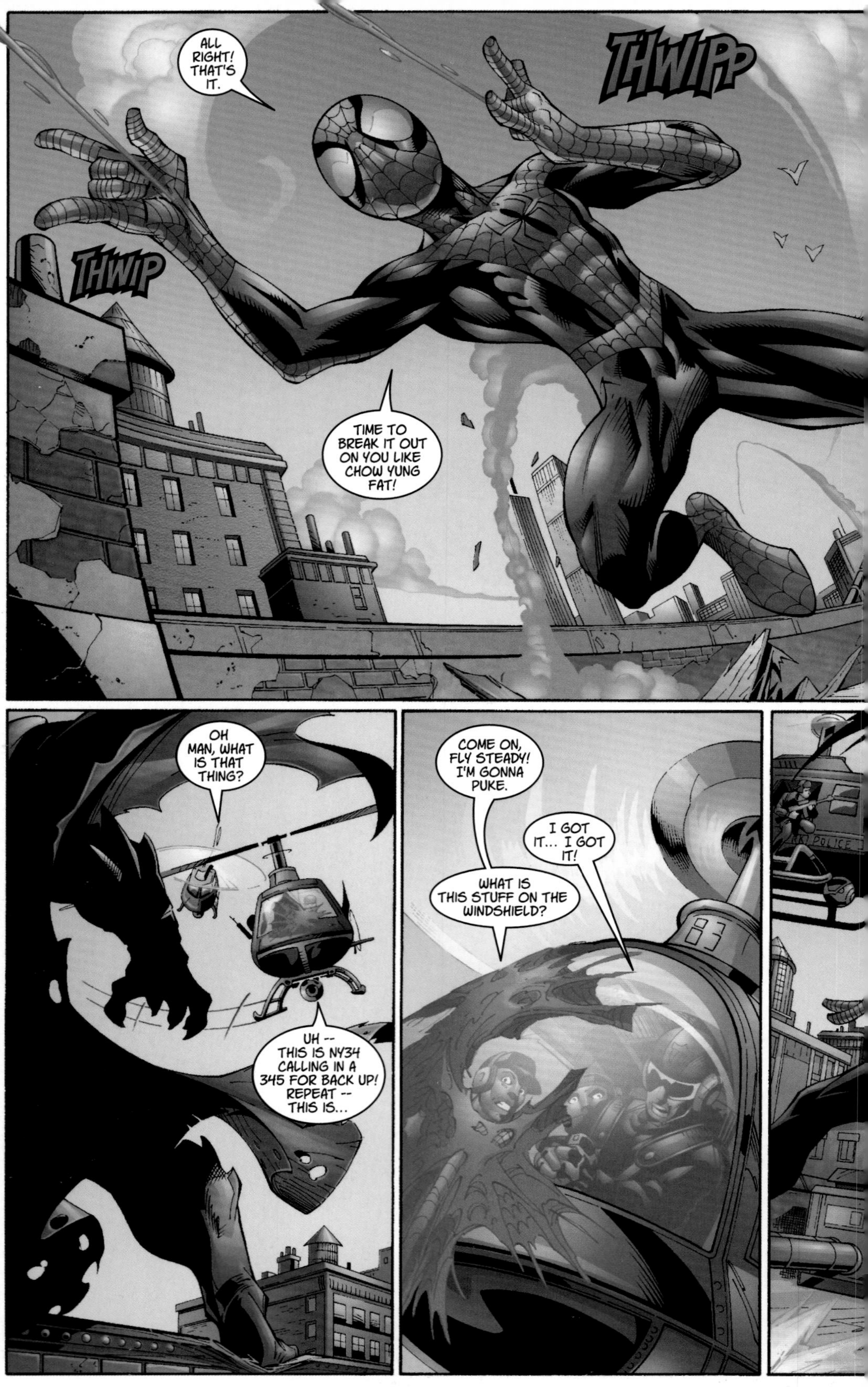
ALL RIGHT! THAT'S IT.
THWIPP
THWIP
TIME TO BREAK IT OUT ON YOU LIKE CHOW YUNG FAT!
OH MAN, WHAT IS THAT THING?
UH -- THIS IS NY34 CALLING IN A 345 FOR BACK UP! REPEAT -- THIS IS...
COME ON, FLY STEADY! I'M GONNA PUKE.
WHAT IS THIS STUFF ON THE WINDSHIELD?
I GOT IT... I GOT IT!

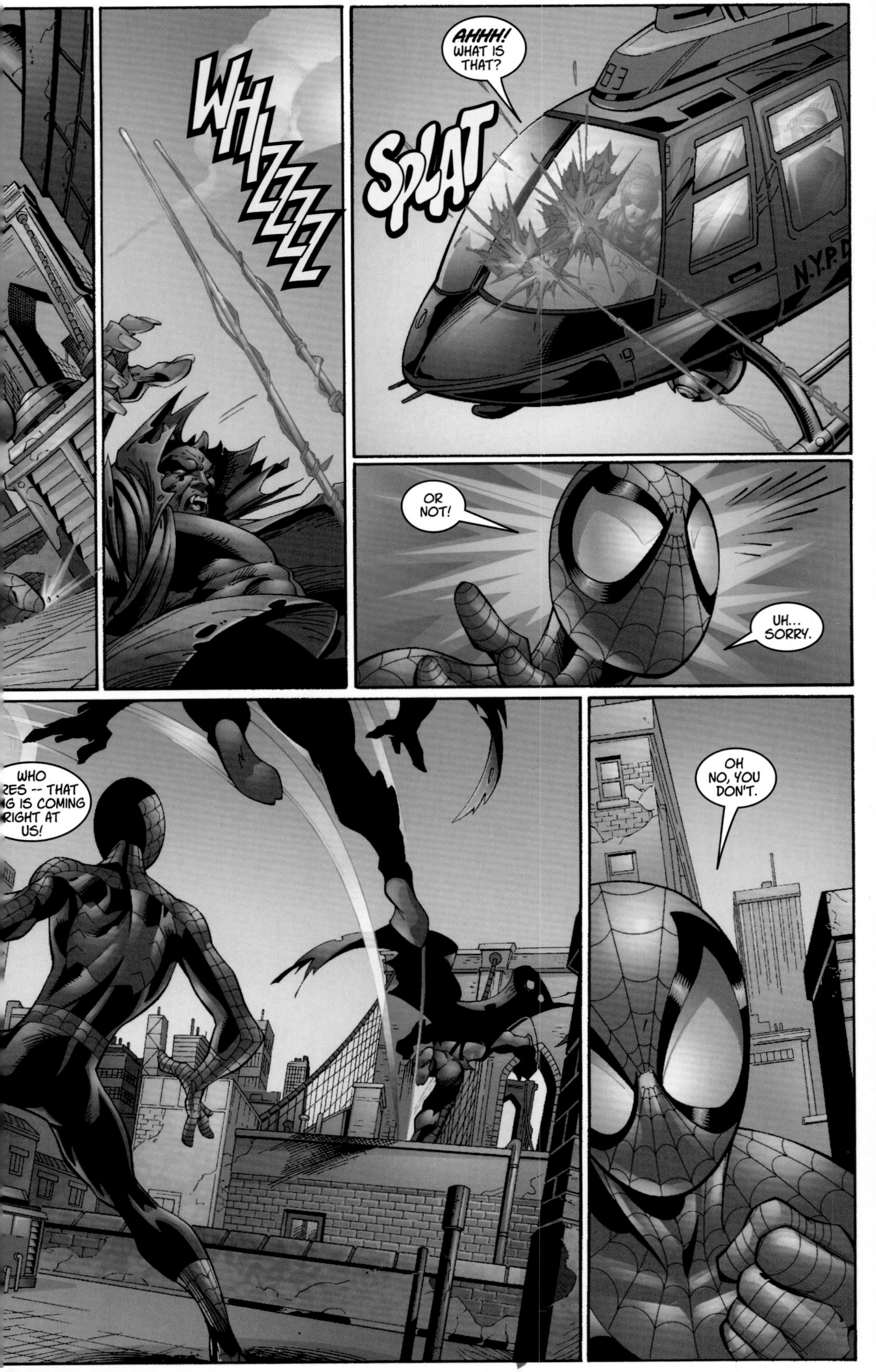
WHIZZZZZ
SPLAT
AHHH! WHAT IS THAT?
OR NOT!
UH... SORRY.
WHO RES -- THAT G IS COMING RIGHT AT US!
OH NO, YOU DON'T.
N.Y.P.D.

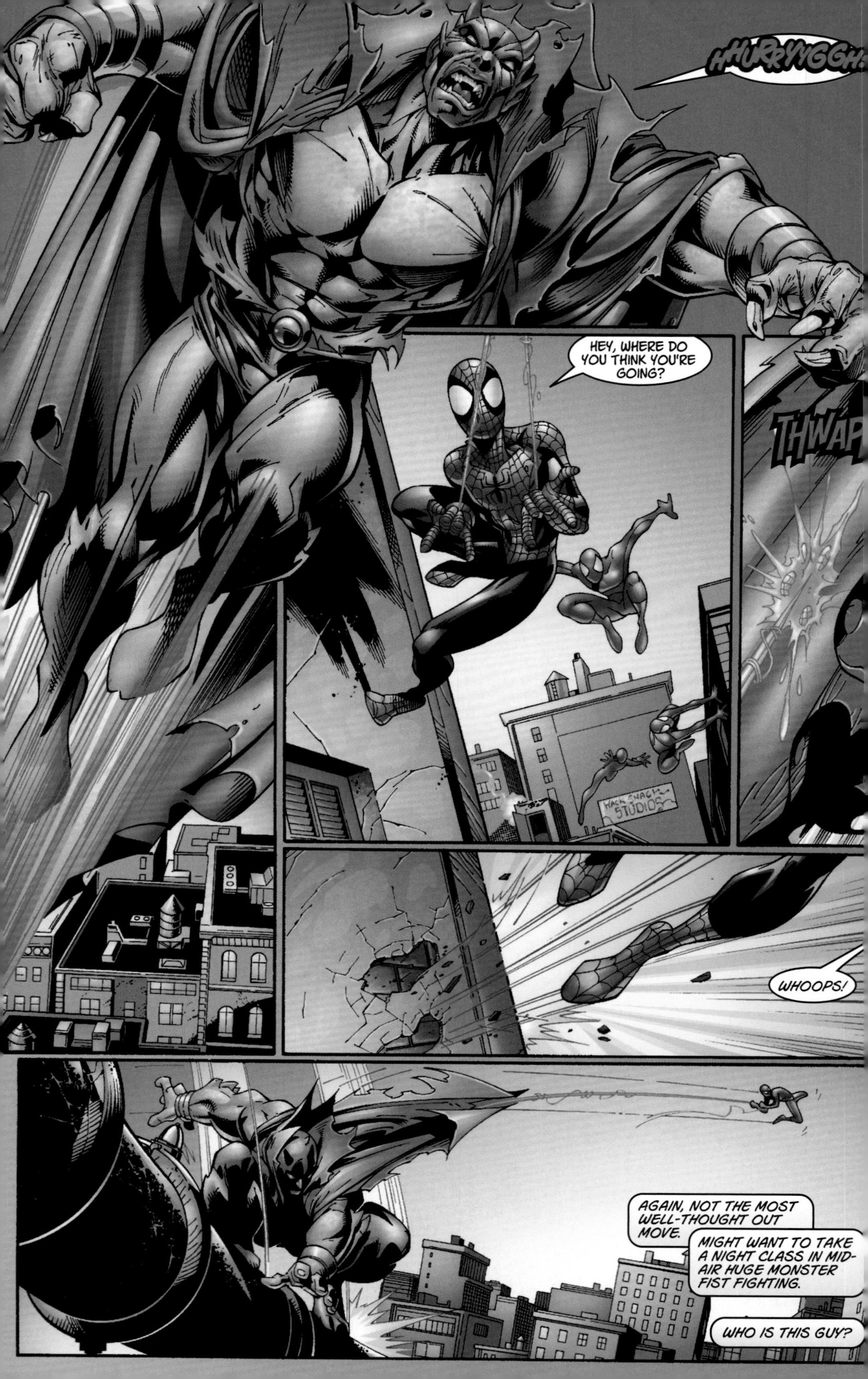
HHURRYYGGH!
HEY, WHERE DO YOU THINK YOU'RE GOING?
THWAP
HACK SHACK STUDIOS
WHOOPS!
AGAIN, NOT THE MOST WELL-THOUGHT OUT MOVE.
MIGHT WANT TO TAKE A NIGHT CLASS IN MID-AIR HUGE MONSTER FIST FIGHTING.
WHO IS THIS GUY?

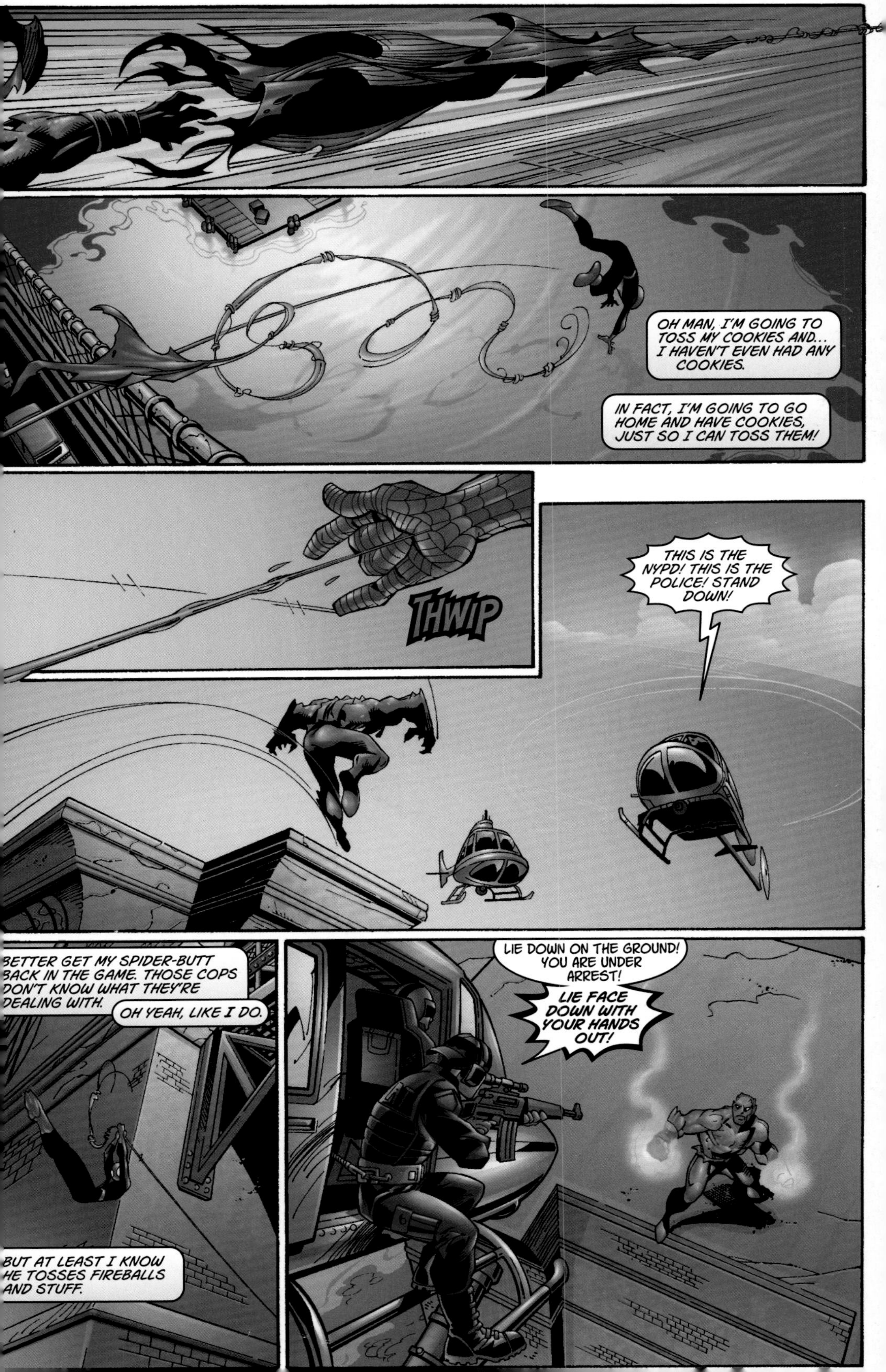
OH MAN, I'M GOING TO TOSS MY COOKIES AND... I HAVEN'T EVEN HAD ANY COOKIES.
IN FACT, I'M GOING TO GO HOME AND HAVE COOKIES, JUST SO I CAN TOSS THEM!
THWIP
THIS IS THE NYPD! THIS IS THE POLICE! STAND DOWN!
BETTER GET MY SPIDER-BUTT BACK IN THE GAME. THOSE COPS DON'T KNOW WHAT THEY'RE DEALING WITH.
OH YEAH, LIKE I DO.
BUT AT LEAST I KNOW HE TOSSES FIREBALLS AND STUFF.
LIE DOWN ON THE GROUND! YOU ARE UNDER ARREST!
LIE FACE DOWN WITH YOUR HANDS OUT!

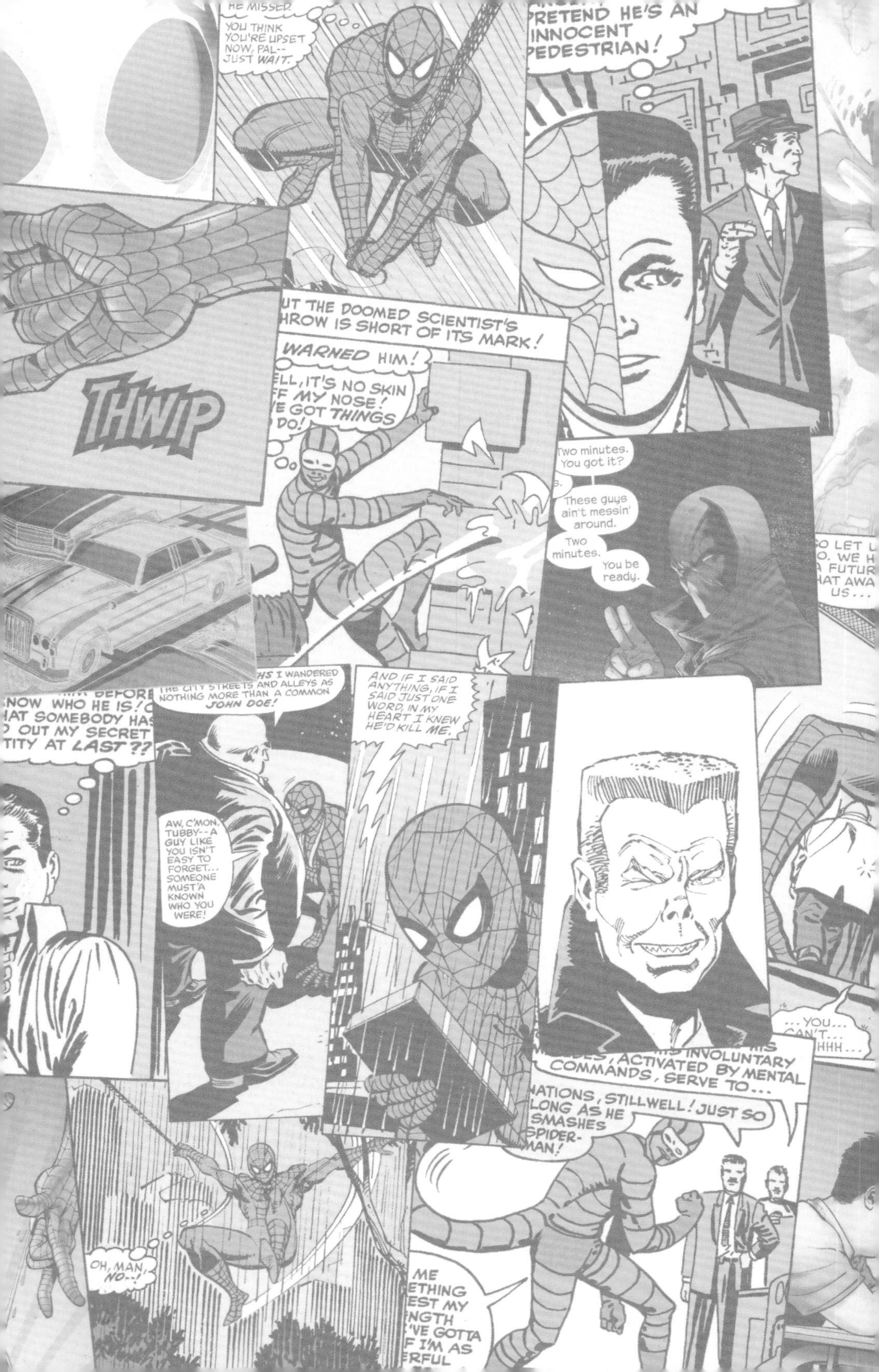
HE MISSED!
YOU THINK YOU'RE UPSET NOW, PAL-- JUST WAIT.
PRETEND HE'S AN INNOCENT PEDESTRIAN!
THWIP
UT THE DOOMED SCIENTIST'S HROW IS SHORT OF ITS MARK!
WARNED HIM!
ELL, IT'S NO SKIN FF MY NOSE! E GOT THINGS DO!
Two minutes. You got it?
These guys ain't messin' around.
Two minutes.
You be ready.
SO LET U O. WE H A FUTUR HAT AWA US...
NOW WHO HE IS!
HAT SOMEBODY HAS D OUT MY SECRET TITY AT LAST??
THE CITY STREETS AND ALLEYS AS NOTHING MORE THAN A COMMON JOHN DOE!
AW, C'MON, TUBBY-- A GUY LIKE YOU ISN'T EASY TO FORGET... SOMEONE MUST'A KNOWN WHO YOU WERE!
AND IF I SAID ANYTHING, IF I SAID JUST ONE WORD, IN MY HEART I KNEW HE'D KILL ME.
...YOU... CAN'T... HHH...
INVOLUNTARY COMMANDS, ACTIVATED BY MENTAL SERVE TO...
NATIONS, STILLWELL! JUST SO LONG AS HE SMASHES SPIDER-MAN!
OH, MAN, NO--!
ME ETHING EST MY NGTH 'VE GOTTA F I'M AS RFUL

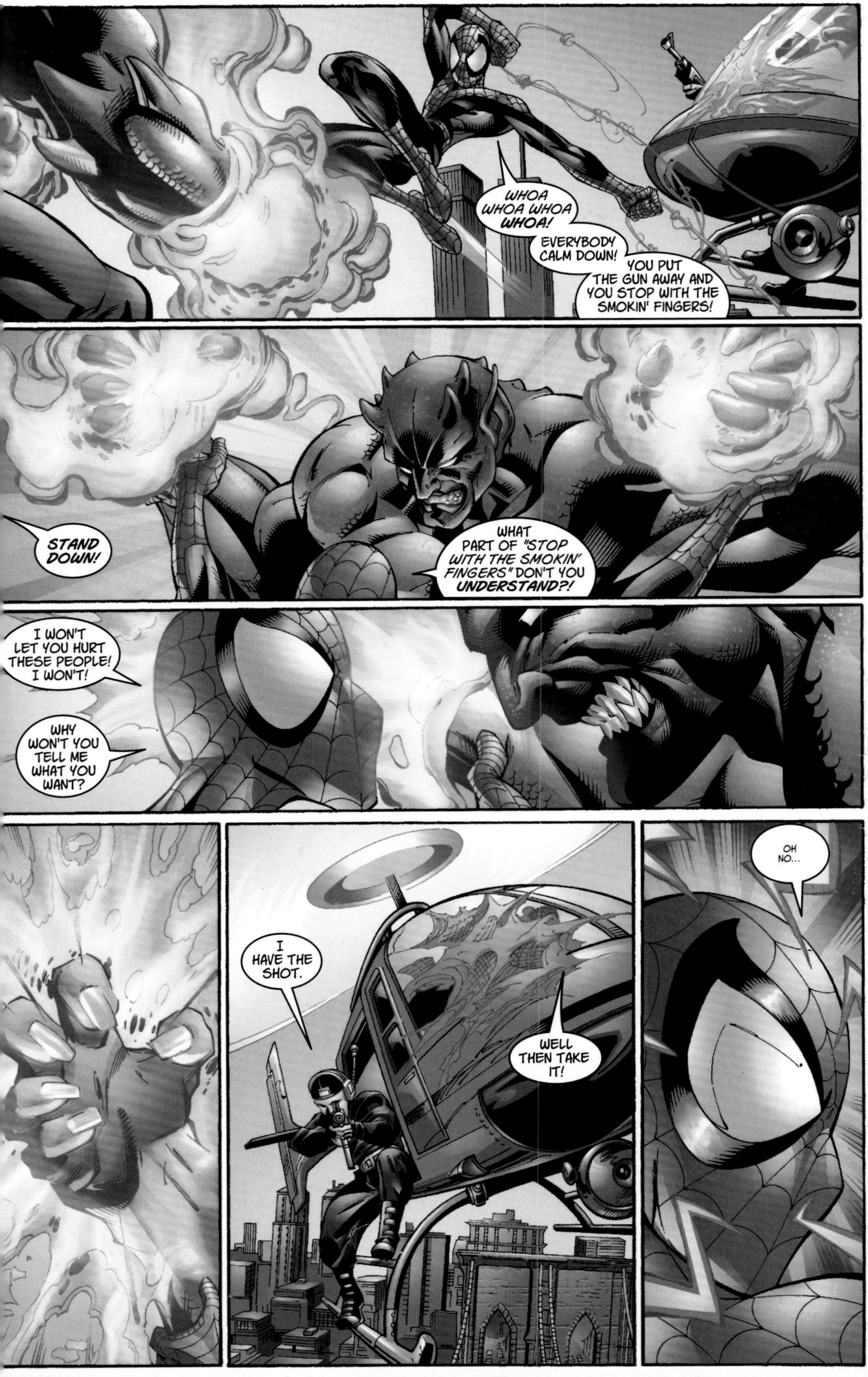

WHOA WHOA WHOA WHOA!
EVERYBODY CALM DOWN!
YOU PUT THE GUN AWAY AND YOU STOP WITH THE SMOKIN' FINGERS!
STAND DOWN!
WHAT PART OF "STOP WITH THE SMOKIN' FINGERS" DON'T YOU UNDERSTAND?!
I WON'T LET YOU HURT THESE PEOPLE! I WON'T!
WHY WON'T YOU TELL ME WHAT YOU WANT?
I HAVE THE SHOT.
WELL THEN TAKE IT!
OH NO...

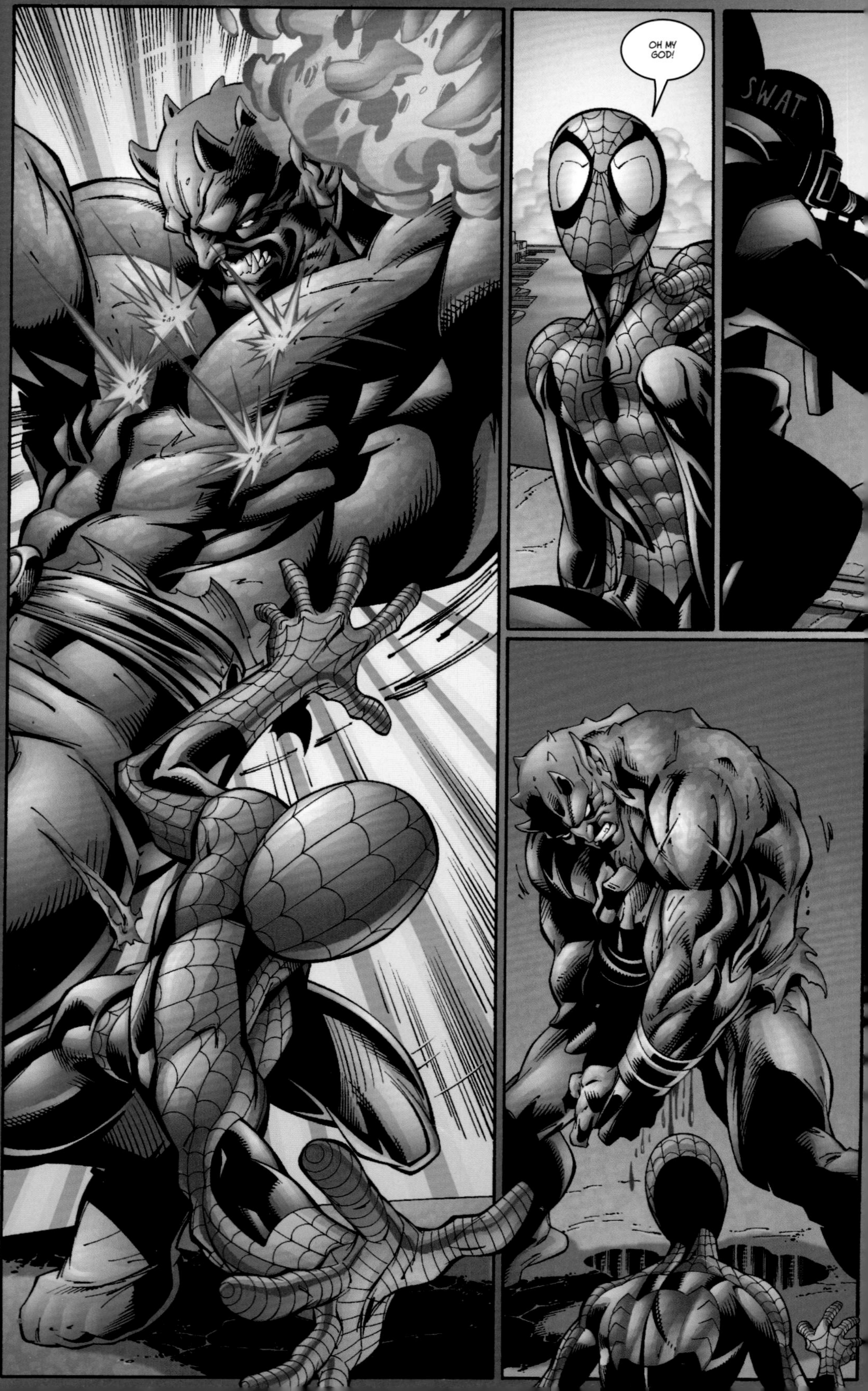
OH MY GOD!
S.W.A.T.

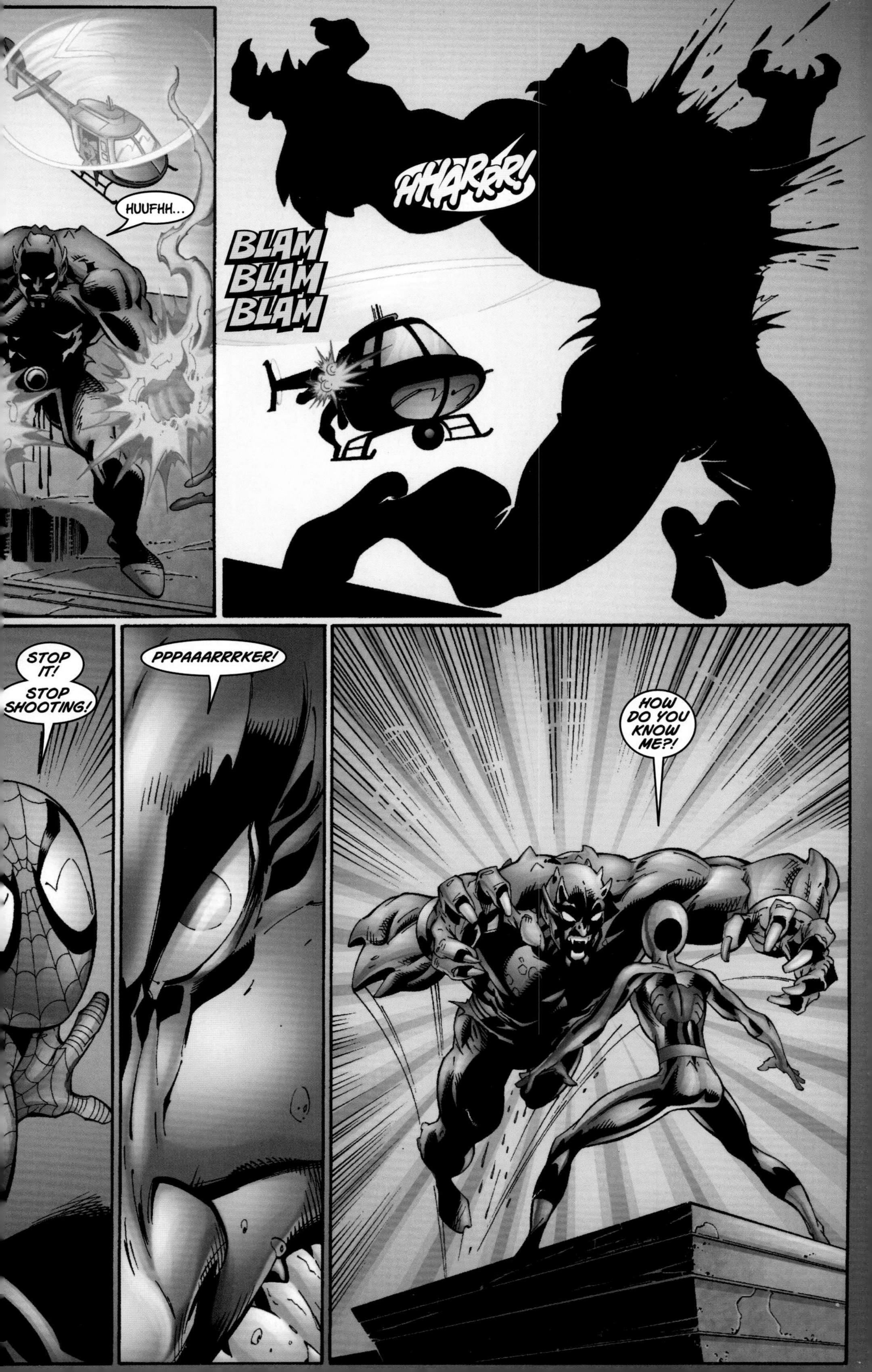
HUUFHH...
BLAM
BLAM
BLAM
HHARRR!
STOP IT! STOP SHOOTING!
PPPAAARRRKER!
HOW DO YOU KNOW ME?!

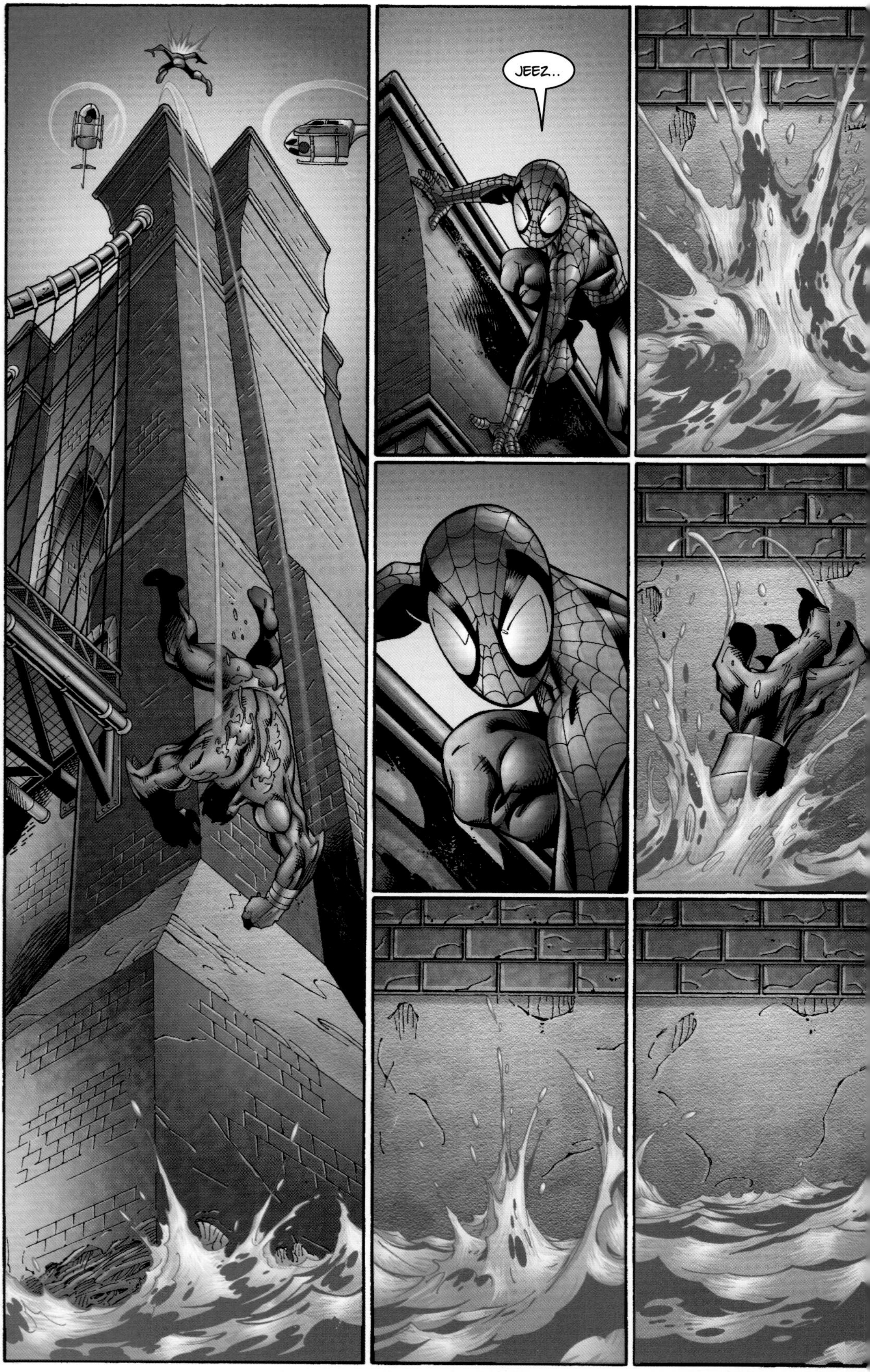
JEEZ..

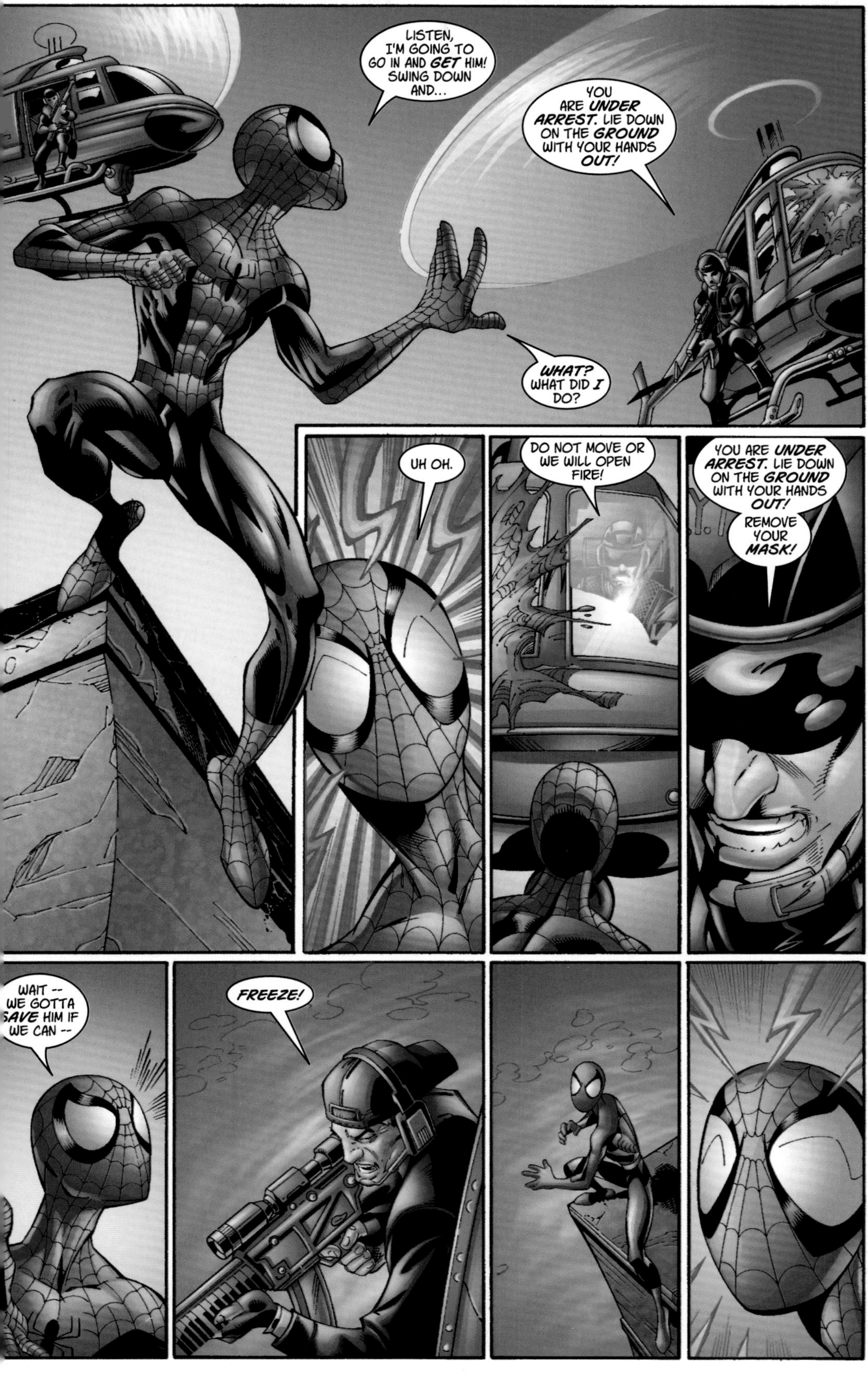
LISTEN, I'M GOING TO GO IN AND GET HIM! SWING DOWN AND...
YOU ARE UNDER ARREST. LIE DOWN ON THE GROUND WITH YOUR HANDS OUT!
WHAT? WHAT DID I DO?
UH OH.
DO NOT MOVE OR WE WILL OPEN FIRE!
YOU ARE UNDER ARREST. LIE DOWN ON THE GROUND WITH YOUR HANDS OUT!
REMOVE YOUR MASK!
WAIT -- WE GOTTA SAVE HIM IF WE CAN --
FREEZE!

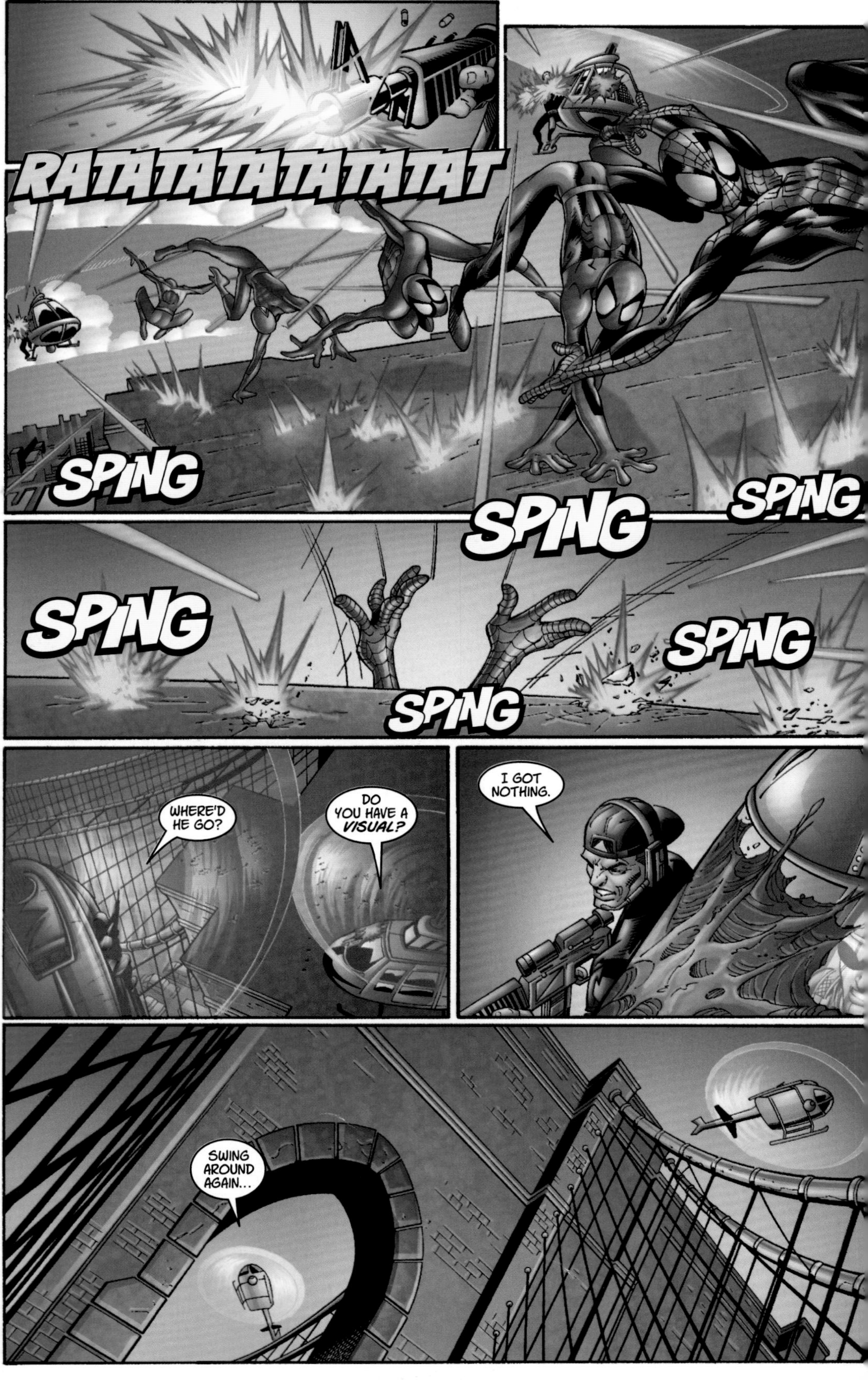
RATATATATATATAT
SPING
SPING
SPING
SPING
SPING
SPING
WHERE'D HE GO?
DO YOU HAVE A *VISUAL?*
I GOT NOTHING.
SWING AROUND AGAIN...

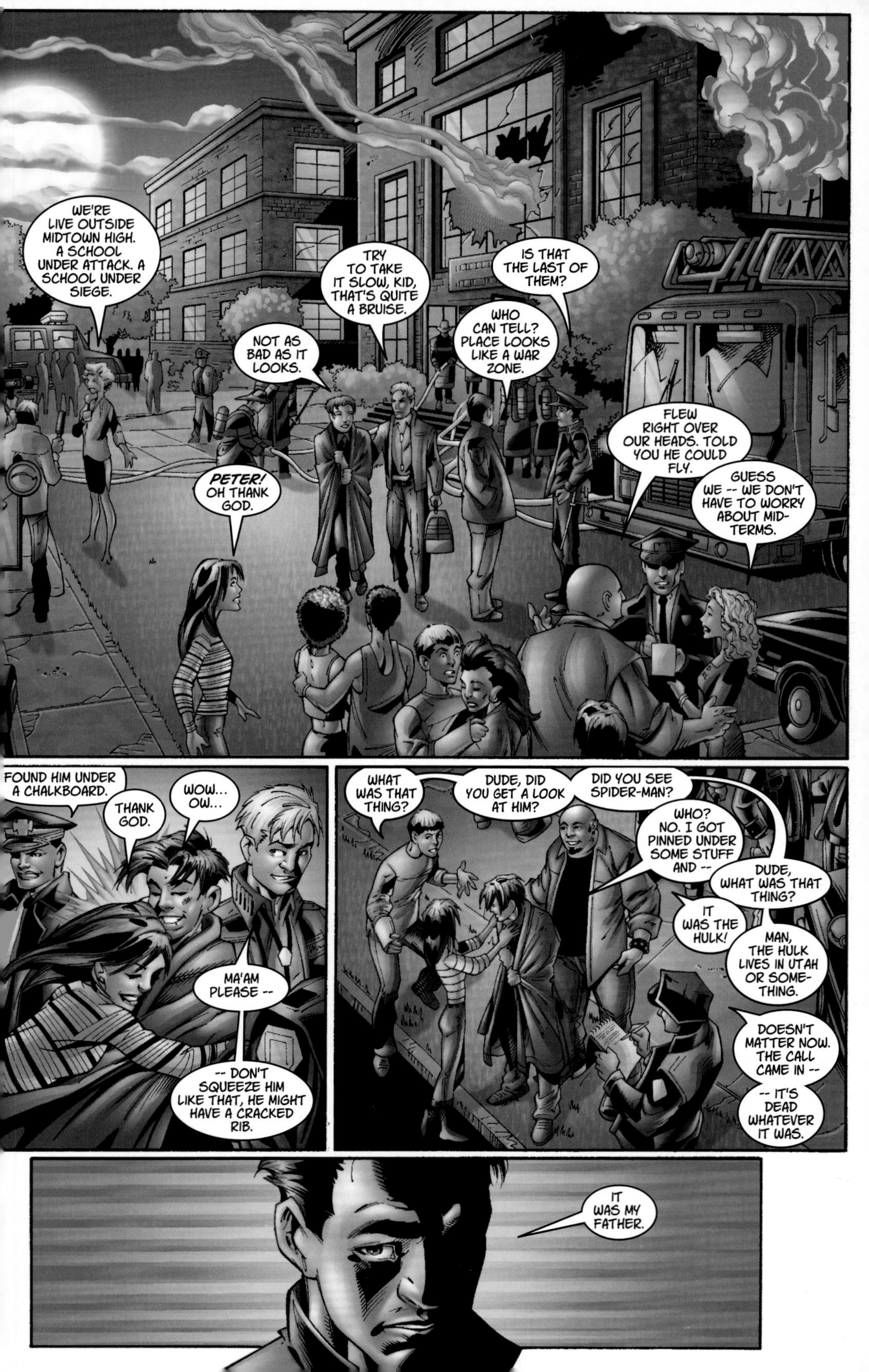
WE'RE LIVE OUTSIDE MIDTOWN HIGH. A SCHOOL UNDER ATTACK. A SCHOOL UNDER SIEGE.
TRY TO TAKE IT SLOW, KID, THAT'S QUITE A BRUISE.
IS THAT THE LAST OF THEM?
NOT AS BAD AS IT LOOKS.
WHO CAN TELL? PLACE LOOKS LIKE A WAR ZONE.
FLEW RIGHT OVER OUR HEADS. TOLD YOU HE COULD FLY.
GUESS WE -- WE DON'T HAVE TO WORRY ABOUT MID-TERMS.
PETER! OH THANK GOD.
FOUND HIM UNDER A CHALKBOARD.
THANK GOD.
WOW... OW...
MA'AM PLEASE --
-- DON'T SQUEEZE HIM LIKE THAT, HE MIGHT HAVE A CRACKED RIB.
WHAT WAS THAT THING?
DUDE, DID YOU GET A LOOK AT HIM?
DID YOU SEE SPIDER-MAN?
WHO? NO. I GOT PINNED UNDER SOME STUFF AND --
DUDE, WHAT WAS THAT THING?
IT WAS THE HULK!
MAN, THE HULK LIVES IN UTAH OR SOME-THING.
DOESN'T MATTER NOW. THE CALL CAME IN --
-- IT'S DEAD WHATEVER IT WAS.
IT WAS MY FATHER.

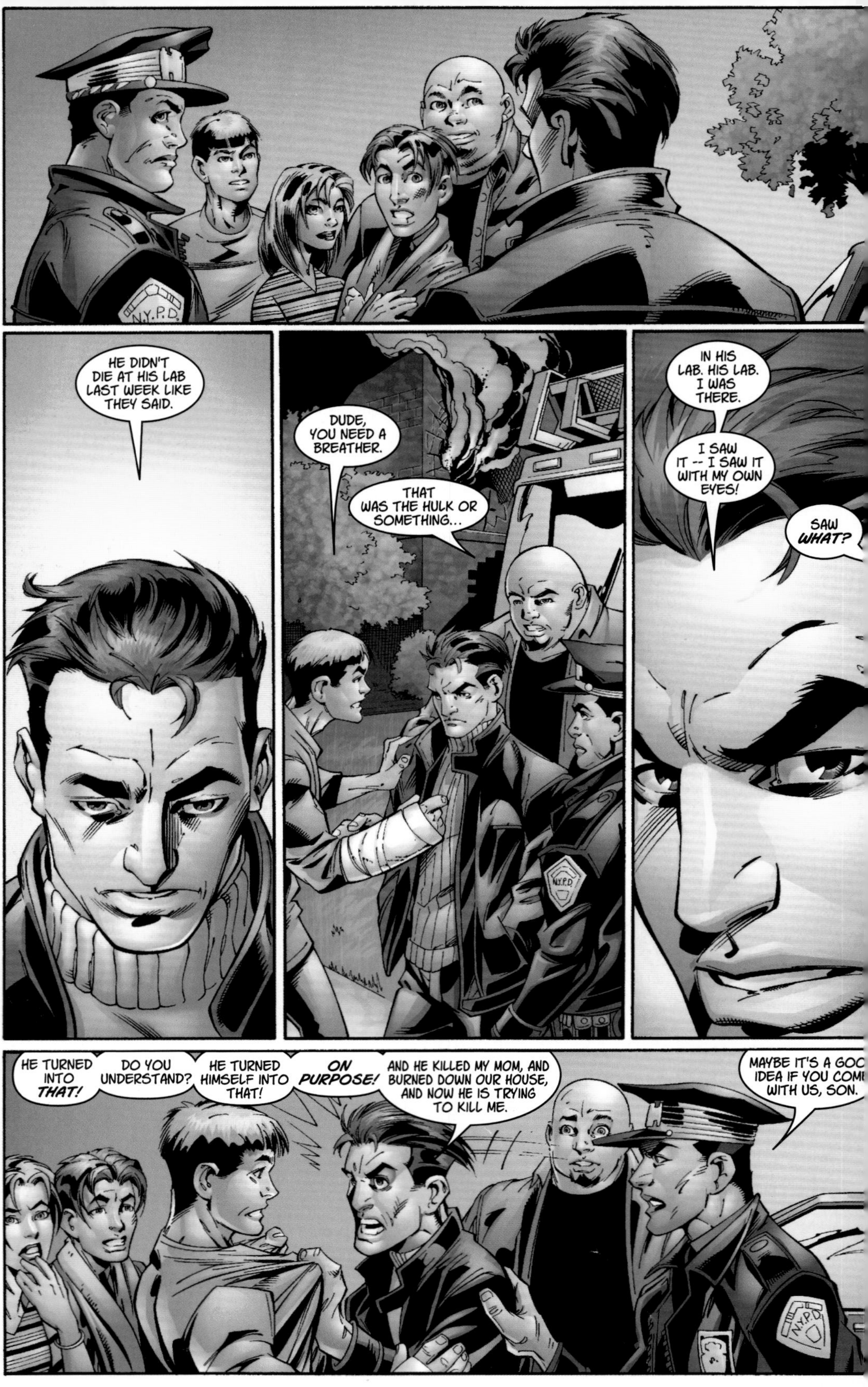
HE DIDN'T DIE AT HIS LAB LAST WEEK LIKE THEY SAID.
DUDE, YOU NEED A BREATHER.
THAT WAS THE HULK OR SOMETHING...
IN HIS LAB. HIS LAB. I WAS THERE.
I SAW IT -- I SAW IT WITH MY OWN EYES!
SAW WHAT?
HE TURNED INTO THAT!
DO YOU UNDERSTAND?
HE TURNED HIMSELF INTO THAT!
ON PURPOSE!
AND HE KILLED MY MOM, AND BURNED DOWN OUR HOUSE, AND NOW HE IS TRYING TO KILL ME.
MAYBE IT'S A GOO IDEA IF YOU COM WITH US, SON.

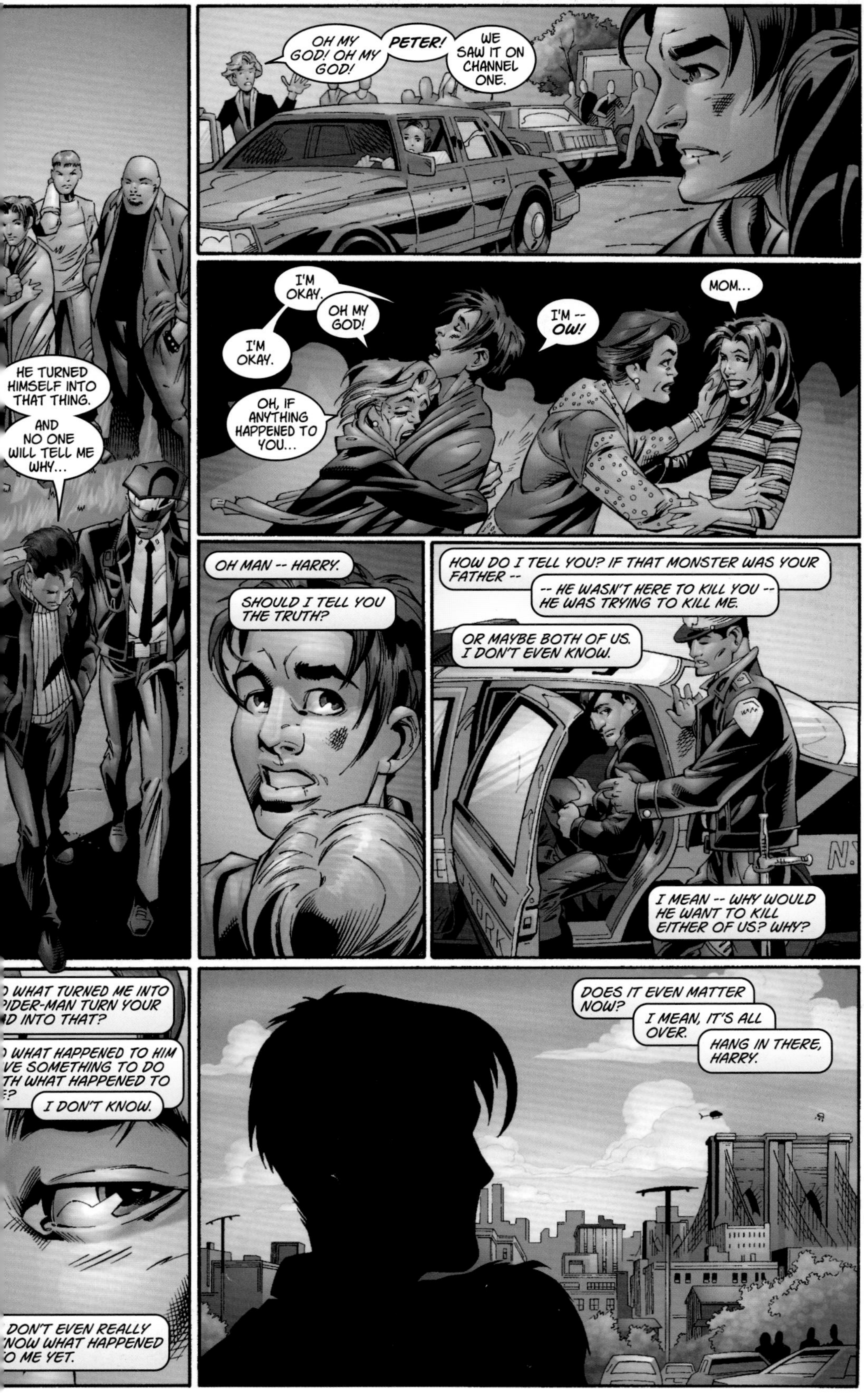
HE TURNED HIMSELF INTO THAT THING.
AND NO ONE WILL TELL ME WHY...
OH MY GOD! OH MY GOD!
PETER!
WE SAW IT ON CHANNEL ONE.
I'M OKAY.
OH MY GOD!
I'M OKAY.
OH, IF ANYTHING HAPPENED TO YOU...
I'M -- OW!
MOM...
OH MAN -- HARRY.
SHOULD I TELL YOU THE TRUTH?
HOW DO I TELL YOU? IF THAT MONSTER WAS YOUR FATHER --
-- HE WASN'T HERE TO KILL YOU -- HE WAS TRYING TO KILL ME.
OR MAYBE BOTH OF US. I DON'T EVEN KNOW.
I MEAN -- WHY WOULD HE WANT TO KILL EITHER OF US? WHY?
D WHAT TURNED ME INTO PIDER-MAN TURN YOUR D INTO THAT?
D WHAT HAPPENED TO HIM VE SOMETHING TO DO TH WHAT HAPPENED TO E?
I DON'T KNOW.
DON'T EVEN REALLY NOW WHAT HAPPENED O ME YET.
DOES IT EVEN MATTER NOW?
I MEAN, IT'S ALL OVER.
HANG IN THERE, HARRY.

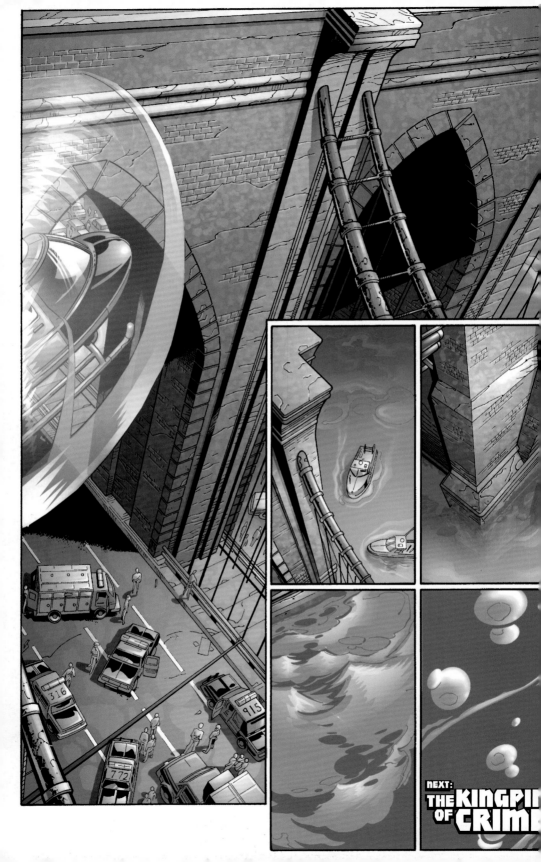

NEXT:
THE KINGPIN
OF CRIME

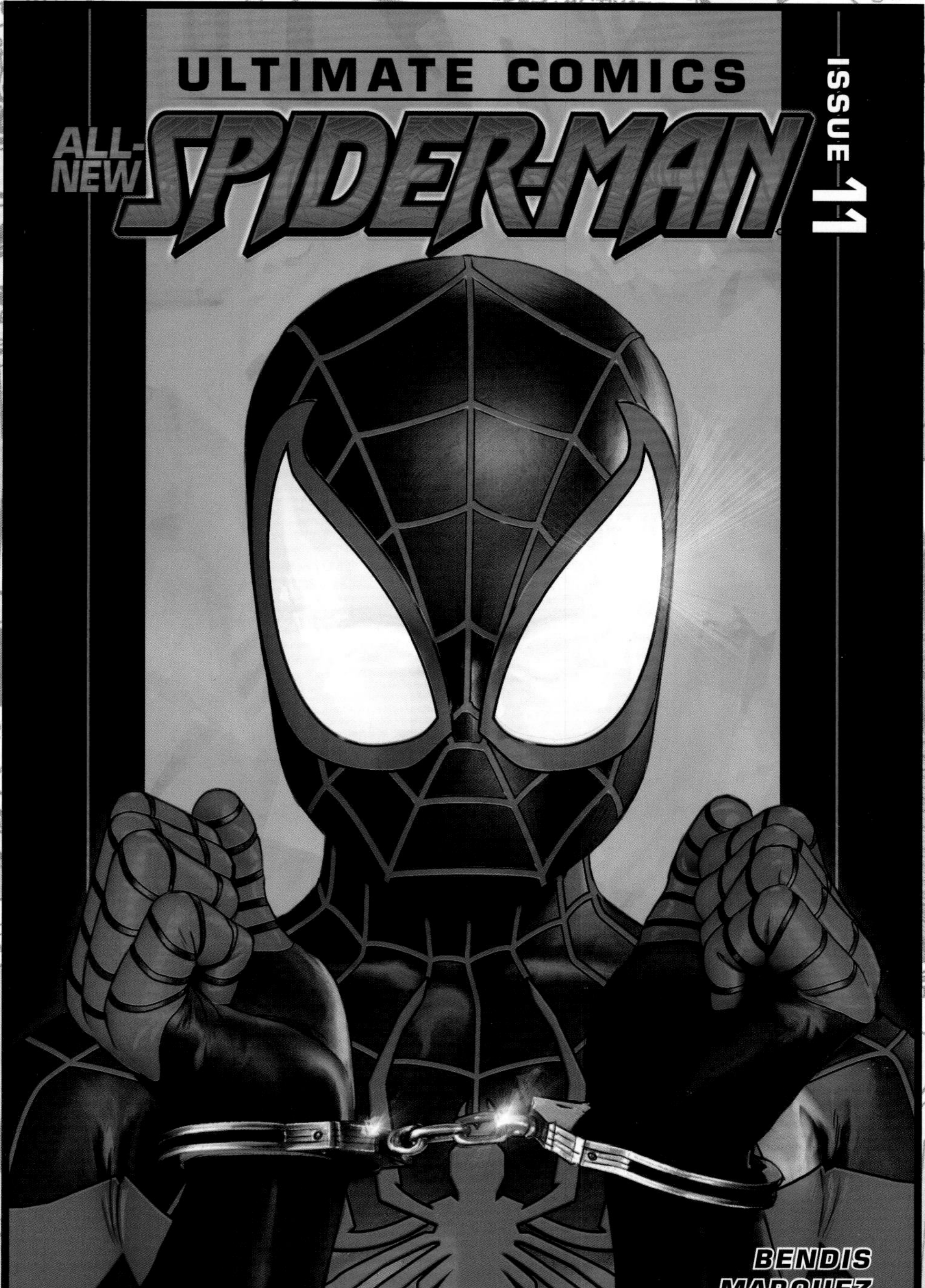
ULTIMATE COMICS
ALL-NEW SPIDER-MAN
ISSUE 11
BENDIS
MARQUEZ
PONSOR

ULTIMATE COMICS SPIDER-MAN (2011) #11

THE ULTIMATE UNIVERSE WAS SHAKEN BY THE DEATH OF PETER PARKER, BUT MILES MORALES STEPPED UP TO TAKE THE MANTLE OF THE ULTIMATE SPIDER-MAN. NOW MILES MUST CONFRONT HIS OWN UNCLE AARON, A.K.A. THE PROWLER!

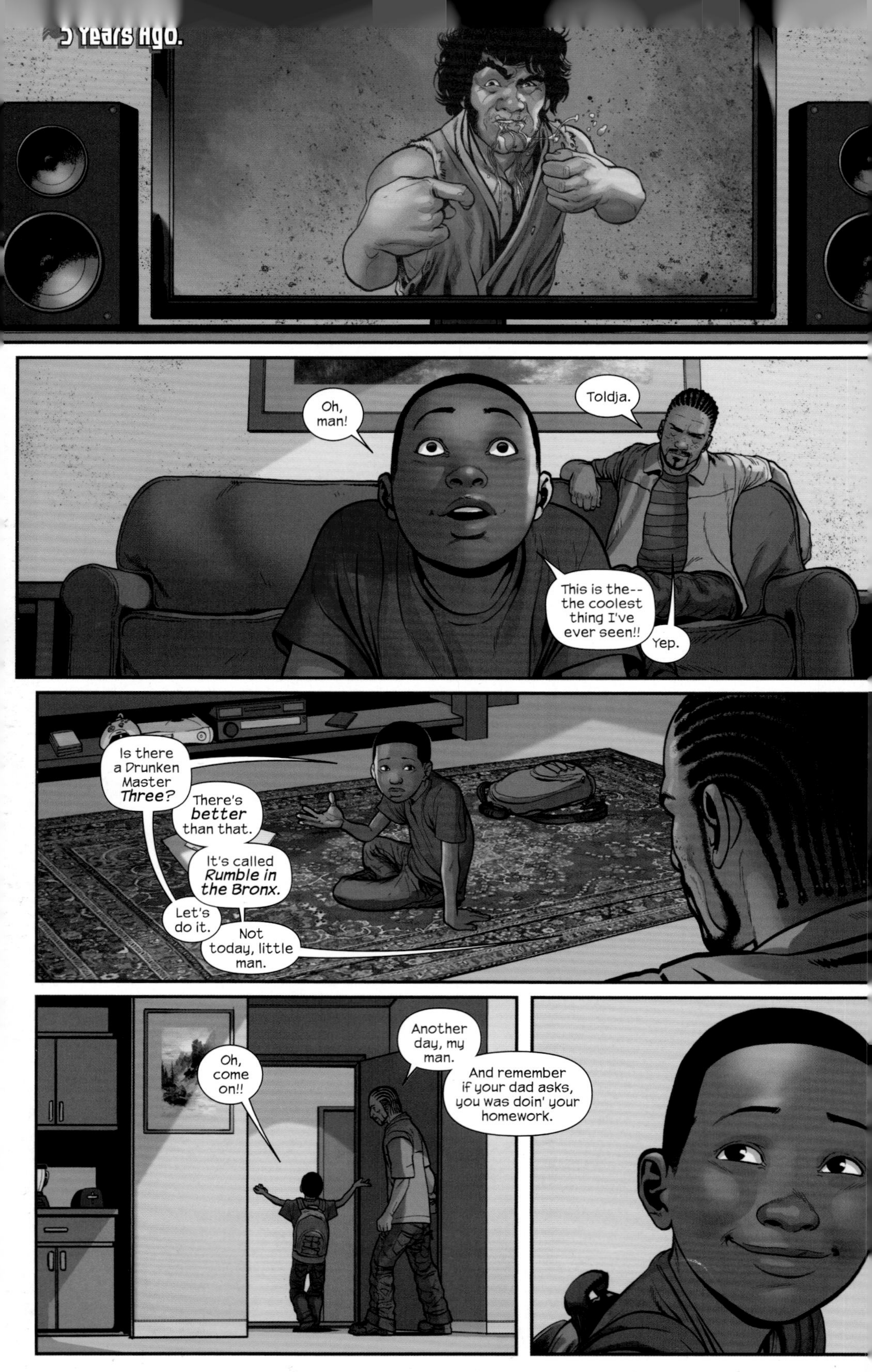
5 Years Ago.
Oh, man!
Toldja.
This is the-- the coolest thing I've ever seen!!
Yep.
Is there a Drunken Master *Three?*
There's *better* than that.
It's called *Rumble in the Bronx.*
Let's do it.
Not today, little man.
Oh, come on!!
Another day, my man.
And remember if your dad asks, you was doin' your homework.

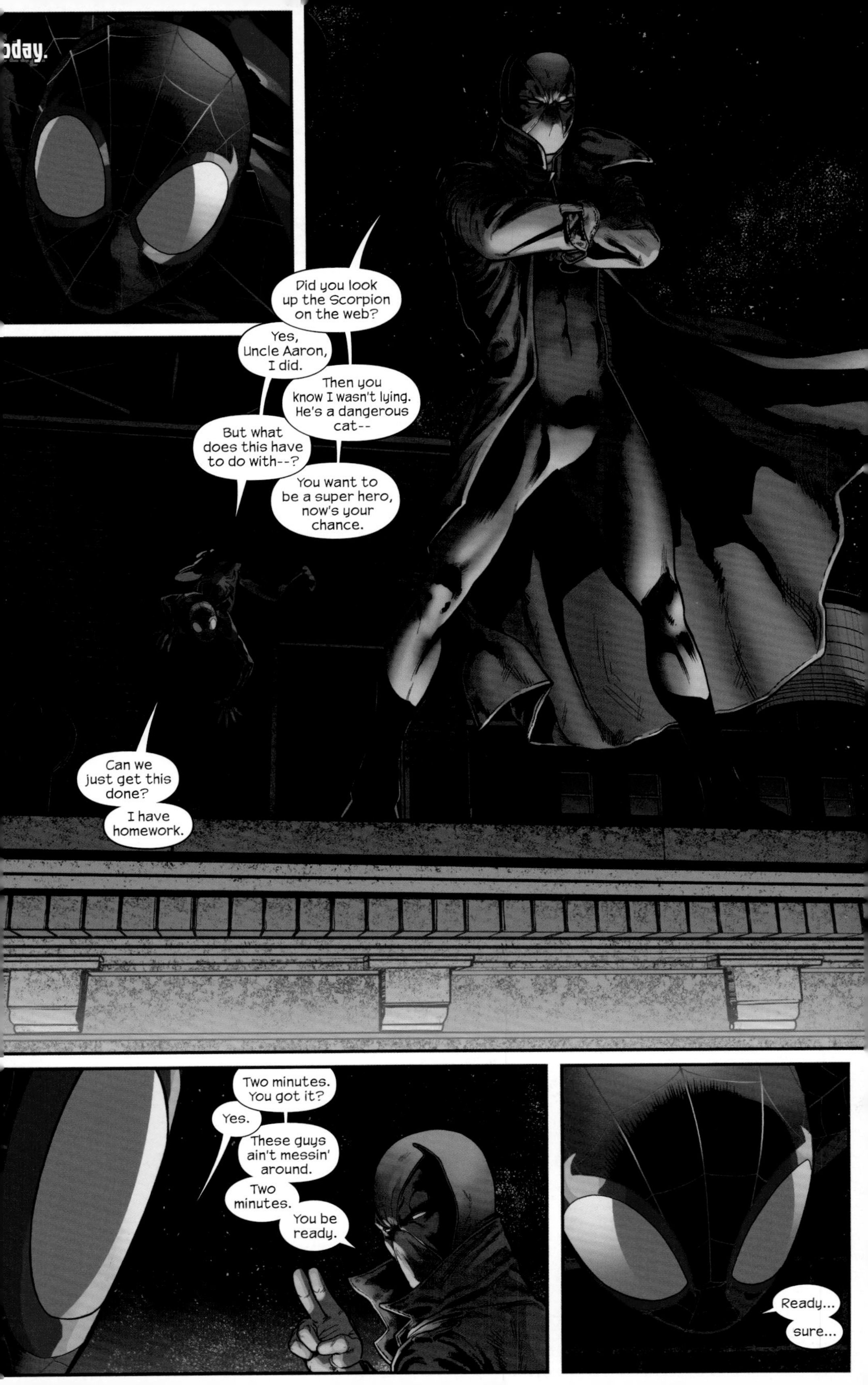

oday.
Did you look up the Scorpion on the web?
Yes, Uncle Aaron, I did.
Then you know I wasn't lying. He's a dangerous cat--
But what does this have to do with--?
You want to be a super hero, now's your chance.
Can we just get this done?
I have homework.
Two minutes. You got it?
Yes.
These guys ain't messin' around.
Two minutes.
You be ready.
Ready...
sure...

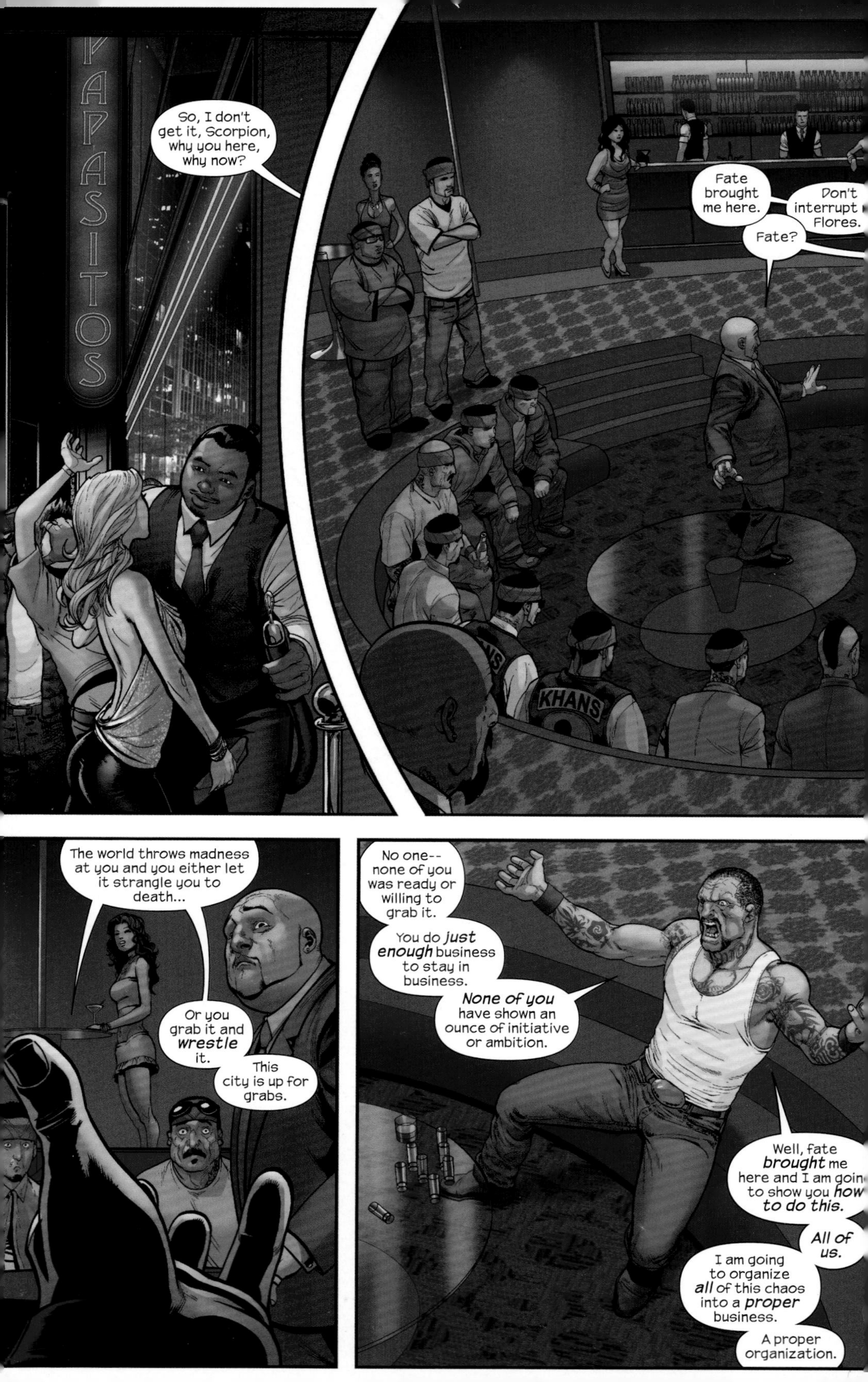
PAPASITOS
So, I don't get it, Scorpion, why you here, why now?
Fate brought me here.
Don't interrupt Flores.
Fate?
KHANS
The world throws madness at you and you either let it strangle you to death...
Or you grab it and *wrestle* it.
This city is up for grabs.
No one-- none of you was ready or willing to grab it.
You do *just enough* business to stay in business.
None of you have shown an ounce of initiative or ambition.
Well, fate *brought* me here and I am goin to show you *how to do this.*
All of us.
I am going to organize *all* of this chaos into a *proper* business.
A proper organization.

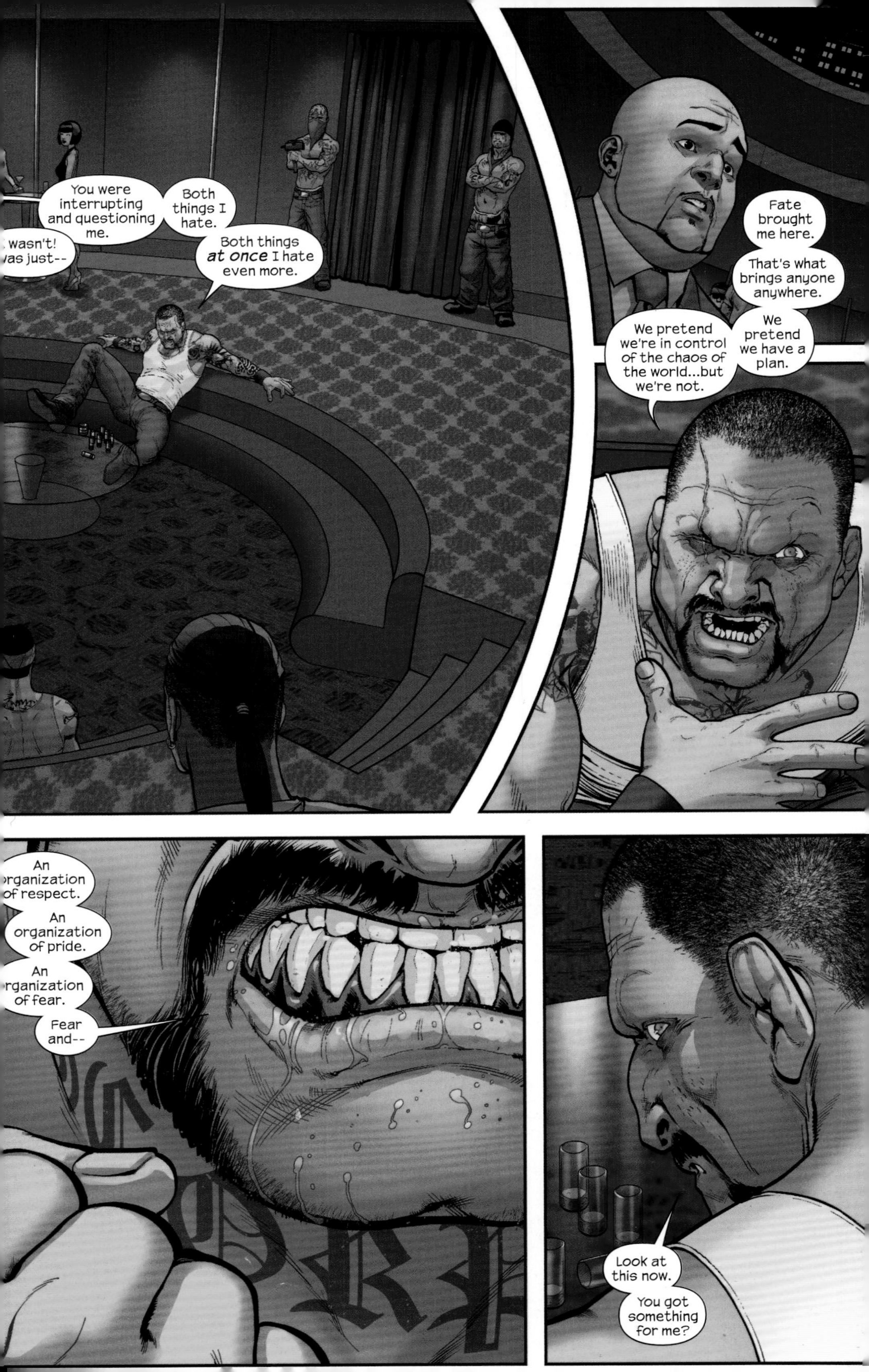

You were interrupting and questioning me.
wasn't! was just--
Both things I hate.
Both things *at once* I hate even more.
Fate brought me here.
That's what brings anyone anywhere.
We pretend we have a plan.
We pretend we're in control of the chaos of the world...but we're not.
An organization of respect.
An organization of pride.
An organization of fear.
Fear and--
Look at this now.
You got something for me?

Fair warning, Scorpion.

Go back where you came from.

Prowler...

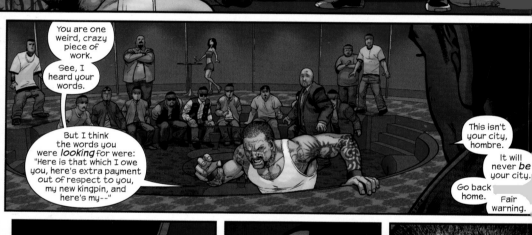

You are one weird, crazy piece of work.

See, I heard your words.

But I think the words you were *looking* for were: "Here is that which I owe you, here's extra payment out of respect to you, my new kingpin, and here's my--"

This isn't your city, hombre.

It will never *be* your city.

Go back home. Fair warning.

See? This is *exactly* what I'm talking about.

Where I come from this would *never* happen. Never.

Now I have to beat you to death in front of my new partners.

You think so, huh?

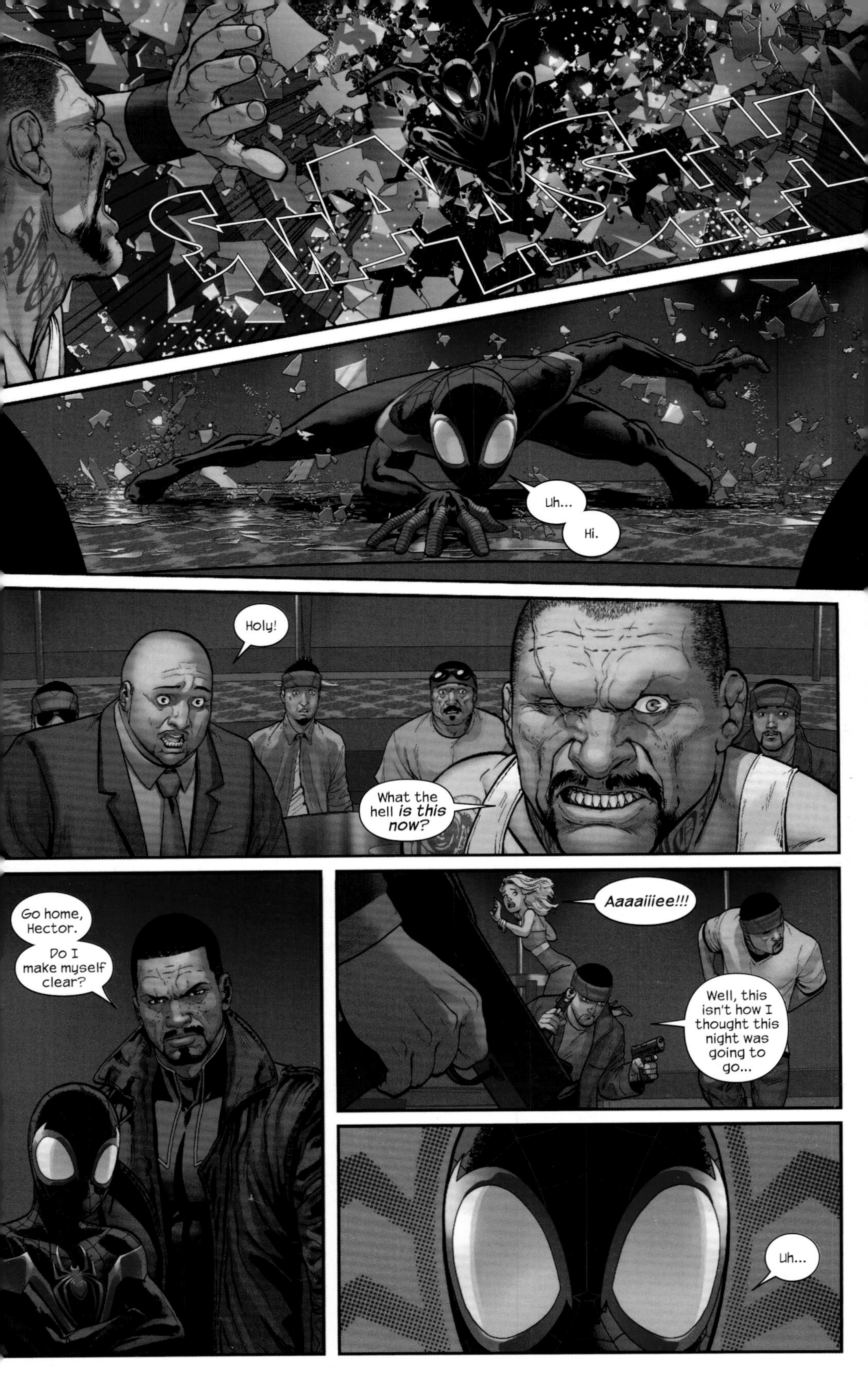
SMASH
Uh...
Hi.
Holy!
What the hell *is this now?*
Go home, Hector.
Do I make myself clear?
Aaaaiiiee!!!
Well, this isn't how I thought this night was going to go...
Uh...

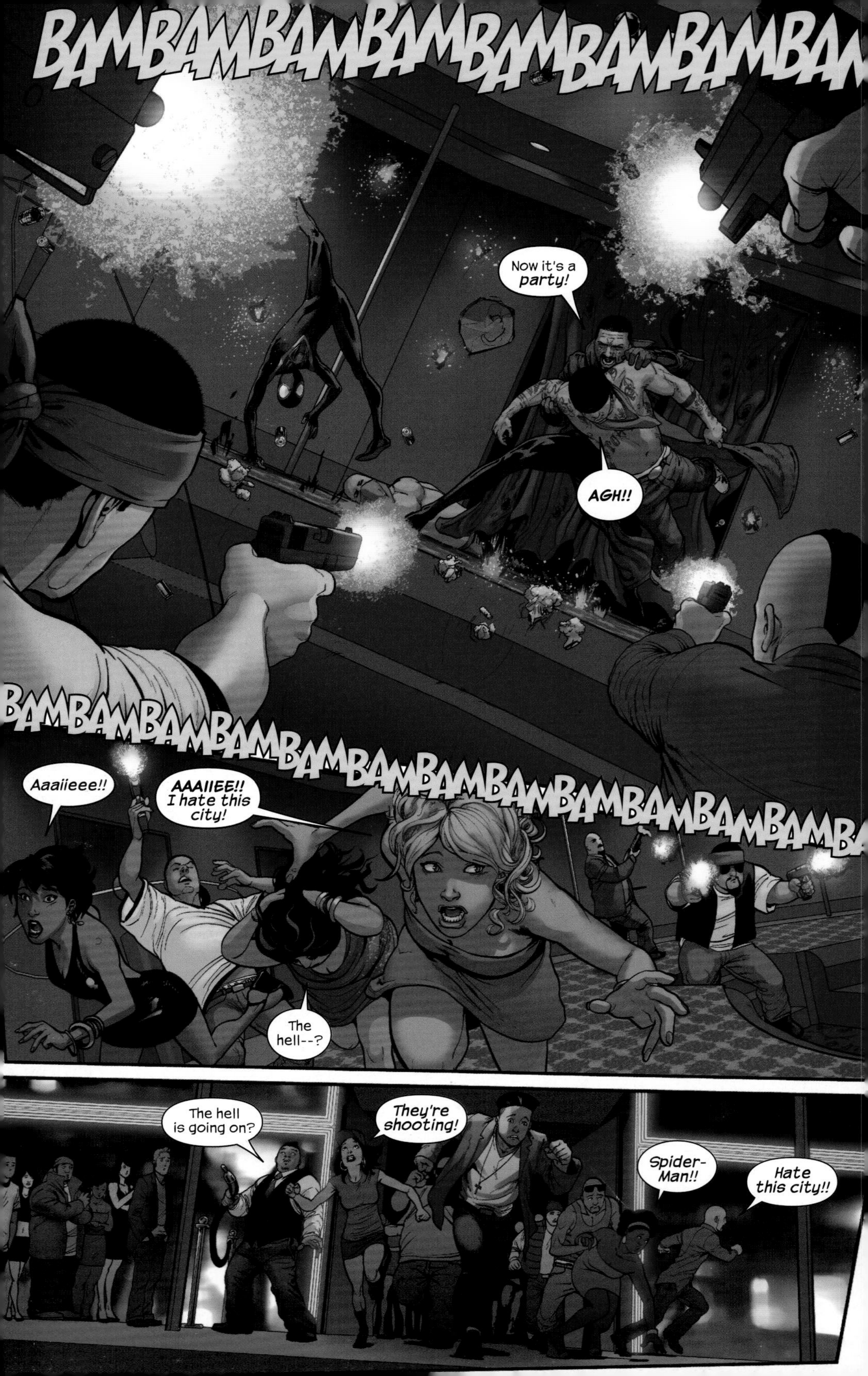
BAMBAMBAMBAMBAMBAMBAMBAM
Now it's a party!
AGH!!
BAMBAMBAMBAMBAMBAMBAMBAMBAMBAMBAMBAMBAMBA
Aaaiieee!!
AAAIIEE!! I hate this city!
The hell--?
The hell is going on?
They're shooting!
Spider-Man!!
Hate this city!!

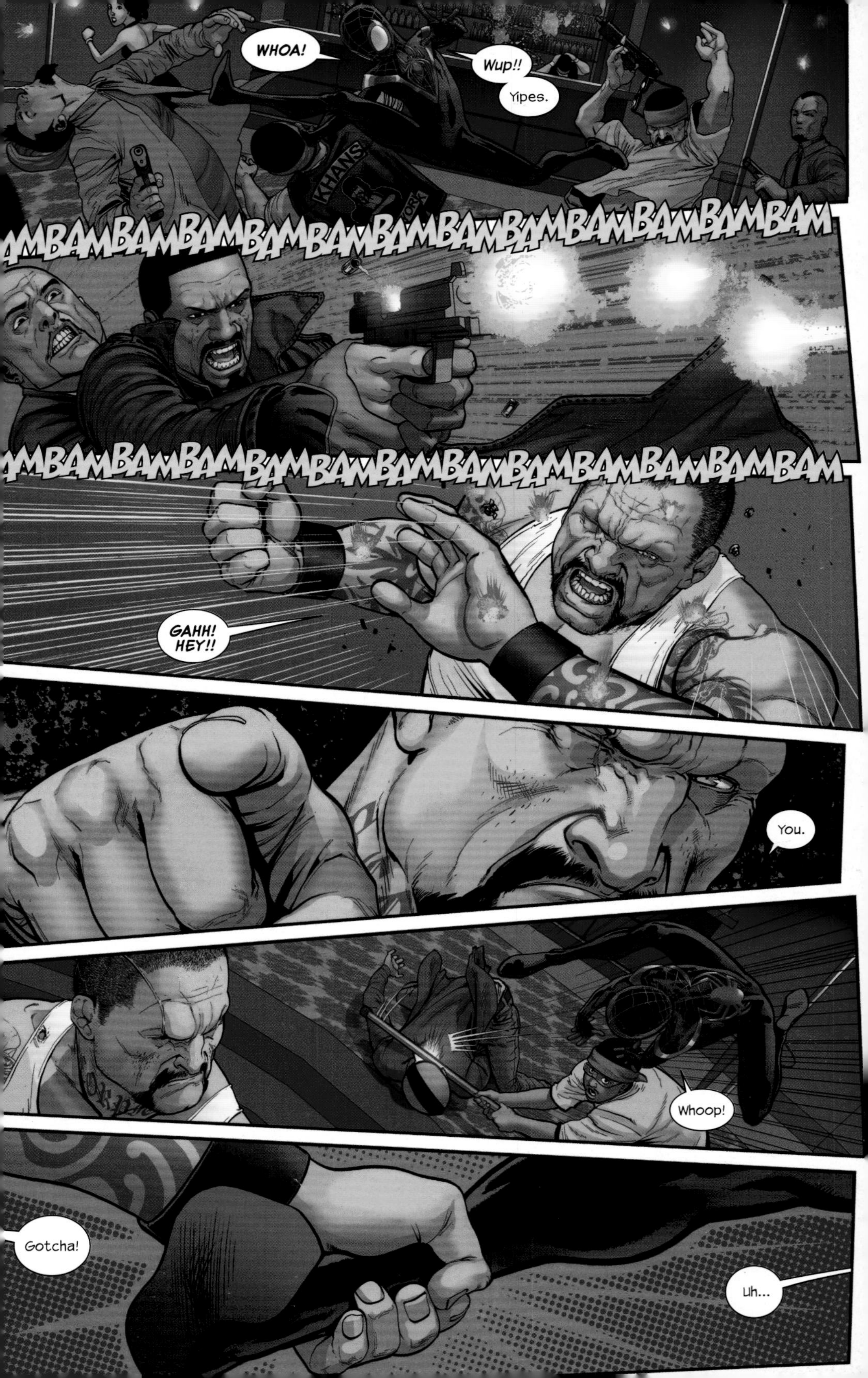
WHOA!
Wup!!
Yipes.
KHANS
BAMBAMBAMBAMBAMBAMBAMBAMBAMBAMBAMBAMBAM
BAMBAMBAMBAMBAMBAMBAMBAMBAMBAMBAMBAMBAM
GAHH! HEY!!
You.
Whoop!
Gotcha!
Uh...

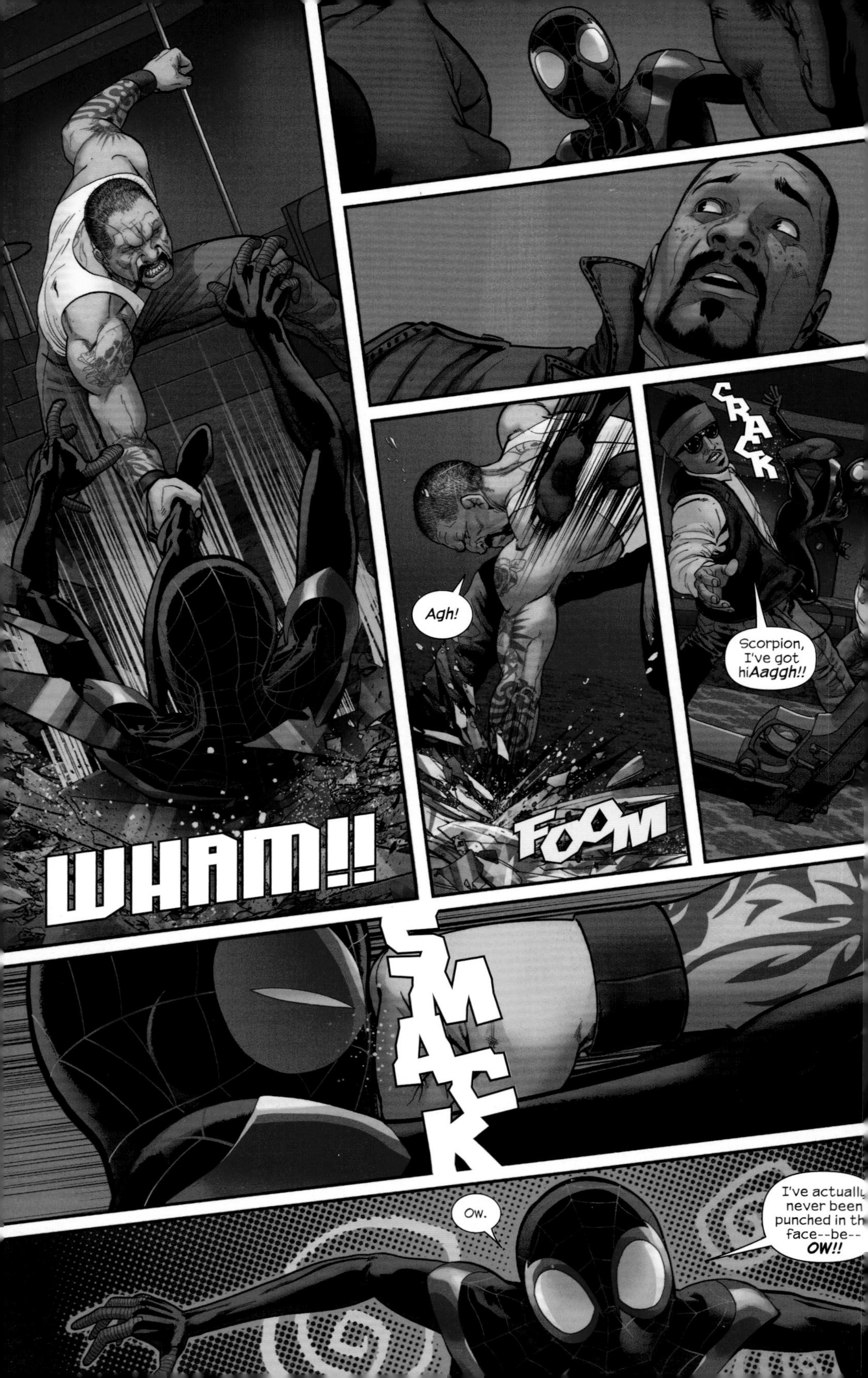
Agh!
CRACK
Scorpion, I've got hiAaggh!!
WHAM!!
FOOM
SMACK
Ow.
I've actually never been punched in the face--be--OW!!

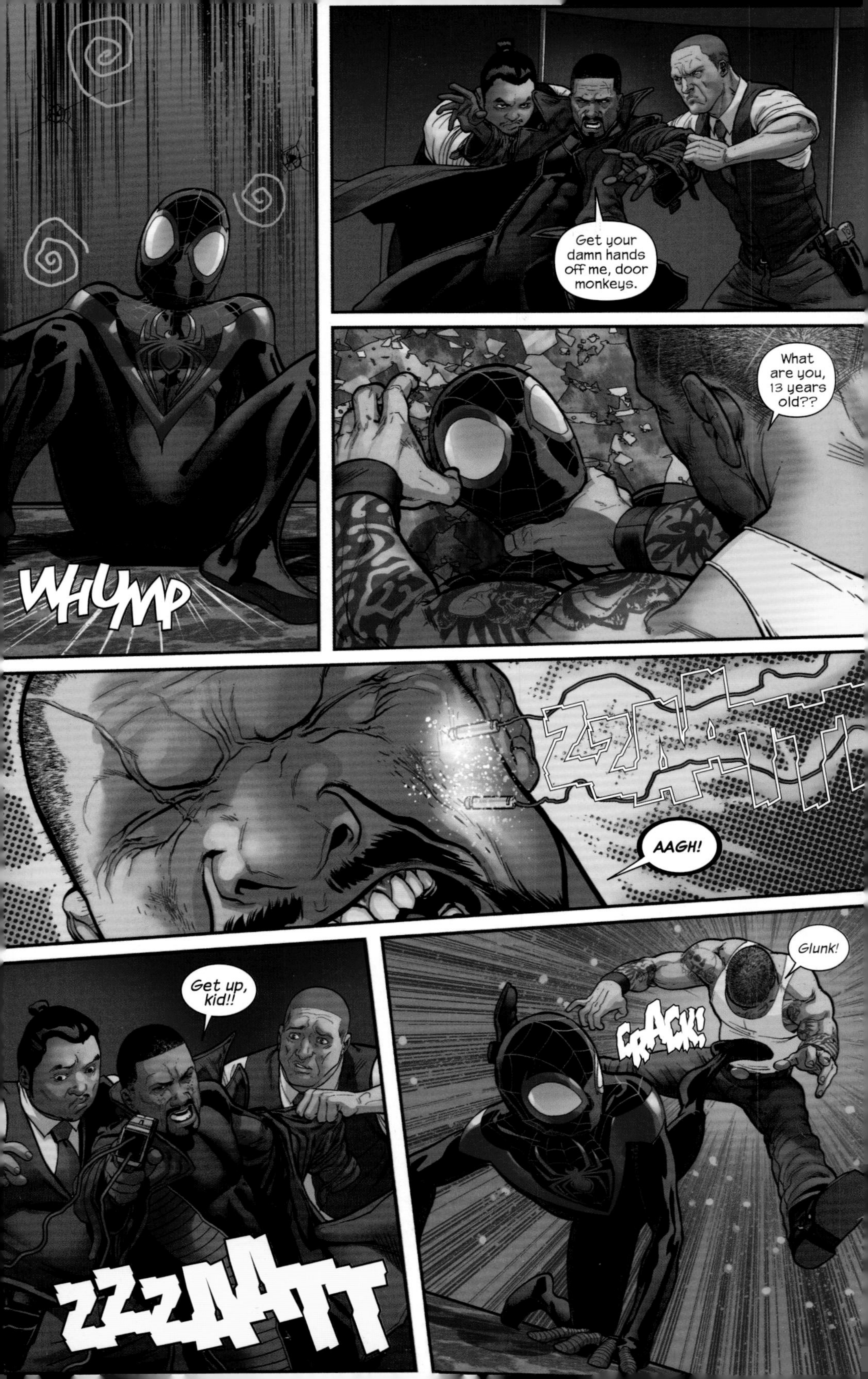

WHUMP
Get your damn hands off me, door monkeys.
What are you, 13 years old??
ZZZAAATT
AAGH!
Get up, kid!!
ZZZAATT
Glunk!
CRACK!

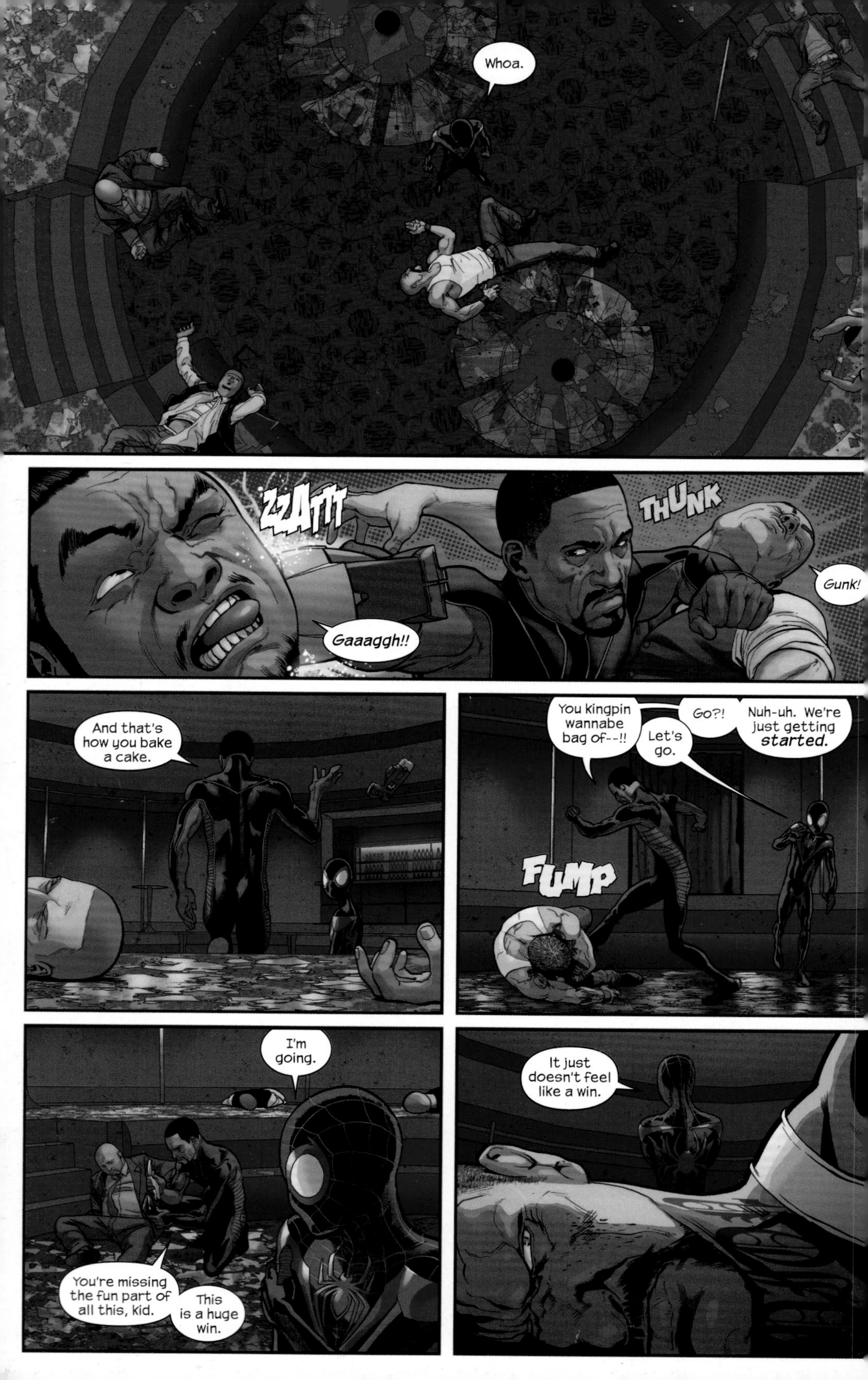
Whoa.
ZZATTT
Gaaaggh!!
THUNK
Gunk!
And that's how you bake a cake.
You kingpin wannabe bag of--!!
Let's go.
Go?!
Nuh-uh. We're just getting started.
FUMP
I'm going.
You're missing the fun part of all this, kid.
This is a huge win.
It just doesn't feel like a win.

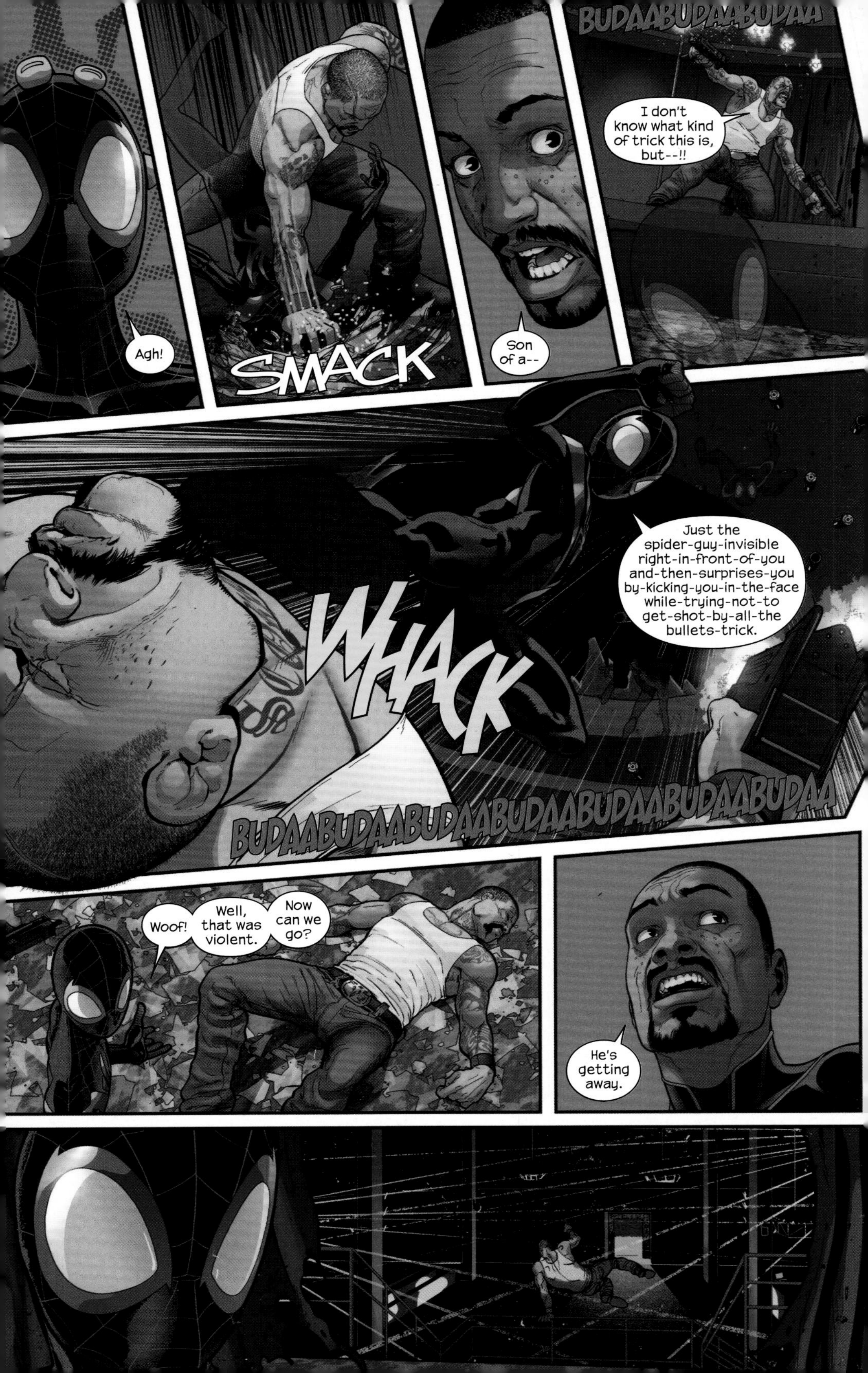
BUDAABUDAABUDAA
I don't know what kind of trick this is, but--!!
Agh!
SMACK
Son of a--
Just the spider-guy-invisible right-in-front-of-you and-then-surprises-you by-kicking-you-in-the-face while-trying-not-to get-shot-by-all-the bullets-trick.
WHACK
BUDAABUDAABUDAABUDAABUDAABUDAA
Woof!
Well, that was violent.
Now can we go?
He's getting away.

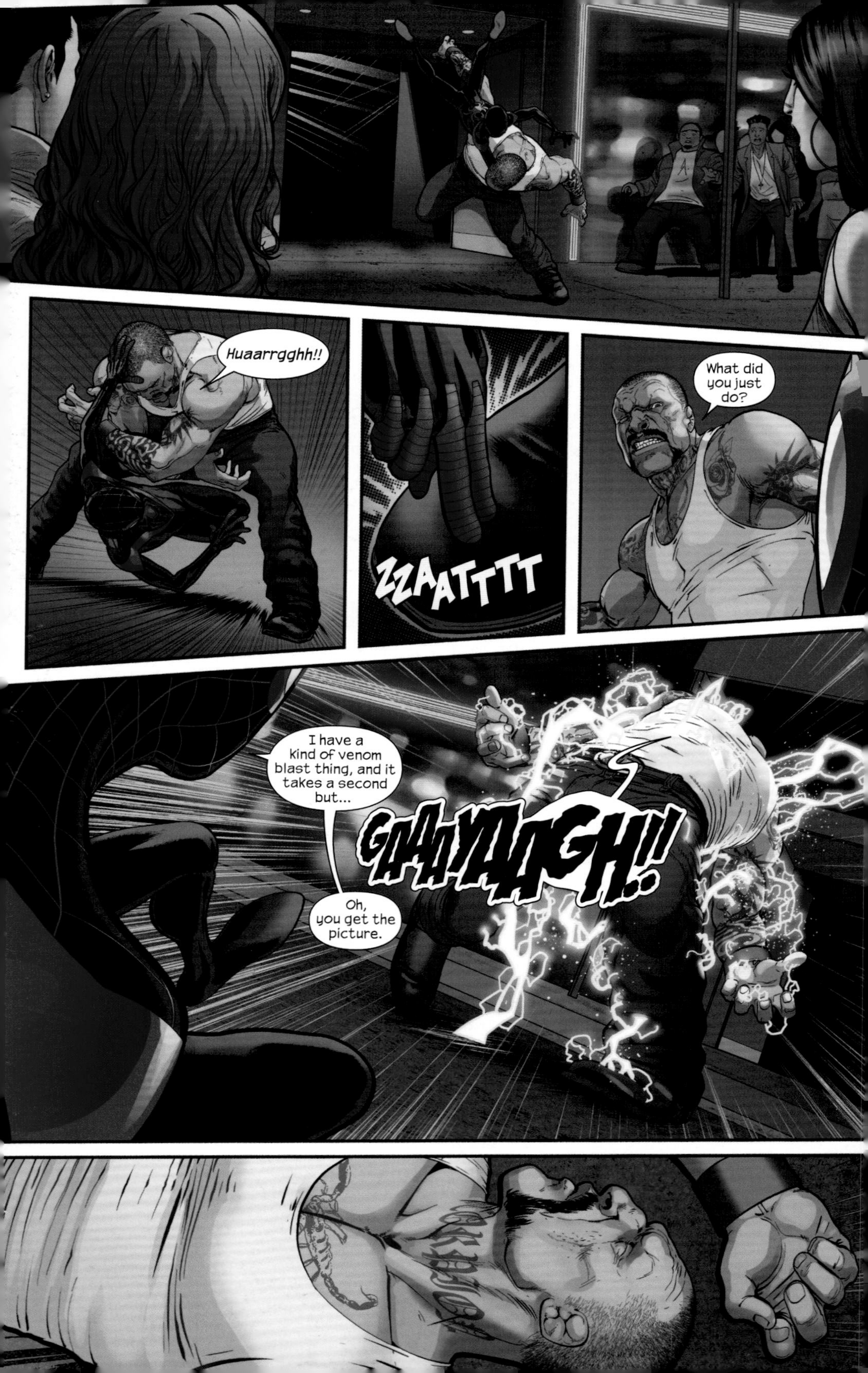
Huaarrgghh!!
ZZAATTTT
What did you just do?
I have a kind of venom blast thing, and it takes a second but...
GAAAYAAGH!!
Oh, you get the picture.

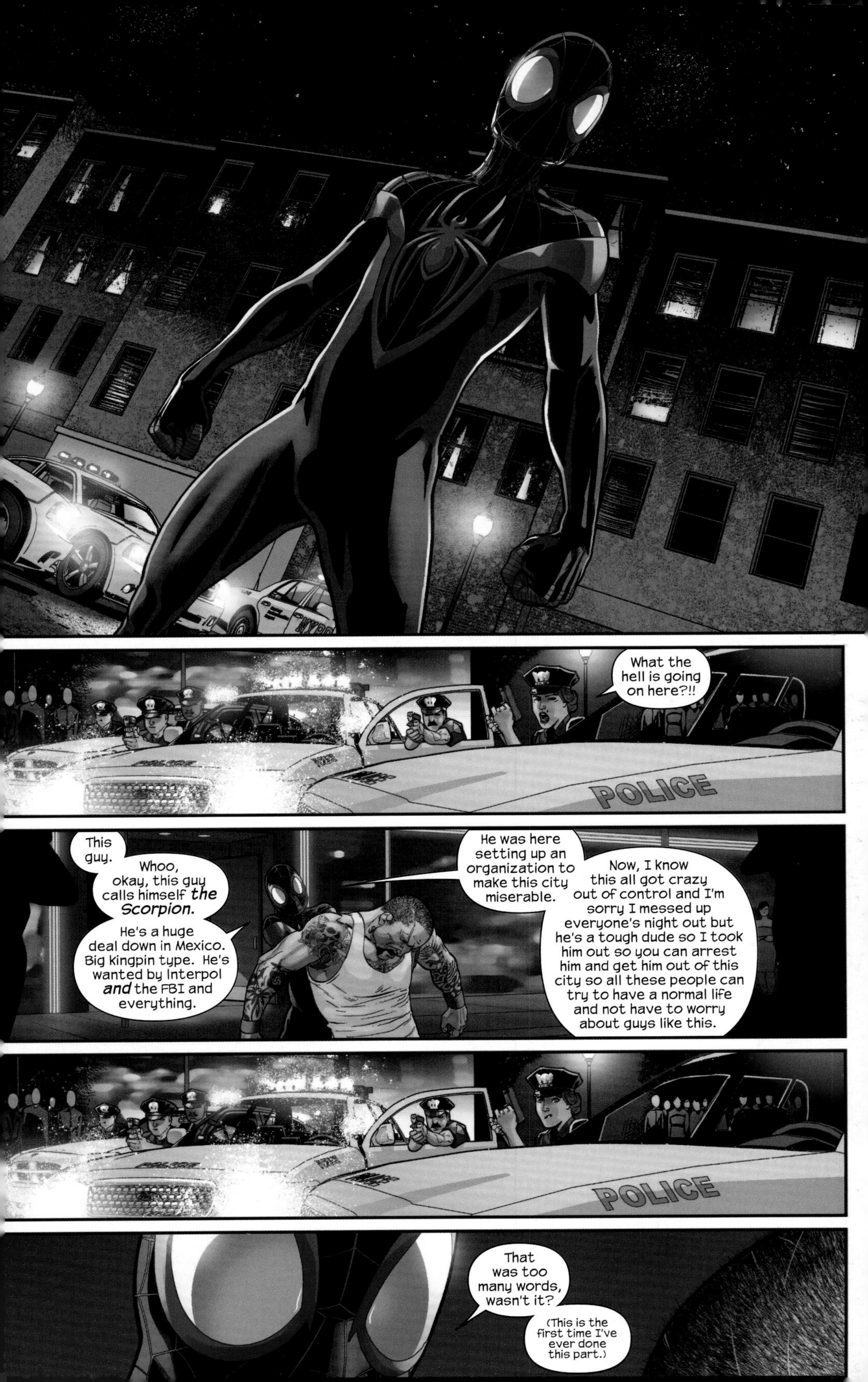
What the hell is going on here?!!
This guy.
Whoo, okay, this guy calls himself *the Scorpion.*
He's a huge deal down in Mexico. Big kingpin type. He's wanted by Interpol *and* the FBI and everything.
He was here setting up an organization to make this city miserable.
Now, I know this all got crazy out of control and I'm sorry I messed up everyone's night out but he's a tough dude so I took him out so you can arrest him and get him out of this city so all these people can try to have a normal life and not have to worry about guys like this.
POLICE
POLICE
That was too many words, wasn't it?
(This is the first time I've ever done this part.)

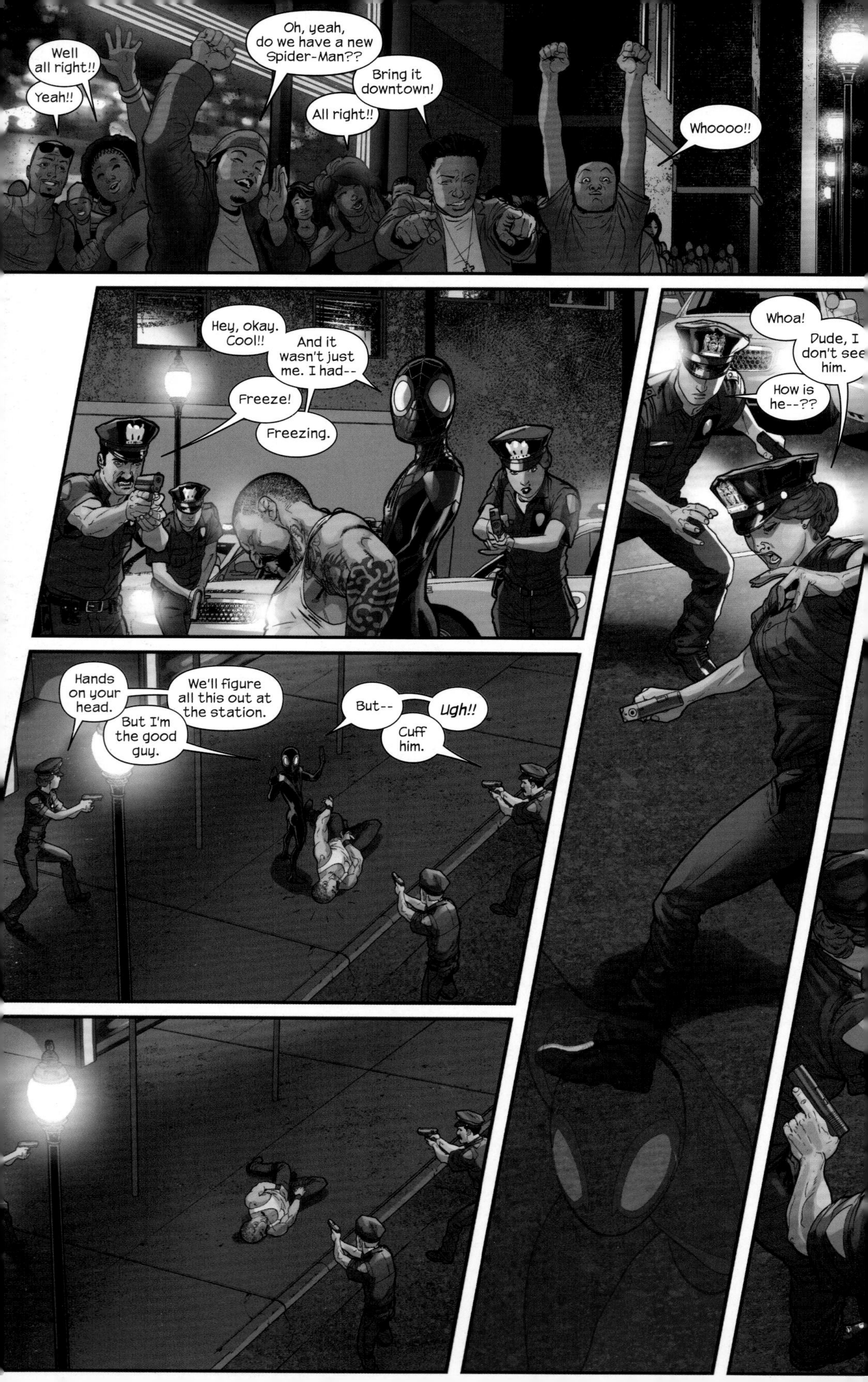
Well all right!!
Yeah!!
Oh, yeah, do we have a new Spider-Man??
All right!!
Bring it downtown!
Whoooo!!
Hey, okay. Cool!!
And it wasn't just me. I had--
Freeze!
Freezing.
Whoa!
Dude, I don't see him.
How is he--??
Hands on your head.
We'll figure all this out at the station.
But I'm the good guy.
But--
Ugh!!
Cuff him.

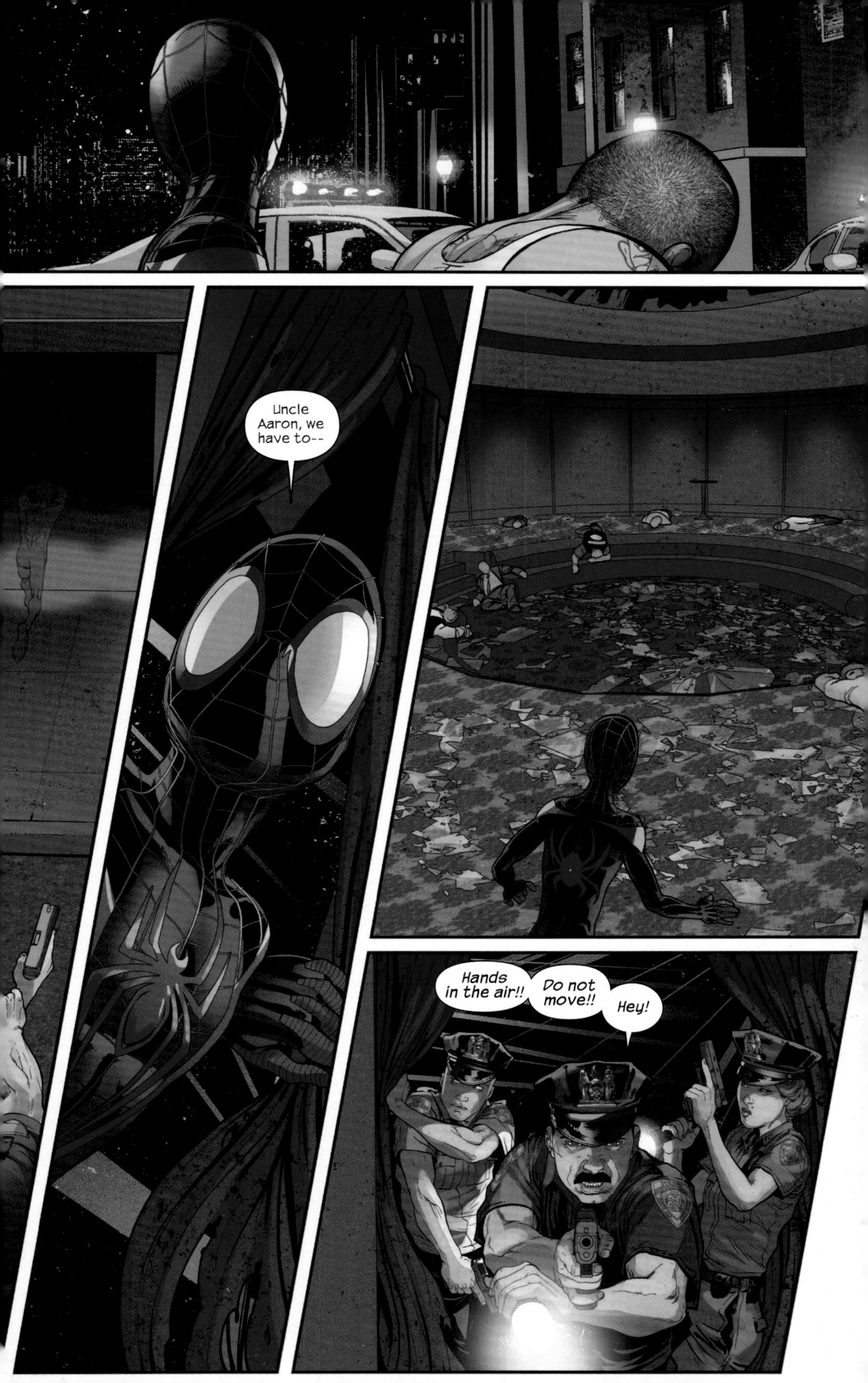
Uncle Aaron, we have to--
Hands in the air!!
Do not move!!
Hey!

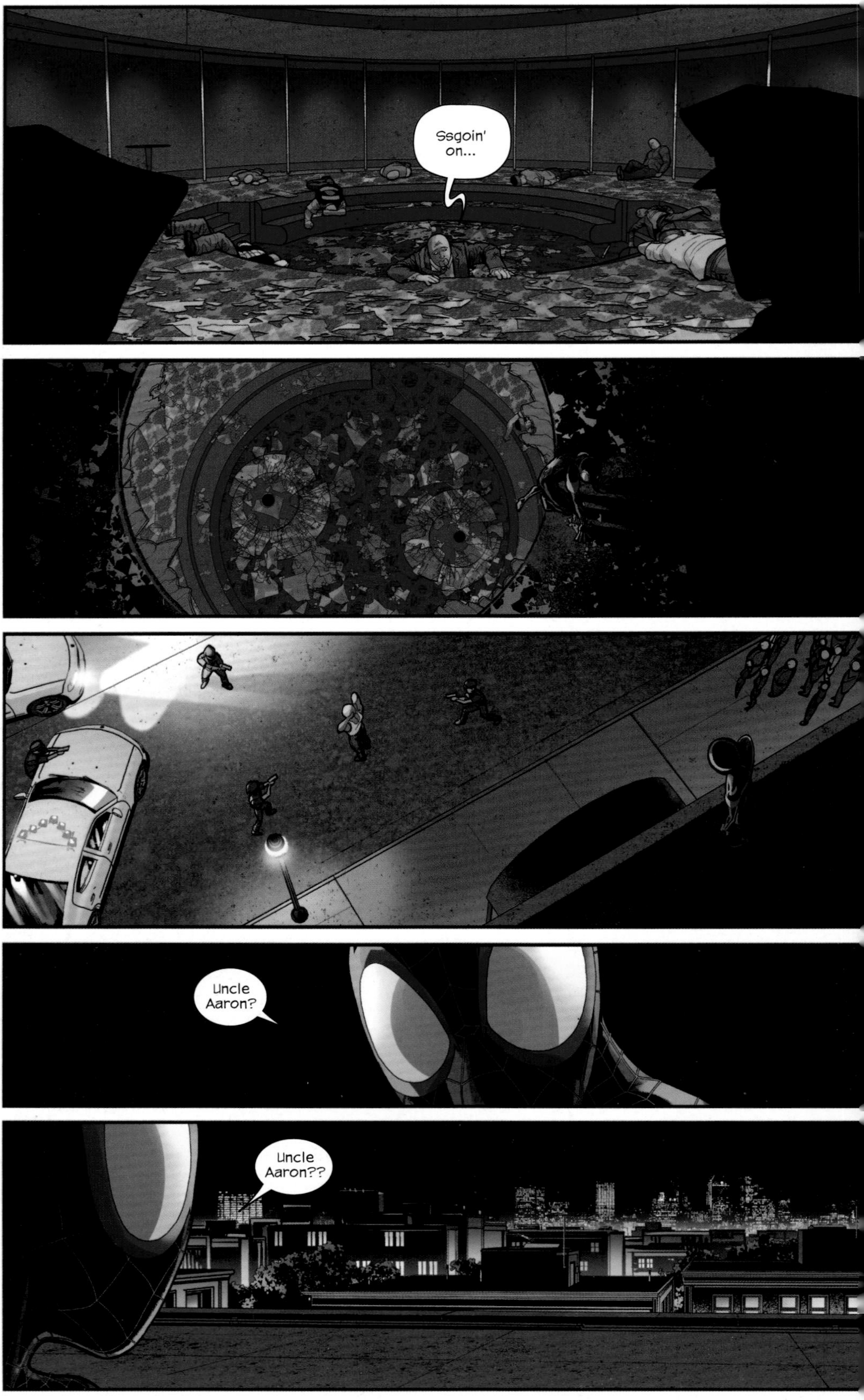
Ssgoin' on...
Uncle Aaron?
Uncle Aaron??

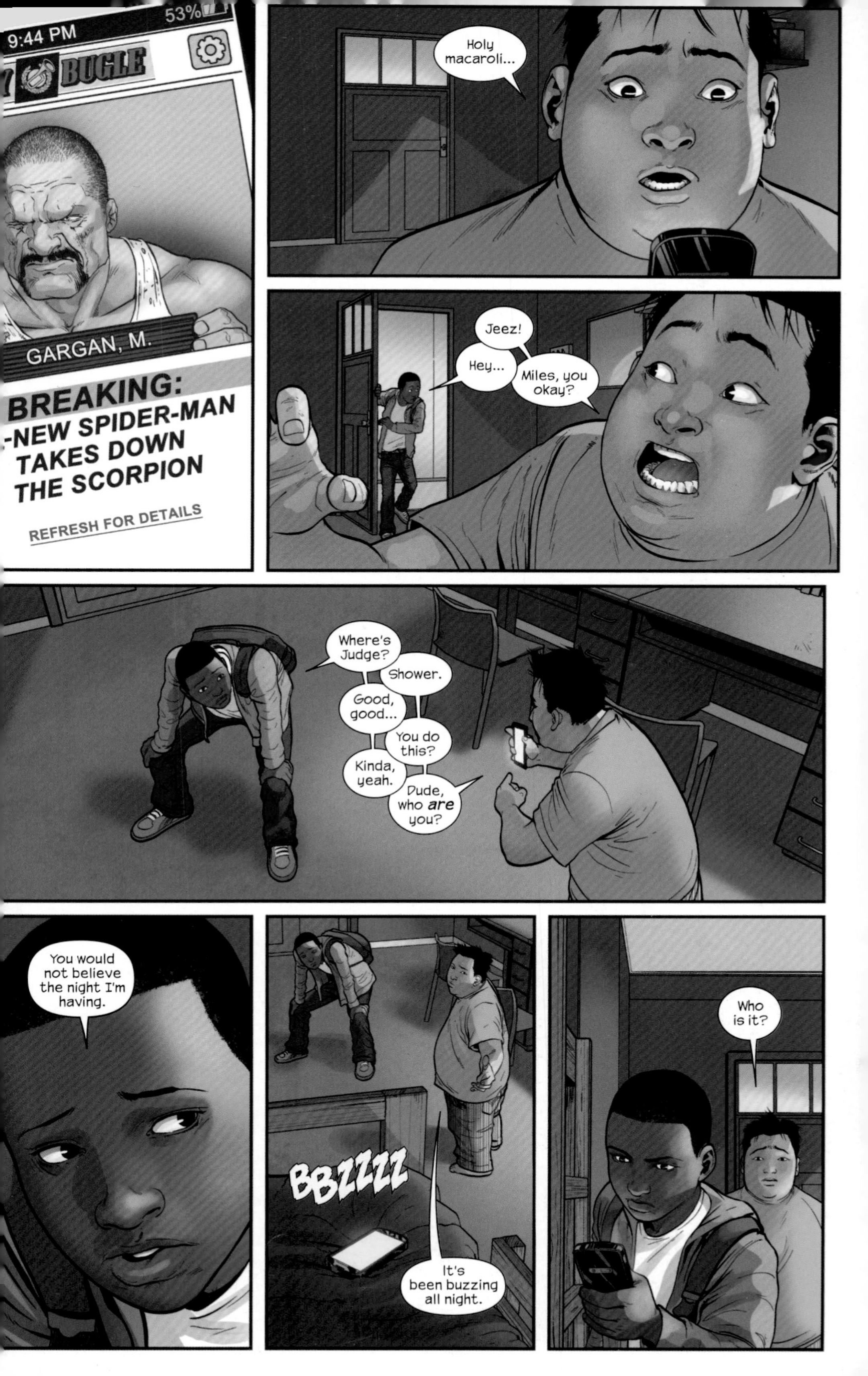

9:44 PM
53%
BUGLE
GARGAN, M.
BREAKING:
-NEW SPIDER-MAN
TAKES DOWN
THE SCORPION
REFRESH FOR DETAILS
Holy macaroli...
Jeez!
Hey...
Miles, you okay?
Where's Judge?
Shower.
Good, good...
You do this?
Kinda, yeah.
Dude, who are you?
You would not believe the night I'm having.
BBZZZZ
It's been buzzing all night.
Who is it?

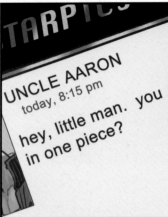

UNCLE AARON
today, 8:15 pm

hey, little man. you in one piece?

SIR MILES
today, 9:47 pm

Where'd you go?

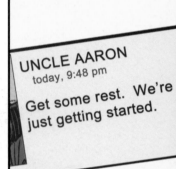

UNCLE AARON
today, 9:48 pm

Get some rest. We're just getting started.

today, 9

no.

today, 9:49

no?

today,

no.

UNCLE AARON
today, 9:50 pm

Then maybe I should call you dad?

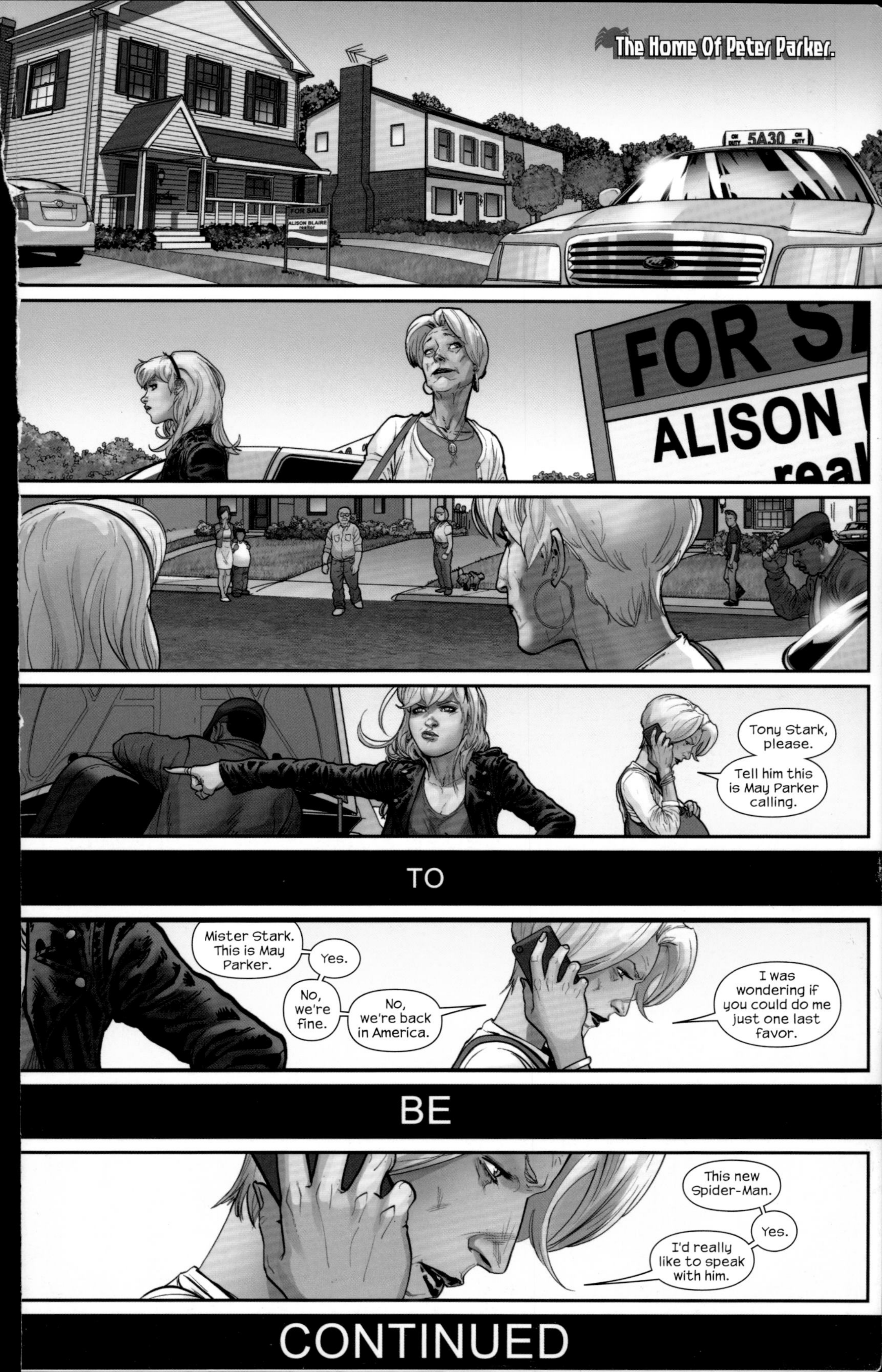
The Home Of Peter Parker.
5A30
FOR SALE
ALISON BLAIRE realtor
FOR S
ALISON
rea
Tony Stark, please.
Tell him this is May Parker calling.
TO
Mister Stark. This is May Parker.
Yes.
No, we're fine.
No, we're back in America.
I was wondering if you could do me just one last favor.
BE
This new Spider-Man.
Yes.
I'd really like to speak with him.
CONTINUED

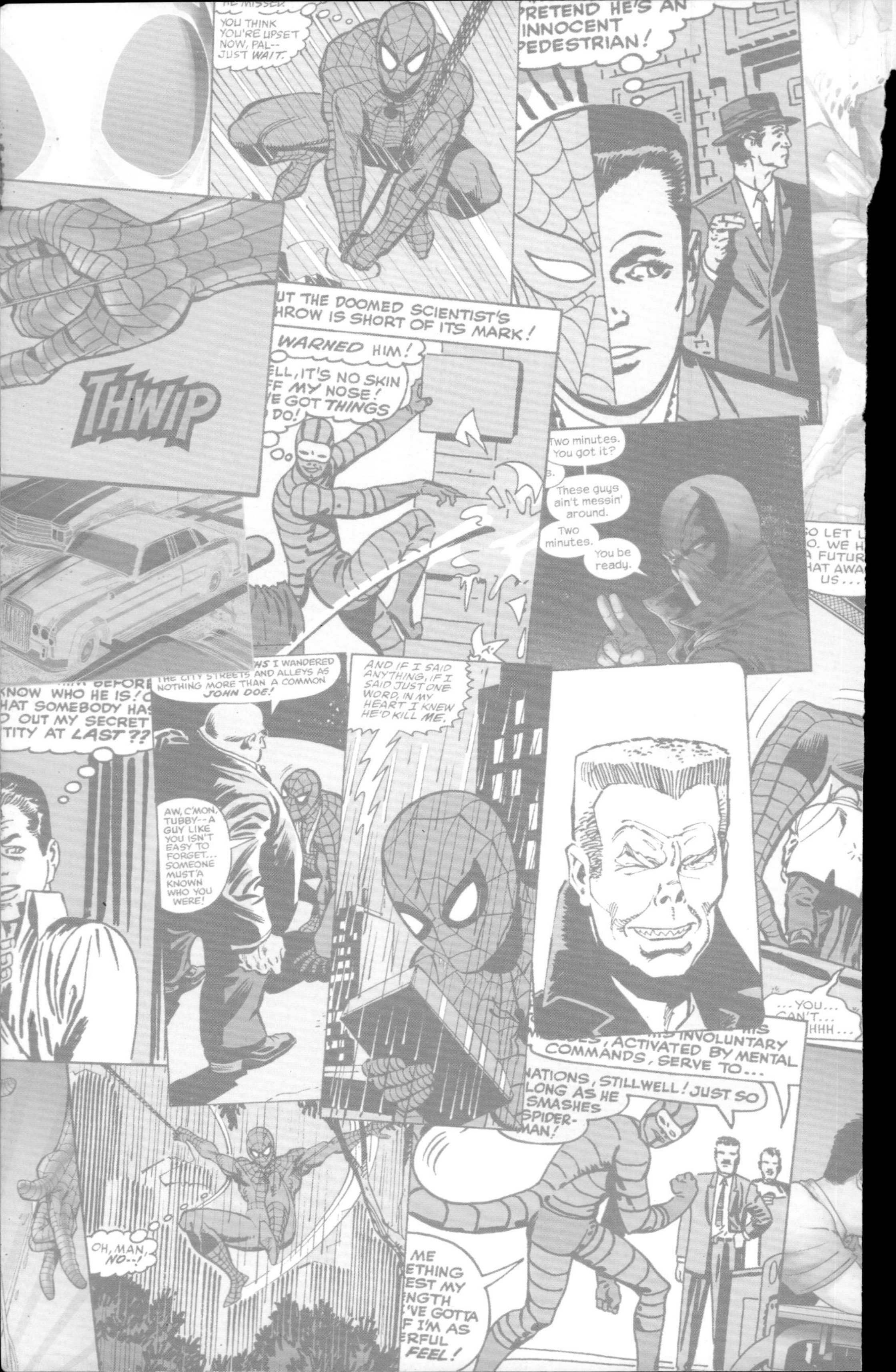

YOU THINK YOU'RE UPSET NOW, PAL-- JUST WAIT.
PRETEND HE'S AN INNOCENT PEDESTRIAN!
THWIP
UT THE DOOMED SCIENTIST'S HROW IS SHORT OF ITS MARK!
WARNED HIM!
ELL, IT'S NO SKIN FF MY NOSE! E GOT THINGS DO!
Two minutes. You got it?
These guys ain't messin' around.
Two minutes.
You be ready.
SO LET U O. WE H A FUTUR HAT AWA US...
KNOW WHO HE IS!
HAT SOMEBODY HAS D OUT MY SECRET TITY AT LAST??
THE CITY STREETS AND ALLEYS AS NOTHING MORE THAN A COMMON JOHN DOE!
AND IF I SAID ANYTHING, IF I SAID JUST ONE WORD, IN MY HEART I KNEW HE'D KILL ME.
AW, C'MON, TUBBY--A GUY LIKE YOU ISN'T EASY TO FORGET... SOMEONE MUST'A KNOWN WHO YOU WERE!
...YOU... CAN'T... HHH...
, ACTIVATED BY MENTAL COMMANDS, SERVE TO...
NATIONS, STILLWELL! JUST SO LONG AS HE SMASHES SPIDER-MAN!
OH, MAN, NO--!
ME ETHING EST MY NGTH 'VE GOTTA F I'M AS ERFUL FEEL!